The
WHITE
MANDARIN

ALSO BY DAN SHERMAN

The Mole

Riddle

Swann

King Jaguar

Dynasty of Spies

The
WHITE
MANDARIN

by Dan
Sherman

 **ARBOR** NEW YORK
HOUSE

Library of Congress Catalog Card Number: 81-66957

ISBN: 0-87795-325-2

Manufactured in the United States of America

10 9 8 7 6 5 4 3 2 1

The author wishes to acknowledge
a special friend from Peking for
his help with this book and his
greater efforts toward peace
between the United States and the
People's Republic of China.

Look a man straight in the face and make no move,
Roll up your sleeve and clench no fist,
Open your hand and show no weapon,
Bare your breast and find no foe.
But as long as there be a foe, value him,
Respect him, measure him, be humble toward him;
Let him not strip from you, however strong he be,
Compassion, the one wealth which can afford him.
LAO-TZU, *The Way and Its Power*

Prologue

FOR MANY years it has generally been acknowledged within the secret world that of all the cold war theaters none remained so obscure as Asia. Asia: it was said that the dimensions of the conflict had a tendency to change shape, the focal point to oscillate, the unreality to spread. Since the culmination of events there have been several attempts to chronicle the story, including the Langley historical department's 1975 China war series. There, under the direction of Lyle Severson, one saw the first detailed analysis of the Formosan overflights, the pacification programs and the darker operations in the southeast. But even with the supplemental series prepared a year later the China warriors still remained an elusive group.

Reading these histories one is left with only vague impressions: agents who spent entire tours without contact in the hills of northern Burma, case officers who worked themselves deep into the social fabric of the secret Hong Kong societies, native teams recruited, trained and left to run amuck. There was continual falsification of documents, money unaccounted for and seven unexplained deaths.

It was in the spring of 1980 that research began on still another chronicle of the Asian wars. Again the task of compilation fell to the historical department and again the initial results were disappointing. Outstanding questions remained unanswered, and there was no sense of a whole. Then in desperation a series of petitions was submitted to the Asian Desk. These petitions were, quite frankly, aimed at the heart of the matter. Let us lay to rest all speculation, argued the historians. Let us see what is in those vaults. There were thirteen weeks of debate, and what exactly was

1

at issue may never be revealed. In the end, however, this much was clear: the vaults of the Central Intelligence Agency were opened briefly and out of that critical portion of the record came the letters of John Polly, · written over the course of his twenty-two years in Peking.

This, then, is the story of John Polly, the one they called the White Mandarin. It has been fitted into the larger scheme of events, but the emphasis lies where it should; with Polly and those people whose lives directly intertwined with his. Regarding those enigmatic letters, all that really need be said at the moment is that apart from chronicling Polly's time in the East, they also reveal in sporadic and momentary images the essential nature of his character.

There are still passages of those letters which baffle readers, areas of obtuse thought, even the occasional untranslated character from the classic Chinese. Additionally these letters speak in length about the women in Polly's life; his wife and daughter, and his loving obsession with them both. Then, too, there are passages of regret, times in his life when he obviously deeply missed his home. Finally, there are also the Chinese, and again all that need be said at the moment is that Polly went a long way in Peking for a man who claimed that he never really understood the Chinese.

Chapter 1

IF THERE is any single event that best seems to serve as an entrance point to this story, it would have to be the disappearance, on July 30, 1971, of John Polly's nineteen-year-old daughter. Of course, there are those who maintain that this story should be told chronologically, beginning with Polly's arrival in Shanghai twenty-two years earlier, but in terms of the existing record, it was the abduction of Maya Polly that remains most prominent in the minds of the Langley chroniclers.

It has been proposed that the abduction of John Polly's daughter represented a full-blown internal war between competing elements within the CIA's Asian division. On the one side there were those indigenous China warriors centered in Hong Kong and Taiwan. On the other side were the Asian Desk directors in Langley, Virginia. At issue was not merely an eighteen-year-old girl. At issue was an entire vision of the Far East.

In terms of a linear sequence to the abduction the record runs like this. In early July 1971, John Polly began to express concern for his safety and the safety of his daughter in Peking. As justification for this concern he cited the various political entanglements that surrounded his life as a spy just prior to Richard Nixon's celebrated meeting with Mao. A letter from the period illustrates his concern:

> There are forces here that do not want this rapprochement,
> powerful forces that even Mao may not be able to overcome. You
> want me to remain still longer, I will. My daughter, however, will
> be leaving for the seaside in a week.

This letter, like others before it, was addressed to Polly's case officer, and one of the leading participants in this story, an elderly man named Simon Crane. Crane was one of the Agency's oldest China hands with a career extending back to before World War II. His role was pivotal.

Ten days after this letter appeared Polly sent his daughter to a summer resort on the Gulf of Po Hai near the Yellow Sea. It is a curious landscape, reminiscent of an older China. Along the main street are whitewashed villas encircled by eucalyptus, banyan trees along the estuary, pools of deep water among the rocks. A photograph, sent by Maya to her father shortly after her arrival, shows her standing on a grassy dune by the shoreline. In the background are the green tiles of a boathouse, a line of junipers and a clump of mottled bamboo.

The next entry in the record concerns the abduction. According to Polly his daughter had apparently been taken from her hotel room in the early hours before dawn. A porter who had tried to stop the abduction was badly beaten with a length of metal pipe.

Given the extent of Polly's involvement in the political maneuvering that had been occurring at this time within the ruling structure of Peking, it was originally thought that the girl had been abducted by members of an ultra-leftist faction that had entrenched itself within the Red Army. There was, however, no concrete evidence of this, nor any indication as to why the girl had been kidnapped, no ransom note or the like.

Polly's grief was inconsolable. He was said to have spent whole nights pacing through the rooms of his home in Peking, eating virtually nothing. It was at this point, three days after the abduction, that the record redirects attention from Peking and Po Hai to Langley, Virginia, where Simon Crane began to develop an elaborate theory concerning not only the girl's disappearance but the entire concept of the story. His theory began on a relatively minor note: the report from the British border watch of an unauthorized crossing from the Chinese border into Hong Kong. The crossing occurred near Lok Ma Chau in the New Territories beyond Kowloon.

It is a moody country. There are long stretches of open marsh, hidden willow ponds and cypress mounds among the hills. At night it is very dark. According to the British, a person of slight build was ferried across the Shum Chun River in the early hours before dawn and met on the banks by three unidentified men. Also of interest was the fact that throughout the crossing the fugitive was in clear sight of Communist border guards but they did not interfere. Attached to this report was a query asking if Langley had had anything to do with the crossing. Crane cabled back that Langley had not.

There are, however, two existing memos written immediately after the crossing that indicate that Simon Crane had already begun to focus his attention on the Agency's field station in Hong Kong and the station's director, Jay Sagan. To understand Crane's thinking here it is necessary to appreciate Sagan's role in events up until this point as well as the role of his longtime friend and power base, a Chinese Nationalist by the name of Feng Chi.

Like Simon Crane, Jay Sagan's involvement in this story extends before the events of July 1971. Sagan first entered the Asian sphere at approximately the same time as John Polly, and he too originally served under Crane in Shanghai. There he made a reputation as one of the few western intelligence officers to be wholly accepted by the Chinese elite.

As for Feng Chi, his involvement also began in Shanghai some twenty months before the fall in 1949. There he was one of the leading figures of the anti-Communist regime under Chiang Kai-shek, and worked closely with Sagan recruiting and training agents and assembling teams for a coastal watch. Later, when the war had been lost and Feng was living on the accumulated wealth from his involvement in the opium trade, Sagan came to him again and said, "We can still play the same game. You supply the people, I'll supply the technical expertise." Within three years there were lines from Macao to Canton, north to Wuhan and all through the southwest. Within twenty years there were lines across the whole of Asia, and technical expertise was still a term that Sagan used whenever he wanted to explain what it was that he had given to the Orient.

As for John Polly's role in this scheme, during those chaotic months in Shanghai just before the Communist victory, Polly became involved in a dispute with Feng Chi's younger brother. Polly killed the brother and fled to Peking, and Feng Chi swore revenge.

Such was the crucial background to that series of memos drafted by Crane in the days immediately following the abduction of John Polly's daughter. In all there would be three memos, each addressed to the Asian Desk's senior officer, Norman Pyle, and each stating that there were possibilities of complicity.

"It is by no means inconceivable to me," Crane wrote, "that Feng Chi was not only responsible for the abduction, but now holds the girl. I further find it not inconceivable that S.[agan] was, if not also responsible, at least knowledgeable in this matter."

To reinforce his theory Crane's next memo listed three occasions during which Jay Sagan had defied Langley policy on Feng's request, most notably in connection with the opium trade.

Initially Crane's theory was received with skepticism. A responsible memo pointed out that Jay Sagan had been a valuable member of the American intelligence community for years, and Feng Chi an equally valuable client. Further doubt about the validity of Crane's theory came up when one considered the fact that the girl had been abducted well within the Chinese mainland, far beyond the reach of either Feng Chi or Jay Sagan.

Crane remained unshaken. Another memo argued that given the enormity of Feng's power in the East, even the Communist border did not represent a barrier. "We have seen before that interplay does exist between Feng and certain Communist elements on the mainland," Crane wrote. "Surely what I am suggesting is not impossible."

To which Norman Pyle replied, "All right then, what do you want to do about it?"

Crane's final memo dealt with the necessity for secrecy. His concern seems to have been twofold. First, he believed that any overt investigation would only succeed in alerting Feng prematurely thus giving him time to bury all traces of the girl. Then, and even closer to the heart of this matter, Crane noted that no action should be taken which by consequence would reveal the extent of Langley's relationship with John Polly. By way of explanation it should be noted that apart from Simon Crane and Norman Pyle, only two others knew the complete John Polly story. They were the director of Central Intelligence and the secretary of state. (That the president was never told would later cause no small degree of embarrassment.)

For these reasons, then, and for what Crane called "the delicate operational balance of Polly's position in Peking," an improbable figure was brought into play. His name was Billy Cassidy, and his story, by virtue of the fact that it threads between all opposing factions, should prove as illuminating a beginning as any.

An item of note regarding young Cassidy appeared in newspapers about twelve years ago. The story told of Cassidy's release from a Chinese prison and his earlier relationship with the Central Intelligence Agency. Other relevant information included the fact that Cassidy had originally been captured when his aircraft, a modified B-17, was disabled and forced down by Chinese interception just south of Peking. Although the flight, which had begun in Taiwan, was initially said to have been part of the CIA's photo-reconnaissance program, later admissions revealed that Cassidy's actual purpose had involved the drop of politically hostile leaflets over the rural Chinese populace. In addition to Cassidy, four Nationalist Chinese crew members were also captured. Cassidy was then twenty-three years old. There were no deaths.

Accompanying most of the newspaper articles was a photograph of Billy. It was taken shortly after his release and showed him stepping from a military transport in Hawaii, a handsome, fair-haired boy with even features and soft eyes and dressed in a light sports coat and slacks. In his left hand he is carrying a canvas flight bag. Behind him stand two Marines in summer tans, while the shadow of a third falls upon the railing. The camera had caught Billy in mid-step, smiling vaguely, perhaps gazing out to a clump of palms at the far end of the airstrip.

Apart from this photograph and those few terse articles in the press there was no other mention of young Cassidy, nor of his experience in Peking, nor of his relationship with John Polly and Polly's daughter. It was assumed that after a brief period of rest Cassidy returned to the bureaucracy from which he came and that his life went on much as it had before. True and not true. There were nine days spent in San Diego with his mother, then another week in Langley for reorientation. Finally he returned to Asia in much the same capacity as before, but he was different. Inside he was very different.

Before the incarceration in Peking, Billy Cassidy had spent most of his time on the island of Formosa in what was commonly called Taiwan Central. This was the hub of the Asian sphere, with thirty-seven Langley employees and many more stringers in the field. But upon Cassidy's release from Peking and his subsequent return to the East, he was posted not in Taiwan but in Hong Kong.

Although smaller, the Hong Kong station had always been considered the more prestigious post. In view of their proximity to the mainland, Hong Kong officers were directly in the line of fire. Agents were run right over the border. Action was fast. On the average there were half a dozen kills a year, and twice that many kidnappings. Hong Kong station employees tended to form close personal ties and to shun outsiders.

Perhaps the most important figure in Cassidy's life at this time was the functional head of the entire Hong Kong-Taiwan sphere, Jay Sagan. Sagan had originally served as Cassidy's sponsor to the secret world, and years earlier had worked with Cassidy's father (and lied to the boy about the Reds causing his father's death).

Occasionally in the evening Cassidy and Sagan would drink together, usually at one of the waterfront bars where there was a view of the harbor junks behind the typhoon shelter. Generally Sagan did most of the talking, using words like "counterforce" and "lateralism," which were supposed to indicate his expansive view of Asia and his own role as white power broker in an Oriental world.

As for Cassidy, there were simply patterns that he was just too tired to change. While Sagan spoke, he would nod and say, "Yes, sir," or "I think I understand." Afterward they would part and Cassidy would stroll out into streets which before Peking had always frightened him but did not frighten him now.

Another figure in Billy's life of this period was a young man about his own age named Johnny Ray. Cassidy had actually met Ray well before Peking but it was not until later that they became friends. In many ways Cassidy's relationship with Ray was similar to his relationship with Sagan. Mostly the two men met in bars, and mostly Billy listened while Ray talked. It seemed that Ray was always involved in some deal or another. One week he would be trying to blackmail a delegate from a Shanghai trade commission, the next week he would be trying to spike an embassy.

There were also deals that had nothing to do with the business of spying. Opium. From Cassidy's first Asian days he had known that the trade routes ran from the southeast in Thailand and Laos, diagonally across Bangkok and into Saigon, Kuala Lumpur, Phnom Penh and finally to Hong Kong. In the beginning opium had been just another abstraction, like Jay Sagan's "counterforce."

Addicts lived in their own lost world with matches, tinfoil and twists of colored paper. These days, though, the trade was no longer so remote. Once a month, sometimes more often, Cassidy would pass a few hundred dollars on to Ray. A week later the money would be returned, doubled, often tripled. Cassidy never asked about these deals. He did not care who bought and who sold. His involvement had started not long after Peking, and now it was simply one of those things that you did like playing horses or saving spare change in a jar. Cassidy was not even certain how much money he had made, which was also indicative of a change since Peking.

Before his capture and meeting with John Polly he had been fairly conscientious about money, but now it was just another abstraction.

As for Cassidy's own use, he was not smoking much anymore. Only occasionally with Ray, or else alone on Sunday afternoons. Although Cassidy's involvement with opium was relatively minor, it did bring him into contact with the third most consequential figure in his life—Feng Chi (the man actually responsible for his father's death). Cassidy did not know Feng well, but like all those who worked in the Hong Kong station he felt the man's presence, his power. In the station records there were memos about Feng's early years in Shanghai, and a few police reports regarding his association with a well-organized criminal society popularly known as the Triads. Of Feng's relationship with Jay Sagan... Cassidy only presumed that the same apparatus that had made Jay Sagan the lord of the Asian intelligence division had also made Feng Chi the lord of opium.

In the main Cassidy lived on the fringes of other people's lives. If others around him did not take him seriously, he did not seem to mind. It was enough that they generally left him alone...

Such was Billy Cassidy's life at the outset of this story. More than a year had passed since his return from Peking, but few had noticed the change. His memory of John Polly was still clear, his memory of Polly's luminous daughter even clearer. Once or twice he had been known to talk about Polly, but he never spoke of the girl. It hurt too much.

Seven days after John Polly's daughter was abducted, on a Tuesday, the second week in August, Cassidy had risen early, boiled an egg, smoked a cigarette by the open window and went off to work as usual at the Agency facility, which made it easy to forget you were in China. Office walls were paneled in rosewood laminate, the floors in gray linoleum. Certain rooms were partitioned with smoked plexiglass, others with fiberboard. There was a view of the consulate courtyard from the lounge.

On this morning Cassidy was at work in finance, sorting through the operational expenditures.

Cassidy did not always work in finance. Only seven weeks earlier he and Johnny Ray had spent four days in Kowloon fishing for agents along the docks. A month before that they had followed a Soviet courier into Macao and wired his hotel room. But mostly he helped out in finance, or else in the telex booth, or sometimes they even had him typing. He had been working all morning like this. For lunch there would be a sandwich in the lounge, either tuna fish or deviled egg. There was a cafe nearby where they more or less knew him. He always ordered rice and steamed vegetables, then ate with a newspaper spread out on the table, although he did not like hard news. He nearly always wore the same raincoat. It was a kind of joke around the station—Billy and this old gray coat with missing buttons and frayed cuffs.

On this Tuesday in August he had just returned from lunch when he received word that the director of personnel wanted to see him, a crabbed little man named Desmond. Desmond also worked with the ciphers, but there was never enough to do in that department so Jay Sagan had given him a converted closet on the third floor where he could handle the staff.

When Cassidy entered his office he found Desmond hunched over some woman's service record.

"Sit down, Billy."

The chair was aluminum with molded plastic. On the desk was a photograph of a woman, probably Desmond's wife, as lost-looking as the wife of any of these consular spies.

"Seems fortune has finally smiled on you, Billy. You're about to become part of what they call the officer's advancement program."

"Sir?" Still gazing at the photograph of Desmond's wife.

"That's right. For God knows what reason you're about to be promoted. Assuming, of course, you qualify, which it seems can only be determined in Langley."

"You mean I have to go to Langley?"

"I'm afraid so, Billy-boy. Testing begins next week."

"What kind of testing?"

"Who knows!"

"How long will I be gone?"

"The order says nine days. That means anywhere from a week to forever."

"And afterwards I can come back?"

"You're asking the wrong man, Billy. I don't know anything more about this crap than you do."

Soon it seemed that everyone knew that Cassidy had been selected for the advancement program, not that they knew exactly what it was all about. They knew only that it was probably important, and for this reason they were jealous. As for Cassidy, he did not know what to think. It had been a long time since he had thought of his career as anything more than a listless tramp through time, and he could not understand how someone at Langley would see it any differently.

On the eve of departure Cassidy attended a farewell dinner at Johnny Ray's apartment. There were a dozen guests, most of them men from the consulate and a few of their Chinese women. Drinks were served on the terrace, then steaks. Through the eucalyptus trees lay the harbor lights, the sloped roofs of Cat Street and the lesser villas. There were remnants of cocaine in the bathroom sink. Someone cut his finger with a knife. When Cassidy was asked to make a speech he said only, "Well I guess even the losers get lucky once in a while." Then everyone smiled and wished him good luck.

As for the flight from Hong Kong to Los Angeles and the next events, Cassidy would only remember the fragmentary impressions of a fog alert and the interminable delay. Then there were moments in the darkened cabin when he nearly convinced himself that what others had been telling him was true: here at last was a real opportunity. Later he would also recall having made the decision to get his hair cut and to purchase a new suit, perhaps something in a charcoal gray flannel.

Passing through customs all he would remember was that the line to the inspector's counter had been short, mainly businessmen and a few frightened students. Perhaps there had also been a rather striking girl, because later he would remember the image of a woman's legs against suede. Until he heard the inspector say, "This is your luggage?"

"Yeah."

"Will you follow that officer, please."

"Why? What's wrong?"

"Just follow the officer through that door on the left."

To a room where they found half an ounce of heroin sewn into the lining of his suitcase.

Cassidy was taken to a detention center where the records show that he hardly spoke at all. Except once to explain that he had been framed, and then to give the barest details of his life. Here impressions were even more fragmented, with a view of a Los Angeles slum through a wire mesh, a concrete cell and country music on a radio. Among his personal belongings were found a book of matches from a Hong Kong nightclub, a slim paperback entitled *The Way and Its Power,* and a street fighter's knife with a nasty spring blade. Finally there was perhaps one brief

11

glimpse into a life that no one could relate to. It was the life of a young American in an Asian wasteland, a life with no more foundation than the life of a refugee. A subsequent interview with police revealed that the other prisoners were apparently afraid of Cassidy, while he behaved as if he were above the law.

Much attention has been paid to Cassidy's initial encounter with Simon Crane. There has been special emphasis on Crane's approach, Cassidy's immediate response, the tactical change midstream, and the final recruitment.

This encounter took place about six hours after Cassidy's arrest. Apparently the theory was that six hours was sufficiently long enough for the boy to become concerned about his legal status, but not long enough for him to panic and so jeopardize the operational security. As it happened, however, Cassidy was neither frightened nor even remotely concerned. He had known from the moment of his arrest that some kind of game was in play, and he was merely waiting to be informed of the rules.

As for Simon Crane, perhaps no more unlikely figure could have been sent to that Los Angeles detention center. Crane was by this time well into his sixties; a short, plump man with white hair. He carried a battered leather briefcase and an overcoat on his arm.

When Cassidy and Simon Crane finally met it was already late morning. Cassidy had been called from his cell and led down a long corridor into a green, windowless room, with only a steel table, two steel chairs and an ashtray. Crane was seated at the table. When Cassidy entered he rose and said, "Hello. I'm Crane."

Cassidy sat down, looked at him. "What do you want?"

"You've heard of me?"

"I've heard of you."

"Well, that simplifies matters. Tell me, how's Jay Sagan?"

"He's fine. What do you want?"

"Well, first off, I think you should know that you're in a great deal of trouble."

"Is that so?"

"These kinds of affairs nearly always end with a mandatory prison term."

Cassidy moved his eyes from the blank wall, to the door, to the edge of the table. Finally he smiled. "Well, you really got me scared."

"May I ask where you got the heroin? Did you get it from Feng Chi?"

"Yeah, sure. Feng always passes me a little something for the holidays."

12

"You're aware that Feng is involved with the trade."

"Really? I didn't know."

"Consequently I was wondering if that involvement extends to the personnel at the station."

"Right. We're always running stuff for Feng."

"Does Jay Sagan know about your involvement?"

"Look, Crane, who are you trying to kid? The stuff was planted and you know it."

There was, at this point, a notation in the record of this conversation regarding a strategic change in Crane's approach. Until this point, Crane had evidently been uncertain as to whether or not the boy truly understood his position. Now, however, there seemed no doubt at all that Cassidy was not even faintly shaken, and so a more direct approach was made.

Crane said, "I think you should know, Billy, that I'm fully prepared to get you out of here today."

"In exchange for what?"

"For answering a few questions."

"You people set me up for leverage. Well that's nice. That must have taken a lot of imagination. How did you plant the junk? Someone in the airline?"

Then Crane just as calmly as before: "We believe that you have certain information that we need. Now surely you have nothing to lose by at least listening to the questions."

Cassidy's hand fell to the table and his eyes moved back to the door.

"I'd like to begin with Jay Sagan," Crane said softly.

"What about him?"

"Do you know what he's been doing lately?"

"Yeah. He runs the Orient."

"I mean specifically."

"How should I know?"

"I was under the impression that you and Jay were rather close."

"Sure. He tells me everything. I'm his right-hand boy. Jerk."

"Do you know if he's been seeing Feng Chi?"

"He always sees Feng Chi."

"How often?"

"I don't know. Once a week, maybe more."

"What about recently? Would you say that Jay has been seeing more or less of Feng recently?"

"Look, I don't move in that company. You got to have an eight-hundred-dollar suit just to get in Feng's front door. Okay?"

"What about eleven days ago? Do you recall seeing Jay eleven days ago?"

"Are you kidding? I don't even remember what I had for lunch."

Crane said, "I'd like to talk about your time in Peking."

"Why? I've already been through all that with you people."

"I realize that, but I'd like to go over a few aspects that might not have been covered in your original debrief."

"What aspects?"

"John Polly."

"Oh, so that's what this is all about."

"I understand that you knew him rather well."

"I knew him."

"Can you describe him?"

"What is this?"

"Please. Just tell me about him."

"What do you want me to say? He's a Red. He's been over there for twenty years, and he tap dances for Chairman Mao."

"I understand that he actually got you out of prison and took you into his home."

"Yeah. So what?"

"Well, are you grateful for that? Do you feel you might owe him something?"

"Why should I owe him?"

"Because he saved your life, saved you from what I understand was rather brutal torture."

"So what?"

"Well, I thought perhaps you might feel that you owe him."

"Well. I don't."

"Okay. What about his daughter, Maya?"

"What about her?"

"I understand that you knew her as well."

"That's right."

"Did you like her?"

"Why should I like her? She's a Commie too."

"I hear that she's very beautiful."

"She's not bad."

"Nineteen and very beautiful."

14

"Okay, so she's beautiful."

"Did you talk much?"

"A little."

"What about?"

"I don't know. Nothing."

"Did she ever express a fear of the political climate in Peking?"

"What do you mean?"

"Let me put it like this. Would it surprise you to know that eleven days ago she was kidnapped and has not been heard of since?"

Cassidy's movements became less precise, with his head cocked to one side, his shirt drenched in perspiration.

"Ostensibly she was abducted by an underground military faction, presumably because her father had been openly opposing them. There has not, however, been any real indication as to what they want with her. No direct threats, nothing like that. In fact there is even some indication that she's not actually on the mainland, and that the abduction was not politically motivated at all."

A silence, broken only by the tap of Cassidy's fingers on the table. "So what? You think Sagan and Feng had something to do with this?"

"Yes, Billy, we do."

"And you thought I was involved too?"

"Well at one time you worked rather closely with Jay, didn't you?"

"Look, no one works closely with Jay. Except maybe Feng."

"Yes, well, I can see that now."

"And I don't know anything about Polly's daughter either."

"But that does not mean you won't be able to help us."

"Help you do what?"

"Establish whether or not Feng really has her."

"Why should I?"

Crane opened his briefcase, removed a brown envelope, and handed it to Billy Cassidy. He opened it and withdrew three black-and-white photographs. Each showed a naked girl and a man's hand resting on her body. The girl was tied to a bed frame by her ankles and wrists. The man's hand lay on her breast in one photograph, her thigh in another and finally her throat. Her face was partially covered by her hair, but her features were still visible. Cassidy looked at the photographs, one after another. Crane watched in silence.

"It's Polly's daughter," Crane said.

"I can see that."

"Polly received them about four days ago. There was no accompanying explanation, just the photographs."

Crane noted that Cassidy's left hand was clenched in a fist throughout the following exchange.

"Why don't you just drag Sagan in and sweat him?" he asked.

"Why? So that he can deny it, and meanwhile Feng will have time to hide his tracks?"

"But you don't know for certain they have her, do you?"

"No, not for certain."

"So it's all really just a lot of speculation, isn't it?"

"In a sense, but as I said there are indications, certainly enough to justify sending in a man."

"You mean me?"

"If you're willing?"

"And if I'm not?"

"It's a stick-and-carrot, Billy. You can play with us, or you can stay here. I might also add that we are prepared to sweeten the deal with a substantial cash bonus."

"How much?"

"It's negotiable."

Then again Cassidy lapsed into a motionless silence, staring at nothing, one hand still clenched in a fist on the table. "What would you want me to do?"

"We'd like to play you back into the station."

"And then what?"

"Our feeling is that if Feng really does have the girl there's bound to be some sort of trail in the records."

"When would I start?"

"Six days. That will give us time for certain preliminary steps, time to brief you fully on the complete story, and it's also about the amount of time you would have actually been absent had you really been in Langley for the program."

"So there really is that officer advancement shit?"

"Oh yes. The program does exist."

"But I didn't qualify, is that it?"

"No. I'm afraid not."

16

There was supposedly an argument at this stage between Simon Crane and Norman Pyle concerning Cassidy's motivation. Crane maintained that, although they were unstated, Cassidy truly did hold certain feelings for John Polly, and particularly for Polly's daughter. As evidence of these feelings, Crane pointed out various moments in his conversation with the boy, moments when there was clearly some deeper emotion in his eyes, in the way his voice wavered, in the movement of his hands.

Norman Pyle, however, who knew Cassidy only from his service record, disagreed. Cassidy, Pyle argued, was nothing more than another Asian tramp, a back-street fighter whose sole motivation in the matter was money and saving his own neck. "If he can be trusted," Pyle was heard to remark, "it's only because we're going to pay him more than the other side."

Regardless, four hours after Cassidy's initial conversation with Crane he was released from the detention center in Los Angeles and formally put on an operational footing. During the next twelve hours Cassidy was kept in a suburban house above the city basin. Here he met a tall, exceedingly muscular young man named Eliot, who would silently follow him to the end. When Cassidy was introduced to the man he was told: "This is Eliot. He's going to be your bodyguard." Cassidy was leaning against a refrigerator, pealing an orange with a serrated knife. Eliot, standing in the doorway, was wearing tight jeans and a shirt unbuttoned to the chest. Their eyes met briefly, then Cassidy continued working even faster with the knife.

In the evening Crane and Cassidy talked in a bedroom with the curtains drawn. Below were the sounds of Eliot in the kitchen and a television set turned to the news. Cassidy had asked how long they would be staying here, was given no answer.

Later in the evening there was a meal which Eliot had prepared with obvious care. There were steaks seasoned with pepper and mushrooms, red wine and a green salad. When the meal was served Cassidy noticed that Eliot waited anxiously for some compliment. Finally Crane told him that the steaks were very good. In the weeks to come Cassidy would understand that this absurd ritual was to be played out every night.

The return to Hong Kong also came in the night, one long night aboard a military aircraft. Meals consisted of bland, freeze-dried food. Everyone was armed. When they landed there was a waiting van at the airstrip. The name of a cleaning company was stenciled on the side panel.

17

The rear windows were blacked out, and when Cassidy asked Crane where they were going he was given no answer.

It was sometime after midnight when they reached the house that would later be the focal point of all final moves. Cassidy was exhausted by this time, and so his first impressions of the house were disjointed. From the road he saw only two dark towers rising above the palms. Then there was a black stretch of land and black rock. There were no lights, and only the sound of waves on a cliff.

Eventually he was told that this house had once belonged to a sea captain. The walls were knotted pine, the furniture heavy oak. Lace curtains hung at the windows. There were paintings of the shoreline and sailing ships. By dawn he saw that the grounds were remote, cut off from the highway by a stone wall. In the rear there was a long grassy walk across the sand dunes, and then cliffs dropping away to the ocean.

In the morning Cassidy had risen early and spent an hour prowling through the empty rooms. Everywhere he smelled wet ash and coffee. He found a brass compass, an hourglass and a pair of dueling pistols. There was a clock that told the phases of the moon, and a map of the South Pacific. Finally Crane appeared, and the two men walked out to the rocks above the bay.

The air was cold. Cassidy wore an old purple sweater and the raincoat he always wore, but still he felt the cold. There was a wind off the bay rocking two sloops in full sail. As he and Crane moved out across the grass and dunes there was the sound of a slamming car door. When Cassidy looked back he saw Eliot unloading groceries from a black station wagon. The man was wearing only a pair of brief shorts.

When Crane and Cassidy reached the promontory they sat down on the rocks. From here lay a long view of the coast and the tide pools below. There was a jetty stretching far out into the water and a few tormented trees on the bluff. Crane was wearing a large duffle coat. Even when the weather grew warmer he would not take off his coat, which led Cassidy to believe that a tape recorder was concealed in the lining.

There was one terse exchange, which took place before the actual briefing began, and although it seems to have no obvious importance, Crane thought fit to include it in his opening notes. Apparently the two men had been sitting only a few minutes when Crane said, "I think you should know that when this is all over there's a very good chance that Jay Sagan is going to take a bad fall. I mean that he's gone way over the edge this time, entirely out of control."

"So what else is new?" Cassidy frowned.

"Well I merely thought that you should know where it stands."

"I know where it stands."

"All right, Billy, then we might as well get started. Unless there's something else you'd like to clear up first?"

Cassidy thought a moment. Then he said, "Yeah there's something I want to clear up. That freak of yours, Eliot. I want him to stay away from me."

"What's the matter? Have you two had some problem?"

"No problem. Just tell him to stay away."

"Very well. I'll tell him. Anything else?"

"No—yes. I want my knife back."

"Your knife?"

"You know what I'm talking about. My knife. Someone took it out of my suitcase and I want it back."

"Oh yes. Well I'll make sure you get it before you leave."

"Fine."

"Now I think we should get started. We have a lot of ground to cover."

There was no other introduction, only a brief silence while Cassidy struck three matches trying to light a cigarette in the wind. Then it seemed that Crane simply started talking, speaking much as he would continue to speak through the days to come, sometimes in great detail, then withdrawing again to the larger scheme. While he spoke Cassidy did not look at him. He looked only at the sea, or farther out to the horizon. Later, when they started to drink out here, Cassidy always threw his empty beer cans into the water.

Chapter 2

IT HAD always been Crane's opinion that in order to understand the life of John Polly it was necessary to understand the political events through which his life progressed. For this reason Crane began with the politics. As Cassidy listened he watched the rising tide and an oil tanker moving out to high sea. There were also crabs stirring among the rocks, some pink, some gray, and clumps of seaweed in vaguely human shapes.

There were, Crane said, several ways to look at the Chinese Revolution. No single view was particularly correct. All contained some truth and some distortion. As for himself he had always preferred the basic historical approach... a logical progression from the fall of the Manchu Dynasty in 1911 through the First Republic under Sun Yat-sen, then again through to the dictatorship under Chiang Kai-shek and finally to the People's Republic. As for the causes of the Revolution, Crane generally described a society as depraved and static as any on earth. The system was feudal, perhaps not in the strictest European sense, although the ultimate domination of the peasant was the same. Gentry families lived chiefly in walled towns, ruling through mortgage and customary obligations. There was some fluidity within the administrative class, but this was small. The disparity between wealth and poverty bred slavery, famine, plague, war.

As for the first revolution and the eventual collapse of the dynasty, Crane described a successive decay and fall of internally linked institutions: the throne, the Confucian orthodoxy, the civil service, land tenure and finally even the formal structure of the extended family. As the father of that revolution, Sun Yat-sen typified the new Chinese. He was born near Canton, then the modern fringe. He attended an English boarding school and was later even baptized in a Congregational church. His sincerity was charismatic, while his opportunism was quite practical, and if the failure of his First Republic was a failure to incorporate the larger mass, then at least it was a later lesson for Mao.

The seeds of the later struggle between the Communists and Nationalists were originally planted during those first chaotic days of the Republic. Years before the war Crane had even written a paper to this effect, basing his premise on the fact that immediately after the fall of the dynasty the Republic had no other alternative than to petition the Soviets for aid. But if Sun's Kuomintang party was to draw its organizational form from Moscow, it was not really a Communist party. Rather it was an authoritarian regime, half imitated from Russia, half from the echo of the fallen empire. So regardless of Sun's Three Principles, there had always been an ideological vacuum for the bona fide Chinese Communists to fill.

With the collapse of the dynasty and the failure of the Republic to consolidate power, the country split into feuding camps. There were continual struggles between rival warlords in the north, while after Sun's death in 1925 the Kuomintang Party in Canton was controlled by a shifting group of military leaders, Chiang Kai-shek among them.

Crane's view of Chiang was a personal one, based upon personal concerns. Chiang, as Crane had known him, was a man of traditional heritage. He had been born in 1887 to a gentry clan near Ningpo. His background was largely military, and to that extent authoritarian. His eventual rise to the head of the Nationalist party was the ultimate triumph of a political infighter. While his final obsession with Mao was the ultimate fixation of a man who could not accept defeat.

Immediately following Chiang's emergence as the dominant force in the Nationalist Kuomintang party there was a brief period of stability. The northern warlords had collapsed, and by the summer of 1926 the revolutionary armies had taken control of the Yangtze Valley. But if there was stability now, it was a tenuous stability, based upon a coalition of the landlord and merchant class with no real representation of the peasant. Even the Communist party, which had been in existence since 1921, showed no inclination to carry the Revolution to the rural areas. Rather they were content to maintain a coalition with the Nationalists, even at the expense of their ideology.

As for the Communist leaders, Crane continued, there was of course, Mao, but he was by no means representative of the party. In fact, it was a fairly heterogeneous base with a scattered leadership, drawing as much from an international student movement as from China. Chou En-lai, for example, first embraced the party ideology in Germany, and then became a figure in the Paris group. If there was any central direction at this time, it had to come from Moscow, with the emphasis on moderation. In fact, at the time Soviet advisors were actually urging their Chinese clients to keep the faith with Chiang Kai-shek in the belief that the embryonic movement could not bring about a revolution without Nationalist support.

So in the beginning, Mao and Chiang were allies of a sort. For a time Mao even worked in the Shanghai bureau of the Nationalist Party. After a brief illness in the winter of 1925 he went to Canton to head the Nationalist Propaganda Congress. Later he even became an alternate member of the Nationalist Central Executive Committee and editor of the party weekly. The alliance, of course, was not to last. By the spring of 1926 Chiang was already growing disenchanted with the Communist element. Then in March of the following year he struck, murdering Communist leaders in Shanghai, and breaking with the Communist-dominated Wuhan government to form his own right-wing coalition in Nanking.

Crane said that this 1927 Shanghai slaughter was really the first engagement of the so-called Chinese Revolution. Shortly after the attack, Chiang began his four campaigns of extermination, with the aim of destroying every remnant of Communist thought and power. Of course, he was unsuccessful. Chou En-lai, for example, managed to escape from Shanghai, as did others.

In that same paper in which Crane had tried to trace the origins of the Revolution, he also proposed that the very campaigns of extermination actually led to the rise of Mao. Out of touch with Moscow, irrevocably committed to survive in the wilderness or not at all, the Soviet-trained element within the party was finally obliged to acknowledge Mao's leadership and his extraordinary theories of guerrilla warfare. Convinced that the revolution could only achieve victory through peasant support, Mao began to assemble a rural army. For a territorial base he chose the mountains of Chingkangshan, and later proclaimed the Chinese Soviet Republic of Juichin. Still later, after continued Nationalist harassment, Mao retreated even deeper into the wasteland, across the northwest to the border of Outer Mongolia. Here in the arid Yenan hills he began to build his party, his army and his vision that would motivate them.

Although there were nominal truces between Communists and Nationalists at the start of the Japanese invasion in 1937, hostilities immediately erupted again once the invasion had been expelled. Yet this time, 1946, the Red Army or Eighth Route Army was a formidable power, particularly in the northeast. With their numbers swollen from the Manchurian prisoners and their firepower increased by captured weapons, they could move at will upon the weaker Nationalist garrisons and the railroads. Red cadres also continued to recruit from the villages, appealing to the peasant sensibility with food and land distribution and an ideological stance that positioned them as representatives of the poor, the battered and the young.

For those like Crane and other fairly distant western observers, these early revolutionary days were perceived with a certain ambivalence. On the one hand, there was the belief that the United States should openly support Chiang and his effort, honoring a commitment from the war. On the other hand, it was increasingly clear that although Chiang held a marginal numerical edge, he was rapidly losing the support of a broad public. His armies had to be pressed into service, desertion became rampant, and his cities were collapsing under the weight of corruption....

Such was the essential background to John Polly's presence in the East, Crane explained to Cassidy. War between the Communists and Nationalists was then, in 1947, in its fourth year, longer in many respects. Mao, of course, was the dominant symbol to the East while Chiang was that symbol to the West. Crane had nothing more to add to his preface than a few personal opinions of the leading combatants, including not only Mao and Chiang, but also the controversial Feng Chi.

Regarding Mao, Crane sketched a portrait of a complex visionary, perhaps even a romantic. There were undertones of the classical romances to Mao's life, elements of the bandit in a water-reed castle. The man had always emphasized the role of women and condemned the tradition of forced marriage and prostitution. Then, too, there were underlying currents of an elemental wisdom from an even older China. He was known, for example, to have read the early Sun-tzu classic on war and perhaps had drawn from it his theories on flexibility and deception. Finally Crane also sketched a clever Mao, a Mao who did not struggle against his countrymen's sense of history, but moved with it, manipulating, always manipulating.

As for Chiang, Crane could only add that the man was decades out of step with his time and probably knew it. The postwar era in question was marked with a hopelessly corrupt system. The rate of exchange was absurd, bribery and extortion were epidemic. Women were routinely sold into slavery or taken from tenant families in lieu of rent. Votes were regularly auctioned, and as part of Chiang's deal with Feng Chi, the opium dens were protected.

To sketch Feng, Crane simply repeated the outstanding events of his life as if these would be enough. Feng had begun his career in 1921 as a member of a Shanghai street gang called the Green Circle. Within two years he had risen to the regional top of the Circle and helped Chiang during the 1927 Communist slaughter by lending Chiang his Circle thugs. From this point on he led a dual life, both as a rising force in the underworld and as a loyal follower of the Nationalist cause. He served on the central advisory board and the municipal office of the Shanghai Electric Company. He also managed the distribution of south China opium, and was known to have loved fine food.

In conclusion to Cassidy, Crane said what he had always said: the China that John Polly entered in 1948 was not a China prepared to receive him or anyone remotely like him. It was essentially a bad time with rumors of smallpox and plague. Money had no relationship to anything it could buy. The nights were often terrible, the days unreal— all of which made even more remarkable what John Polly was able to accomplish during all those long years as the White Mandarin.

John Polly entered China in the summer of 1948. He was then twenty-four years old. He came by way of Manila on a military transport and reached the city of Shanghai on a muggy, velvet evening. He was a thin man of medium stature with light brown hair and delicate features. Women generally found him attractive, while men, particularly older men, were often taken by his modest, shy way of speaking. A photograph of the period shows him vaguely smiling on the docks by the Whangpoo River. He is wearing a white tropical suit, a maroon tie and a newspaper is tucked under his arm. In the background stand the broad steps of the Cathay Hotel. All in all he appears to be just another pale stranger.

Polly had originally come to China as a representative of the United States Intelligence Service. This was critical. In that summer of 1948 he was officially attached to the newly formed Central Intelligence Agency. He had joined four months earlier—he was recommended by a history professor at Yale. Polly had all the markings of a career man. He had requested a China posting because someone had told him that it would look good on his record.

There is a story of John Polly's first night in Shanghai, a story which

Crane occasionally told others. It concerns an experience which Polly was supposed to have had with a fortune-teller, one of the disreputable street magicians who read palms or astrological charts. A few hours after Polly had arrived he actually consulted one of these people out of boredom and on the spur of the moment.

He had been in his hotel room, reading by the window, occasionally stopping to watch a line of coolies moving down the gangplank of a rusting tramp steamer. Then after several hours of this he decided to take a walk. He walked until the streets became narrow, flanked by chipped plaster walls and rotting timber. Above the upturned eaves ran nests of telegraph wires and bamboo laundry poles hung from every window ledge. Then halfway down a long, sloping alley he saw the fortune-teller.

Exactly what method of divination was employed, Polly never said. He was told that he would soon be swept away by a vast and uncompromising love. It was a love that would have the potential of changing the very fabric of his life, and if he was not careful it would also destroy him. Polly later explained that he had been only faintly amused; every client was told that sort of story, he felt.

Regarding Polly's first encounter with Simon Crane: it took place at four o'clock in the afternoon, the second day after Polly's arrival. Before the meeting Polly had spent a long time laying out shirts on the bed, posing in front of the mirror, looking at images of himself that would soon become irrelevant. Then he moved down into the lobby of the Cathay Hotel.

There was a sultry, languid atmosphere in the bar, the walls in dark mahogany, the furniture in cracked red leather. Crane had taken a table by the window. From here there was a long view of the docks with junks moving slowly upstream and jetties like fingers in the brown water. Behind a row of potted palms someone was playing a sad piano.

Crane's first impression of John Polly was that the young man was like others who had been sent east in some official but limited capacity. He had made a rudimentary study of the language and customs, read most of the standard Oriental texts, accepted certain theories, discarded others. But above all he was concerned with being well thought of. Entering the bar he even paused to straighten his tie in the mirror.

As for Crane, he was slightly drunk on lukewarm gin. His suit was wrinkled and his trousers damp from perspiration. He had also laid his left sleeve in a puddle of beer. At other tables men were watching the river as if in a trance.

"So this is your first time east?" Crane asked.

"Yes, sir. First time."

"Well in that case—welcome to China." Although it sounded pretty dreary.

"Oh. Thank you, sir."

"No, don't thank me. Don't ever thank anyone who welcomes you here. This place is a sewer. Inflation is running four hundred percent. A fifth of the city is starving, and there are more refugees arriving every day. Apart from all that the Communists are massing just across the Yangtze and Chiang Kai-shek doesn't have a chance in hell of winning this war. So don't thank me, son. Whatever you do, don't thank me."

At counterpoint to the piano strains were the river sounds of bells and a passing barge. There were also faint voices of coolies on the docks. Crane watched them for a moment, then tapped the windowpane.

"They hate us," he said.

"They hate us?" Polly had been watching a girl in a rhinestone cape.

"The natives. They hate us. That's the first lesson you should learn, son. The natives hate us for all that they're worth. Not that one can blame them. We colonize them, corrupt them, bomb them and spit on their culture. And now we're trying to keep them from going Red when all they want is Red. Do you know what happens when the Red Army enters a village?"

Polly shook his head. "No. I don't know."

"The peasants applaud them. They actually applaud them. And why?"

"I guess I don't know that either."

"Because the Reds understand what they want. Chiang's army enters into a village and rapes all the women. The Red Army goes in and distributes land and rice. To peasants, mind you. To peasants who have been treated like dirt for a thousand years. And people ask why we're losing this goddamn war."

A silent man with heavy eyes was chatting with a Chinese girl. Finally she settled on his knee, slipped and overturned a glass of beer.

"I assume you haven't had a chance to meet my young demon, have you?"

"Demon, sir?"

"My other junior officer, Jay Sagan."

"No, sir. I haven't met him yet."

"Well, I expect he'll give you a different view of all this. But then Jay is a believer. He thinks we're actually going to save these people. Ever heard of Feng Chi?"

26

"Feng Chi? No, sir. I don't believe I have."

"You will. Spend some time with Jay and you'll hear a lot about him. Feng is one of Jay's clients. His word, not mine. Client. I assume it means that they scheme together."

"So Feng is a Nationalist?"

"No. He's a crook. Ever heard of the Triads?"

"I believe they're some sort of secret society, aren't they?"

"Criminal society. They work the opium routes south of here. Feng is the regional head of a faction known as the Green Circle. But he's also a celebrated anti-Communist, which is why Jay loves him. Every now and then one of Feng's people hacks up a Red for Chiang. In exchange Chiang has given him a commission in the army. It's all very cozy."

Now there was a girl in green sequins moving to the music underneath the lanterns. There were other ladies in the corridor, their laughter mingling with a slavic voice.

"Look, Polly, I don't mean to give you the wrong impression about Jay. He's a good boy."

"I understand, sir."

"It's merely that he's from a different school. You know the crowd. Dulles, Luce, Chennault. Not to mention their Agency counterparts. In their view Chiang is the last hope, while Mao is the Beast of Revelations. That's why they sent Jay. He's to be the liaison between them and Chiang's people."

"But you don't approve, sir?"

Crane smiled. "What's to approve? Jay has another set of orders. I don't control him. If he wants to spend his time courting someone like Feng Chi that's his business. I just think it's a damn shame."

"May I ask in what sense?"

"To cut ourselves off from the future. And make no mistake about it, the Communists are the future here. It's only a matter of time."

Another freighter was edging into the quay. Someone was talking about a dog race in Canton. There was a crash of breaking glass.

"Incidentally we have a house for you," Crane said suddenly. "It's all arranged."

"A house, sir?"

"On the outskirts of town. I haven't seen it, but I understand it's very nice. Of course if you don't like it . . ."

"Oh no, sir. I'm sure it will be fine."

"And as far as your duties go, we can discuss that on Monday."

"Of course, sir."

"In the meantime just stay out of trouble."

"I intend to, sir."

"You don't know what I'm talking about, do you, Polly?"

"Sir?"

"Trouble. I'm talking about the streets. They're not safe. Only last week the British lost a man. Some poor savage cut his throat and tossed him in the river."

"I see."

"So watch your step. Regardless of what they told you in Washington, this city is overrun with Communists. It's particularly bad at night."

The following afternoon Polly moved into the house. It was a small, two-story villa on the outskirts of the city. The grounds were surrounded by camphor and flame trees. A stream ran through the garden and there were groves of bamboo. Inside the walls were white stucco. The hardwood floors were covered with faded rugs. The furniture was European and also badly worn. There was a crude imitation of a Sung Dynasty landscape on the wall, a lacquer chest in the entry hall, a bronze horse on the window box. Apart from these objects the only other trace of China were the odors.

In addition to the villa Polly was given a housekeeper. She was a heavy, middle-aged woman from a northern province. Her name was Chan Shu-ying, but she told Polly to call her Mary, which was the name she had been given by missionaries with whom she had lived for many years. When Polly first met her she told him that certain rooms were occupied by ghosts. She said that she had been trying to drive them off, but so far she had had no luck. She and Polly were standing in the kitchen, and through the dusty window above the washbasin was a narrow view of the garden. Mary pointed to the window and said that there were also walking ghosts out there. She said that she had heard them walking through the bamboo, singing in the leaves. Later that night, while he sat in his room at the top of a twisted staircase, Polly also thought he heard the sound of someone singing. But this was only his second night in China, and he was still in a position to tell himself that all he had heard was the wind.

Polly reported to the office on the following Monday. He spent an hour with the security officer, who gave him a three-page list of rules and issued him a .38 Colt revolver. He was then shown to his desk in the corner of a drab beige room. He waited the rest of the morning for Crane, but the man never appeared.

At noon he crossed the street and entered the first restaurant he saw. It was a dark basement cafe with silent Chinese. It seemed to take a long time before anyone was willing to seat him, and then the food was greasy, the vegetables limp. While he ate the other patrons kept looking at him, so he kept his eyes fixed on the painted design of a bat on the wall.

When he returned to the office he found that Crane had still not arrived, and so he sat, smoking, reading the list of rules again. Finally he even began a letter to no one in particular. It was three o'clock in the afternoon, and the food he had eaten now made him nauseated. An hour before he had opened the desk drawer only to find it filled with dead flies. He desperately wanted a drink of water, but for some reason did not have the courage to ask.

This, then, was the setting for Polly's first encounter with Jay Sagan. He was sitting at the desk, hot, faintly dizzy. Then Sagan walked into the room. He was wearing a suit in bone white cotton, a tight budded rose in his lapel. Briefly he introduced himself, then suggested that they have a drink. Polly hesitated a moment, then agreed.

Once again Polly found himself overlooking the river docks, although here the furniture was chrome, and smoked mirrors had been set into the walls. Again there was a piano, and a sailor tapping out notes to an old song. There was a steady drone of traffic from the street below.

"I understand you've already met Simon," Sagan said.

"Yes. We had drinks the other day."

"And I imagine that he told you that I was in league with the devil."

A girl with a red flower in her hair was standing motionless in the doorway.

"Look, Polly, I know what Simon told you. He told you that I work with Feng Chi, right?"

Polly nodded. The girl's eyes were black in the meager light, her hair like animal fur.

"And I suppose he also told you that Feng is involved with mud?"

"Mud?"

"Opium."

"Oh. Yes, I'm afraid he did say that."

Now a second girl had joined the first with a green wrap around her shoulders.

"Did he also tell you that Feng's brother runs the prostitution rings?"

"Uh, no. I don't believe he mentioned that."

"Well, it's true. But what you've got to understand is that opium is part of these people's lives. Their culture actually. Prostitution too for that matter. One day Chiang will cut it out, but right now he's got more important things on his mind—like stopping communism."

A man in gabardine had laid his arm around the girl with a flower. He was whispering in her ear. She grinned and wet her lips.

"See, what you've got to understand, Polly, is that these people are primitive. I know how that sounds, but it's true. Take their attitude toward women, for example. Every time a woman is about to have a baby they always bring in a pile of wet newspapers. You know what that's for?"

"No. I'm afraid I don't."

"In case the baby is a girl. The Chinese think it's a waste of time trying to raise girls so they smother them in wet newspapers. Either that or they sell them to the brothels. Now of course that's not always true, but it happens enough to make you sick. First week I was here I saw the body of this little girl. She was floating in the canal not two miles from here. It was pretty disgusting."

Polly bit his lip and nodded. "Yes. I can imagine."

"That's why it's vital that Chiang maintains control here. He's the only internal force capable of civilizing these people. The Reds talk a lot about reform, but they're animals. First month I was here I saw this landlord they had caught. They had given him the hungry rat treatment. Know what that is?"

Polly breathed and shook his head. From the end of the bar came the solitary clap of hands, then cold laughter.

"That's where they stick your head in a cage with a starving rat in it. When the rat gets hungry enough it starts eating your brains out. They've also got other tricks. There were a couple of missionaries picked up the other day. The Reds had pounded bamboo stakes through their ears."

Through the window the light was fading, while fog was rising from the river. A waiter had slumped against the far wall. There were odors of cheap perfume.

"Look, Polly, I don't want to give you the wrong idea about this place. There are actually a lot of fine sides to this city. Are you married, Polly?"

"Pardon me?"

"Married?"

30

"No. No I'm not."

"Because there are a lot of very attractive women around here. And do you like good food?"

"Uh, sure."

"Because there's some very good restaurants if you know where to look. Remind me to take you to dinner sometime."

"Yes. I'd like that."

"And Polly?"

"Yes?"

"Don't listen to everything Crane tells you. He's a little over the hill. Know what I mean?"

In the days that followed Polly fell into a routine which would carry him through the first stage of his life in Shanghai. He rose early in the mornings and ate his breakfast on the veranda above the bamboo grove. Mary Chan always served bacon and eggs, which she had learned to prepare while living with the missionaries. Usually she and Polly would have brief conversations about the rising cost of food, the weather or mice in the attic. She also talked about ghosts. She said that she kept hearing them moving through the house at night. She claimed that one of them had a mouth like a fish, while another was a beautiful woman who had died eighty years ago of a broken heart and now walked the earth looking for her lover. Polly would listen and nod, but rarely had anything to add.

After breakfast he would drive to the office in a Buick that had been issued to him from the consulate motor pool. The road to the city was lined with magnolia trees and behind the trees lay marshland. On clear mornings he could see the ocher walls of distant villages. On other mornings there was only white mist rising. Then returning in the evenings he often saw bluish lights moving through the reeds. He did not know what these lights were.

His time at the office was mostly spent with paperwork. Crane ran nineteen agents in the city, and although none of them were reliable, their weekly reports had to be processed anyway. There were also the Nationalist field reports, which were usually little more than rumor and speculation, and were sometimes even intentionally falsified in the interests of morale and maintaining American enthusiasm. Consequently the estimates of Communist troop strength were routinely lowered and their victories minimized. Still, Polly was also required to process this material, and there was a lot of it. Sagan would bring in twenty to thirty pages a week.

In his spare time he liked to read and wander out to the fields around his house. From the edge of the trees he could look across the mulberry groves to the whitewashed huts of the river towns. Beyond lay the blue hills and the scalloped tiles of a ruined temple. This was empty country with unpaved roads, bamboo and swamp.

Finally there were evenings in the city. These were mostly spent with Jay Sagan and the other men from the consulate. They would usually begin at dusk and drift from one nightclub to another. In the streets the air was motionless. In the clubs the gloom was cut by colored lamps. There were rooms with lacquered doorways and ideograms on the stucco walls. Older men chatted with young girls, then left empty champagne glasses on the enamel.

With Stone and his friends the conversation always turned to women. They seemed particularly fascinated by the prostitutes along the Nanking Road. All these girls wore narrow hobble skirts, slit to the thigh or silk dresses that unzipped from the armpit in a single stroke. Polly usually remained silent during these conversations, for although he thought about women, thought about them all the time, he did not like talking about them with these other desperate, lonely men.

But one night after days of declining, Polly accompanied Sagan to a brothel in the old city. Polly did not know why he had agreed to go, and once arrived he regretted it. The brothel lay past an iron gate, then there was a path in the shadows of palms. A servant girl in clinging silk was moving like a sleepwalker. Another stood on the landing, turned to meet Polly and then turned away again.

Eventually Polly found himself in a room with a young Chinese girl. She wore a pleated skirt, a white blouse and white knee socks. Polly faced the open window as the child began to undress. From the garden came the sound of crickets, and through the trees were bluish lamps. When the girl was finally naked she stood in front of him with her hands on her hips. He did not move to touch her. He did not even look at her.

"What's wrong, Johnny. Don't you like Chinese girl?"

"No."

"Then why you come up here? You just want to watch?"

"No."

"Then what do you want?"

32

He wanted to go home. Suddenly, desperately, he wanted to go home to America.

Once a week Polly and Sagan attended the Nationalist briefings held at the Kiangwan Arsenal. Nothing of consequence was ever said at these briefings. They were like the filed reports that Sagan brought in: bad news was deleted. Good news exaggerated, sometimes fabricated. Yet from other sources, stories from refugees, articles in the foreign press, it was clear that the war was not going well. The garrisons at Mukden, Chinchow and Suchow on the Yangtze Delta were now entirely surrounded by the Communists. Nationalist morale continued to waver. Defection was increasing daily.

But these events had little impact on the foreign residents in Shanghai. Sometimes in the evenings Polly would step into the Columbia bar for a drink with Crane. Here the talk was rarely political, or at least not Chinese political. Rather, attention was focused on Europe, particularly Berlin and Athens. More usually the topic of discussion was still commerce. At the cocktail hour one stood at the windows and watched the unloading steamers.

These were slow evenings, these evenings with Crane. Eventually they began to dine together in the French Concession or else in one of the White Russian cafes. They did not discuss anything in particular. Mostly Crane would simply ramble on about whatever came into his mind. Some nights he would talk about an older China, which he called the world's greatest example of a rule by the few over the many. Here, he said, had been a society as intricately structured as an atom, and entranced by its own perfection, it had turned inward and grown stagnant. Thus, said Crane, communism was not such a departure from the past as some would think. The Chinese had always defined themselves as individuals only in terms of the masses. "If I not be a man among men," said Confucius, "then what am I to be?" Crane quoted.

On another night he talked about the alternative to the Confucian doctrine as contained in the five thousand characters of the *Tao-te-ching.* According to tradition this text had been written in the sixth century by a mystic called Lao-tzu a few days before he disappeared into the mountains. Crane called the work transcendent and eternal, although he said that its power was only rarely understood. This was Polly's first actual exposure to the *Tao,* which he would later translate in his letters as *The Way and Its Power.*

In time, and through a string of these evenings, Polly came to see that Crane held a progressive view of history wherein the past could not be divorced from the present. It was a view which Polly himself would one day adopt, and that too would be reflected in the Peking letters.

It was not long after Polly and Crane began spending time together that Crane began to work the boy into the actual process of running live networks. First Polly began to familiarize himself with the field. Apart from Crane's station there were three intelligence services actively opposing the Communists in the Shanghai area. There were the British, the French and the internal security police of the Nationalist Chinese. None of them had been particularly successful in penetrating the Communist cells, at least not at the higher levels. Furthermore the life expectancy of the agents was painfully short. Hardly a month went by without somebody dying.

As for Crane's agents, they were neither better nor worse than anyone else's. They were generally young, cynical; they spied only for the money, expecting nothing else in return. They lied when they thought they could get away with it, and told the truth when they had to. None of them believed in Chiang Kai-shek, democracy, the United States or even Simon Crane. They believed only in themselves, and perhaps their next meal.

But if there was a larger theme to these days, it was probably best revealed to Polly in a conversation that took place about six weeks after his arrival. It was a Friday, and earlier news had come in that an agent had been killed. As usual there were no details other than the medical report, which stated that the victim had been clubbed to death and then thrown into the canals. The British identified the body and called Crane. After the telephone call Crane sat alone in his office for a while. Then he asked Polly to take a walk with him. The two men left the consulate and began moving up the Bund. They turned east along the creek without any destination in mind.

Earlier there had been rain. Now the air was moist and warm. This was a neighborhood of open sewers, and on the muddy rise above the creek there were hundreds of shacks in corrugated iron. Water dripped from the horned roofs of decaying factories. The sky was vaguely yellow.

They had walked in silence for a long time. Then Crane said, "We hardly knew him, did we?"

"No, sir. I suppose we didn't."

"I ran him for almost two years and what did I really know about him?

34

His name was Lin Tee-hsu. He lived with a cabaret girl. He liked English cigarettes."

"We also knew that he was a security risk, always had been. You told me that he could never remember things and so he had to write them down."

Crane sighed. "Yes. That was true. He used to pull out these little slips of paper. I must have told him a hundred times that nothing should be written down, but of course he didn't listen."

"Well, maybe that's what happened then. Perhaps he left one of his notes lying about. I mean, it wasn't necessarily your fault. In fact it might not have even had anything to do with us. I mean, these people are always murdering one another, aren't they?"

Crane stiffened. "Who told you that? Did Jay tell you that?"

Polly shrugged. "I don't know. I suppose I just heard it somewhere."

"Well, it's not true. These people kill for the same reasons and at the same rate as anyone else."

They passed a brick foundry, built on a foundation of rammed earth. Broken pottery lay scattered in the mud.

"You're wondering why we do it, aren't you?" Crane said suddenly.

"I'm sorry?"

"I said you're wondering why we even continue the game."

"I'm afraid I don't follow, sir."

"Oh come on, John. Here I've just lost another boy and you've been trying your best to console me, but all along you've been wondering what it's all for. Isn't that right?"

Polly shrugged again. "Well, I suppose there have been times when things did seem a little..."

"Absurd?"

"I wouldn't have used that word, sir."

"How about pointless then?"

"All right. Maybe there have been moments."

"Of course there have. You don't have to be ashamed to admit that. If I were in your position I'd have thought that it was all pretty pointless too. One only need look at the success of this station, not to mention the death rate. But there are other factors, John."

"Yes, sir. I'm sure there are."

"Only you don't have the faintest idea what those factors are, do you?"

"No, sir. I suppose I don't."

There was a movement in a clump of nettles, then the cry of another bird. Ahead lay a fallen gate and a lump of stone half eaten by black ivy.

Crane said, "I imagine that within a year the Communists will control the entire mainland. When that happens the country will be completely lost to us. The Communists have no use for us now, and they certainly won't have any when they've won. You and I will be posted in Taiwan or Hong Kong, but we might as well be in Washington. We won't be in any position to deal with these people, not in any position at all. Consequently if we're going to make any sort of long-term arrangement, then we'd better do it soon. Do you understand what I'm saying, John?"

Through the gate lay a splintered trellis, scattered bricks and the headless form of a statue. There were also stirring shadows in the ivy.

"I'm not sure, sir. What exactly do you mean by a long-term arrangement?"

Crane kicked at a loose brick. "Ah. That would be a placement, wouldn't it?"

"A placement?"

"Someone on the inside. Someone in the party. Perhaps even someone close to Mao."

Polly turned suddenly to look at the man. "You're serious, aren't you?"

"Completely."

"And you think it's possible?"

"Why not?"

"But how?"

"Oh I think it could be done in the usual way. Either we recruit an existing party member, or else build our own—from the ground up."

Then, softly, "The Russians call it a mole, don't they, sir? I mean that's what they would call a long-term placement. Say someone who has to be developed over fifteen years."

Crane nodded. "Yes. Now that you mention it, I suppose they do call it a mole. So you see there is a precedent. It has been done."

Far in the distance there seemed to be smoke rising from the mountains, and the drone of heavy aircraft.

"Do you have anyone in mind?"

"Ah. That's the key, isn't it? Whom do we play? It can't be just anyone. It has to be someone with the potential to go far, to make a name for himself, to rise to the top of the heap."

"And that boy? Lin? He was working on this?"

"Yes, as a matter of fact he was. That is, they're all working on it to some extent. It has to be that way, because time is running out. If we're going to play a man in, then it must be done soon, while the war is still

36

going on, while the party is still in flux. Right now the Reds need people. They'll take anyone. It's the perfect opportunity. You see that, don't you?"

"Yes, sir. I guess I do."

"That's why I'd like you to begin working on it as well."

"Me, sir?"

"Why not? You learn fast."

"But I wouldn't even know where to begin."

"Oh, that's easy. All you have to keep in mind is that our choice can be narrowed down to one of eight hundred million Chinese."

Which was only ironic in retrospect, when five months later the concept of the White Mandarin was formed.

In opposition to Crane's world, and all that it actually stood for, there was Jay Sagan's world, as generally found among the Chinese elite. Here one saw Feng Chi, his brother and the other Nationalists. On occasion there was even Chiang Kai-shek, and always his presence was visible. Social affairs were usually somber. Emphasis was on respect properly paid. One was also expected to bring gifts, and to refrain from discussing the underworld.

Polly's first encounter with Feng Chi occurred about three months into his stay in Shanghai. This encounter took place at Feng's home near the airport beyond the city limits. Here lay a vast, whitewashed estate, surrounded by walls and tall trees. Polly had accompanied Sagan to the affair, and they arrived in the late afternoon. There were tables of crayfish, crystallized apples and egg custard. Beneath a garden pavilion three girls performed a dance, while a forth sat behind to play the single-stringed violin. Later there was even a song about the mandarin duck which never left its mate and so became a symbol of love.

Toward evening Polly wandered out into the garden, and found himself on a lacquered bridge above a pond. He had thought he was alone, the other guests scattered below among the dwarf pines. But then he heard a footstep from behind, turned and saw a man in the shadow of the mulberry vines. The man was standing with his hands in the pockets of his coat. A red cravat was knotted at his throat. For a moment they merely looked at one another. Then the man moved closer, and by the lantern light Polly could see the smooth face of Feng Chi.

"Are you enjoying yourself, Mr. Polly?" Feng's head had never seemed so prominent, entirely bald and glistening.

"Yes. Thank you. It's very nice."

"Too bad Mr. Crane could not have also come."

"Yes. Too bad."

Feng placed his hands on the railing, his enormous eyes fixed on the water.

"Tell me, Mr. Polly, how do you find my country?"

"I find it very beautiful and interesting."

"But there are a great many problems, wouldn't you say?"

"Yes. I'm afraid there are."

"And for every problem there are many possible solutions, isn't that also true?"

"Yes. I suppose it is." And also supposed that Feng was trying to size him up.

"I mention this, Mr. Polly, because it has been my observation that among your colleagues there are two very different opinions as to how my country's problems might be solved. So I wonder if you favor the solutions offered by Mr. Crane, or those offered by my good friend Mr. Sagan?"

A second passed, and Polly remained absolutely still. He had briefly wondered if there wasn't something clever he could say, some ironic and evasive reply. Both men's fingers were tight around the railing. They were waiting.

Then, "I suppose I'd have to say that I generally favor Simon Crane."

His answer jolted them both, as if each understood that this would mark the start of all the pain that would follow.

In a letter written at the end of his fourth month in Shanghai Polly noted that the Chinese especially feared the ghosts of drowned people because these ghosts were believed to wait by the rivers and lakes to pull in those who passed. He further wrote that it was becoming increasingly clear to him that there were three, not two, distinct worlds in China. There was the old, the new and the unreal, and each was like the ghost of a drowned person trying to pull him under.

Of this third, unsubstantial world, Polly would only say that he had seen it in glimpses, like the marginal hallucinations one experiences when tired or hungry. But it was in both the city and country. It was in a vision of rickshaws waiting by a red clay wall, in the skyline of pagodas, in the peaked roofs. Most of all it was in the eyes of the impoverished Chinese.

Since his first night in Shanghai Polly did not like to go into the streets that lay behind the Bund. Sometimes, however, agents had to be met on their own ground, debriefed in a ruined factory or a one-room tenement apartment where the windows had been boarded up with cardboard. Then one walked in alleys filled with windblown paper, bits of rotting fruit, sometimes even the skeletons of fish. And if walking through these streets was sometimes like walking through a dream, then it was a dream that would eventually lead him into the main body of his story.

One Sunday afternoon Polly's housekeeper started to tell him about the dragons. She said that you could faintly see them rising like steam in the mornings along the marsh. They were also in the bottoms of canals and in the wind and the rain. But mostly, she said, the dragons were in the mountains. They were also the sound of the mountains.

"What do they sound like?" he asked.

"Like giants groaning," she replied.

"If I were to stand at the foot of the mountain would I hear a dragon?"

She thought a moment. They were standing in the garden. The colors of water and bamboo were washing together.

Finally she said, "No. Even if you stood next to the mountain you would not hear dragons."

"Why not?"

"Because you don't have Chinese ears yet."

But if he did not have Chinese ears, a few days later he began to wonder if he might not be developing the Chinese eye.

Late one evening while returning from a dinner party his Buick broke down about five miles from his home. It was an uncertain hour after midnight and he had no other choice but to walk. The road ran straight for several miles across the swamp and between the magnolia trees. After walking several minutes he thought he heard a nightingale calling. There was also the strident hum of cicadas.

Then on the last stretch before his house he saw a figure in the shadows ahead. Whether man or woman he could not tell. It was moving slowly, almost gliding as if blown toward him by the predawn wind. Closer now he heard its footsteps and saw that it was wrapped in a dark robe. Even the face was concealed. He vaguely thought of calling out, but was afraid somehow that it would not reply, and he would be left with his own echo. Only later, much later as he lay in bed, did he recall the moment of passing, and the almond eyes of a Eurasian girl, glancing up in terror.

When he woke in the morning the image of that girl was still very much on his mind. Not that he really knew what to make of it all, other than the fact that she had been very beautiful. He supposed that it would be enough to say, possibly at a dinner party, "The strangest thing happened to me the other night on the Hungeo Road..." Then everyone would have been intrigued and amused and the matter forgotten. But as it was Polly could not forget this girl, and the memory of her made him very still and quiet.

Later, while he sat at the wicker table with his untouched egg in a porcelain bowl, the image of her still remained. He had not felt like eating. Finally his housekeeper came out through the screen door, frowned and started piling his dishes on the tray. She was wearing a flowered blouse with the faces of dragons in the petals.

"You work late last night," she said.

"Yes. I worked late." He had also wakened with a headache and his legs were knotted.

"You work late, and now you don't eat. That's very bad."

The morning light was flat and pale. The entire landscape seemed drained of color.

Suddenly he said, "Mary, who is that woman who lives down the road?"

"Woman? What woman? Chinese woman?"

"Half Chinese."

"There's no woman."

"But I saw her last night. She was walking along the road about a mile from here."

The housekeeper started to smile. "Ah. I know what you saw. You saw a ghost."

"No. It wasn't a ghost."

She shrugged. "Okay, no ghost," and left him sitting among the steaming bamboo.

In time he began to realize that the memory of that girl might never fade. Whenever he drove the road he thought of her, slowed a little to watch carefully through the windshield. He tried very hard to envision her face as he remembered it, peering out from the hood of her cloak. Sometimes he could picture her quite clearly, while at other times there was only a feeling. But even after several days the memory remained.

So in the end he came to think of this memory as a focal point to everything in China that he did not understand. In the streets there were magicians selling spirit names, boys flying kites to take away the evil. He had been told that certain trees had spirits in the shape of oxen, and that

40

there were demons that sucked the breath out of babies. Once he had seen an old woman holding up the little jacket of her grandchild. She was letting the jacket fill with wind in the hope of catching the child's spirit that had flown away after a long and painful illness.

But if this inner world remained elusive, it also remained pervasive. There were moments in the morning or at twilight along the marsh when it seemed as if the whole landscape was filled with shuddering ghosts. Until finally Polly even grew to wonder what would happen if that unreality were ever to eclipse the reality, which in a sense was exactly what happened as he began his fifth month in Shanghai.

Each year the elite of Shanghai gathered at the home of Feng Chi to celebrate his birthday. In addition to the Chinese guests, a few American and European Nationalist supporters were also invited, and among those was Jay Sagan. Sagan received his invitation on a Friday and that evening he invited Polly for a drink at the Columbia bar.

Ever since Polly had become close with Simon Crane he had not seen much of Sagan, such were the office politics. One was either a friend of Sagan and the Kuomintang, or else a friend of Crane and the old China hands. In Washington there were the same kinds of divisions among the Orientalists. Either one believed that Chiang Kai-shek was the only possible savior of China, or else one believed that he was a corrupt and incompetent tyrant who was soon to be crushed by the Communists. There was not supposed to be any middle ground.

But that Friday evening in the Columbia bar it seemed to Polly that there may have been a middle ground after all. It was well past the cocktail hour and the noises around them were soft. There was only the sound of ice in the glasses and the turning pages of the evening paper.

"I want you to come to Feng's birthday," said Sagan. His cuff links were cut into the shape of tiger's claws.

"It's two weeks from this coming Sunday, and I think it's important that you come."

"Why?" Polly asked.

"Lots of reasons."

"Name one."

"Well, I think it's important that we show my people that just because you're in tight with Simon it doesn't mean that you're necessarily at odds with the Nationalists."

"But I am at odds with the Nationalists."

41

"No you're not. The Communists are at odds with them. You simply disagree with some of their policies. Besides, you wouldn't even be in disagreement at all if you hadn't been listening to Simon."

It was true, and every now and then it worried Polly. What if he wound up as just another listless China hand?

"So how about it? Will you come?"

"Let me think about it."

Sagan began to rattle the ice in his glass. There was a faint echo of a low clarinet from an adjoining room.

"Look, if you're concerned with what Simon will think, don't be. He doesn't give a damn if you spend an afternoon with the bad guys."

Polly was also rattling the ice. "I still want to think about it."

"What's there to think about?"

"Well, for one thing Feng doesn't like me."

"Why? Because you told him that you were a friend of Simon's. He won't remember that. Anyway that's the whole point. I want to show him that my station isn't divided."

But Polly still shook his head. "I don't know, I don't think it would look right."

"Sure it would look right. In fact not only would it look right it might just be the best thing you could do—career-wise."

"What do you mean?"

"It's like this. You don't want to be seen exclusively with Crane's people. What if Crane is moved out next month? You could be up the creek. It's much better to circulate. That way if the roof falls in on one house you still got a place to go to get out of the rain. You understand what I'm saying?"

Polly finally agreed to go. Not perhaps because he wanted to, but at this early stage of his life, Polly was still under the illusion that he would always be a regular sort of career man.

In retrospect Polly would write that on the morning before the party he had had the strangest feeling that something vital might occur. While shaving he thought he had seen the reflection of a face in the mirror. It had startled him and his soap mug slipped out of his fingers. He had had that mug for years, and now it lay in pieces on the tile all because the wind had caught the muslin curtains. Then on the veranda he had seen two sticks floating down the stream and for an instant thought those sticks were mating snakes. But whether a good omen or bad he could not remember.

He and Sagan arrived at Feng's home in the early afternoon. They came in the consulate limousine, because appearances were vital here. Lanterns were strung in rows above the garden, the willows hung with streamers, guests were mingling in the shadows of larger trees. Sagan had brought a gift, a panther carved in jade. There were children on the lawn. The light was almost transparent.

Soon along the gravel path Polly found himself discussing politics with a silk merchant from Canton. The merchant said that the Communists were like a north wind. Overhead one side of the sky was already black and a wind was moving in from the sea.

Next there was a clerk who worked in the British consulate. He was a wizened creature who had spent some twenty years in the East. They discussed opium and the philosophy of Yan Chu, who believed that there was no God, no afterlife and that men were at the fate of blind forces. The clerk went on to say these two subjects were very dear to Feng. Then he added that he had hated both brothers for years and had only come to this party because he had been ordered to do so.

By the early evening Polly found himself queasy, possibly from too much shrimp. So he broke off another vapid conversation and began drifting through the crowd in search of Sagan. He passed several rooms, but heard only the nasal tones of the local dialects. There were moments when he hated this language, hated the sour kitchen smells and the lingering odor of rosewater and almonds.

In the end he was wandering randomly, past an inner courtyard, through a latticed gate to the remote ends of the garden. Here the limbs of trees were unnaturally twisted. There were tulips withering on a muddy slope, and a cypress grove beyond a field of willows. He thought he was entirely alone.

Then he saw the girl. She was high on the terraced hillside, but moving down, sliding her hand along a bamboo railing. Greener stalks of bamboo stood behind her. She wore a simple dress, blue with white lilies. He could hear her footsteps on the wet leaves. He took a step himself, and she saw him. She walked like loose silk blown in the wind. It was all he could do to keep from staring.

"I'm looking for my friend." He had to say something. But she did not seem to understand. Her head was cocked at an angle. There was the oddest half-smile on her lips.

So he added, "I thought he might be up there," while the blood drained from his face. "Did you see anyone up there?"

"No," her voice was soft and breathless.

"Well I suppose I'll have to look elsewhere."

But neither moved. He was rooted to the sandy path. Her hand was still on the railing. Their eyes kept darting away and meeting again.

Then, before it was too late: "You look very much like someone I saw the other night on the Hungeo Road. You see, I was walking around midnight and..."

"Yes," she said. "That was me." But so casually, he could hardly believe it.

"Really? Isn't that incredible. My car had broken down and..."

"My car too."

"Your car too? Isn't that remarkable? I mean what a coincidence."

"Yes. It was a coincidence." But she did not seem impressed. Her voice was still cool and soft.

"And now the two of us meeting like this," he blurted.

"Yes, very unusual."

Then it seemed she had had enough, and left him on the path, feeling fairly limp and cheated.

In all probability Polly knew that he would have eventually forgotten about that girl, or if remembered it would only have been in passing, an idle memory of her framed between the cypress branches. By now he had been in China long enough to know that every visitor had certain strange encounters. At the time you believed they were significant. Then after a while they became just another old China story, which you thought about at odd times in your life.

Still, in the days that immediately followed his meeting with this woman, Polly made a point of staying close to Jay Sagan in the hope that there might be another party and another chance encounter. In fact there was another affair with the Chinese elite. Guests were assembled at the docks and then ferried out to a sloop in the harbor. The deck was filled with women, and Polly spent a long time wandering among them. But he did not find *her.* So in the end he simply killed the night with champagne and small talk, while an orchestra played a medley of show tunes.

There were also the occasional evenings at the clubs, although by the end of a week Polly was merely tagging along out of boredom. He liked to watch the sing-song girls cadging drinks and the prostitutes under the lamplight. On any given night there were lots of girls who met Polly's gaze from across the bars, through the cigarette smoke. They had all learned to smile over the rim of their whiskey glasses just like the women in the American films.

Then there was the evening when he found himself in a club where the conversations were more subdued and a saxophone played softly in the background. Earlier he had been ill and vomited in the washroom. Now it was half-past midnight and he was just staring into the bluish gloom. Someone called his name. He nodded, and they brought him another gin and tonic. Finally a woman started singing "The Saint James Infirmary," and before it was over he had the briefest thought that he had reached the end of something. Then he looked out across the room and there was the girl again.

She was standing by the beaded curtains, talking with a waiter. As he rose from the chair she looked at him, glanced away, but then had to look again. He had never seen her more substantial, simply leaning against the door jamb in a dark green dress, toying with a string of pearls. She was wearing the same perfume she had worn that day in the garden.

"Hello," he smiled. "Do you remember me? I'm the one from the Hungeo Road, and then the party."

"Yes. I remember." But she seemed a little dazed.

"I'm glad to see you again. I started to wonder if you really existed."

"I exist."

"I mean I thought perhaps you were just a ghost," and he laughed, but stopped when he saw that she wasn't even smiling.

"You thought I was a ghost?"

"Well, not really a ghost, but . . ."

"I thought you were a ghost too. When I saw you on the road that was what I thought."

"I guess neither of us are ghosts," and tried to force another laugh as a filler.

"I have to go now."

"But can't I buy you a drink?"

"My friends are waiting."

"But just one drink?"

"I have to go."

She began to walk away. She was actually walking away.

"But I don't even know your name."

Then she stopped and glanced back over her shoulder. "It's Kim," and smiled.

Through the rest of that evening he spoke only when spoken to, and

45

occasionally did not answer at all. Once he even excused himself and stumbled to the men's room where he slumped against the wall and shut his eyes to remember.

It was nearly dawn when Sagan finally drove Polly back to his house on the Hungeo Road. Mist lay in sheets above the marsh and clotted among the banyan trees. Mostly there was silence, except for the tick of the cooling radiator.

Suddenly Sagan said, "I want to talk to you about that girl in the club."

"What girl?" As if he didn't know.

"The one you spoke to in the club tonight."

"Oh, that girl." His stomach was starting to knot.

"Do you know who she is?"

Polly shrugged. "Yeah. She's just some girl. Her name is Kim."

"She's not just some girl."

"What do you mean?" Now his mouth was starting to dry up.

"I mean that she's not just any girl. She's Danny Feng's mistress."

"What?"

"You heard me. She's the mistress of Feng Chi's brother."

Polly felt the blood pounding in his ears, thinking: *this could have happened only in China.*

"So I want you to stay away from her, John. She's the property of the Fengs."

"What do you mean property?"

"I mean just that. They own her. She used to work in one of the brothels. Then Danny Feng took a liking to her and made her his mistress. So I want you to stay away from her. We don't need trouble from the Fengs."

"Look, I was only talking to her."

"Fine. Just make sure you don't do it again. Okay?"

"Come on, Jay."

"Okay?"

Polly clenched his teeth and nodded. "Okay. I'll stay away from her."

And for a while he actually managed to keep her out of his thoughts. Until he fell into bed and shut his eyes. Then she came to him quite clearly, unconsciously biting her lower lip, her eyes shining through dark strands of hair. He did not fall asleep until dawn.

The next day was Sunday, and Polly spent the morning in his garden. He had always liked walking under the nets of leaves. Once he had found the bleached bones of a cat, which his housekeeper had said was a sure sign of spirits. But he had also found a rusting shovel and in the outer fields there was the chassis of an old tractor.

In the evening he sat in the kitchen while his housekeeper chopped vegetables which she would force him to eat later. But he loved to watch her handle food. He had never seen such reverence. Rice sifting through her fingers might have been gold. She looked especially pious dissecting fish.

While she worked she also talked. She would tell him about her family. There were brothers that she hadn't seen in years, and a sister who lived in San Francisco. She also talked about people she had known, and these stories often twisted from one event to another until Polly could not be sure who was alive and who was not. But mostly she talked about the ghosts, and tigermen and apemen and a forest where your shadow stuck to the trees. There was also a land of vampires and a place without time beyond the sky.

But tonight he had his own question, a question that had been with him all day. He waited until she sat down for tea. Then he casually asked, "Say, Mary, who is Feng Chi?"

She did not raise her eyes. She did not stop pouring the tea.

"Mary? Feng Chi?"

Then her voice was very cold. "Why you care?"

"Oh he's just someone I met the other day. So I was wondering if you've ever heard of him."

"Everybody hear of Feng Chi."

"What about his brother, Danny Feng?"

"Everybody hear of him too."

"What are they like?"

"Very rich. Very strong."

"Strong?"

"Like warlords."

"You mean powerful."

"Yes. Very powerful."

"What makes them so powerful?"

She hesitated a moment. Then she began to pantomime the ritual of lighting an opium pipe.

He nodded and then said, "Oh I see."

"So you keep away from them, okay?"

"Why?"

"Because they are bad people, Mr. Polly. Feng Chi and his brother both bad people. Everybody know that."

"Everybody? Who's everybody, Mary?"

Then she used a Chinese word to describe the masses. It was a word that had become very popular with the Communists, and it was the first time he had ever heard her use it.

On the following Monday morning Polly requested four volumes of files from the consulate archive room. The first volume consisted of documents compiled from the late 1920's and were concerned with the formal structure of the Shanghai criminal gangs, particularly the Green Circle. Next there was a volume dealing with the early years of formation when Triad societies largely drew their membership from smugglers along the Grand Canal. This material continued through to 1918 when the Green Circle appropriated the opium routes from the British concession. The third volume contained extensive details on the Nationalist government's use of the Circle in the suppression of the Communist cells, including the employment of torture on Communist party members. Finally there was also material on Feng Chi, his brother and their gradual rise to regional supremacy.

Today those records which Polly reviewed are stored in the Langley archives along with all later material on Feng Chi and his role in the secret China wars. Also in the archives is the actual log, complete with Polly's signature, showing what files he had taken from the consulate shelves and how long he had kept them. This log later became a critical document, because it clearly suggested that from the start Polly had marked Feng Chi as an enemy.

If Polly's inner thoughts at this stage were still focused upon the girl there was nothing in his outer life to suggest it. Soon after his encounter in the nightclub he stopped accompanying Sagan to those places where the Chinese elite were known to gather. Instead he once again began dining with Crane, or else simply remained home. It was about this time that he had begun to read *Our Oriental Heritage,* and at the end of three weeks the margins were covered with his spidery notes, attesting to the fact that if nothing else he had certainly tried to understand these people.

Also a factor of these days was the Communist offensive in Manchuria. Reliable accounts of the fighting were scarce, but it seemed fairly clear that the Nationalist Army was performing badly. Not that there was any undue alarm within Shanghai. Rather, people seemed fairly unconcerned, except for those like Crane who continually muttered that the end was near.

But regardless of the war, for Polly these were generally controlled days, days filled with the tedium of espionage. Every morning he carefully chose a tie to match his shirt. Every evening he practiced writing Chinese characters in a notebook he had purchased especially for that purpose. He kept a bottle of shaving lotion in his desk, and had begun to count the number of cigarettes he smoked with the aim of stopping by the end of January.

Only the odd hours were bad, afternoons in the torpid heat, nights in his bedroom when he could not sleep. Then the disquietude, which was also part of his life in China would start closing in.

Yet this was the time in which Polly came closest to living the life he had originally envisioned for himself. Those who knew him well during this period would later recall him as a reasonable, conscientious young man, as reasonable and conscientious as any in the foreign community. When he borrowed books he always returned them on time, and with an appreciative note. Notes were also sent to the homes of those who had invited him to dinner, and it was about this time that he ordered his first business cards—discreet, embossed on white linen. As for those secret thoughts, Crane would later swear to the end that Polly had still been primarily concerned with being well thought of, while probably believing that the entire East was merely a stepping-stone on the road to a brilliant career.

But then on Thursday morning Crane casually mentioned that certain friends of his were giving a picnic to be held at the home of a shipping director. Crane asked if Polly would like to attend. Polly replied that he would be delighted. He did not give it another thought, because nothing of consequence ever happened among Crane's friends.

The day of the party was warm and clear, with a breeze blowing from the south. The guests assembled under striped cabanas that had been erected on the lawn. The grounds were ringed with magnolia trees and high shrubbery, while on the rise of a hill stood a white gabled house with blue shutters.

For a while Polly sat by the reflecting pond, chatting with some women from the Red Cross. They discussed the problems of disease among the impoverished natives, while he prodded the lily pads with a stick. Finally one of the women began to complain about the heat, and Polly offered to bring her a glass of lemonade. This was precisely the sort of act that he wanted to be known for. Also, he was bored with these women and their millions of dying peasants.

A flagstone path along the hedgerow led to the center of the garden. Here every leaf was still and limp. There was a glare off the broad lawns, and a clump of lavender flowers in the distance. A dozen guests lingered in the shade by a cricket pitch. A child was examining a daffodil bulb. Then gazing out farther, fifty feet across the lawn, Polly stopped. And raised his hand to shade his eyes. And then he saw her.

She stood with her back to the others. There was a glass of champagne in her hand. Her dress was very much like the one she had worn that night in the bar, but her hair was gathered behind. For several fragile seconds neither moved at all. There was only a sense of others moving and the white light of the late afternoon. Then slowly she nodded and began to move off toward a mirage of eucalyptus trees in the distance. He lit a cigarette, waited, then followed.

It was cool under these trees, and beyond lay the flat, open land of a marsh in tall reeds. The light off the marsh looked like steam. But where she stood the light was faintly gray. Once again there were several seconds of silence: she simply standing beneath the branches, he moving toward her. It was a brittle moment.

He said, "Hello. How are you?"

She did not smile. "I'm fine, thank you. How are you?"

He shrugged. "Why did you meet me here? You don't even know my name."

And then she smiled. "Yes I do. It's John. I asked and they told me."

He saw a flight of geese in the blanched sky. The light was both still and moving. Her eyes were very moist.

"They told me about you too," he said. "They told me you were Danny Feng's mistress, and that I wasn't to see you."

"Yes," she whispered. "We shouldn't be doing this."

"So why did you come?"

She shook her head. "Do you want me to leave?"

"No. I'm glad you came. I've been thinking about you."

Then again that same half-smile. "I know. I've been thinking about you too."

"You have?"

"Yes, John. I have."

Somehow they had drawn closer, and now both stood in the same

50

circle of trampled reeds. When he started to speak again she laid her finger on his lips. Obviously there was nothing more to explain.

Even later they hardly spoke. He asked only, "Will I see you again?"

She answered, "Do you know the bridge at the Broadway Mansions? Come Tuesday at seven o'clock."

As for the rest of the day, it passed nearly like a dream. He even forgot about the lemonade he was supposed to have brought to the woman from the Red Cross.

The night she and Polly met by the Garden Bridge there was a cool wind moving in from the bay. She wore a simple black dress, a black handbag on her shoulder. When Polly first saw her, she was standing by the silhouette of humped iron. There was a faint sound like low wailing from the river.

Without a word they started walking along the half-deserted streets. There was alternating light and darkness between the shadows of the trees, and the streetlamps. There was also the occasional rattle of a passing tram, and bells from incoming steamers.

She began speaking with no introduction. They had been walking in silence, and then suddenly she was talking about her life. As she talked he had the impression that she had been waiting a long time to tell someone, although her voice was very flat.

Her mother, she said, had been a poor girl from the northeast. Her father had been a White Russian who had fled the Soviets from Vladivostok. As a child she had loved to hear the stories of how her father had arrived with the remnants of his army. Only later did she learn that some of what she had been told was untrue.

In those early years she had lived in a small apartment in the French Concession. Her father had worked in a restaurant called the Blue Swan. She said that it had been an elegant restaurant, serving only Europeans and Americans.

When it became time for her to attend school she was sent to a private class in the British section. Her father had been adamant that she learn English, which he believed was the language that would open any door. There were months when she did nothing but practice forming words in the hopes of sounding like her instructors. In the end, however, it came to nothing. She still spoke English like a girl from China.

Her father died when she was twelve. Most of the money went to the funeral, which she claimed was quite extravagant. A month later her mother gave up the apartment in the French Concession, and they moved into the old city. Here they survived minimally, gathering wood in vacant lots, pounding out tin in a factory. Of these days she remembered the voices of old people chanting the lunar prayers, the view of the horned roofs through shutters, little else.

When she was thirteen her mother made a deal with a woman who ran an entertainment house along the Foochow Road. Here she slept in a room with nine other girls. From the beginning there was always talk of men. Her first was a boy from Nanking. He was barely older than she, and he called her Little Mother. Two months later she began formal training. Sometimes she was beaten with a willow branch. Her mistress had eyes that twisted up like crooked pins.

She was seventeen when she met Danny Feng. He came to the house on Foochow Road, just as the others had come. He was accompanied by friends, all relatively drunk. She said that whenever she heard men climbing the stairs it was like a small drum pounding in her brain. She would sit on the edge of the bed and wait.

With Danny she said that she had to get down on her knees and open his trousers with her teeth. Then he casually bent her over a chair. He was neither gentle nor rough, although once he kissed her and then wiped his hand across his mouth.

He returned to her room every week for almost a year. In the beginning he rarely spoke. He would just sit in the chair, watch her undress, then ask her to kneel. He always asked. Even when she knew perfectly well what to do, he still insisted upon asking first. After he had gone she would clean his cigarette ash off the mat.

Then one day he came with another man whom she was later to learn was his brother Feng Chi. This time Feng Chi sat in the chair and smoked a cigarette. Danny told her to take off her dress and pose for his brother. He had her turn slowly this way and that. He had her cup her breasts and run her hands along her thighs. He had her lie down and then stand on her toes with her arms over her head. After about an hour of this Feng Chi nodded approvingly. Then both men left the room. Later Kim learned that a bargain had been made with the house mistress, and now she belonged to Danny. Within the trade, she said, this was considered the best fortune imaginable.

Now she again lived in the heart of the French Concession. She had a spacious apartment with modern furniture, thick rugs and a view of the river. She also had pocket money, jewelry and beautiful clothes. In return for all this she remained at Danny's call. She slept with him, listened to him and accompanied him to those affairs at which he wanted to be seen with a beautiful woman. It was an open and defined relationship. Danny's wife knew all about Kim, and tolerated her because she knew that Kim would never be anything more than a slave. Within the milieu, however, Kim was afforded a surprising amount of respect.

It was nearly midnight when Kim finished speaking. They had come to a park by the river's edge, and sat on an iron bench. The shadows were shifting in the wind. Polly was thinking that he had never been with someone who made him feel so removed from the world. All over China people were dying in one another's arms, while he was just sitting here with this girl.

After a long silence she said, "I know a place we can go."

"A place?" He might have been talking in his sleep.

"It's on the road out of the city. It's near that spot where we first saw each other and I thought you were a ghost. It's a cottage. No one knows about it, not even Danny."

He started to speak, but stopped. Then he managed to say, "We don't have to go anywhere. It would be all right if we just stayed here."

"No. I want to go there with you. I want to."

"But maybe we should think about it first."

"I already thought about it."

"What about Danny?"

"He won't find out."

"But what if he does?"

"Please."

The cottage lay well off the road among the banyan trees. All around grew tall reeds and bamboo. Farther on were the canals, then the limitless marsh. The walls were mud brick. The roof was thatched. Reed mats had been laid on the dirt floor. They undressed by the light of a kerosene lamp, then lay down on the mattress. When he saw her naked she was so beautiful he had to catch his breath. When she fell into his arms he felt as if his life had begun to unravel. At first they clung to each other, and time seemed to stretch to the breaking point. But when they were no longer afraid it was enough to be still.

After that first night they met again on a Friday, then again on Monday. Initially they told each other that it could not go on, that they had to stop. Although he had not told her the details of what he did at the consulate, she knew that he was jeopardizing a great deal by seeing her, not only his own life, but also the lives of others. Away from her the risk seemed even more acute. There were moments at the station when he could not believe what he was doing, moments when he was deeply afraid. But whenever he entered her cottage it was like entering another world. It was a world of simplicity and static hours. There were always birds. It was as if this was a China of a thousand years ago.

Often she would ask him to talk about America. She wanted to know what his parents were like, what kind of automobile they drove, what sort of house they lived in. She conceived of America as one vast metropolis from horizon to horizon. Or else she thought of the open range where cowboys vanished into the distance. Once he asked if she would like to live in America. She thought about it a long time. Then she said that they might not have any choice. It was the closest they had come to mentioning Danny Feng for quite a while.

In many ways he realized that Kim was a very simple girl. She dreamed of going to Paris one day and marrying John and having children. Once she told him that beyond a life with him and their future children all she really wanted was a house full of good furniture. Furniture, she said, was important.

But there were other times when he sensed a deeper, introspective Kim, a girl who understood what was wrong with modern China more than anyone else around him. She once told him that all of China was like a ghost, intractable, stubborn, entirely stuck in the past. Women had the worst of it, living out their lives feeling unworthy of the food they ate, ashamed of their menstrual cycles and the bad luck they brought. She said that she wanted to live for a year not cooking, not cleaning. She wanted the kind of home that brought embarrassment to her husband and male children. She would not live like this out of spite. On the contrary, she would live like this out of love for herself, which was the one kind of love that was forbidden of women in China.

One afternoon in the cottage Polly fell asleep and when he awoke he saw Kim kneeling on the matted floor. It was dark and the yellow light from the kerosene lamp flooded her body so that she looked vaguely spectral. The crossbeams overhead threw a shadow on the clay wall. There was the wind under the door. She was gazing intently at the mat where a handful of tiny sticks lay in a random pattern.

"What are you doing?" he asked.

She answered distractedly. "This is the future."

"What do you mean?"

"These tell the future."

"Those little sticks?"

"Yes. They tell the future."

"Whose future?"

"Mine."

"What do they say?"

She began to point at the various configurations which the sticks formed. "This is heaven, this is thunder. This is dangerous and this is keeping still."

"What does it all mean?"

She shook her head. "I think it means that we must be very careful. I think it means that we are living on the edge of a knife."

"Do you really believe in this?"

She smiled, but said nothing.

Eventually he came to understand that tradition to Kim was like an old earthen jar filled with scorpions. She hated that jar and would have smashed it, crushing the scorpions as they tried to scamper away, except she was afraid that one or two of them might survive and then come back to sting her in the night.

Soon it became clear to Polly that the more time he spent with Kim the less real the outside world became. By the last days of summer inflation in Shanghai had reached tragic proportions. An egg cost ten thousand Chinese dollars, a pint of milk four hundred thousand. Prices rose every day. Money was spent as soon as it was earned. No one knew where it was going to stop. For those with foreign currency the inflation was hardly more than an inconvenience. Except that there were murders for a few English pounds or a pocketful of loose change.

Occasionally there was political violence: a bit of plastic wedged into the exhaust pipe of a bus, gasoline in a warehouse. People rarely talked about it, and the newspapers ignored it. But one afternoon Polly saw the body of a Kuomintang general who was widely hated by the Communists. The man had been shot and killed as he stepped out of a restaurant on the Yu Yuen Road. A crowd of laborers gathered around as they carried the body away. It was difficult for Polly to tell whether the crowd was indifferent or secretly glad.

In addition to the political deaths there were always the bodies of those who died of starvation in the night. Every morning the municipal trucks drove through the shantytowns and picked up the corpses. One morning Polly saw a truck piled so high with bodies that two or three fell off when the driver turned too sharply around a corner. It was not long after dawn. Polly had been on his way to the office after a night in the cottage with Kim. He was thinking that he would shower and change clothes at the America Club, then join Simon for breakfast. Then he crossed the intersection of a deserted, windblown street and saw the bodies. They were half naked and their limbs were entangled. Obviously the driver of the truck had not noticed that they had fallen out because the truck just kept moving slowly down the boulevard into the gray morning.

But regardless of famine, sporadic violence or even the inflation, life among the foreign residents generally went on much as it had before. Conversation usually centered on trivial incidents: a piano recital in the afternoon, a lecture in the evening, an endless stream of meals. The weather that autumn was mild. Days were clear with cooling breezes from the river. After the office Polly would join Crane for a drink in the club. Then standing at the plate glass above the oily river he would pretend to be that courteous, eager boy who was so concerned about his career in the American intelligence establishment. While a thousand light-years away there was Kim in her cottage by the canals. He would meet her at nightfall, hold her very tightly, then wake in the morning and do it all again.

Toward the end of autumn, however, the pattern of life in the city slowly began to change. There were rumors or renewed fighting in the Yangtze Delta, then verified reports that the Communists had attacked the Nationalist garrisons at Changchun, Mukden and Chinchow. Defenders in those garrisons were said to have been living on rats, dogs and cats, and against the crack divisions of the Red Army they stood no chance at all. It was rumored that Chiang had requested additional heavy bombers from the United States. There was also apparently talk that American troops might be sent in for a single tactical strike. Simon Crane, however, who was at this point very close to the center of things, told Polly that no such American commitment was in sight. He said that everyone in Washington with any real standing knew that the country was already lost.

On the night that the first reports of hard fighting came in Polly met Kim at the cottage. It was nine o'clock in the evening, and they had strolled out to the banks of the canals. There were traces of moonlight on the water, and Kim explained that those reflections were actually traces of ghosts. Then she began to tell him a long story of ghosts fighting demons for possession of a wasteland. As she spoke he could not help thinking how the Communists battling Nationalists in the north was no more relevant to his life than ghosts battling demons in the wasteland. But it was only a momentary thought.

By the end of October both Changchun and Chinchow had fallen, and with them fell the Seventh Nationalist Army. Yet even more shattering to Nationalist morale was the alarming rate of defection. Although there was no mention of it in the Shanghai press, it soon became clear that hundreds of government soldiers were willingly joining the Red Army.

Now in Shanghai came the first whispers of what was to come. Within the diplomatic circles there was already talk of evacuation. Families of consulate employees were quietly urged to prepare to leave. There were also rumors that Chiang had begun fortifying the island of Formosa as his last bastion of resistance. Then, too, money began to leave the city, and there was no rice in the shops.

For Polly the fall of the garrisons meant that he had to spend more time at the office and less time with Kim. In the mornings he read through the field reports. All of them spoke of a crumbling government and a monolithic wave of communism. In the afternoons he encoded dispatches which would go out that night in the diplomatic pouch. In the evenings he and Crane met with agents, debriefed them and then analyzed the raw intelligence. It was a time filled with long hours waiting for the telephone to ring, hoping that no one else would be killed.

There was a space of about two weeks during this first period of intensive fighting when Danny Feng left the city, presumably for Hong Kong. In his absense Kim was free nearly every night. Then no matter how late Polly had to stay at the station, he would always meet her afterward. When Feng returned, however, it seemed that he wanted to make up for lost time. At least three nights a week he took Kim to dinner and then back to her apartment in the French Concession. On these nights wherever Polly was, whatever he was doing, he kept seeing images of Kim lying on a bed with her eyes shut tight while Feng lowered his mouth to her breast. Then it was like glass breaking inside Polly's stomach.

In all the time they had spent together they had rarely talked about Feng. If his name was ever mentioned in passing it would fall like a dead weight on the floor between them. Then there would be silence and they

57

would talk about something else. But one night Polly began to ask her about the man and would not stop. They were sitting on the mattress in her cottage. It was late and the wind had died. There was an empty bottle of wine on the floor, two glasses and a deck of playing cards.

He said, "Why can't you just leave Feng? Why can't you tell him that you met me and you want to marry me?"

She had picked up the deck of cards and began idly laying them out on the mat. "You don't understand, John."

"What's to understand?"

She had found the jack of diamonds and was holding it up to the light. "In order to leave I must first obtain his permission."

"Why?"

"Because that's the way these things must be done."

"But he doesn't even love you."

And still examining the jack of diamonds: "Love is only one form of desire."

"What the hell is that supposed to mean?"

Now she had the queen of hearts. "It means that I cannot leave him without his permission."

"I think that's crazy."

"I knew that you would not understand."

Finally she held up the joker to the light.

"Is it money?" he asked suddenly. "Is that it?"

"No, John. It's not money."

"Then what is it?"

She turned her head away. He had always loved her profile in the lamplight. After a moment she said, "It's pride. The Fengs are a very proud family. If I were to leave without their permission it would seriously injure their pride, and they would be forced to come after us to save face."

"Then we'll go out of the country. I'll take you back to the States."

"No, John. They would even follow us there if it were a matter of pride."

Later that night as he watched her sleep he heard mice in the thatch above, and a dawn wind across the landscape. He also had the strangest feeling of a presence in the room.

The battle for the Suchow garrison began the following week. From the start the Nationalist defenders were plagued with misfortune. There were shortages of food and ammunition, quarrels among the commanders. Then the cold set in and disease swept through the city streets.

By the end of November a hundred thousand Nationalist troops were either dead or wounded. Supplies were lost to graft. Relief columns were attacked and decimated en route to the city. When the food ran out surrounding fields were stripped bare. Photographs of the area showed skeletal figures against muddy plains. Rodents, dogs, cats, leather, the bark from trees—anything that could be chewed and swallowed was eaten. There were even reports of cannibalism, parents eating the unwanted female child.

Winter was also bad in Shanghai. Refugees continued to pour in from the north and northeast. Every night there were deaths from starvation. Every morning the trucks collected bodies. The poor wore coats out of rat skin, shoes out of cardboard. By December the streets were glazed with ice. Then footsteps at night became more prominent. Those with strength were always wandering in search of something to eat. The authorities feared plague.

Politically the chaos was no less severe. There were continually rumors of peace, but no one believed in them. Fortifications were built on the west bank of the Yangtze, but no one expected them to hold. Nationalist officers spoke of victory, but more and more equipment was diverted to Formosa. Everywhere there were youths milling in the doorways. Knives kept disappearing from kitchens of restaurants.

As for Polly's life with Kim, he eventually came to see that they were only living from moment to moment, usually at night, always with an underlying sense of desperation. At the end of December she spent a week in Formosa with Feng. Twice Polly woke suddenly and called her name. When she finally returned she seemed distant, tense. When he asked her what was wrong she said that Feng may have begun to suspect that she had been unfaithful.

They were sitting on the mattress in the cottage. Again the clay walls were washed in the lamplight. Earlier there had been thunder from the south, but now it was still.

"What makes you think he knows about us?" Polly asked. "Was it something he said?"

"No."

"Then what was it?"

"It's the way he looks at me."

"How does he look at you?"

"I don't know. He just looks at me strange. Yes, strange."

The wind began to sound under the door, through the thatch. Or possibly it was only a rodent in the leaves.

"Look, it doesn't mean anything. You're probably just imagining that he suspects."

But she shook her head. "No, John. I can see the suspicion in his eyes. I can see it there."

In the morning there was a dead mouse lying in the corner of the cottage. Polly saw it as soon as he opened his eyes. He assumed that the mouse must have fallen from the thatch above, but if Kim saw it she would take it as a sign of misfortune. So he rose quietly, carried the tiny body outside and threw it as far as he could into the surrounding reeds. When he returned she was still asleep. Her hair was a dark storm on the pillow.

Finally there were moments when it seemed to Polly that events were about to reach some kind of a climax if only because things could not go on this way much longer. All around him people had begun to act erratically. One evening there was a suicide on the fifth floor of the British consulate. Then someone defaced a monument to Hope. Red paint was splashed on the steps of the Anglican cathedral. There were rumors of a prostitute who had been butchering her victims with a razor blade, and one night Polly saw the shank bone of an ox hanging from a traffic light. There were sounds of women screaming in the night, and glass breaking on empty streets.

Even in the office there were new undertones of anxiety. It was not uncommon to see Crane brooding at the window, chewing on the end of his pipe. If spoken to at these moments he would take a long time to reply. He had also taken to snapping at the junior clerks, and complaining about drafts. In a matter of weeks he seemed to have aged years.

Jay Sagan also seemed caught in the riptide of some pervasive fear. Whole days would pass when he would not come into the office. Then he would appear suddenly, looking knotted and angry, drinking cup after cup of rank coffee. Whenever he saw Polly he was either overly friendly, grinning and speaking very fast, or else he would hardly say a word. He had also started carrying a gun, a tiny Beretta with a pearl grip.

Only with Kim was there peace, and even then it was fragile, transitory peace. They talked about rumors they had heard, and were afraid. Sometimes they were even afraid of the unseen birds behind the rushes, the

60

turning shadows, everything but the stillness. Now and then she continued to talk about her suspicion that Danny Feng had discovered that she and Polly were lovers. Once she said that Danny had questioned her about what she had been doing with her nights alone. On another occasion she said that she thought she saw someone following her. Whenever she spoke of her fears Polly tried to reassure her, but he barely succeeded in reassuring himself.

It went from bad to worse. By April the Communists had crossed the Yangtze and taken all of the northern plains. Not long after the crossing martial law was imposed, but still the city nights were filled with violence. By the middle of the month all roads to the city were jammed with refugees. Rain fell continuously, and for the homeless there was no shelter beyond doorways, wagons, scraps of canvas and wood.

Among the foreign community the exodus had also begun. Polly would see them in the afternoons, lined on the docks awaiting ships. He liked to imagine himself among them, Kim in a fur coat clinging to his arm. He saw her framed against the foaming wake of a steamer, her face changing from sadness to relief.

This was Shanghai in April of 1949. During the nights there were arrests. In the mornings there were executions. The dispossessed wandered aimlessly, whispering together, then moving on. Garbage lay uncollected. Edicts were posted every day. There was an emergency tax on automobiles. Children carried razor blades. Finally there was an announcement that an evacuation of all consulate staff could be activated at any time. Valuables were to be stored in vaults, personal belongings crated. It was a Monday morning when this announcement was made, and in the evening Polly returned to the station.

For a long time he sat and watched the evening crowds, waiting for the day shift to leave. Then when the halls were quiet he smoked another cigarette, rose from his desk and moved down the corridor to the operations room. There in the vault were seven blank passports and about three thousand dollars in cash. He decided that Kim would probably not need the money, but one passport he stuffed in his pocket.

Later that night he went to the cottage. She was waiting for him with fish cakes in a basket. When he showed her the passport, she nodded, then kissed him. After that they were quiet, locked in each other's arms beneath a blanket they had hung above the mattress like a tent. Their hands briefly touched to express what they could not describe. They sensed that the end was very near.

The end came on a Tuesday, on a rainy afternoon that was no different from any of the days that preceded it. In the morning there was a general staff meeting at the station. The tone was jocular, even hopeful. It had been three weeks since the Yangtze crossing and still there was no sign of the Red Army. Over lunch at the Columbia Club, Polly and Crane discussed the war. Nothing was said that hadn't been said a hundred times before. Crane lamented that he still hadn't found a foothold in the Communist camp. Then he began to complain about Jay Sagan and the Nationalist command. He called them rats deserting a sinking ship, and referred to the fact that the Nationalist gold reserves had already been transferred to Formosa.

In the early evening Polly had a drink with Sagan at a bar called the Fox and Hounds. Sagan seemed evasive and nervous. They discussed Formosa. Sagan explained that the retreat to the island would only be temporary, but all the while he kept fingering a rabbit's foot that one of the Nationalist officers had given him as a joke.

Then it was full night, and Polly passed through the sentries and out onto the open road. There was fine mist breaking in the headlights, blurring the cypress groves. He had not seen Kim for three days, but he could imagine her very clearly now, waiting for him in the stillness of the cottage, kneeling by the lantern, reading a movie magazine.

Off the main road the narrow path ran between the reeds. Polly drove slowly, following the tire tracks he had left on other nights. When he reached the rise of stunted pines he saw the cottage; he noticed that there was no light, but thought that it only meant that she was asleep. Then he was standing in the doorway. His eyes moved from object to object. There was a battered teapot, her comb, her canvas shoes and plastic raincoat. It appeared that she had not been here in days.

He lit the coals in the iron pot and made himself some tea. He smoked a cigarette, and leafed through a magazine. An hour passed. Once he thought he heard her car on the path but it was only the wind. Then he threw a little water on the coals to watch the steam rise. Finally he walked out to the canals. There was a full moon, and he saw a cloud of insects. Then he went back into the cottage and sat down again on the mattress. He had never been here alone. She had always been waiting when he arrived.

At some point he fell asleep, and then woke suddenly, again sensing a presence in the room. But there were only the shadows on the clay wall, and a dying moth on the floor.

It was some indefinite hour after midnight when he finally left the cottage. The dew glazed on the windshield of his car. Even when he was warm again he could not keep his hands from shaking.

He knew that something was wrong the moment he pulled into the drive in front of his house. The lights were burning. The door was ajar. Inside he saw that a vase had fallen from the alcove. The pieces still lay on the parquetry. There were odors of antiseptic. There was also a slipper on the staircase, a trace of blood and the sound of boiling water.

He moved up the stairs slowly until he heard soft voices. Then he called out his housekeeper's name, and heard her call back, "Come quickly, Mr. Polly. Come quickly." Even before he took another step he knew what he would find.

Kim lay in the bedroom at the top of the stairs. Polly's housekeeper was kneeling beside her. For a moment after he entered the room Kim did not seem to recognize him. Then she murmured his name and reached out her hands. There were wads of bloody cotton on the table, a bottle of iodine on the floor. Kim's face was swollen and her eyes were black. When she parted her lips he could see that two teeth were missing.

It took her a long time to tell him what had happened. As she spoke he sat perfectly still on the edge of the bed and pictured every incident; the rooms, the movement, the expressions on faces; he saw it all in his mind. First she told him how Danny Feng had come to her apartment. But he had not come alone. There was his chauffeur and bodyguard. While these men held her down, Danny showed her a stack of photographs. There was one of her and Polly entering the cottage, and another of them both hand in hand among the reeds. She said that the photographs were blurred, and Polly imagined that they had been taken with a telephoto lens from the cypress grove.

After the photographs had been laid on the table again, Danny watched while the chauffeur and the bodyguard raped and beat her. She said that she particularly remembered Danny's eyes, and his hairless wrists on the arm of the chair. The radio had been playing in the background, songs from the cabaret. They had also flogged her with a leather belt and burned her feet with cigarettes.

When they had finished with her she was only half conscious. They had to carry her to the car. Then they drove her to Polly's house and left

63

her on the doorstep. After a while, maybe a quarter of an hour, the housekeeper heard her moaning and brought her upstairs.

When she finished speaking she remained motionless, gazing into the empty space past Polly's left shoulder. Once her lips moved, but there was no sound. Then her eyes filled with tears. The last thing she told Polly before drifting off again was that now she belonged to him. She said that Feng had given her to him, because she was no longer worthy of an Oriental gentleman.

Polly remained at her side while she slept. There was the rhythm of her breath, the ticking clock and smells of the night through the window. He supposed that he was very tired, but he did not want to shut his eyes. He knew what he would see if he shut his eyes.

Twenty minutes passed. He did not move his hand. The curtains were stirring in the breeze, occasionally billowing out to meet the dresser. And he knew what was in that dresser. Now he would fix his eyes on the porcelain vase, now on the telephone, but always he returned to the top drawer of that plain, unvarnished dresser.

For a while he tried to put his mind on other things, on certain conversations, certain phrases he had heard or read. But there was just no way of getting around it: that Colt revolver in the drawer.

He could not recall ever having fired it. Although once, out of boredom on a Sunday afternoon, he had examined it, spun the chamber, inserted the cartridges, sighted into the light. When they issued it to him they had said, "Keep it handy. You never know when you might need it."

There was a moment before he rose from the chair when he told himself that he should consider the consequences. Then that moment passed, and now every movement was mechanical. He poured himself a glass of scotch, spilled some on the rug, dragged an old coat from the closet, and put the gun in a pocket. Descending the stairs he heard his housekeeper call to him, but he did not answer. On the open road the magnolia trees had never seemed so ghostly, rising up in the tunnel of headlights, then falling away again.

At the edge of Danny Feng's estate he felt calmer, parked in the shadows of the trees. Through the branches lay a white pavilion, the garden in tangled vines and spiked leaves. There were also clumps of orchids, and some other unidentifiable plant.

Another minute passed. He lit a cigarette and let his head fall back on the seat. Half an hour ago he had seen himself reeling through Feng's door. But now he felt exhausted. The revolver in his pocket kept gouging into his ribs. He told himself that he would wait another minute, then return to Kim.

But suddenly a light went on in the window. Then the front door opened, and he heard broken voices from across the lawn. Two figures appeared on the path down from the portico. Their faces were hidden in the shadows, but they were moving closer. One was tall and thin, while the shorter man was gazing at the sky. There was a moment when Polly knew that he should not even look, a moment when he knew that he shouldn't have even come here in the first place. But then that moment passed. The two men stepped out of the darkness, and Polly saw that the shorter one was Danny Feng.

Polly moved stiffly. He might have been in a trance. Leaves brushed against his shoulder. The air was cold, almost liquid. Feng and his companion had stopped.

"Is that Mr. Polly?"

Polly nodded, but said nothing.

"Go home, Mr. Polly. You only make more trouble. Go home or I set the dogs on you."

Kim had never liked dogs, always said that she was afraid of them.

"Go home, Mr. Polly. Go home before I give you a night that you will never forget."

As if he would ever forget this night as it was, gazing into Feng's eyes, feeling his fingers curl around the butt of the gun, drawing it out of his pocket.

"Just what do you think you're doing, Mr. Polly?"

He hardly knew, except that when he briefly shut his eyes there was one clear image of Kim's face.

"Mr. Polly. Mr. Polly."

Polly shot rapidly with his eyes wide and dull. He was conscious only of the muzzle flash and Feng's crumpling form. Then it was over, and he stood very still in the ringing silence. The slender man was staring at him, and slowly backing away. Feng's hand kept opening and closing in the grass. Later on the road, and then again beneath the shuttered branches, Polly realized that he was crying, but because he was neither sad nor angry he assumed that the tears were merely some sort of physical reaction, like the movement of Feng's hand after he had died.

How Polly spent the remainder of that fractured night he would never clearly remember. At one point he telephoned Simon Crane, and Crane met him on the road a mile west of his home. From here they drove in Crane's car northwest until they passed the outskirts of the city. Then came the ruins of some sort of temple. Here Polly was left with two drab green blankets and a canvas satchel filled with tinned food. Crane said that he would return later. But earlier, moments after Polly had telephoned, there had also been a minute with Kim. Of this Polly would only remember peering into the darkened room and gazing at the outline of her face.

The temple lay on the rise of a hill, not far from the banks of the farthest canal. From the road he saw a wedge of stone and a few shingles the color of dried blood. There were also tall willow groves on the slope. Fern spores lay scattered on the bricks and lacquer dust from the overhead beams.

It was not until the following afternoon that Crane returned to the ruins. Polly saw him first from a long way off, the car leaving dust on the road. The old man took the steep path up the hillside, and Polly saw him resting in the white sunlight. He seemed to be carrying another canvas bag. Finally they sat together on a fallen block of stone. There were rat pellets in the sand.

"I'm afraid it's pretty bad, John. Feng died this morning. The man who was with him last night gave a full statement."

"I see."

There was silence. Then Crane said, "Why don't you tell me what happened again."

Polly shrugged. "I shot him."

"Because of what he did to that girl?"

"Yeah. Because of what he did to her."

"I suppose you realize that your motive does not constitute a legal justification."

"Yeah. I realize it."

"But there's a possibility that we could use the circumstances to build a case of temporary insanity. Maybe get the charge reduced to manslaughter."

Then Polly thought: *Is that what I did for her? Slaughtered a man?*

"On the other hand we might be able to make some sort of deal with them. Say a reduced sentence in exchange for certain military appropriations. It all depends upon whether or not Washington will play along with us."

Two crows circled in the sky above, rose and then fell to the trees, the few dominant trees to the west.

"This girl," Crane said suddenly. "How long have you been seeing her?"

"I don't know. Months."

"But you knew what her relationship was to Danny Feng?"

"I knew."

"Did she ever come to your house?"

"No."

"So you only met her at the cottage?"

"Yes."

"Didn't you realize that sooner or later Feng was bound to find out?"

"I tried not to think about it."

"But what about when—"

"Look, can't we keep her out of this? She doesn't have anything to do with it."

"All right, John. If you say so."

In the last failing minutes together they stood on the edge of the rise. Here the silence was immense. The western sky had begun to darken. There were long shadows on the open land.

"I'll come tomorrow," Crane said. "In the meantime you had better keep out of sight. Apparently they've got a special unit looking for you, not to mention Feng Chi's people. So don't wander off the hill."

"I won't."

Then as Crane was walking away: "Simon, wait."

"What is it?"

"If you see Kim, will you give her a message for me?"

"Nothing written, John. It's not safe."

"No, just tell her... that I love her. Will you do that for me?"

Crane nodded. "Sure, John. I'll tell her."

When Crane had gone, Polly walked back to the ruins and sat down. Here there was a partly sheltered room in red sandstone. With his back to the wall he could see far out across the willows to mountains and swamps in the hollows. After a while he slept, but woke an hour later and found that there were fern spores in his hair.

There were bad hours here, hours when he could not help but think about her, particularly certain memories of her profile, a white blouse slipping over her shoulder, her hands holding some small, meaningless object. But among the things that Crane had given him—the blankets, the tins of meat and sardines, cigarettes, crackers—there was also a copy of the *Tao*. It was one of the Modern Library editions, bound in gray and dog-eared. He read only a few pages at first, a chapter called "On Stealing Light." Then he put the book aside, but picked it up again and read: *Gravity is the root of grace.*

Later he heard dry thunder, then there was rain. For a while he watched a beetle in one of his discarded sardine cans. Toward evening the shapes of things around him became more defined, and out of sheer boredom he started to read again. Until at some point he was left with the oddest image of a dragonfly, a pearl, interwoven roots and the face of a woman rising out of steam. Then later, just before dawn, he woke suddenly with the strangest sense of peace. So that by the time that Crane returned he was fairly resigned to whatever would happen. He told himself that he would see Kim again, and beyond that nothing mattered. But never once did he imagine that what seemed like the end of his career in China was in reality only the beginning.

Crane returned again toward the end of the second day. He wore an old trench coat with coffee stains on the sleeve. Again there was hardly any greeting. The two men just sat down on another block of stone. Crane said, "I'm afraid that Washington won't play ball with us. The consulate staff has been ordered to cooperate with the local authority. I'm not even supposed to have seen you."

Polly nodded, but said nothing. He had grown used to the silence here.

"But you've got to understand how it is, John. Washington had no choice under the circumstances. Danny Feng had a lot of friends. His brother has a lot of pull. That's just the way it is."

Polly breathed deeply. "I understand."

"Of course there are still several variables. We still might be able to work a deal."

Polly ran his hand through his hair. "What kind of deal?"

"Say a minimum sentence of about ten years in exchange for certain political favors."

"Ten years?"

"Well, I'm afraid it's going to be at least that."

"Ten years?"

68

"I'm sorry."

Polly shut his eyes, and for a moment he was absolutely still.

"The problem is, John, that the only one who can effectively negotiate any sort of deal is Sagan, and I'm afraid he's not too willing to help right now."

"No, I don't imagine that Jay would be too willing to help."

In the distance was another flight of migrating birds. Polly was watching the sky. Crane was looking at his hands. There was a brief moment of silence. Then Crane said, "Listen to me carefully, John. There is another way we can go with this."

Polly was still watching the horizon. "What are you talking about?"

"I'm talking about the fact that not everyone is mourning Danny Feng's death. Yes, he had friends in the foreign community. And yes, his brother carries a lot of weight. But really who are these Fengs? They symbolize everything that the common man resents: dependence on foreign interest, corruption, favoritism, not to mention the opium. So it's a question of politics really. That is, by killing Danny Feng you may have quite honestly made more friends than enemies."

Then softly, slowly turning his head: "You're talking about the Communists, aren't you?"

"Look at it this way, John. If you stay here you face a possible sentence of twenty, maybe thirty years. And I don't have to tell you what the Nationalist prisons are like. You'd probably never make it. But if you cross the line—well, I think there's a very good chance of your survival."

Polly rose and stepped to the edge of the hill. His hands were jammed in his pockets. To the north lay black mountains and the water meadows of the lowlands.

"What you've got to understand, John, is that what you did was heroic in the eyes of the Communists. Yes, heroic. You shot and killed Danny Feng because he abused a young girl. Their ranks are filled with young women who have been beaten and raped, filled with young men who have had to run from the law. What kind of people do you think make up the backbone of the Red Army? They're all outlaws. They've all spent time in prison. I honestly think they'll take you in, John. After all, you've just killed a man who stood for everything that they're fighting against. They just can't turn you away."

Polly looked up at the sky again. He was still facing the limitless plain and humped mountains. "How long would I have to stay?"

"I don't know. A year, two years. Just until things calm down a little."

"And what would I tell them? I couldn't tell them I worked in the station."

"Why not? You're a defector. An American intelligence officer joins the Red Army. I really don't think they'll be able to resist that one."

Again Polly was silent, watching something on the horizon, either light off a pond or the faint trace of a village fire.

Finally he said, "So. It's going to be me, huh? All these months you've been looking for a man to place inside their camp, and now you want to send me."

"John, listen to me. This is workable. We'll never have another chance like this. They'll take you in. They'll send you to Peking. You can't imagine how valuable that could be to us. With any luck..."

"What about Kim?"

"Take her with you."

"No, not until I know it's safe."

"All right then, I'll look after her and you can send for her later."

"And what about my status with Washington?"

"Officially you'll be a defector, but a few of us will know the truth, and when the time comes for you to return we'll make sure you're taken care of."

"And my link to you?"

"I haven't worked that out yet, but I'll get something established."

"But until then I'm on my own, is that right?"

"Yes, John. You'll be on your own."

"When do I have to give you an answer?"

"I'm afraid it has to be now, John. Right now. I've made contact with some people who can take you over to the Red lines, but every hour is critical. So if you want it, you've got to tell me now."

After another minute of thought, Polly said, "Okay. I'll do it," and then shrugged.

Of Polly's last hours in Shanghai all that he would remember was a final meeting with Crane and then his farewell to Kim. Both conversations took place at dusk when the whole landscape seemed to be dissolving. Mostly Crane talked about how Polly should conduct himself once he reached the Communist lines. Once again they stood on the bluff.

Crane said, "There's no need to try and withhold anything from them. There's nothing you can tell them that will hurt us now. So feel free to talk. Details about the station, your training, even personal relationships.

70

I expect they'll ask you all of that. And you must tell them. There's no sense in spoiling the entire operation because of some silly lie."

Far to the north there were shifting rain clouds, the scent of rain in the air.

"Now I can't promise what sort of reception you'll receive, but if all goes according to plan they should be expecting you. So don't be surprised if they already know the details of what happened. And remember one doesn't maintain a cover, one lives it. So give them what they want."

As for their actual goodbye, there simply came a point when Crane did not have anything else to say. So for an awkward moment the two men just looked at each other. Their emotions were undefined.

As Crane descended the hill he passed Kim moving up. Obviously she had been waiting in the car. As she climbed through the reeds Polly watched from above. She wore a leather coat and a scarf. When they finally came together she seemed ashamed of the bruises on her face.

At first they did not speak. Polly merely held her in his arms. There was the scent of her perfume, her hair, her breath.

"How are you?" His voice was raw.

"I'm okay." There were tears in her eyes, but she managed to smile. "I guess Simon told you that I have to leave for a while."

"Yes."

"But I'll be coming back for you. So no matter what happens..."

She nodded. Her face had never seemed so fragile.

They walked several feet to the edge of the hill. Then she suddenly turned to him and began speaking softly. She told him that when two people were in love they were bound together by an invisible red string. So regardless of the distance she would really always be with him, and sometimes she would even appear to him as a ghost appears—briefly, in the corner of a darkened room.

Polly left for the northeast around midnight three days after the murder of Danny Feng. He was escorted by two men in an arrangement Crane had made. There was no moon and it was very cold. Polly's guides spoke only minimal English, so there was hardly any talk between them. In the darkest hours there was still the whisper of running streams and occasionally lightning.

Chapter 3

"WHAT WAS Sagan doing through all this?" Cassidy asked.

Crane shook his head. "I hardly saw him."

"But he must have been pretty upset?"

"He was concerned that his relationship with Feng Chi had been jeopardized by Polly's actions."

"And was it?"

"To some extent, yes."

It was their second day on the point. Earlier, just after dawn, Cassidy had walked out to these cliffs alone and had seen a gray fin cutting the water. He threw a rock, but missed. Now he continued to scan the bay.

Suddenly Crane said, "Look, I'd rather not discuss Jay Sagan right now. It will only cloud the issue. So if it's all right with you I think we should stay with Polly."

Cassidy shrugged. "Sure. We'll stay with Polly."

At the time of Polly's flight, the People's Revolutionary Army totaled nearly three million men. Most were young, not over thirty, and had come from impoverished farms. Few were literate, although reading classes were held by the political directors. Neither soldiers nor their commanders received fixed salaries. There were, however, small grain allotments which could be pooled and traded for vegetables. In addition to the grain the soldiers were also given one winter and two summer uniforms, a rifle, two hand grenades, ten clips of ammunition, one blanket, underwear, a cake of soap, a rice bowl, a sewing kit and a notebook. Morale was high, discipline near-perfect. Rarely did—or could—a soldier put his own interests before the interests of the group. There was no belief in personal liberty. There was only belief in the supreme right of the people.

It was cold the night that Polly reached the Communist lines. Spring had come late that year, and by March the north China plain still lay barren, suspended between freezing and thawing. Distances were obscured in ice and blue shadows. There had been intermittent rain for days.

Polly's first vision of the lines came from the rise of a hill. He saw campfires spread out across the narrow valley, and figures moving in the darkness. At the edge of camp he was met by sentries, and then taken to an inn along the main street of the village.

Here a dirt floor was sprinkled with manure. Burlap sacks of grain were stacked in the corner. Half a dozen soldiers sat cross-legged on a low platform and spoke softly among themselves. One of them seemed to be describing a rat the size of a man's arm. There was also something about a crow and a woman in black. As the others listened they kept glancing at Polly. Moths kept beating themselves against the oil lamps. Finally the rain stopped, then the wind.

More than an hour passed. Twice there were faces at the window, peering in and then vanishing. When Polly tried to speak he was ignored. When he offered cigarettes no one took them. Finally the door burst open and two soldiers entered. They seemed to hesitate a moment, then motioned for Polly to come.

Outside the village street lay awash with mud. There was water dripping from the eaves. Most of the huts were dark. A dog was barking from behind a wall. A line of men crossed the road in the distance. Polly followed the soldiers along a planked boardwalk until he came to a low clay building.

The room was lit by another oil lamp. Sitting in the light at a packing crate was a small thin man. He wore what the others wore: khaki trousers and a blue winter tunic. He had a young man's face and cropped hair. When Polly entered he rose and extended his hand.

"You are John Polly?"

"Yes."

"I am Ling Sheng, political director for this section. It is apparently my privilege to welcome you to the liberated zone."

Polly sat on a gunnysack. The small man brought tea. There were two chipped cups on the packing crate, a dry slab of bread, and a bottle of water. Straw had been spread on the floor. A rope hung from the rafters and threw a long shadow on the bricks. There was a faint odor of gasoline, a picture of Mao on the wall.

"Do you think I speak good English?" Ling asked.

"Yes, pretty good."

"That's because I attended university in the United States. This was in California. I studied advertising. What did you study, Mr. Polly?"

"Political science."

"Oh, then your instructor would undoubtedly be surprised to see you here."

"Yes. I guess he would be pretty surprised, all right."

"Although I understand that it was not a political act which led to your predicament."

"Excuse me?"

"I said that it was not a political act which led to your presence here. It was an emotional act."

"Yes. I suppose you could say that it was an emotional act."

"They say you killed Danny Feng because of a woman, isn't that correct?"

"Yes. There was a woman."

"Not that it makes a particular difference to us. All that matters is that you dealt a blow against an enemy."

"Thank you."

"Although I do personally wonder exactly what your true sentiments are?"

"My true sentiments?"

"Yes, your true political sentiments. After all, you originally came to this country as a spy. Isn't that correct?"

"Yes. It's correct."

"And now you seek sanctuary among us. It's a strange predicament, wouldn't you say?"

"Yes. It's pretty strange."

"And so I wonder what are your sentiments?"

"You mean my political sentiments."

"Yes, political."

In the corner of the room was an iron cot, a coil of wire and a pair of goggles. There was also a crude red star painted on the mud brick. Polly glanced from one object to another. Then his mouth began to spread in a slow, lumpy smile.

74

"You know something, Mr. Ling. I really don't have the faintest idea what my political sentiments are," and he laughed.

Later that night he was given a plate of greasy vegetables and pork. While he ate Ling talked obliquely about what he called the Communist Ethic. There were only two concrete images: land and food. The rest was an abstraction. Finally Polly fell asleep on a pile of grain sacks. When he woke again it was still dark, and there were rats moving along the rafters.

In the morning he was given a fountain pen and notebook. He was told to write down his experiences in Shanghai with a particular emphasis on his confrontation with Danny Feng. At first he did not know what to write, and sat for an hour sipping tea, smoking cigarettes, doodling in the margin of the page. Then slowly he began to describe how he met Kim, the night he had spent searching for her through the Shanghai bars. He described Feng Chi, the house, the servants, those dinners with the Nationalist elite. Interspersed with these descriptions were images of the slums around the old city, the bodies lying on the dawn streets. Eventually the words were coming to him as fast as he could put them down, perhaps not his own words exactly, but phrases he had heard, concepts he had read in some of the Communist newspapers that Crane had always been bringing into the office. In the end even Danny's death had overtones of the political allegory.

When he was done there were more than twenty pages of drivel that he could not even read himself without wincing. Although he had to admit that some of the lines did have a certain ring to them, what with his imperialist steamrollers and proletariat turbines of the heart. Later that afternoon Ling Sheng read the pages while Polly waited outside on the warped steps of the supply shed. In the courtyard three soldiers were trying to start an old weapons carrier. They kept grinding the gears and from the sound of the engine it was pretty clear that the valves were shot.

Finally Ling came outside and also sat down on the steps. There was a windless cold and, there were chickens shrieking from the edge of the village. Ling took out a pack of muddied cigarettes and handed one to Polly. After they sat smoking awhile Ling suddenly said that based upon those pages it would seem that Polly's prospects for success were very promising in this new People's Republic of China.

In all Polly spent three weeks in that village, and his initial impressions were to later comprise an entire series of the China letters. There was an odd placidity to these days, a feeling that was captured in his letters. From the end of the village was a long view of the muddy track into the hills. Nights were spent around adobe ovens. Afternoons were devoted to study, tracing characters in his exercise book. He loved the symmetry of the completed page.

Occasionally he would help with small jobs around the camp. He especially liked caring for the horses. Sometimes in the evening he would walk them out to the edge of the plateau. Once he helped dig a truck out of the mud, and afterward lay panting in the grass with seven other young men. They passed a cigarette among them, and later even slices of watermelon. The future was still incalculable, but at least there were the rudiments of life.

In time, just as Crane had predicted, Polly came to see that he was to serve various political functions. Within the first week he had written another article for Ling, this one regarding the exploitation of the western intelligence establishment in Asia. Many of the facts were garbled, and he could not recall dates or proper names. Ling, however, seemed pleased with the overall effort, especially the turn of certain phrases, like the dog-faced lackey and the peanut-headed servant of the degenerate palace.

On another night Polly addressed about two hundred soldiers on the subversive capabilities of the foreign espionage rings. Ling acted as interpreter. Initially Polly was nervous, halting. He kept absently brushing his hair from his eyes. But then, as with his articles, the sentences started coming to him almost automatically. In the torchlight, leaning slightly out from the podium of ammunition crates, one hand was outstretched, the other clutching a wad of notes.

Toward the end of most evenings Polly would meet Ling for tea and idle talk in the allotment shed. Here, slouched on gunnysacks, sipping tea or hot water if there was no tea, Ling and Polly would chat for hours. Ling did most of the talking, and mostly the talk was political.

There were stories of men buried alive because they could not pay their debts, stories of entire families who committed suicide because they lost their land. During the famine in Taihan people ate dung and female children. There was even a landlord who blinded the first-born son of every village family. Eventually Polly came to see that each of Ling's stories was like a backward, half-glance over the shoulder toward a primitive and timeless horror. Often the stories were elliptical. There was one about a boy who had never kissed a girl, another about the revenge of a young mother. In the end Polly had no idea if these stories were true,

76

but he reasoned that if this country could inspire them then things must have been pretty bad. Besides, everyone had stories like these. One only had to ask a soldier how he had come to join the Red Army, and he would tell a story about pain that no mind could understand.

Finally there came a night when Ling began to talk about himself. Earlier there had been news of another victory in the south. In celebration there was a little wine, rank yellow stuff with sediment at the bottom of the bottle. But after several glasses Polly found himself very nearly drunk, once more slouched on the gunnysacks, once more listening to Ling.

Ling said that his father had traded silk in Canton, but at an early age had taken the family to San Francisco. There he dreamed of becoming a fisherman, but at seventeen he was back in China again. His first exposure to Marx had been in Shanghai, and then again while at the university in Los Angeles. When he returned to China for a second time he joined the party, and worked in a basement editing one of the underground journals. At the end of nine months the Nationalist Special Service Section found the press, and he was forced to flee north to the Manchurian hills. Here in the open, barren country he led a platoon recruited from the provinces.

"Of course life was very hard at that time," Ling said.

"I can imagine," Polly replied, half listening, staring at the oil lamp and a beetle on the packing crate.

"Not only were there Nationalist patrols, but there were bandits too. And Chinese bandits are very bad."

"So I've heard." He wasn't sure if the beetle was dead or alive. It hadn't moved for an hour.

"But of course we were eventually able to kill the bandits with superior firepower. Or else recruit them to our cause."

From beyond the wooden door came the faint sound of a banging shutter in the wind, then the footsteps of passing sentries.

"I will tell you something else about me," Ling said suddenly. "When I lived in the United States I had a different name. It was Tommy. That's what all my American friends called me. They called me Tommy. Tommy Ling. Now tell me what you think about that?"

Polly smiled. "I think it's a good name."

"I tell you this because I thought perhaps you might also like to call me Tommy."

"Sure."

"And maybe I could call you John?"

77

"Sure, call me John."

Later that night the two men walked out to the plateau. There was a warped quarter-moon above the muddy road between the hills, and something burning in the distance. Of these early days Polly would write that he could not understand why these people trusted him.

Toward the end of the month word came that the advance units were starting to organize for the continued march west to Shanghai and Canton. For days Polly lived under the impression that he would be allowed to accompany them, and the thought of returning to Kim made everything bearable. But two days before the camp was to break, Ling casually mentioned that he and Polly would not be leaving with the army. Instead they were to continue east to Peking. They would travel with about nine men. There would be a flatbed truck if the axle didn't break. Otherwise there would be mules until they intersected with the railroad. When Polly protested all Ling said was that now he was part of the Revolution, and within the Revolution one did as one was ordered to do.

Later Polly walked back out along the muddy track until he came to the rise of the hill. Here there were a few solitary pines and a patch of grass that had not been washed away. For a long time he just sat, pulling at the root of some plant. Then he heard the sound of footsteps, and Ling calling his name.

When they drew closer Ling said, "You were thinking about that girl. I can always tell when you're thinking about her."

"Yes," Polly breathed. "I was thinking about her."

"And of course the reason that you want to go to Shanghai is to find her. Isn't that true?"

"Yes. It's true."

Farther down the slope two soldiers were hacking at an uprooted tree. There would probably be more rain.

"Believe me, John. If it were my decision I would allow you to see her now. However, it's not my decision. I wrote them about you, and now they want to meet you."

One of the soldiers seemed to have cut his hand with the ax. He was kneeling in the mud with his fist jammed under his arm.

"Who?" Polly said. "Who wants to see me?"

"My superiors at the Propaganda Ministry, and some others in the Foreign Intelligence Ministry."

"What do they want?"

78

"I imagine they want to ask you questions. Perhaps they want you to write articles for them. I believe they were very impressed with what you've done so far."

"But why can't they just wait a few weeks? Shanghai will fall in a few weeks."

"I'm sorry, John. The decision has been made."

Again there was the clear echo of an ax on wood, and an approaching truck miles up the black road.

Suddenly Ling said, "You're a strange person, John. I like you, but you're a strange person."

"Yes?"

"Yes. You are very strange. In fact you're one of the strangest people I've ever met."

"Is that so?"

"Yes. Here we are all involved in momentous events. Victory is at hand. The entire mainland will soon belong to the people of China, and yet all you think about is this girl. Sometimes I wonder how I'm ever going to make a good Communist out of you."

"Doesn't a good Communist ever think about the person he loves?"

"Of course, but never does he put his personal feelings above his duty to the Revolution."

"Is that so?"

"Yes. A good Communist thinks only of the Revolution and the welfare of the majority."

"And you really believe that?"

"Wait until we get to Peking, John. Then you will see for yourself."

Which was exactly the sort of sentiment that led Polly to a theme found in many of the China letters. These people, he would write, were also chasing a dream that might very well kill them in the end.

Polly and Tommy Ling left the next morning in the back of an old flatbed truck. The first day was spent moving through open, windy spaces. Polly hardly spoke to the others, although occasionally their eyes met his. Then they would nod and smile a little, like strangers on a train. The first night they spent in another blacked-out village. It was hardly more than a row of clay huts on a dusty street. The inhabitants seemed afraid.

On the second day the landscape seemed greener. All around lay terraced fields and mulberry groves. In the afternoon, Polly and the others sat in the shade of the truck and ate watermelon. The first spring breeze was sweeping in from the west. At night there was another village, this one in a forest of bamboo. Sometime before dawn Polly faintly heard a woman call. Hopelessly and half-consciously he whispered yes.

Of Polly's first impressions of Peking, he would write only that he was very tired, and the Forbidden City seemed smaller and dirtier than he had imagined. He also noted that there had been no one to meet them at the station. Ling said nothing about this, but it was clear to Polly that the man's feelings were hurt. While all around people seemed to be walking in a kind of dead patrol.

At this time the visible center of Peking was still the Forbidden City. Built as the royal palace of the Ming emperors, there were more than a hundred acres of perfect symmetry within the walls. Each pavilion lay in accord with others, linked by promenades, encircled by gardens where the willows hung over the ponds. There were more than nine thousand rooms here to house the imperial family, their aides, retainers, concubines and eunuchs. In the year of Polly's entrance, however, one pavilion was already in conversion for government use.

Extending from the palace, the city formed a rectangle criss-crossed by streets and enclosed by high walls. On his second evening here Polly strolled out to the edge of the palace walls. The light was almost silver, and between the sounds of passing trucks it was quiet. In an empty courtyard he saw an old man treading across a humped bridge. The man was framed between black cherry boughs and the green moat. Then again this may have been the China of a thousand years ago.

Polly began working in the Propaganda Ministry on his third day in Peking. Mostly he wrote articles for what would later become the *Peking Review*. The office was on a quiet street not far from the old legation. There were water stains on the ceiling and flaking paint. Furniture was crude: block desks, unpadded chairs. There was also an acute shortage of stationery, and it was cold in the mornings, very cold.

Polly shared an office with an intense but polite young man named Wang Hsu-tung. Wang was barely twenty years old. He had joined the cause in 1945 after running away from an unhappy marriage. The first time Polly saw him he was sitting behind a desk that was much too large for him. He spoke a lyrical, stilted English that he had learned from reading Shakespeare. Consequently he was always saying things like, "What says the clock?" or "How goes the night?"

80

As Polly later learned, Wang's father had arranged his marriage solely for financial reasons. Wang's wife had been nearly twenty years his senior. She had also been a harsh, occasionally perverse woman who controlled almost three thousand acres in the heartland of the province. At the time Wang had only been fifteen. Generally his wife treated him like a servant. When she became displeased he was stripped and beaten with a bamboo cane. These beatings seemed to excite the woman sexually, and for a long time Wang believed that pain and love were inseparable.

One night after a particularly bad beating Wang climbed through a window and fled into the hills. Eventually he met a contingent of the Red Army. Soon he was attending lectures, often held in gorges deep in the wilderness. He read continually, not only Marx, but also French. At the end of three months he had learned to wire explosives, and how to delay the timing mechanism on a hand grenade. Also his fundamental outlook on life had changed.

Now Wang Hsu-tung was like many of the young Communists whom Polly had met and would continue to meet as time went by. He was unquestionably loyal to Mao and the Revolution. He saw the universe around him as finite and ordered. It might have been a sort of mystical vision, but there was no belief in any kind of immortal spirit. There was only a belief in things that could be seen and touched.

Also a part of the early Peking days was Polly's first introduction to the others of the foreign community. There were two Englishmen, a Frenchman, a New Zealander and an Italian. Later there would also be a few Americans and Canadians, but Polly would never become very close to any of them. They had all come for ideological reasons, and in some ways they were more zealously communistic than the Chinese. Only the Russians were there because of circumstances beyond their personal control.

Most of the foreign residents lived in a compound near the Tien An Men Square. Here lay a block of European-styled apartments, originally built by the imperialist interests. Although the rooms were in need of repair they were large with high ceilings and ornate fixtures. Plane trees grew in the courtyard, mulberrys on the walls. There was also a fountain shaped like a lion, although maybe it was supposed to have been a dog.

The day that Polly moved into the compound the other residents came by his apartment to welcome him. It was a fairly stiff affair. He was given small gifts: pencils, toothpaste, toilet paper—all indications that things were lean. As for the rest of the evening, Polly sat rigidly in a soiled

81

armchair, his guests toasting his political stance with a bottle of flat champagne that someone had saved from the war.

Polly's first experience with a struggle that would follow him through to the end came nine days after his arrival. A summons, on cheap paper and handwritten, was delivered to his office on a Thursday morning. Tommy Ling assured him that there was no cause for alarm. Certain people in the party's formative intelligence service wished to see him. Through the remainder of the morning Polly sat at his desk pretending to work, chain smoking, then staring at the keys of an ancient typewriter.

Later that afternoon he went to the offices of what was then the Foreign Ministry, but had once been the residence of the French Consul. He was taken to the counselor's parlor. There were six bulging chairs wrapped in cotton slipcovers. A single light bulb hung from the ceiling. On the walls were portraits of Mao. On a card table was a tray with a pot of tea and cigarettes. The windows had been shattered months before and never repaired.

After Polly had been sitting a few minutes a tall thin man walked into the room. He had a smooth face, dominated by a very high forehead that swept back to thick black hair. He wore a blue cotton boiler suit, worn at the elbow and stained. He said his name was Han Chow.

After tea was served Han began casually asking about Polly's experiences in Shanghai. He seemed most interested in the activities of Jay Sagan and the Nationalist elite. He wanted to know who in Washington supported Chiang, and who did not. He was also interested in the organizational structure of the Shanghai station.

Next Han wanted to know the details of running agents. He wanted to know how they were recruited, how much money they were paid, and how they were serviced. If Polly's answers did not satisfy him, he would approach the question from a different angle, but his demeanor never changed. He remained friendly and polite, although his voice was flat and dry.

To Polly this conversation was unlike any he had ever had thus far in Peking. There was no mention of political theory, no condemnation of the capitalist system, no praise of Mao. Han was only interested in the pragmatic realities of the secret world.

"I understand you ran into trouble in Shanghai," Han said.

Polly answered, "I shot a man."

"Yes. You shot Feng Chi's brother. How do you feel about that now?"

"How do I feel?"

"Yes. How do you feel emotionally?"

Polly began to rub his knuckles. His hands were moist with perspiration. "I don't know. I guess I never really thought about it."

"I understand there was also a woman involved. A prostitute."

"Yes. I guess you could say that."

"And now my sources also tell me that Feng Chi has taken an oath to avenge his brother's death."

Polly nodded. "Yes. Well, I guess that doesn't surprise me."

"Which is why I have decided to have a few of my men watch you for a while."

"Watch me?"

"Yes. In this way they will be able to tell us whether or not anyone is trailing you."

Polly wet his lips. His mouth was dry. "Who would be trailing me?"

"Perhaps an assassin sent by Feng Chi."

Through all this Han had been leaning across the table, his eyes never leaving Polly's face. But now he withdrew and smiled. "One can never be too careful, Mr. Polly."

A few days later Polly noticed two young men walking behind him as he made his way to work. The two men remained at a distance, and when Polly turned around and looked at them they pretended to be browsing in a shop window. For nearly a week Polly was followed wherever he went. Then one day he noticed that the men were gone, but just as suddenly they were back the following evening. So it went for almost a month. Sometimes there would be men walking behind, watching from street corners, following on bicycles. Then there would be no one. Although Polly was not sure exactly why he was being followed he was certain that the reason had nothing to do with his personal safety.

Now once again Polly found himself living out a routine which would mark a definite stage of his life in China. He rose early each morning, because he could not sleep through the sounds of people moving through the streets on their way to the factories and offices. When there was no tea he drank hot water. When there were no cigarettes he smoked butts he had saved and rolled himself. There were also shortages of soap, and what Polly could buy was rough, tawny, smelling of disinfectant.

Each morning Ling would give him a theme on which to base his articles. Sometimes Polly would be asked to write in praise of Soviet tractors, or a speech by Mao. On other occasions he was asked to criticize some aspect of western civilization. Capitalism, materialism, military policy, the banking system, racism in the American south—eventually Polly got around to attacking them all. Finally he was asked to describe his own reflections of life in the new regime. He learned fairly soon that what the ministry wanted in these articles was a sort of paean to the Revolution from the viewpoint of a man who knew at first hand how terrible it was to live under the yoke of the imperialist running dogs.

At first these articles gave him the most trouble. He just couldn't seem to adopt the proper viewpoint. In time, however, he was able to knock out four or five of them a month. After a while the ministry was so pleased with his work that they wanted the articles as a regular feature in both the domestic review as well as those foreign tabloids that were starting to circulate all over the Orient. When Polly was asked what he wanted to call his column he said, "How about 'My Window on Peking'?" It was the stupidest name he could think of, but the ministry loved it.

Soon everywhere that Polly went he kept meeting people who complimented him on his work. They were always telling him how much they enjoyed reading this or that article, how they were taken with this or that turn of phrase. He knew that they weren't lying because every now and then he met someone who actually quoted part of his article. The fact that there were people who were not only reading but also memorizing his stuff never ceased to amaze him. Additionally the articles that drew the most praise were those that struck him as the most ludicrous. One piece that was particularly popular dealt with the secret network of American concentration camps wherein Negroes and other undesirables were incarcerated and left to rot. Polly had no idea what inspired him to write that piece. He supposed it just came to him one evening while he was having dinner.

Also of note during these formative days, when Polly's reputation was still unblemished, was Polly's first encounter with Chairman Mao. The encounter was terribly brief. Hardly more than a dozen words were exchanged between them. The encounter took place at a reception for Mao held in one of the inner palaces of the Forbidden City. In all there were more than one hundred guests, and Mao appeared only for a few minutes, circulating once around the garden and then disappearing with Chou En-lai and others of the inner circle. But at some point during those few minutes in the garden Mao and Polly were introduced by Ling.

The chairman had seemed to be familiar with Polly's story inasmuch as he made mention of the fact that Polly had once been an American intelligence officer, and was currently generating material for the Propaganda Ministry. The only other words of consequence was Mao's offer of assistance should Polly ever run into difficulty in Peking.

The end of the initial Peking phase came with the fall of Shanghai, then Canton, and the final victory of the People's Army. From Polly's viewpoint in Peking the final victory came very suddenly. The remaining Nationalist forces surrendered with only token resistance, the bulk of Nationalists having already fled to the island of Taiwan, formerly Formosa, which Chiang Kai-shek had been fortifying steadily over the previous six months. There were also reports of refugees pouring into Hong Kong, leaving the mainland clear for the Communist consolidation.

As for Polly's personal thoughts on the victory, these were best expressed in a conversation he had with Tommy Ling on the morning after the victory celebration. There had been a party at the Soviet embassy. Later the two men found themselves wandering through the predawn streets. Here was another neighborhood of crumbling walls and cracked tiles. The road was cobbled, lined with tiny houses in clay-brick. The gutters were littered with firecracker casings and watermelon rinds.

Polly said, "You told me that when Shanghai fell I could go and get Kim."

"Ah, so that's what you've been thinking about all evening."

"Yes. That's what I've been thinking about."

"I knew that you were preoccupied by something, but I wasn't sure what it was."

"Well, now you know."

"Yes, John. Now I know."

"So how about it? Can I go?"

There was the clap of a limping horse, cartwheels over the cobbles.

"I don't think this would be a propitious time, John."

"Why not?"

"First there is the question of your safety. Although we have officially liberated Shanghai, it is still probable that many of Feng Chi's people continue to reside there."

"I'll take that chance."

They had come to the edge of an empty square. There were terra-cotta

85

figures on the walls, twists of crepe paper and dust blown across the paving stones. By midday a mobilized brigade would sweep the streets clean.

Finally Polly said, "All right. If you won't let me go, then at least have someone contact her for me."

Ling did not answer. He seemed to be watching a gray form moving across the roofs, a bird or some rodent.

"I said if you won't—"

"John, please. There are very few people in authority who can spare time to look for one girl. I will, however, present your problem to the ministry. It may take a little time, but I think they'll be sympathetic."

"How much time?"

"Please, John. I don't know."

"A month? Two months?"

"I would say about a month."

"All right. I'll give it a month."

Later, just before falling asleep, Polly saw an image he had been seeing quite a lot these days. Kim, standing in this shabby room, feeling for dust on the window ledge. He would have to make her into a Communist so that the state would leave them alone.

The consolidation of the new regime began immediately after victory. First the mass organizations were formed. There was the All-China Federation of Democratic Youth, the Students Federation, the Association of Industry and Commerce and the Young Pioneer Corps. In general the party set policy and the government carried it out. Power ran vertically, extending through the lower branch agencies directly into the factories and the communes. There was also a direct flow of instruction from top down, while reports went from the bottom up. Everyone was responsible for someone.

Behind the entire apparatus were the secret services within the party, the army and the Ministry for Public Security. Neighborhood committees were encouraged to report the day-to-day activities of their members to the police. Any sort of abnormal behavior aroused suspicion. Family quarrels turned into political issues with serious consequences. Wives were encouraged to inform on their husbands, children on their parents. Every now and then someone would disappear. Litigation was meaningless, legislation unimportant. Criminal codes remained unpublished.

Generally the most severe cases of extremism were promoted by the official government campaigns. Usually these campaigns appeared to start spontaneously, but in reality they were carefully directed by the Central Committee. A campaign could be directed against anything—heterodox ideas, undesired activities, individuals and groups. There were also campaigns to rid the city of rats. Polly watched the children all over Peking walking to the sanitation centers with gunnysacks filled with tiny corpses.

One of the earliest campaigns was the Elimination of Counterrevolutionaries. To Polly it began innocently enough. One morning the walls of the city were plastered with posters denouncing counterrevolutionaries in the bureaucracy. No names were mentioned, and the rhetoric was mild. Next Polly heard that the discussion leaders of the indoctrination centers were focusing more and more attention on the problem of supposed Nationalist sympathizers among the civilian population. Then the arrests began. Then the executions. No one knew how many people were taken. Polly estimated that there were thousands in Peking alone. Now and then he would see a demolished storefront and the seal of the Security Ministry fixed on the door. There were also suicides, and people gathering in the streets. Even late at night he would hear the chant of the crowds moving through the neighborhood.

Then came the thought reform movements. These were subtler, and directly aimed at the children. Every week there were posters praising children who had proven their allegiance to the state by denouncing their parents. The papers carried editorials condemning the extended family as feudal and romantic love as bourgeois. Occasionally there were condemnations of sexual love, although these were usually veiled in political imagery.

Eventually Polly came to realize that survival meant conforming. True, the Chinese expected him to be a little eccentric. They approved his shambling walks at all hours and the solitary meals in the courtyard. They had become used to seeing him stare out the window of his office, and used to his clothing, now a little ragged. He was also known to read potentially subversive books, which might have accounted for his occasional lapse of political propriety. But in the main he was expected to conform, and conform with at least some enthusiasm.

Soon it seemed that everywhere events were occurring that had no relationship to reality. One month there was a campaign to kill all the flies. Organizations competed with one another to see who could kill the most. Every afternoon squads of schoolchildren could be seen patrolling the marketplace. The city walls were covered with squashed flies. There were also rumors of mass trials and executions. Throughout the city posters urged citizens to criticize themselves for failing to uphold the precepts of Mao. Literature and art were officially proclaimed to be tools of the class struggle. Critics continually fought among themselves as to which writers best represented the universal principles of the new order.

Now and then Polly would imagine himself living in Peking entirely alone for the next fifteen or twenty years, the society becoming more and more robotlike. Soon there would be nearly a billion of these people, all dressed in drab colors, all thinking alike, with Polly among them in the deepest alienation possible.

And so he continued fixing his thoughts on Kim. Sometimes he became frightened because he would try and picture her face and see nothing. There were moments when he felt so close to her that he was almost certain he could read her thoughts. Once he dreamed that she had entered his room, but it did not feel like a dream. He could have sworn he heard her footsteps and her clothing falling softly to the floor. The more time he spent in China, the harder it was to determine what was illusion and what was reality.

At the end of the month there was another conversation with Ling. This one took place on the ministry balcony. The light was brown off the broader roofs. Ling was sipping hot water from a tin cup. There had been a dust storm the night before. There were people coughing in the corridors.

Without turning around Ling said, "I've heard nothing about your request today, John. Perhaps tomorrow."

"You've been saying that for over a week."

"I'm sorry."

"Don't be sorry. Just get me some results."

"As I said, these things take time, John."

"What's to take time? All I want is for someone to send me Kim. If they won't do that then I want a travel permit to Shanghai."

"This girl is not a priority as far as the state is concerned. As for your travel permit, I'm told that space is limited on the trains."

"One seat? You tell me that they can't get me one seat?"

"I'm sorry, John."

Now more than ever Polly felt as if he was living a bad dream from which he could not wake. The day after he spoke with Ling on the balcony he began a series of his own petitions, moving from office to office, waiting, filling out forms, then waiting again. Every room was the same, gray with benches along the wall, silent people at the door. In the evenings he was left with images of shabby halls, blank faces behind counters, listening passively, then waving him on for the next in line.

At the end of two weeks Polly realized he was drinking every night alone in his room. He would sit on the edge of his bed or at the window, always a candle burning on the table. One week they kept turning off the water. The next week it was the electricity. There was no aspirin for headaches, no insecticide for cockroaches. The trucks were filled with political prisoners. The sanitation department was supposed to be poisoning the dogs.

Finally one evening when he thought he could not go on any longer, Tommy Ling led him down the ministry steps out along the back streets near the water park. Here grew a row of eucalyptus trees, and through the trees was the outline of a fallen pagoda. The sky was deepening to salmon tones. There was white mist on the edge of the city. A child with smallpox cracks on his face was sitting on a drainage pipe, rocking back and forth, clasping the soles of his feet.

Ling and Polly had been walking in silence for several minutes. Then Ling suddenly stopped and said that he had been lying for seven weeks.

He said, "You must understand that I did what I believed was best for you. I thought perhaps that eventually you would forget about this woman. Only now I see that you can't forget, and so I've decided to tell you the truth.

"The truth?" Polly's voice was hollow. His mouth was suddenly very dry.

"I know where the woman is. I've known for some time."

"But you—"

"She's in a prison, John. It's a prison for enemies of the state."

"What are you talking about?"

"Kim Lee has been charged with crimes against the state."

"What *kind* of crimes?"

"Serious crimes, John. I've seen the list of charges. Apparently she was arrested attempting to smuggle valuables out of Shanghai."

Then Polly grew very still. "She was framed," he said softly. "You know that, don't you?"

"Please, John."

"Feng Chi did it. He knew that she was waiting for me, so he set her up. He did it because I killed his brother."

Ling shook his head. "This theory was considered at the trial, but apparently discarded as irrelevant."

"I don't care—what trial?"

"There was a trial about three weeks ago."

"But you didn't tell me. Why the hell didn't you tell me?"

"There was nothing that you could have done, John. These matters are not handled the same way here as they are handled in your country."

"Well, how are they handled then? What happened?"

"She was found guilty by the people's court."

Then barely loud enough to be heard, "What's the sentence, Ling?"

"Please try and understand that we are a struggling new nation, John."

"What's the sentence?"

"Thirty-five years."

Sinking to his knees, Polly saw only the swimming leaves and the angular skyline.

Now came a still-point. The panic subsided, and Polly passed the hours wandering the back streets or lingering in the gloom of his apartment. People looked at him and he did not care. He supposed they were only trying to estimate the cost of his clothing. Sometimes whole days passed without his moving from his rotting sofa. When he had enough to drink he sometimes saw himself with her, actually felt her presence, and when he turned quickly enough he could almost see her in the darkness.

After a week of these nights Polly began to suspect that his health was going; he suffered spells of fever, then bad chills. Objects he would look at would suddenly begin to blur. His eyes were ringed with red, and he had no sense of time.

Then early on the morning of the ninth day he was wakened by a knock at the door. It was not yet fully dawn, and he had been up half the night drinking, smoking, holding on to the windowsill. As he moved to answer the door he vaguely thought: this was how they took you away. They came for you just before the first light. Then he had the door unlatched and was blankly looking at Ling.

"Get dressed, John. We haven't much time."

"Time for what?"

"You said you wanted to see that woman. Well, I've arranged it."

90

"Now? We're going now?"

"Yes, now."

"But you told me..."

"Permission has been granted as a special favor in acknowledgment of your work. Now get dressed. We don't have much time."

Outside it was cold. The night winds had left another layer of red dust from the Gobi. Ling had come in a Russian car, one that Polly had never seen before. It was some sort of gray sedan. Ling drove it very badly. He kept grinding the gears whenever he shifted. Polly sat in complete silence. There was only dead road, mud factories, patches of slipping tiles.

Beyond the city the country was unlit. There were hills back from the road, and pines. Once Polly asked what this road was called, but he was given no answer. There were only a few signs, telegraph poles and the occasional steel tower against the sky. The wind blew strongly, shifting dust clouds above.

The prison complex lay at the edge of a wooded valley. There were long corrugated iron shacks, like barracks and a central compound of cement, surrounded by barbed wire. The guards were young, armed with automatic weapons. Ling and Polly had to get out of the car for a search. Later, waiting inside the compound, there was a view of parallel walls and a concrete track between. One wall was bullet-pitted. An open trench might have been for graves.

"I have to tell you," Ling said suddenly. They were standing by the car, facing the desolate yard. "I have to tell you."

"Tell me what, Tommy? What?"

"I didn't bring you here so that you would continue to live on hope. I brought you here so that you could say goodbye."

Moments later Polly was following a young guard down the track. There were steel doors, then a cement corridor. Cold drafts alternated with warmer, foul air from the ventilation shafts. There were also swamp odors, and water dripping from the pipes. Finally Polly came to a bare room, nothing more than a concrete cube, divided by a wire screen. There were no windows, no chairs, only a light bulb recessed in the ceiling.

They brought her in without ceremony, two guards in uniforms like all the others. They led her by the arms, and shut the door behind her. At first she seemed frightened and confused like a half-awakened child. Then she saw him standing there in his old raincoat with his hands at his side. For several seconds they could only gaze at each other. Then they fell to the screen, and pressed themselves against it to touch as best they could.

"How are you?" he whispered.

"Okay."

He could smell her hair, feel her skin. Nothing mattered now.

"How did you get here?" she asked.

"A friend."

"And he told you what happened?"

"Yes. He told me. But I've got to know, Kim. I've got to know if it was Feng Chi. Did he do this?"

She nodded, and again he saw that she was crying.

"How? Tell me how he did it."

"It doesn't matter, John."

"Yes it does. I've got to know how he did it."

"He paid people. He paid them to say that I had diamonds hidden, and that I was going to take them to Hong Kong. He did it to get even with us. He wanted you to hate these people, but you shouldn't hate them. It's not their fault."

"Where's Feng now?"

"Leave him alone, John. He lost. He wanted them to kill me, but they're not going to kill me. And maybe they'll even let me go before it's time. So we can hope for that, can't we?"

He wanted to tear the screen away, to hold her for just a moment, even for just a moment. "Yes. We can hope for that."

In the end they were clinging on to the screen with their fingers intertwined. The last thing she said to him was, "You'll see. The time will pass like a dream." But Polly was only twenty-five, and she was talking about thirty-five years.

By the time Polly and Ling left the prison the morning light was green, distilled from the foliage along the road. Ling drove slowly over the dragon's spine of mountains. It was said that before the Revolution this land had also been filled with ghosts, particularly the ghosts of women who had killed themselves so that in death they could avenge themselves on men.

After a long time Polly said, "I was right about Feng Chi. He had her framed."

92

"You should try not to think about it, John. It will only be worse if you think about it."

Polly's hands gripped the dashboard. He was staring at the passing rocks. "Apparently Feng bought the informants. He knew that the Shang-hai Authority was particularly tough on smugglers, so he set it up for Kim. I imagine he must have loved the irony."

"Please, John. You must look at the future now. You must accept it. There's nothing that can be done."

"There's always something that can be done."

"Not in this case."

"What about that guy Han? The one in security?"

"Han Chow?"

"Yes, him. Couldn't he do something?"

"Han is an undersecretary to the internal police. His jurisdiction does not extend to the penal system."

"But he could do something, couldn't he?"

"Han is a hard man. I doubt that he would help you."

The passing landscape had grown stranger, with gnarled trees at odd angles, fields of mushrooms in the shade of green-backed trees, elephant vines in the branches.

"What about Mao?" Polly said suddenly. "Mao could get her out, couldn't he?"

Ling stiffened. "You shouldn't even think something like that, John. It's dangerous to even think it."

"Is that so? Well, it happens that Mao told me to contact him if I ever had any trouble. He *told* me."

"The chairman was simply being polite, John."

They passed a sunken forest hollow, scattered with white stones. The air was damp.

"How do you know he was just being polite?"

"I know, John. You took a great risk when you petitioned the state in your first effort to locate this woman. You will be taking a greater risk if you petition the chairman."

"What sort of risk?" He was watching Ling's hands. They were tight around the steering wheel.

"It is bad to draw attention to yourself asking for favors."

"Fine. Now if I wrote him will you see that the letter is delivered?"

"John, you must not even contemplate such an action."

"Will you see that the letter is delivered?"

"John, you must listen to me."

"Okay. I'll deliver it myself."

Polly began the letter that night. He worked until dawn, alternately dozing and drinking. Then the next night he wrote until he was exhausted, slept, and rose again in a panic to write more. At times he was only imperfectly aware of what he was putting down. At other times he was so tired that he just sat at the rickety table and stared into the burning candle. The winds from the Gobi Desert left the whole city smelling of the desert and the red-yellow dust lay everywhere. The white hours of the morning were cold, the afternoons hot. Through it all he had to remind himself that he had nothing more to lose.

At the end of those extraordinary nights Polly discovered that he had written nearly seventeen pages. From these seventeen the final letter would be reduced to nine. He had begun with a brief synopsis of how he had come to be in Peking, then had moved simply and quickly into the body of the plea. There were no politics, no underlying moral issues. He simply told the story of how he had met Kim and how, in a fit of rage, he had killed a man. Next he enumerated his theory of how Feng Chi might have paid the informants that led to Kim's arrest, and he used the concept of revenge as a bridge into the idea of compassion. The Revolution, the party: these could not prosper without compassion, he wrote, and compassion was the only real measure of greatness.

The last paragraphs contained sentiments that he would never have included had he not been so tired, desperate, maybe drunk too. The tone was wholly personal. He might have been writing to a friend. He said that, yes, he understood that people were starving and, yes, he realized that the Revolution may well have been the only hope for almost a billion Chinese, but it was also important to understand how it was whenever he thought about Kim. In the end he supposed that this petition was the only completely honest message he had written since he had fled from Shanghai.

He sent off the letter on a Thursday, a day when the yellow light made the city look particularly insubstantial. Afterward he did not go to the ministry, but lingered in a park under the arch of a disintegrating temple. There were children watching from behind the gates. Later he found himself on the banks of a pond where the grass had turned to rutted mud. From across the water came the sounds of heavy construction. Obviously

94

the Russians were building another hotel without concern for the dragon paths or ghosts that waited in the temple columns. Toward evening he returned to his apartment and waited for a knock on the door that never came.

Now, rising in the morning, lying down in the evening he kept returning to a vision of her that he had had a few nights before. A dream, in which he had seen himself in some sort of empty station filled with dust and parallel shafts of light that diminished with distance. Kim had been drawing closer from across the marble wastes. There had been a suitcase in one hand, an old coat draped over her arm.

So it stood that in the first few days after his petition was sent to Mao, Polly found himself living entirely on hope and the oddest sense that dreams in China were always signals of the future. Then one evening, a Tuesday like all the other Tuesdays, he began to suspect that perhaps Ling had been right after all. Perhaps he shouldn't have sent that petition, perhaps this was the end.

He had just returned from the ministry, from another day of pounding out some diatribe on the failing capitalist system. He had stopped at a market stall, and bought a wad of vegetables and rice. While he waited for the water to boil, he lit a cigarette and wandered to the window. It was a night full of moths and pale moonlight. He was just about to turn away when he saw a man leaning against the courtyard wall below.

Over the next few days Polly saw a figure behind him nearly everywhere he went. It was not always the same man, although they all looked the same, thin and young. As before they watched while pretending not to watch, although some were pretty bold, just staring up at his window in the night.

Then one evening he returned to his apartment to find that his room had been searched. They had tried to make it look as though it had not been searched, but their efforts were crude. The binding of a book was broken. Papers were out of order. They had not been able to refold his shirts, and a bar of soap was missing.

Polly only saw Ling once during this time. It was in the morning after another night of dust. Ling had been waiting on the steps of the ministry, and the moment Polly arrived he led him into the back streets. Occasionally in these alleys one saw all the heaped trash that the new regime was not supposed to have wasted. There were piles of twisted scrap iron, cardboard that the rain had reduced to pulp.

"You sent that letter, didn't you?"

Polly nodded. "How did you find out?"

"I received a telephone call from Han Chow. Apparently he wanted more information about you."

"I see."

"This is bad, John. This is very bad. I told you not to send that letter. I told you. I think you'd better tell me what was in that letter, John."

"What was in the letter?"

"Yes. I think I'd better know."

"I don't remember."

"You don't have a copy?"

"No."

"But essentially you requested that the chairman intercede on your behalf and release that woman."

"Her name is Kim, okay? It's Kim."

Then Ling ran his hand across his eyes. "I'm sorry, John. Her name is Kim."

Later, there was again a man behind him when he left the ministry, down his usual route, past the old observatory and the Gardens of Divine Pride. In his room he stayed away from the window, and drank a glass of whiskey in the sagging burlap chair. He also ate a little rice, and picked the scraps off a chicken carcass. Still later, he finally fell into a patchy sleep. There were no sounds but the ticking of a cheap alarm clock and water moving through the pipes.

It was after midnight when he woke again. There was the wind sounding through loose tiles and the rainspout. For a long time he sat in total darkness. Then he lit a candle. There had been moments in the last few days when he decided that whatever they did to him was really quite inconsequential. Imprisonment, exile to the provinces, execution—without Kim, all of it was inconsequential. So that by the time he finally heard the knock on the door, he hardly even cared. If they had come to take him away, he simply did not care. So he rose, pulled on an old terry cloth robe and moved to the door. There were three men on the step, another waiting by the car in the street.

They drove fast through the back streets so that Polly was not sure where he was being taken. It was not the prison, not the security compound either, but some sort of converted hotel on the southern edge of the city.

Within the walls lay a circular court that may have once been a garden. Now it was filled with weeds.

He was led up two flights of steps. One man walked in front of him, the others behind. They entered a long corridor smelling of stale food. The walls were blank, in certain places the plaster had fallen to reveal the rusting pipes. Finally they came to a cracked, glazed door which opened onto a large room. Here there was only a desk, two metal chairs and a row of filing cabinets. Behind the desk sat a short fat man in a boiler suit. He smiled as Polly entered and motioned to the chair. Through the dirty window lay a swimming pool, caked with algae and half-filled with green water.

"I am Deputy Assistant Wong," said the man. "I'm sorry to have had to bring you here at this inconvenient hour."

Polly shrugged. It was dawn, or nearly dawn. His watch had not been running for days.

"I have a list of questions to ask you, Mr. Polly. Please answer them as truthfully as you can."

"What sort of questions?" Although he knew that he shouldn't have asked.

"These are questions from the city functionary committee."

"What's that?"

"This is the committee concerned with the local welfare in this district."

On the wall hung a crude poster of an American soldier bayoneting an Asian child. The soldier had a pig's snout and jackboots.

"The first question is this: to your knowledge has the woman Kim ever demonstrated counterrevolutionary tendencies?"

"No." He had played this game before.

"What was the woman Kim Lee's employment before the liberation of Shanghai?"

"She was an entertainer."

"Wouldn't it be more accurate to say that she was an entertainer of men?"

"Okay, she was an entertainer of men."

"And what was your relationship to her?"

"Fiancé."

"There was no political relationship?"

"What do you mean?"

"She was not connected to your work at the imperialist espionage station?"

"No."

"Did you ever discuss politics with her?"

"No."

"Who advised you to petition the party chairman on the woman's behalf?"

"No one advised me. It was my own idea."

"You were given no encouragement from anyone? Not even from the Propaganda Section director?"

"No."

"Thank you, Mr. Polly."

"That's all? That's all you wanted?"

"Yes. Those are the only questions."

"You brought me down here in the middle of the night for that?"

Except that it was not the middle of the night. Already the first light was breaking through the windows, leaving the room faintly silver.

"The questions were merely a formality, Mr. Polly."

"What kind of formality?"

"The committee requires that the questions be answered truthfully before the actual release of the prisoner."

Then Polly felt his stomach tighten. He had absently picked up a pencil, one of the cheap domestic brands. It was right on the verge of breaking. "What prisoner?"

"The woman Kim Lee."

"She's to be released."

"Yes, of course."

"Now? Right now?"

"Yes."

"But they didn't tell me. No one told me."

He supposed there were tears in his eyes. At least the walls were blurring, the light fragmenting into spears.

"If you'll be good enough to come with me, Mr. Polly."

"Excuse me?"

"If you'll come with me I'll take you to the room where she is waiting."

Now there were the overtones of that dream he kept having. He moved along a corridor through parallel shafts of light. Desks, chairs, a fire extinguisher, all seemed insubstantial, almost flimsy. Even the walls seemed ready to dissolve. Finally he came to an empty hall that might once have been a place where dances were held. There were remnants of a chandelier, a bandstand, a microphone on a rusting pole. But this room was also a little like his dream station, what with the expansive gloom and the echo of his footsteps on the floorboards.

At some point Wong had fallen behind so that Polly was reentering his dream alone, waiting for her to materialize out of the darkness. In fact she was simply waiting with some others awaiting release. They were all sitting on folding chairs. When she saw him approach she rose slowly and then started to run toward him. But she did not have an old coat draped over her arm or a suitcase in her hand. Also, there were a number of papers that had to be signed before she was allowed to leave the premises.

But they did have one moment together alone, standing in the ruined garden, while the driver went to fetch the car. Their breath was white on the air. The overhead branches were still, reflected in plum-colored pools of rainwater. He held her as tightly as he could and whispered her name over and over. She was wearing that same prison uniform, and when he realized that she was shivering he wrapped her in his filthy belted raincoat, the one he had purchased an eternity ago at Brooks Brothers.

So ended the second stage of Polly's career in China. Whatever happiness he had now crystallized. Spring burst out on the first of April. Grasses rose among the unpruned trees. There were blossoms all along Chang An Jie. After a rain there was the damp redness of the branches, wet leaves clinging everywhere. The willows of the inner yards sounded in the wind. Of these days Polly would eventually write that he was a rich man in a poor country.

At the end of March Polly and Kim Lee left the foreign compound and were given a house which would eventually become permanently associated with Polly in the minds of those who knew him. The house stood on the edge of the city behind a high sandstone wall. There were surrounding gardens, and from the upstairs windows one could see for miles across the city. In later years this house came to be the most salient extension of Polly himself, although in the beginning it was simply another whitewashed Peking villa, built by the imperialists, confiscated by the state and presented to favored city residents.

The house was furnished piecemeal over a long period of time. Initially there were only two rosewood chairs, a pine dresser, a laminated breakfast table and the bed. Then Tommy Ling found a desk for Polly's study, lamps, fiberboard bookshelves and a low settee in blue with a pattern of lilies. In all, the decor was clean and simple. The cool white walls contrasted with pastels. Kim would stand and gaze at rooms for minutes on end, then suddenly rearrange an enamel vase.

During that spring Kim and Polly were married. The license was granted without delay, which was taken by all to signify a blessing from the state. The ceremony was brief, attended by Tommy Ling and others from the ministry. Among the gifts were two cicadas imprisoned in tiny bamboo cages. Polly hung the cages outside the bedroom window and through the first night he heard them singing. In later years, however, the selling of cicadas and goldfish would be labeled bourgeois and condemned.

Soon after they were married Kim Lee began working at the Cultural Ministry, initially as a film editor's apprentice, then as an actress and production assistant. In her first role she portrayed a village girl who had been given a job castrating pigs on a commune. In the opening sequence the girl was scorned by the men who had the peculiar idea that castrating pigs was not fit work for a woman. Kim was shown eating alone in the community dining room, then wandering out sadly among the terraced fields. Eventually, however, she began to read the works of Mao, and drawing strength from them became the best pig castrator on the commune. In the end she was shown happily receiving the respect and affection of all peasants, while an enormous moon rose above the mountains.

In another film she played the role of a construction worker who fell in love on a building site. Her lover was a young machinist with serious political misconceptions. The action alternated between Kim's efforts to reeducate her young machinist and the two working happily against a background of heavy equipment. In the end the machinist sees the errors of his ways and embraces Kim on the bamboo scaffolding while the face of Mao is superimposed against the clouds.

As for Kim's personal feelings about the new regime Polly came to see that she genuinely believed in most of the Revolution's basic tenets. Time and again she would point to some aspect of life and explain how much better things were since the Communist victory. Women, she would tell him, women had especially profited from the Revolution. But her vision of the new Chinese woman was a little like a child's vision of a fairy-tale hero. It was a vision mostly formulated by what she saw on the posters and in the theater where all the women were strong and beautiful, perched on tractors or holding rifles.

There were moments when Polly would catch a glimpse of Kim Lee and it was like looking at her for the first time. She could be several women depending upon her mood, whether it was day or night and which dream rose to the surface. He knew that she had secrets he would probably never know. He looked forward to the day when the garden would become so thick and high that he could wander along the paths and come upon her by accident.

His own days were spent writing articles for the Peking press, and even in this work he found a sort of pleasure now, toying with the metaphors until they were right. At night Kim would come to him, take his hand and place it over her breast until they were part of each other. Then later he might watch her sleeping beside him, and on warm evenings, draw back the sheets to see her naked body. If the Communists could produce something like this, he would tell himself, they couldn't be all bad.

So by summer Polly found himself in a life he refused to believe would ever end. True there were still those odd moments when he deeply missed America. Also there were moments when the power of this Chinese state honestly frightened him. But in the main he had come to feel that he would be content if nothing ever changed, which he knew was too much to hope for.

Now the various threads of Polly's life began to come together. It was still another day of dust storms. Polly had seen the clouds in the morning from his bedroom window. By noon the streets were covered with silt. There was even grit in his typewriter, jamming the keys. At the end of the day he took the long route home, because Kim had her production meeting and would not return until late. So he was walking through the western district along the Lishi Road. Dust had caught the failing light, and the sky was indigo with a red welt. As he climbed the last hill and looked back over his shoulder he saw that the city had grown even stranger. There were clouds unraveling in a gale, trees bending, the crowds flowing mechanically over Wang Fu Jing.

Then approaching the gates of his home, he saw a man, clearly European, standing against the gray wall. The man wore a dark coat and a homburg. He had a handkerchief pressed to his nose and mouth, presumably against the dust. He was squinting into the light, watching Polly draw closer. When there were only twenty yards between them he raised his arm in greeting; Polly had never seen him before. He was quite certain of that. The man was round, bookish, about thirty, perhaps a bit younger. He had fair skin and red hair. He waited until Polly came closer. Then he said, "You are John Polly?"

Polly nodded, studying the face, wary.

"My name is Neil Dray. Is there somewhere we can chat?"

"What about?"

"Please, not here."

"What about?"

"All right, if you must know. I believe we have a friend in common."

"Who?"

"Simon Crane."

They passed through the garden gates to a stone bench beneath one of the older magnolias. While they walked Polly said nothing, and there was no perceptible emotion in his eyes.

Even his voice was empty. "Where's Simon now?"

"Washington," Dray replied. Then smiled nervously, "He had a bout with the flu, but he's doing better now."

Polly frowned. "So you're the cutout? You're my link to Simon?"

"Yes, I suppose you could say that. Although actually it's a partnership. You see, I'm with the British effort."

"At the consulate?"

"Yes."

Behind them lay three moss-covered rocks and a pool of water that the storm had left with a skin of dust.

Suddenly Dray added, "Well, what did you expect? Simon couldn't have very well sent one of your own people, not here. So he worked a deal with London. We handle you and split the product."

To which Polly only smirked, "Sounds nice."

"Look, Polly, I know what you're thinking. But you needn't worry. I've had experience with this kind of thing before. In fact, I've actually run quite a few."

"Quite a few what?"

"Agents."

Then again Polly's voice was dead flat. "All right. What do you want?"

"Well, you're to be activated, aren't you? Now of course Simon will still be your ultimate control. I'll merely be supplying the field support."

"What the hell does that mean?"

"Suppose you need a camera. Say a sub-miniature with an infrared. All you've got to do is ask."

The wind had died. It was very still again.

"I'll also be making the pickups for you," Dray continued. "Simon thought a monthly schedule would be reasonable, and I believe I've worked out a very nice drop system."

102

A mouse or a rat was sliding through the ferns. Polly could see its shadow.

"Now of course you won't be able to speak with Simon directly, not for the moment anyway. But he will be sending you a brief."

Now a second rodent had slipped out of the grass, definitely a rat.

"In the meantime, however, you might try to keep your ear to the ground as far as Korea goes. Try and get some idea of the prevailing winds."

Then Polly nodded, and the rat, which had also been watching him, slid into the vegetation.

"Incidentally, you might be pleased to know that as far as Washington goes you're now legitimately on the books as a foreign operative. They're calling it China Shore."

Polly turned. "What?"

"The operative name. It's China Shore. And as operative source you're to be known as—and I think you'll like this—White Mandarin."

"White Mandarin?"

"Yes. It's a sort of pun. Get it?"

But that night in his spectral garden the subtleties were lost on Polly. It hadn't even occurred to him that the die was cast.

Chapter 4

IT WAS now the late afternoon. The tide had fallen to expose the more delicate algae. Another oppressive fog was moving in from the bay. Earlier Cassidy had grown restless, and walked south along the palisade. When he returned Crane was still waiting for him on the rocks.

Cassidy said, "This guy Neil Dray. Who was he?"

"No one special. We mainly chose him because he was available."

"And he's still there?"

"Oh no. There's been two since him. A fellow named Roger Hall, and now there's Dart."

"So the British are still in on it."

Crane nodded. "Yes. They're still in."

"Must have been hard pushing that one through."

"Not really. At the time we hadn't any choice. We needed a resident to service John, and the British were the only possible ones with a diplomatic staff."

"And what about Polly?"

"How do you mean?"

"What did he think about all this?"

Crane shrugged. "Difficult to say really. I like to think that he recognized the importance of what we were doing, but—well, John has always been a rather enigmatic person."

Later there was fog and the sound of harbor bells, then another strange meal of baked fish, beer and a salad with anchovies. At one point Eliot took offense because Cassidy snubbed out a cigarette on his plate. Afterward Crane and Cassidy walked back out to the point.

104

There was no end to the drifting refuse here: bottles, paper, cork, splintered packing crates. Once Billy had even found a lady's slipper down among the tide pools. But tonight the beach had been left with nothing but a clump of seaweed and a sand shark. As Crane began to talk, Cassidy watched the jetty lights.

Within the scheme of Simon Crane's story, it was now 1951 and Jay Sagan had begun to make a name for himself as a bonafide China warrior. Properly the story of Sagan began the night that Feng Chi's brother was shot. Earlier that evening Sagan had met with three Chinese for drinks at the Shanghai Mansions. They had been discussing military appropriations for Taiwan, and while they spoke a willowy girl could occasionally be seen moving through the apartment, the lateral slit up her dress revealing the favored lighter skin, a string of pearls to show that she had already been taken. Afterward Sagan decided that he also wanted a woman, and went to a club on the poor side of the docks. By midnight he had not found anyone intriguing, and in the end simply went home to bed. Then, just after eight o'clock in the morning, he was awakened by a telephone call and told that Danny Feng was dead.

The weeks that followed the shooting were uncertain weeks for Sagan. He spent hours watching the river from a table in a bar, walking the streets in search of women, brooding in his office. Messages sent to Feng Chi were unanswered, telephone calls not returned. Even a note of condolence and a wreath of hothouse orchids was ignored.

Yet perhaps the most disturbing development of these days were the rumors, rumors that Polly had not gone east at all, but was in Hawaii with both Agency knowledge and consent. Of course Sagan denied all this, but denied it to no avail. It seemed that Feng's circle was closed to him now. It seemed that he was guilty by association.

So Sagan remained in a kind of political limbo. Once out of boredom he drove out to Polly's home, and there wandered freely through rooms where nothing had been disturbed. There were Polly's suits in the closet, even crusted soap in the bristles of his shaving brush. Sagan probed through the house for an hour, peering into drawers, leafing through old papers, finding nothing of consequence except perhaps a photograph of Kim.

Jay Sagan's role in the incarceration of Kim Lee was the least understood aspect of these days. All that was really known was that at some point shortly after Polly's disappearance the girl was also said to have vanished, whether to Hong Kong or across the Yangtze no one knew. It was further said that Feng Chi was as interested in finding her as were the Nationalist Police. But on the whole Sagan did not think about her very much, except in passing and then his thoughts were ambivalent. He supposed in one sense he partially blamed her for what had happened, although perhaps that was only a little of the Chinese morality rubbing off.

Then one evening, quite by accident, he discovered that she had not fled the city, but was in fact living secretly in one of the consulate residences on the edge of the city. It came about this way. Four weeks after Polly's flight, Simon Crane was hospitalized with influenza. Normally Crane's absence from the station would have had no bearing on Sagan's life, but since Polly was also absent, Sagan naturally became the only intelligence officer with authority. Consequently certain matters which Crane had been handling now fell directly into Sagan's jurisdiction, and one of those matters was Kim Lee.

In all probability Sagan discovered the girl's whereabouts by going through Crane's payment ledgers. Whether or not Sagan had been actually looking for the girl at this point has never been determined. But the fact remains that on the last week of the month, undoubtedly in the evening, he found that the girl had been moved into one of the larger consulate estates normally reserved for staff.

Two nights later he contacted one of Feng Chi's closest associates, a tall handsome man named Jerry Woo. Woo had been educated in America on Feng's behalf, and before that had worked for the Feng organization for approximately seven years. He was further considered one of the most approachable in the organizaiton, and at the time of Sagan's dealing with him he was serving as Feng's personal secretary.

The conversation took place under adverse conditions. It was late and the streets were washed in yellow fog. Earlier in the evening Sagan had torn his sleeve climbing out of a taxicab. There were also grease stains on his trousers. After a few fairly cold words Woo finally agreed to step into the adjoining alley.

"I understand that Feng Chi wants to find Kim Lee," said Sagan.

Woo shrugged. "Maybe."

"Will you give him a message for me?"

"Mr. Feng is still in mourning."

"Which means that he doesn't want to talk to me, right?"

Again Woo shrugged.

106

"Okay, just tell him that I know where the girl is. If he wants the information he can contact me."

Woo telephoned three nights later. He met Sagan in a teahouse near the South Station. On the wall was a poster of a demon surrounded by starving children. The characters in black read: *Hunger.* Woo said that Feng Chi would be very grateful for any information regarding the woman. Then Sagan wrote down the address. The following week Sagan received an invitation to join Feng and his guests for dinner. The main course consisted of chicken with snow peas and shrimp.

Also consequential to that night was Kim Lee's imprisonment and a commendation to Sagan from a chief lieutenant of the Nationalist Army. The commendation stated that Julius Sagan was a valiant anti-Communist, and would always be welcome in Free China. Although four months later the Red Army took over the entire mainland so that Free China meant only Taiwan and Hong Kong.

Jay Sagan left Shanghi about six weeks before the fall. He spent two weeks in Taiwan conferring with Chiang Kai-shek, and then continued to Washington by way of Hawaii. By January the British had recognized the Communist regime. By February Chou En-lai had signed a friendship treaty with the Soviets. At the signing he was quoted as saying that between Moscow and Peking there were now over a billion Communists with an army that would be impossible to defeat.

After another three months in Washington Sagan flew to Miami for his first vacation in almost two years. Upon arriving at his hotel he telephoned a prostitute who had been recommended by an associate at the Agency. But by the time she arrived it was well after midnight and he was too exhausted to use her. So he started to tell her about China. He did not know why. He just compulsively rambled on about China.

For nearly six months Sagan remained in Washington. He was living in a Virginia suburb in a sterile apartment complex among other Agency employees. His days were filled with paperwork, rewriting raw intelligence that was still trickling in from the south China border. Occasionally he heard rumors that he would soon be given another Asian posting, but those rumors never came to much. It seemed that the American policy in Asia had entered a floundering stage. No one was quite sure how to stop communism in the Far East.

There remains a paper of Sagan's from this era, supposedly intended as an answer to those like Simon Crane who continued to argue that the Chinese Revolution had been inevitable and the only proper course of action now was diplomatic recognition. At the heart of the paper were several controversial solutions to the Asian problem, including a massive military investment. As it happened, however, the paper never received more than a modest, low-level circulation. Among other things, it was rather poorly written.

Twice that summer Sagan drafted formal requests for an Asian posting and twice the requests were ignored. There were apparently open slots in South Korea and Japan, but not within the China sphere. So in time Sagan began to tell himself that luck was simply against him, although in reality it was politics that were against him, and eventually those politics changed.

The events which finally led to Sagan's return were the darkest of the Asian wars. Even now there are still unanswered questions, still portions of the story which have never been explained. In essence the story involved not China particularly, but Southeast Asia, and those remnants of the Nationalist Army who, after defeat at the hands of the Communists, fled across the south China border into Burma and Laos where their descendants remain today.

Secret-world historians have always had difficulty placing these Nationalist or Kuomintang refugee armies in proper perspective. Part of the problem undoubtedly stems from the fact that no one was quite sure what their real intent had been for staying in the southeast rather than moving on to Taiwan. Ostensibly their story was this: when the Red Army pushed south into the Yunnan Province the 93rd Nationalist Division, the 26th and General Li Mi's Eighth all fled into Burma where they immediately entrenched themselves in the remote mountains of Mong Hsat. There were a few halfhearted Burmese attempts to expel them, but these were unsuccessful. Officially the Kuomintang refugee armies claimed that their mission was wholly to fight Communists, and to this end they appealed to the United States for military aid.

From the start the Asian intelligence warriors generally viewed these armies with ambivalence. On the one hand there was a tacit understanding that they could be useful as a buffer against the Red Chinese, particularly if one saw China as a nation that could only be contained with force. On the other hand there were diplomatic questions involving the legalities of aiding a military force which had entrenched itself in an allied country. Finally there was the even more problematic aspect of

Feng Chi's relationship with these armies and what is today popularly called the Golden Triangle opium route.

Jay Sagan might never have entered this chapter of the story had those refugee armies never involved themselves in the cultivation of Burmese opium. There were dozens of intelligence officers far more qualified than Sagan. But as events eventually started to unfold it seemed that Sagan was the only one with the necessary relationship with Feng Chi and that organization loosely called the Triads.

Sagan's entrance into this chapter and his later return to the East is also perhaps notable because it marks the entrance of Norman Pyle. Pyle was at this time in his first year as tactical head of the Asian Desk. He was comparatively young then, with a strong background in Oriental languages and some actual field experience in French Indo-China.

The initial conversation between Pyle and Sagan took place on a Tuesday morning, presumably after an earlier high-level debate. The briefing was fairly typical, with Pyle immediately asking what Sagan knew about the Shan states in northeastern Burma. Sagan replied that he had heard that the country was pretty rough with regular intertribal warfare and territorial battles over the opium fields. Pyle then laid a buff folder on the desk and said that it contained a directive from the Joint Chiefs enumerating the theory that Burma, and specifically the northeast, was "the hole in the dike as far as Red Chinese expansion is concerned." Sagan expressed no surprise over this statement as the theory had also been discussed in his previously mentioned paper.

At this point the conversation was directed toward the main issue at hand, namely the entrenchment of the Kuomintang refugee army and their potential use as a defensive wall against Communist expansion.

Sagan wholeheartedly endorsed this proposal and all underlying theories behind it. (What may today be called the Domino Theory.) Then regarding the problem of the illegal infringement upon Burmese soil by the Kuomintang and the question of whether or not the United States had a right to endorse that infringement by sending the Kuomintang aid, Sagan said only: secrecy could be stressed.

At this juncture there was a brief pause. Up until now Pyle had been toying with a crystal paperweight, but suddenly laid the object down. He then put the folder aside, and said that it was time to discuss one of the more delicate aspects of the operation: opium.

According to the Rangoon station the Kuomintang refugees had begun to involve themselves with the cultivation of opium almost as soon as they had crossed the border. Of course, Pyle admitted that opium had always been an economic reality in that area, but until the arrival of the Kuomintang, production had been relatively small, mainly consisting of village plots in the naturally formed valleys. The Kuomintang, however, changed all this by methodically reorganizing tribal srtructure and markedly increasing poppy harvest.

In response to all this Sagan said virtually nothing. Obviously he knew what was coming next—Feng Chi.

According to reports, also from the Rangoon station, Feng Chi had met with Kuomintang leaders in Burma on three occasions. The subject of these talks was of course opium, specifically distribution and refinement. With increased production Kuomintang leaders had obviously discovered that new access to markets was needed, and for this reason they had turned to Feng. Precisely what agreements had been made was not known, but it was clear that a formal partnership had been drawn. The Kuomintang would continue to insure production, while Feng Chi and the greater Triad organization would handle distribution and laboratory refinement.

Once again Sagan remained silent. Then came a brief exchange:

"Tell me about Feng, Jay. Would you say that he trusts you?"

"Yes, sir. I think he trusts me."

"And how do you feel about him? You trust him?"

"Oh I believe so."

"Because trust is a crucial word here. I mean the Chinese have different standards than we do, don't they?"

"Yes, sir. I suppose they do."

"Now, we're contemplating arming a large number of trained men in a remote area of Burma. I'm talking about advanced weapons, Jay, weapons which will virtually make those people the law of the land. Consequently the question arises as to how much power are we going to have over them? You see what I'm getting at, don't you?"

"Yes, sir. I think I do. You want Feng as a handle on those people."

"It's a matter of personal relationships really. I think if those Nationalists knew that Feng was completely our man it would strengthen our position all the way around. I mean they need Feng, don't they?"

"So you want me to speak to Feng?"

"I want you to bring him into the fold. Give him what he eats. Make him part of our team. I know he's got a stable of people in that area, so let's see if we can't use them."

110

Following this exchange there was a secondary discussion on the tactical potential of Feng as an Agency client as well as the larger potential of the Triads. Here Sagan again reiterated his viewpoint that Feng was essentially a trustworthy man, while Pyle merely smiled, "Well, let's hope so." Then: "I want you to know that the opium is to be temporary," Pyle said.

"In what sense, sir?"

"In the most literal sense. You make it clear to those people that we do not like it, and will not support it."

"Yes, sir."

"And Jay?"

"Sir?"

"I'm serious about this, okay?"

Supposedly this was the end of the conversation, or at least the end as regards Pyle's later summary. In fact, however, it was not the end, but for obvious reasons Pyle made no mention of these words in his summary.

"I understand you knew John Polly, Jay."

"Uh, yes. We were in Shanghai together."

"Did you know him well?"

"No, not really."

"But you did work with him?"

"Yes."

"What would you say he was like?"

"Oh I don't know. I guess he seemed nice enough on the surface, but then one never knows, does one?"

"Well, listen, Jay. If you should ever hear anything about him, you just ignore it, okay? Anyone ever asks you about him, keep your mouth shut. Know what I mean?"

"Yes, sir, but I was under the impression—"

"Just do what I say, okay?"

Then followed another awkward silence wherein Pyle once again began to toy with his paperweight and Sagan simply watched him.

Sagan spent three more weeks at headquarters. His eventual recommendations called for a supply line from Taiwan to the Burmese hills consisting of airdrops from C-46's and C-47's. Although these recommendations were later amended, they formed the basis of what was eventually to become the Air America system which, along with the politics of heroin in Asia, would one day become a story in itself.

At the end of the three weeks Sagan then left Langley and returned to Hong Kong, stopping first in Los Angeles, then in Hawaii. The afternoon of his arrival he spent in a hotel bar talking with some missionary's daughter who had recently escaped from Canton. While watching her profile in the mirror he listened to the usual horror story of Communist brutality. The woman was plain, thirty, and possibly a little mad. But after two or three whiskeys she seemed to lose her more haggard dimensions, so that Sagan was tempted to tell her that he also knew a thing about the Communists, then take her to bed. But the moment he started sliding closer, she panicked and started talking about the Pentecost. In the end he was left alone through the whole deteriorating night.

In many ways the Hong Kong that Sagan had entered in this summer of 1950 was much more the China of his dreams than Shanghai had ever been. He was soon settled into an apartment high up on Victoria Peak where he was surrounded by people like himself—Americans and English who lived amid orchids, playing the horses on weekends, dealing with China the rest of the time. His apartment was modern and white, and it had a magnificent view of the harbor. The bad moments were mainly those without women. One did not bring prostitutes to one's own apartment.

Beneath the peak lay areas where he was told that he should never go alone, or at least unarmed. In Shanghai he had been told that you could die by looking at the wrong man the wrong way. This was also said to be true of certain quarters in Hong Kong.

But regardless of what may have been said about Hong Kong, Sagan would always look back on these two weeks as among the best weeks of his career. Most days he spent at the consulate. His office lay in the west wing of what was called the isolation ward. It was small and there were no windows, but it was clean and comfortable.

In the evenings when the doors were shut and there were no sounds except the hum of the coding machines, he could lay out maps of the China coast and in that silence it seemed that the whole of Asia was accessible. There remain notes he had written at this time explaining how courier routes could be laid throughout the south China sphere, with links to mainland agents through the fishing fleets. Or else agents could be run with high frequency radio links over the Burmese border. There was also a map with potential trouble spots slashed in red crayon, while blue drawing pins represented the listening posts. Sometimes he would just sit with his hands spread around the entire continent.

In the later evening he would wander down to the Wanchai bars. Here the girls were like the girls in Shanghai, no less desperate. One night he went to a place called the Luk Kwok Hotel. There was a dance floor filled with swaying couples, girls waiting by the jukebox, men watching them from the tables. Eventually he found a girl wearing a white fringed scarf. He saw her first clutching a narrow party bag to her breast, and liked her because she looked frightened. Then came a slow elevator up to her room. He liked the anticipation as the music faded away, the elevator anchoring on the residential floor. When she was naked he had her kneel on the floor between his legs. All these girls were kids at heart. Through the shutter lay an indigo skyline, and faintly moonlit ivy. Romantic China.

At the end of these two weeks, time brushed aside as orientation, Sagan began his more formal entry into the second phase of his career. Appropriately enough this entry was signaled by a reunion with Feng Chi.

Like Sagan, Feng left the mainland shortly before the Communist victory. For a time he lived in Taipei, but by the summer of 1950 he was also in Hong Kong near the bay and the Headland Road. Here stood a white villa amid pines and rows of cultivated tulips. The morning of Sagan's visit the west grounds were blooming with azaleas and roses by the outer gate.

As always the curtains were drawn, the rooms set in perpetual stillness. There were undertones of emotion that Sagan could never identify, odd mixtures of fear and serenity.

He was met by a butler and led down a long hall. A woman's dreamy voice sounded from beneath a door. She was softly singing to a plucked violin. There were dried flowers in a vase, the stems wrapped in silver paper. Feng was waiting in the drawing room. He wore a velvet jacket and red tie. On the wall above hung a landscape of leaves stuck to wilting trees. The water was suggested by only three brushstrokes.

"So you have come back to us," Feng said. "This is good. I'm truly glad to see you."

"I'm glad to see you too," replied Sagan.

"I take it that you spent the time that you were away conferring with your superiors?" Feng asked.

"I was in Washington, yes."

"And now you come to me with an entirely new set of proposals?"

Sagan smiled. There was something undefined about the light in this

113

room. "I wouldn't say that I've got a proposal. I'd say that it was more of a political arrangement."

"Political arrangement? But I'm no longer a political man."

"All right. Then let's just say that what is business to you is politics to me."

Tea was served, laid on a black table bordered in pearl. Along the rim of the cups were interlocking tigers.

"What is your proposal, Mr. Sagan? Please tell me."

"It concerns Burma."

"Burma? Burma is an insignificant country. I don't believe that I know any Burmese."

"Perhaps not, but you know Chinese who are living there."

"Do I? Who told you that?"

"My superiors."

"They are mistaken."

"I don't think so. In fact I think that you know a great number of Chinese who are presently living in the hills of northern Burma."

"And supposing this is true, please tell me what your superiors believe I have in common with these people?"

"Opium."

"Opium? But, opium is currently illegal in most of the world. Why would I be dealing in opium?"

"I don't know, Mr. Feng. Why would you?"

They had stepped into the garden, through a gallery in shadows to a terrace that fell away to the trees. Here lay a pond underneath the maples, and three plaster geese on the lawn.

"We're concerned about Burma," Sagan said softly. "We're concerned about that entire region."

"Who is we?"

"Washington."

"Ah. So this is definitely official business, no?"

"Yes."

"And why is Washington concerned?"

"The usual reasons. It's possible that the Communists will not respect the border."

"So we are back to politics. First we talk about geography, then the danger of narcotics, and now we are again back to politics."

"Well, it's a political world, Mr. Feng."

114

A servant was moving between the trunks of the tall trees, leading a small dog on a leash. There was no wind, only static heat.

Sagan said, "We would like those soldiers to work for us. We will offer any and all material assistance, but we want them to work exclusively for us."

"They are independent people," Feng replied. "They are proud and independent."

"We are hoping that you would talk to them."

"Me? Why would they listen to me?"

"Because they need you—financially."

"Ah. So you think you know all the answers. You think you have us entirely understood."

"No, sir. We only think you might be able to influence them."

"And supposing this is true, why would I concern myself with the matter?"

"Because you are a great champion of the Free Chinese."

A second servant appeared below them, a thin girl in black. She was carrying a bucket and a coiled garden hose.

Suddenly Feng said, "You must understand that of course I would normally be only too happy to help you politically, Mr. Sagan. But under the circumstances I am worried that there may be certain conflicts of interest."

"Such as?"

"Well, for example, my people have informed me that your people disapprove of certain business arrangements that I have been forced to make recently. Now, is this true?"

Sagan nodded. "To some degree, yes."

"So if I am to help you now, how am I to be sure that your people will help me later?"

"What if I were to give you my word? What if I were to promise you that my people, regardless of their personal feelings, will not interfere with your business arrangements? Would that be acceptable?"

"Oh yes. That would be acceptable. Assuming of course that your word is good."

"I'll make sure that it is."

"Then perhaps we have just reached a new plateau of understanding."

"I certainly hope so, Mr. Feng."

In his subsequent report on this conversation, Sagan wrote only that

115

he had obtained Feng Chi's agreement on all points previously discussed with Norman Pyle. There was no mention of the opium routes, nor the implication of a future debt.

Now Sagan began to live the life he had always imagined was possible. In the weeks that followed he met seven times with Feng and Feng's secretary Jerry Woo. By the end of July the skeleton of the first extensive China network had been laid. Most of the information collected was relatively low grade: rumors from refugees, unverifiable sightings of troop concentrations. But the fact remained that Sagan had at least made a step in penetrating what they were by now calling the Bamboo Curtain.

During this period Sagan began the formal organization of the Nationalist Chinese in Burma. By the end of the summer unmarked aircraft were routinely making drops of food, clothing, small arms, bazookas, mortars and heavy-caliber machine guns. By the beginning of autumn another eight thousand soldiers had been recruited from the hill tribes. As was expected there were protests from the Burmese government, but after the first round of drops, it seemed that the Burmese were too weak to take any overt action.

Two months after the airdrops began, Sagan made the first of several trips into the northern Burma hills. He flew in with a Chinese pilot from Taiwan. There was a crucifix stuck to the instrument panel, and the pilot prayed before they took off. They landed in a tiny jungle airstrip in a place called Mong Pa Lioa. From the air this village appeared to be only a string of crude huts near a stretch of slashed forest. On the ground, however, it was clear that the village had already begun to assume the likeness of a military installation.

Upon landing Sagan was taken to the largest hut where he met with the local unit commander and General Li Mi's personal aide. By noon there was rain, and the conversations were held against the sound of water on the thatch and damp gusts through the palms. There was jasmine tea, rice and some sort of fried meat. Talk was wholly political, and generally theoretical. Li Mi's aide kept pointing to the north and saying that the enslaved masses were only waiting for a sign to rise up against the Communist regime. Through the doorway of the hut three tribal children were carrying an anteater which they had trapped and clubbed to death. Later there was an embarassing moment when Sagan failed to recognize a field of poppies, and inquired as to why so much land was given to the flowers.

116

It was not long after Sagan returned from Burma that an idea was born which would dominate his life for the greater part of the remaining year. The idea involved nothing less than a full reconquest of south China. As first envisioned the conquest would begin in Mong Mao, on the Burmese side of the border. General Li Mi's Fifth Army would be reinforced with regular Nationalist troops from Taiwan, and as many local tribesmen as could be pressed into service. The entire operation would be supplied by the C-47's, and although American advisors would be present, they would carry French papers.

Exactly who was originally responsible for conceiving the Yunnan invasion still remains a mystery today. In the beginning everyone wanted credit. When it was over no one wanted it. Jay Sagan's role has been called everything from critical to peripheral. What is known for certain, however, is that from the very start he had been one of the operation's keenest supporters. There are still existent maps containing notations in his own handwriting relating to the strategic theory of launching an operation of that size. There are also his tactical recommendations, including his ideas of troop deployment and supply, all of which were later discarded as hopelessly optimistic.

A conversation of note on the subject occurred not long after the idea was born. Norman Pyle had flown into Hong Kong by way of Singapore and came together with Sagan in the early evening. It was a warm night, and there had been talk of a typhoon. All day the sky had been dead white. After meeting Pyle, Sagan suggested that they go to a bar, but Pyle felt that it would be safer to speak in the station. So they sat in Sagan's office, amid a litter of notes, empty coffee cups and crude sketches of the border land.

Sagan began simply enough by saying, "There's been some talk that it might be time for people in Burma to take an offensive posture."

Pyle, who was exhausted, merely smiled. "What's that supposed to mean?"

"A sweep. A thrust right into Yunnan."

"Why?"

"To take it back. To take the whole damn thing back from the Reds."

Until now Pyle had been idly playing with a cigarette lighter. "I assume you're kidding."

"No, sir. I'm not. I can get five thousand men on that border. The

117

offensive can be coordinated with a leaflet drop over the south so that by the time the Reds can counter the entire country will be up in arms."

To which Pyle replied. "What arms, Jay?"

"Preliminary program calls for three dozen advance strike teams and enough weapons to make everyone happy."

"And if the peasants don't play?"

"Well, sir, I think they will. I mean it's a question of political climate. I think those people are pretty sick of the Communist regime."

There was a long pause and again Pyle began to fumble with his lighter. Finally he said, "You're talking about political climate, Jay. I'm talking about real death. Know what I mean?"

As a result of this conversation, Sagan spent three nights drafting a request for a broad intelligence survey of the political stance of the Yunnan peasant. His proposal included requests for a refugee interrogation program as well as a comprehensive study of the south China press. He also suggested that efforts be intensified to place at least one reliable source into the Peking establishment. He had heard while in Shanghai that such an operation existed, but of course he had no idea that the slot had been filled months ago by the White Mandarin.

The request was sent out on a Thursday, and the reply came back ten days later on a muggy afternoon when the consulate air conditioning unit was barely functioning. Earlier Sagan had called down for ice, but none had come. Spirits seemed low all over Hong Kong. Returning from lunch he had watched a crowd gather around the bodies of an elderly couple who had thrown themselves under a tram. The night before, the Communists had splashed pig's blood on the steps of Government House.

The reply filled barely a page. There was no indication of the source, nor a reliability grade. The language was terse, and the entire analysis took the classical form wherein the request was briefly stated at the top of the page, and then the answer followed. The following conversation ensued between Sagan and one of the junior officers in the station, an inconsequential figure named Ross.

"Tell me what you think of this crap?" Sagan asked.

Ross quickly read the paper, then laid it back down on Sagan's desk. "Well, sir. It seems that someone back home doesn't think that the Yunnan move has much chance of sparking a peasant revolt."

"That's right, son. Someone doesn't believe we have much of a chance. Someone seems to think we should scrap the entire operation. *Someone.* Who the hell is *someone?*"

"I'm sure there's a source, sir."

"Yeah? Who? God? Chairman Mao? You go down to communications, Ross. You go down there right now and tell them that this crap is unacceptable. You tell them that I want a verification of the source, and I want it now."

But no verification came, nor would it ever come. What Sagan had received following his request for an analysis of the internal political climate of mainland China had been, in truth, one of the earliest submissions from the White Mandarin.

The analysis had apparently been drafted by Polly following written instructions from Simon Crane. Those instructions were coded, and then placed behind a loose brick on the Fuchen Road, which was one of the two dead-drops that Polly had been using at the time. After receiving the instructions Polly immediately began working on the analysis, the main body of which was drawn from a Security Ministry report on potential unrest in the southern rural areas. Supposedly Polly had received this report after claiming that he needed it for an article he was preparing for the *Peking Foreign Journal.* It was a method of obtaining information that he was to use over and over again.

If nothing else, this small incident helped prove that effective intelligence had always been a question of careful focus. The Polly analysis conceded that there were indeed pockets of disharmony within parts of Yunnan and the rural south. However, this disharmony was solely the result of the near famine conditions prevailing after the year's crop failure. There were no political overtones to the discontent, nor any solid indication that an armed revolt would succeed.

But at that time, the autumn of 1950, Jay Sagan still enjoyed the overall blessing of the secret world. John Polly, on the other hand, had yet to prove himself, not the least beyond the inner sanctum. As time went by, the Polly analysis, the only substantial argument against the Yunnan invasion, became less and less an issue. Momentum took over. By the end of the year the Yunnan plans had reached a stage wherein the sheer numbers of men involved, the amount of paper and the money all tended to give the plan a sense of inevitability from which there was no turning back.

In the final days before the invasion Sagan's existence reached a kind of fevered pitch. He would wake suddenly each morning, roll out of bed, splash water on his face and then turn confidently to the mirror. He had

119

never lived through a wartime situation, and when he stopped to think about it, he supposed that he loved it. Meals were eaten quickly. Drinking was minimal. Every wall of his office was dominated by a map, which was his window into the action landscape.

On the eve of the invasion Sagan invited two junior aides into his office and opened a bottle of scotch. He told them, "We have done all we could." And then later, "I wish I could be with them now." All around lay papers bound for the shredder, candy wrappers, wadded packs of Lucky Strikes. Later there was rain, and wet leaves plastered on the consulate steps.

As for the battle itself, early the following morning two thousand Nationalist troops under General Li Mi crossed the Burma border into China. They moved northward in two columns, capturing Kengma without resistance. Simultaneously aircraft from Taiwan dropped thousands of leaflets over south Yunnan, proclaiming that China was soon to be free and the time had come for the people to revolt.

In response the Red Army assembled to the east, drawing up howitzers that had been captured during the Revolution. The guns caught the Nationalists as they were trying to flank the Communist lines, and immediately cut them to shreds. Beyond these few details, no other account of the battle remains. General Li Mi's notes were supposedly lost in the retreat, and an American technical advisor who was also supposedly recording events was killed in the initial bombardment. As for the leaflets, winds carried most of them far out into the treeless wastes, while others were used by villagers for toilet paper.

News of the disaster began trickling into Hong Kong about seven hours after the defeat. First reports were sketchy, even contradictory. Early on the morning of the sixth day Sagan was awakened by a telephone call and told only that the invasion force had met the Communists, but was still holding the field. Later that story was to read that the invasion force had suffered moderate losses and was expected to regroup by night. Then came the final reports of full retreat and heavy casualties.

For Sagan the disaster was finally reduced to precise gestures and carefully phrased sentences. He played his final scene at midnight underneath the fluorescent lights against the attenuated clack of a typewriter. The air was faintly blue with cigarette smoke. Another cigarette lay burning in an ashtray. Sagan had been sitting for a long time, alone with a pencil in his hand. Then an aide entered and laid another telex on the desk. Sagan read it without touching the paper, rose and moved slowly

120

to face a map of China still tacked to the wall. He withdrew the blue pin, representing General Li, and dropped it into the ashtray. Finally he spoke without turning around. "Fucking Chinks," and said nothing else all evening.

There were those who after the failure at Yunnan seemed to lapse into a wasting grief. All over Southeast Asia there were lonely China Warriors who spent the tropical nights drinking, or staring at the yellowed plaster from underneath mosquito netting. In Burma jungles there were nearly two dozen American advisors who waited weeks in thatched huts without whiskey or tobacco, bitten by flies, certain of nothing but their automatic pistols. There were case officers in Taiwan who spent their time waiting by their radios and telephones, asking one another useless questions, toying with paper clips.

So in a way it was to Sagan's credit that within a few days after the defeat he had already begun trying to extricate himself from any responsibility, covering the bad card with new ones as fast as he could turn them over.

In the end, however, there was a price he had to pay, and it came about two weeks after the disaster. He had been working quietly in his office when he received word that Feng Chi's secretary wished to see him. Ordinarily Sagan took these requests from Jerry Woo rather casually. Lately he had even been making a point of not answering them too quickly, because there were limits to how far one went to please a client. But since the Yunnan disaster he had been feeling particularly propitiative toward the Chinese elite, especially those who had been involved with Yunnan. So after receiving this invitation to the Feng home, Sagan promptly cleared his desk and left the office.

The afternoon began much the same as other afternoons of this kind. Sagan was met at the door of the Feng home by a reticent servant, then taken to the drawing room. There through the window were the blanched faces of flowers, and a wider view of the cliffs in rising fog. Sagan was standing at the window when Jerry Woo entered. They shook hands and moved smoothly to their chairs. Woo was wearing a black silk suit but no tie. He had never looked so severe.

Their first words together were cordial, but even from the start Sagan had a feeling that something bad was going to happen. Woo asked if he was well. Sagan replied that he was, and asked the same. Woo nodded and said that he was also in good health, but lately he had been concerned

121

about Feng Chi. Sagan then asked if Feng had been ill. Woo replied no, but explained that the man had been very disturbed about a particular matter. On the table was an ivory dog with cracked haunches. There were figures like this all over Feng's home: tigers, dwarfs, fish, monkeys— all somehow disturbing. Finally Sagan asked what it was that was upsetting Feng.

Then Woo answered: "It concerns John Polly."

Sagan felt his stomach tighten. He was staring at the ivory dog. "What about him?"

"As you know, the death of Danny has been a great source of grief to the entire family. Mr. Feng particularly has been pained by his brother's death, and this pain has not been lessened by the outrage of injustice. If you understand my meaning?"

"Yes," Sagan murmured. "I understand." Still staring at the creature on the table.

"Now we are not vindictive people, Mr. Sagan. However, we have recently been informed that this John Polly is living in Peking. He is living there and prospering, while the family continues to grieve."

Then again in the same hollow voice, "I understand."

"We have given this matter a great deal of thought, and we have decided that something must be done now. So we have come to you for help."

"Help? How?" He was numb.

"Well, for example we will need certain travel permits like the ones now used on the mainland. These would have to appear perfectly authentic, and I know that your office is capable of producing such forgeries. Also we may need certain information regarding the Communist terrain, information which your office is also capable of supplying."

Then softly, vacantly, "You want to put a man in, don't you?"

"Yes, Mr. Sagan. This is what we want."

"To kill Polly?"

"To punish him."

"That's impossible."

"Nothing is impossible."

"I could never get approval for that kind of thing."

"We are not asking for approval. We are asking for assistance."

"I'm sorry. I can't do it."

A minute passed. Sagan did not move. Then he heard Woo say, "I did not want to bring this up. However, it appears that I have no choice

122

now but to tell you that it would be very advantageous for your personal position in the East if you were to help Mr. Feng. I say this because at the moment he is also very upset about what happened in Yunnan. As a matter of fact there has even been some talk between Mr. Feng and his associates that you were responsible for the military disaster that took so many lives."

Sagan thought: *I should smash that dog against the wall.*

"Now I'm sure you understand me, Mr. Sagan?"

Or grind it into his face.

"Mr. Sagan?"

And into Feng's face too.

"Mr. Sagan?"

"I'll do what I can."

Two weeks later, on a Monday evening, Sagan returned home from the office and found Jerry Woo waiting for him in the twilight underneath a palm tree. Sagan said hello. Woo said that the time had come to deal with John Polly. Instead of entering Sagan's apartment, the two men felt that it would be safer to talk inside of Woo's silver Rolls-Royce, which everyone knew had been purchased with dirty money.

Chapter 5

BY THE third day Billy had lost all perspective on this story. At one point, he began to exhibit all the signs of preoperative stress. He slept erratically, drank and smoked excessively. A typical conversation on the third morning of his briefing began when Cassidy asked Crane why he could not return to the station immediately.

Crane replied, "I've already told you. You're not expected back until Friday, and an early arrival might arouse suspicion."

"So what?"

"So there is much more at work here than you're aware of."

"Like what?"

"You shall be told when the time comes."

"I think you're full of shit."

Following this conversation the boy climbed down to the tide pools, where Crane observed him spearing crabs with a sharpened stick. When he returned, Crane was again waiting for him on the rocks. There were a few preliminary words of no consequence: Crane asking if Cassidy was hungry, Cassidy replying that he was not. Then after a brief discussion regarding the political dynamics of the Korean War, Crane formally began the next phase of Polly's story.

By way of introduction Crane explained that according to any standard, Operation China Shore was one of the classic operations of all time. It was marked by a steady flow of dependable intelligence, all of which was good, some of which was exceptional. Of particular note in these early years was Polly's prediction of the Communist spring offensive in Korea, and his initial reports on the Chinese atomic tests. Naturally there were those within the secret world who claimed that Polly's material could have been better, that the man displayed too much caution, often failing to pursue a target because of some imagined threat. As Crane pointed out, however, those critics were not there. They did not actually have to calculate the risks of a particular action while watching Kim Lee sleep.

As for Polly's personal vision of his work, it was known that in the beginning he suffered as any spy suffers at work in a strange country. So many things frightened him: a glance of patrons in a shop, footsteps behind him on an empty street, crowds moving toward him. Once a month he met with Neil Dray, always in accordance with a rigid procedure. Flowers in the window box meant that all was safe. A hand in the trouser pocket was a fall-back signal. Nothing was ever written down, except of course those China letters, which were coded and immediately passed out of the country to Crane.

There remain dozens of passages in the China letters reflective of the quiet terror that lay at the bottom of John Polly's secret life. Fear, he wrote, was sometimes felt as hunger, sometimes as cold, sometimes as a lingering illness. The worst of it was never knowing what was imagined and what was real, what lay behind a smile that seemed to fade too quickly or a glance upon leaving a room.

In response to these letters Crane exhibited the classic handling of a seasoned controller—he continually tried to reassure Polly, but did not discourage his vigilance. Then in the fall of 1951 there was an event that was a calculated Chinese test of Polly's loyalty to Peking. The incident centered around one of the Soviet advisors stationed in the capital, a Russian colonel named Viktor Morozov.

Polly's first encounter with Morozov came in October, on a Thursday evening at the Rumanian embassy. About fifty guests had come to welcome a new ambassador. Cocktails were served on the second floor. There was no formal introduction. At some point Polly found himself facing an oval window with the reflection of the Russian in the glass. Morozov was a heavy, flabby man with red hair. Polly would later describe him as a jovial cossack, always laughing from the corner of his mouth. On this night of their encounter Morozov was drunk, or else pretended to be drunk.

He began by saying only, "John Polly, I presume?"

Polly turned slowly to face the man. Past the Russian's shoulder was a half-lit chandelier.

"My name is Morozov. Viktor Morozov. Perhaps you've heard of me?"

Polly smiled and shook his head. All night he had been trying to avoid the Russians.

"Well, I've heard of you, Mr. Polly. In fact, I've heard a great deal about you. Now what do you say to that?"

Polly shrugged. "I guess I don't know what to say."

Which started the colonel laughing.

On the balcony above the guests stood three Chinese like wax figures. A Rumanian girl was descending the staircase. The colonel watched her, then leaned closer. "Tell me something," he said softly. "How do you like Peking?"

"How do I like it?"

"Yes. How do you like living here?"

"I don't know. I guess I like it all right."

"You don't miss your home?"

"Not particularly."

"Ah! Then in this way we are different. I miss my home terribly."

A servant passed with a platter of dried fish. There were long pale evening shadows falling from the upper gallery.

"May I ask you a personal question, Mr. Polly?"

"What's that?" Although he couldn't have sounded less interested.

"Are you fond of American jazz?"

"Huh?"

"American jazz music—are you fond of it?"

Polly glanced up to the ceiling. There were water stains in the plaster. "I don't know. I guess so."

"Because I have an excellent collection of phonograph records in my apartment, and I would be honored if you would come some time and listen to them."

Later that evening Polly passed the colonel once more in the garden. When their eyes met the colonel winked and began to whistle the fragment of an old song called "Desperation."

Except perhaps for that lingering memory of the song beneath the vines Polly probably would have forgotten that Russian within a couple of weeks. He had never seen the invitations as entirely relevant, or at least not within the greater scheme. "There are," he once wrote, "traditional differences between Moscow and Peking that supersede any transitory relationship." But inasmuch as they could not be completely ignored,

126

Polly accepted an invitation eight days later to dine with Morozov.

Morozov lived in the diplomatic quarter, in a once-ornate apartment now fairly shabby. The furniture was heavy burlap and badly jointed pine. The rugs were worn, and in places the molding had fallen away. While sipping unchilled champagne the colonel mentioned that the previous owner had shot himself, and he pointed to a stain at their feet.

"Now I believe I hear his spirit in the night."

"Really?" Polly was gazing at a landscape in oil of the Russian steppes. Another of the Black Sea hung above the fireplace.

"Do you believe in ghosts, Mr. Polly?"

But Polly only shrugged.

Later they listened to Morozov's collection of postwar jazz, which the colonel claimed was actually rather expressive of revolutionary spirit. During the long piano solos they both seemed to fall into a trance. Although once when Polly laid his head back he caught a glimpse of the colonel watching him from the corner of his eye.

To Polly's credit there was one itemized request for information concerning the colonel's political background and possible connection with Soviet intelligence. This request was filed on the morning following their evening together, and Simon Crane responded six days later with a lengthy cable to Neil Dray. At the heart of Crane's cable lay a British Secret Service report detailing Morozov's residency in Korea two years earlier, and a rather shady tour of Kabul. There were also indications that the man maintained a professional tie with Han Chow's Ministry of Internal Security, as well as the foreign intelligence department of the Red Army. Crane advised Polly to continue to see the man if for no other reason than to determine what sort of game was in play.

Their next evening together was again spent in Morozov's apartment with another melancholy record on the phonograph. For a while conversation was incidental. The colonel described an expedition he had made through Tibet. He said there had been four days of treeless plain, then lines of dolmens and finally the ruins of a dead city. The villages were filthy, the inhabitants addicted to superstition. As he spoke he stared at the burning tip of his cigar. Then he said, "Tell me, John. How does someone like yourself adapt to a place like this?"

"Adapt?" His own cigar had made him slightly ill.

"You seem to be a sophisticated young man, so I wonder how you manage among these people—these Chinamen."

"I manage all right."

"Do you? Surely there must be moments when you are left exasperated by the sheer stupidity?"

Then again in that young man's voice, "I'm afraid I don't know what you mean, sir."

"Oh please, John. I promise you that these rooms are free from hidden recording devices."

In the morning a tin of caviar was delivered to Polly's home. The attached note from the colonel read: *I present you with a real taste of civilization.*

The final play came unexpectedly twelve days later. The previous week saw the publication of two Polly editorials on the Korean conflict. The first was a long tirade against imperialist aggression. The second was concerned with the death, in combat, of Mao's son. For those who knew Polly well, those with sensitivity and understanding, this latter piece would always be remembered. There was no obvious condemnation of the United States, no political or ideological sentiment. It was simply about death and the sorrow for which there is no consolation.

Among the congratulatory notes following publication there was another invitation from Morozov, somewhat more cryptic than the other. Apparently the colonel very much wanted to explore with Polly certain ideas only touched upon in his recent article. In a postscript the colonel wrote: *And come prepared to tell the truth.*

Polly later wrote that there had been something oddly unsettling about Morozov's room that night. An electrical failure in the afternoon had left the entire district black. A windstorm had ruined the garden. The colonel placed candles on the mantel. Another patch of rotting plaster had fallen, exposing the pipes in the wall.

Once more the initial conversation was relatively harmless. The colonel explained that he had been deeply moved by Polly's essay on the death of Mao's son. He said that only a man of great compassion could have written such a piece.

"Which is why I cannot help wondering," he added.

"Wondering?"

"As to how you can endorse this war in Korea when it's all really so pointless."

"I don't know that it's pointless."

"Oh come now, John. What are the issues here? A political abstraction and a few hundred miles of hills? Of course it's pointless."

But what Polly thought was pointless was this conversation.

128

Until Morozov said casually, "Let me share a little secret with you, John. In six weeks' time the North Koreans are going to launch an offensive. Not a large affair, just a little thrust a few miles east of Seoul. Naturally the soldiers will be told that their mission is vital to the war effort, but this will be a lie. The real purpose of this offensive is simply to provide an opportunity for Moscow to test the performance of a newly modified tank, one of the T-34 series. Thus you have a situation in which hundreds of American soldiers will die, not to mention the Koreans, merely so that Moscow can assess the tactical performance of a tank. Now tell me, John, what do you say to that?"

John Polly's ensuing memo to Simon Crane represents one of the most controversial sequences of the era. It was composed in the early hours of November 14 and passed to Neil Dray the following evening. In essence the memo maintained that Morozov had deliberately leaked the information regarding the North Korean assault as a covert test of Polly's loyalty to the Peking regime. For this reason any effort to warn the United States forces in Korea of the planned offensive would effectively blow the entire White Mandarin operation. Unstated, but clearly implied, was also a question which would continue to haunt John Polly throughout the affair: was the White Mandarin really worth so many lives?

Three black weeks followed. In that time Polly received two cables from Crane, and dined once more with Morozov at the Soviet embassy. Among the issues raised by Crane was the question of whether or not some way could be found to warn American commanders of the impending offensive without jeopardizing Polly's position. In response Polly wrote, "I am not tactically or morally able to decide such a thing." Additionally Crane proposed that there was a distinct possibility that the whole story had been fabricated, because surely, if Morozov believed Polly was a spy, he would not have risked such an operation to prove it. In response to this Polly wrote nothing.

There were by turns dozens of opinions, recommendations, theories and expressed fears. All told they comprised weeks of intra-agency discussion. But for Polly, alone and at the center of it all, there was only that quiet terror and a deeper sense of remorse. Twice in the passing days he felt the presence of figures trailing him, but when he turned he saw no one.

In an effort to maintain appearances he attended a reception at the Albanian embassy, only to find Morozov watching from the doorway to the dining room. Once more the man was partially drunk, or else pretending. He put his arm on Polly's shoulder and led him to the garden. Below lay flowers in the darkness beaten down by rain. The few trees were nearly bare.

"You look tired, John. Are you tired?"

Polly shrugged. He hadn't felt this listless in months.

"Do you know that I've been worried about you, John?"

"Me?" He could feel the colonel's breath on his face.

"Yes. I thought perhaps I upset you the other night."

"Upset me?"

"Because of what I said about Korea."

"Oh that..."

"Yes. I thought perhaps you were disturbed."

"No. I wasn't disturbed," although his fists were clenched inside his pockets.

"Good. Then perhaps we can have dinner again sometime? Is next Wednesday good for you?"

It was a Wednesday like any other Wednesday. News of the offensive was carried on the radio. There were claims of nine hundred American casualties south of Pusan, but as always Polly supposed that the Peking radio had probably exaggerated the figure in the interest of popular morale. There was more rain in the afternoon, deepening the green light, leaving the back streets awash with mud. In the predawn hours of Thursday Polly began a letter to Crane which he did not send because there was nothing essential to add. It seemed that his cover was again intact, and four months later Morozov returned to Moscow, but did not say goodbye.

Now every evening Polly sat in the center of his garden. From here the flame trees radiated outward until they formed a circle. He often sat here while his rice was boiling, and loved the feeling that each leaf and rock was resonant of deeper meaning. He also liked the concept of himself out here: an expatriate sitting in his garden in a land where hardly anyone had his own garden.

By this year, 1952, Polly's garden had begun to achieve the more formal scheme he had always envisioned. There were dwarf pines by the pool of lilies, bamboo leaving upright shadows on the moss. The branches of larger trees had interwoven to form a net. Chrysanthemums opened twice a year.

As for Kim, she had planted orchids on the terrace. One evening while sitting in the kitchen she began to talk about her childhood. She said that in winter she used to walk the banks of frozen streams to see the sleeping dragons underneath the ice. When she had finished talking it was dawn. A whole night had passed and it had seemed like only an hour.

That Kim could embrace the tenets of communism and still discuss the supernatural was one of those mysteries that Polly assumed he would never completely unravel. One afternoon in the garden she told him that if he placed his ear to the trunk of certain trees he would hear the heartbeat of a dragon. He tried it, heard nothing, and when he told her she said, "That's because it's only a myth."

"But you heard it. You heard the heartbeat."

"That was a long time ago. That was when I was young."

"But if you're certain you heard it then it's not a myth."

She thought about this for a moment. Then she said, "Before the Revolution there were many things we saw that were not as they seemed."

But he could tell from her eyes and the tone of her voice that she was merely repeating something she had heard at the ministry or the indoctrination center. So he asked, "Does that mean that there were never any dragons?"

"Maybe a long time ago."

"What happened to them?" She was gazing intently at an unfolding rose. "Did they die? Did they die when the Communists came?"

Suddenly she took his hand. He had rarely seen her look so much like a child. "The dragons are only symbols, John. That's what they are. They're symbols."

"Symbols?" He had never heard her use that word. "Symbols for what?"

"For something."

"But what?"

"I can't explain," and that was all she would tell him that day.

But after many months he began to understand that the dragons were indeed symbols. He was still not exactly sure what they were symbols for, but it had something to do with an elemental power, a power of the earth and sky. It was a power so great and pervasive that even the Communists could not entirely suppress it, and if they tried it may have been because they secretly feared that these dragons would outlast them.

Most evenings after a day at the ministry the conversation was about the small events of their lives, the people they worked with, the various projects that came along. In autumn Kim was involved with two films. One was a kind of industrial training film. The other was a romance about a young girl who falls in love with a soldier bound for Korea. The soldier is killed in combat, but the young girl's grief is abated when she learns that he died a hero. In the final scene she is smiling at a landscape superimposed with the faces of children, implying that her lover has died for the coming generation.

Like Polly's office, the ministry where Kim worked was filled with petty jealousy, silent feuds and the undercurrents of sexual tension. People discussed politics and how to increase production, but their emotions and obsessions were the same as in any office anywhere in the world. At the end of the day Kim would sit with Polly and tell him who was in love with whom and so on.

Yet what they never seemed to discuss was the future. Polly supposed that he was responsible for this. He supposed that regardless of the happiness he now had, he still could not imagine living here for another twenty years. So the future remained indeterminate. They never talked about what might happen in the years ahead.

Suddenly, Polly began to notice that Kim was slowly growing more and more anxious about the future. She did not speak about it directly, but from the drift of her conversations, from the occasional questions she asked, he could tell there was something on her mind. Finally one night in the bedroom she started speaking more openly than she ever had before. She said that she wanted to know if they would always live in China. She also asked about money and his position with the party. She seemed concerned about his ability to provide, although her voice was soft and undemanding.

"Why are you asking me all this?"

They were lying side by side on the bed. There was a vase of fresh flowers on the window box, shadows of ivy on the wall.

"Sometimes it's good to plan for the future," she said.

"But you never worried about it before. What's changed?"

"Nothing has changed. It's just good sometimes to plan ahead." But she wouldn't look at him. She was pulling a stray thread from a lilac blue quilt.

"You can tell me what you're thinking," he finally said. "Whatever it is it'll be okay."

"I'm not thinking anything special. It's just that there are certain things we never discuss."

132

"Like what?"

"Like children."

Then he understood. "You're going to have a baby, aren't you? You're going to have a baby."

She nodded, half-smiling, still pulling at the thread. These perfect moments in China were always so much more than he felt he deserved.

All through that fall and into the winter Polly continued to respond to requests issued from Washington and relayed by Neil Dray. The majority of these requests concerned the softer targets. One month he was asked to assess the mood of the People's Congress, another month to evaluate the economic repercussions of the Korean effort. On the whole, however, the fundamental direction of Operation China Shore, even during these early years, was not directed at destroying Chinese society, but toward understanding it.

With the first cold spell there were more reports of famine in the countryside, now aggravated by collectivization. Yet even in these hardest times it seemed that Tommy Ling was able to get anything: eggs, meat, dried fruit, even sugar. Kim found onions, radishes, and some sort of grub that Polly had never seen before.

In February there was another brief campaign to abolish superstition. Citizens were discouraged from placing food for ghosts at the crossroads. One night Polly was awakened by what sounded like a woman weeping in the garden, but when he rose he saw only black branches and moonlight on the snow. In the morning he told Kim what had happened, and she said that the ghosts, driven out of other homes, had probably come to stay in their garden. Later she explained that she had only been joking.

In April the days grew warmer. The first buds appeared on the trees. Polly would always maintain that there was something unique about the north China sky. It was a pale, distant sky, sometimes slate gray, sometimes deeply colored. By the end of April the unborn child had developed enough so that he could hear its heartbeat whenever he laid his ear to Kim's belly. She still believed it would be a boy, while he had no idea at all.

As he approached the summer of 1952, Polly believed he had at last achieved a kind of balance between his secret life and the life that everyone around him saw, between politics and love, between Revolutionary China and the China in his heart. Things always seemed very simple. He did not like leaving Kim in the morning. He loved returning to her in the

133

evening. He no longer thought that the past had any relevance to the future, and believed that this state of happiness was permanent rather than just another stage of his life that must end like all the others.

The night that this stage of his life came to an end was a hot night in the second week of June. Toward the early evening Polly and Kim sat in the garden and drank jasmine tea, a gift from Tommy Ling. As usual they talked about the baby, which was now due at any time. If the child was a boy they had decided to call him Alex after Kim's father, who had always wanted a grandson to bear his name. If the child was a girl they would call her Maya, because it meant illusion and was neither Chinese nor American.

By nine o'clock a southern wind had risen, leaving dust on the windowsill and under the doors. The air smelled of red soil, also faintly of dung. Kim said that she was tired, possibly even feverish. An hour passed. The wind grew worse. The landscape was reduced to boiling forms, while hot gusts spread seeds and an occasional insect.

By ten o'clock she went to bed. Polly kissed her, then drew and tied the mosquito netting. After wandering for an undetermined time in the darkened house, he finally found himself in his study. At some point he fell asleep, but wakened suddenly in the aftershock of a bad dream. It was a dream he had had before, but could never fully remember. There was something about a sloping lawn, white columns and the receding face of Danny Feng.

He was not sure what eventually drove him into the garden. He was warm, terribly warm, and his mouth was filled with some bad taste. So he walked, first down the staircase, then out along the gravel path until he came to the black water. Here he could see the path of seeded cabbages that Kim had planted a month before. The stalks were long, ringed like stone, and he vaguely thought this heat would kill them. And when he turned he saw one clear image of her bending over the leaves. Then he heard her scream.

Running up the path he heard her scream again, but thought only that it was the baby. She was going into labor and was frightened. Except that the door was open and there were muddy tracks on the floorboards. The house had never seemed this still with moonlight and the billowing curtains. He called her name, but heard only his own voice. Then he started moving up the stairs. He was nearly to the bedroom when he saw the figure ahead in the half-lit hall. It was a man, squared off, knees

134

bent. Some kind of club was dangling from his hand.

Polly froze, first thinking about distances, and how that club was really just a sock with a stone. But then he saw the open bedroom door, and understood, fully understood.

The intruder tried to spin away, but Polly was much too fast now. He felt one blow on the side of his head, shook it off and kept coming. He was clawing for the eyes, then the throat. Until he had the thing in both hands, wrenching it in a trance.

Polly rose when he was certain that the man was dead, rose and stumbled down the hall to the bedroom. There Kim lay on the floor. One arm was coiled above her head. There was blood in her hair, and down the side of her face. Her nightgown was torn at the shoulder. He knelt and whispered her name. She did not respond, but when he laid his ear to her breast he could hear her heartbeat and slow breath. After he telephoned for help there was nothing else to do. He wanted to hold her in his arms, but they had told him not to move her. So he lay down beside her and held her hand.

She was taken to one of the newer hospitals, built under Soviet supervision. Here there was a drab, rectangular courtyard with a poor garden of trailing ivy and a misshapen tree by a fountain. The fountain was dry, and the morning very still. An hour ago Polly had requested a glass of water from a passing orderly, but the boy must have forgotten.

When Kim had first been admitted to the hospital Polly had stood by the door to the operating room. They had told him that waiting was prohibited there, but he did not care. He wanted to be as close to her as possible. Then Tommy Ling came, and he persuaded Polly to move downstairs to a room that had been specifically designed for waiting. To pass the time they had set up a Ping-Pong table, but there was only one paddle. Then two old women came. After a while the women began to cry. Then Polly went out to the courtyard just as the sun was rising.

Now at least another hour had passed, and he had not moved his hands. Once he closed his eyes and felt himself half drifting, entangled in the misshapen tree. But mostly he just sat. A line of ants moved along the wall. Then he heard footsteps behind, turned and saw Ling.

"There's been no change," said Ling. "She still hasn't become conscious."

Polly nodded. "What about the baby? They told me she might lose the baby."

135

"It's still too early to tell."

Ling sat down on the concrete bench next to Polly. He was also watching the ants tear apart a stricken cricket.

"We have some information on the assailant," said Ling.

"Yes?"

"The man you killed last night."

"Oh."

"His name was Lui Sun-tuan. He was originally from Shanghai, but since the liberation he has been living in Hong Kong. We understand that he crossed the border three weeks ago. He carried forged papers, but we're not certain how he made his way to Peking."

"But you're sure that he was from Hong Kong?"

"Yes."

"Then Feng sent him."

"But we do not know this for certain, John."

"I do."

From beyond the wall came the voices of passing children. They sang in unison: *"The red sun will engulf the world."*

"Perhaps you should try to eat," Ling said softly. "And maybe you should sleep too."

But Polly shook his head. "Just tell me what else you found about that man."

"I've told you everything, John."

"What about his papers? What was the quality like?"

"I don't know what you mean?"

"You said they were forgeries, right? Well, how good were they?"

"I don't know. I didn't think it was important to ask."

"It's just that you can tell a lot by the quality of things like the papers."

"But does it matter, John? Does it really matter now?"

Again Polly shook his head. "Maybe not."

Toward the middle of the day hunger and exhaustion finally drove Polly indoors again. He was given a bowl of thin soup and rice. Then he was taken to a bare room with an iron cot, and he fell into a patchy sleep. When he woke the light was softer, the air cooler. He stopped a doctor in the corridor, but there had been no change.

At some point in the late afternoon, when the smell of disinfectant became too oppressive, Polly left the hospital and started walking randomly, vaguely heading south. He came to a neighborhood that he had never seen before. There were rows of deteriorating houses in sandstone

136

and terra-cotta. Farther on lay a ditch of black water covered in scum with the texture of gauze. By the ditch grew a dying persimmon tree and a patch of unattended scrub. A man was squatting by a telegraph pole, tearing the husks of vegetables.

But at the end of the lane the air was filled with the scent of crushed flowers. There were also sparrows calling from beyond the windbreak. For a mile now he had been thinking alternately of Kim and a future without her, but now he found himself with the oddest sense of hope, with a vision of nothing worse than a long convalescence. He would take a leave from the ministry, perhaps arrange for an air conditioner. In the evenings they could sit in the garden. Everything would be all right. He just felt it would be all right.

When he returned through the hospital gates to the drab courtyard he found Tommy Ling was sitting on the bench. In the darkening light he looked frailer than usual. He had changed his clothes, but his suit was just as shabby as what he had worn earlier. When he heard Polly approach he rose, then stood framed against the brown wall. Polly started to speak, but something in Ling's eyes stopped him.

Now both men stood unmoving, facing each other across the dry fountain. The light was almost green, translucent through the ivy.

"Where's Kim?" Polly asked. "Where is she?"

Ling shut his eyes. "They managed to save the baby, John. It's a girl."

While Polly mechanically kept asking, "But where's Kim? Where is she? Tell me where she is."

That night Polly returned to his house alone. Ling had offered to stay, but Polly wanted to be alone. He wanted to sit in the darkness and explore what possibilities remained. He wanted to call her name, then listen to the trailing echo. Around midnight he lay down on what used to be their bed. There may have been a nightingale outside his window, but when he looked he only saw an audible shadow. Just before dawn he rose in complete terror, remembering that he did not even have a photograph of her face.

The funeral was held two days later. It was a simple affair in keeping with the new campaign to abolish superstition. There were none of the traditional tricks to keep the spirit from haunting the loved ones; no firecrackers, no paper money burned. But then Polly did not want to keep her from haunting him. He wanted to wake up night after night and feel her presence beside him.

To the astonishment of the other mourners there was a wreath of flowers and a note of condolence from Mao. The note read simply: *We share your grief.* After the funeral Polly was driven to the hospital to see his daughter. It had been decided that the child would remain in a state nursery for a few more weeks. When Polly told everyone that the child's name was Maya, they all agreed that it was a good name. Then he held her in his arms, and looked into her eyes, searching for a shred of meaning he felt he must have missed.

Now Polly entered a deteriorating existence of solitude and lingering sadness. At times he thought he was living only out of habit: sleeping when tired, eating when hungry, occasionally walking through his house. He was always preparing meals and then leaving them untouched on the table, picking up objects, examining them, then putting them down again.

Mostly he spent his time sitting by the window, dozing, leafing through books and old magazines. He did not go into the office. He did not go anywhere. He had his food delivered. There were, however, a few articles from this period, dry mechanical pieces he produced to keep the column alive. But apart from this work he did nothing, and whole hours would pass when he would not take his eyes off a vase or the sunlight falling across dead leaves.

But if the days were empty and still, the nights were something very different. More than once he woke and felt compelled to wander through the house, peering into rooms, almost believing that her ghost would be waiting for him. In the darkness a patch of moonlight on the porcelain looked like her gleaming teeth, or a curtain filling with wind was like her profile. Finally he even saw her in a dream, standing on some lonely stretch of road, not unlike the road where he had first seen her.

In time he realized that he had grown shockingly thin, horribly thin. His suits did not fit him anymore. Passing a mirror he was almost afraid of what he saw: eyes ringed with dark circles, the whites streaked with red. If he stood too quickly he began to feel dizzy. When he brushed his teeth his gums bled. There were also spells of nausea, headaches and a low but persistent fever.

There were dreams he could not account for: dreams of snakes that talked of suicide, a humped mountain, and something about a frog, an island and a pile of rotting bones. Finally he was sitting by the window again. He had been trying to read, but he had not been able to concen-

138

trate. He was also thirsty, but too exhausted to get a drink of water. He remembered vaguely that Kim had had a remedy for fevers, with some sort of root that you boiled. But she also believed you could cure cancer with roots, and that time could be controlled by thought. Then he heard the latch on the garden gate, looked up and saw Ling moving between the poles of bamboo.

Polly did not get up to answer the door. He just called out Ling's name. Ling pushed in the door, and entered slowly. All around lay the shambles of the last two weeks. There was a dish of overflowing cigarette butts, empty bottles, rice grains scattered on the floor. Polly tried to smile, but he only managed to bare his teeth. He wore no shoes and the soles of his feet were black.

"How are you, John?"

"I'm okay."

"I've been worried about you. The boy who delivers your food said that you weren't eating. Are you ill?"

"I'm okay."

Ling was holding a package wrapped in yellow paper. He kept toying with the string. "Everyone at the ministry sends their regards. They always keep asking when you are coming back."

"Tell them I appreciate their concern."

At the end of the room was a shattered mirror, broken in the night in some sort of fit. Ling kept looking at it. "Also I read what you wrote for the journal. It seemed very good, and I was glad to see that you've still been able to work."

"Yes. I've been working."

"How is the article for this week going?"

"Fine. It's going fine." Actually he hadn't started it.

"Did you read those magazines I sent you?"

"No, but I'll get to them."

"I think you'll find some interesting ideas in them."

"I'll get to them."

Then Ling's tone was suddenly desperate. He was leaning forward, nearly touching Polly's arm. "Listen to me, John. I really came to talk to you about your daughter."

"What about her?" He had forgotten her.

"Maybe it would be good if you took her home now. I spoke with the doctors. They told me she is strong enough. So maybe it would be good for you to bring her home."

139

Polly wiped his hand across his mouth. "How can I take care of her? I can't take care of a baby."

"I've engaged a nurse. It's someone you once knew."

"Yes?"

"Mary Chan? Your housekeeper in Shanghai? I managed to find her, and when I told her about your present circumstances she agreed to come."

"Mary is here?"

"She's in Peking, yes. And she has agreed to live here and take care of the child."

Polly's eyes suddenly grew moist. He was gazing out the window at transitory blossoms that the heat would soon destroy.

Finally he said, "I appreciate what you've done, Tommy, but I need more time. I just need more time."

"All right, John. But I know that it would be good for you to have the baby here. You'll see. It will be very healthy for you to have the baby."

"I'll do it, but I need more time."

Ling started to turn and leave, but stopped. "Oh, I nearly forgot. I brought you this," and he handed Polly the package.

Polly took it, and began to tear back the yellow paper. It was a book. The *Tao*.

"An English translation," Ling grinned. "Don't you remember? You told me that you had enjoyed this book. Of course it's no longer a work that is in favor now, but I thought..."

"Thank you." There was a dragon on the cover.

When Ling left, Polly laid the book aside, then picked it up, then laid it down again. But at some point during the night he found himself reading thirteen pages. Then he shut his eyes and felt the muscles in his neck unknot. Every object in the room seemed insubstantial, almost transparent. Finally he fell asleep and dreamed of walking in a forest, but it wasn't like a normal dream. It was like actually being there.

In the morning he read again until he was left with three images of water: undisturbed, running and deep. Then he rose and cut a watermelon in one perfect stroke. He ate it on the veranda, tilting back in the rattan chair, spitting out the seeds into a clump of ferns. There was something about time he kept trying to remember, something about time passing that was important. Also, the fever had died.

Finally late at night he woke recalling a single image from a passage he must have read the day before: a man singing and beating a copper

140

basin to keep time, while the body of his dead wife lay in a thatched hut by a river. *Why are you singing when your wife has just died? Because if I should break down and cry aloud, I would behave like one who does not understand destiny.* Then it might have been the moon, or maybe something else, but the whole room filled with silver light.

So began the most enigmatic stage of Polly's life. There are only the merest hints in the China letters as to what really occurred in his house during those extraordinary nights. He wrote: "Something is happening to me. I am losing all sense of time." While another passage described how there were no absolutes, nothing completely good or evil. Ostensibly he was referring to the political structure of Peking, but may also have been referring to something far more fundamental. Then, too, there was a lot he did not write.

Among his personal papers of this period there were several sheets of yellow foolscap filled with sketches and odd notations. He seemed to have become intrigued with the concept of empty space, which he said was only a viewpoint of dimension, while time was the apparency of change. It also seemed significant to him that the Chinese had discovered gunpowder while looking for the Philosopher's Stone. He wrote: "Every moment is new and shocking." Then, "I'm only trying to understand these people."

Often in the mornings he would sit at his window and watch the incoming fog. For three days there was the strangest weather that anyone could remember. It was winter yet with the disturbance of spring. "There is something about this place," he wrote, and in the margin drew a tiny dragon with a pearl in its claw.

It was also about this time that Polly may have begun to formulate his idea for what would eventually become one of the most celebrated China letters, essentially dealing with what Polly called, "the underlying political strategy of the Communist regime." He described that strategy as pliant, as always taking the line of least resistance, like water. It did not batter itself against the rocks, but percolated through the cracks, and the more you tried to clutch it the more it slipped away.

What else occurred during those nights even Polly himself did not fully understand. Although once on a windless night a sudden flurry of wind rose up from nowhere and sent the cassia seeds pinging against the windowpanes. Then there was the night he thought he heard a hollow rumble of beating wings passing overhead. Then the night in the garden.

141

For a long time he had been standing among the ferns. There had been a warm breeze from the south, spreading pollen and odors of human fertilizer. All the roses hung withering. There was no moon, only the movement of darkness on darkness. A rat or a toad may have been moving in the water grass.

Earlier he had been trying to recall every detail of his last night with Kim, what she had been wearing, what she had said. Had her sweater been green? Had there been some special meaning he had missed? Until finally he thought: this happened and that happened, and what he had missed was nothing. Nothing. There were simply the brown shells of her cabbages that he had neglected to water, a row of dry onion stalks. Although later still another letter would describe a flight of descending birds, mice emerging from the underbrush and a final vision of her eyes.

The following morning Polly called Tommy Ling and said that he was ready to have his daughter brought home. Then he put down the telephone, and began to clean his house. There were still those empty bottles, crumpled cigarette packs, noodles caked to the sides of bowls, a pitcher of congealing milk. In the end he discovered that it all had to go, all except a few scraps of notes he had made. And when it was over it did not feel like his house anymore, but then he didn't feel like himself anymore either.

The child arrived that afternoon, brought by one of the hospital attendants. An hour later Mary Chan arrived, carrying two suitcases with broken locks. She had had to tie them shut with twine. But in that hour between the time the hospital attendant left and before Mary arrived, Polly sat with his daughter in that same rattan chair where he had passed so many of the previous nights. It seemed that he had a quiet baby, and he could not stop looking at her face. Only a few months old and already there were traces of her mother.

Before long Polly came to realize that he had fallen into still another stage of life, different from any of those that had come before it. At the end of a week he had returned to the ministry where everyone was apparently glad to see him. His first assignment was a kind of paean to the soldiers in Korea with images of disciplined ranks of young men, fists in the yellow sky. In the evenings he would return to his house, and if it was warm he would sit out on the veranda with the child in his arms. He liked to feel her grasping at his fingers. He liked the moon in the trees, the light in the black pond.

142

Then later he would sometimes return to the veranda with Mary Chan. Early on he had come to realize that three years under communism had really made no effect upon her. She still believed that the nights were filled with ghosts, still believed that the fog was a dragon's breath, still saw signs everywhere. But mostly on these nights they just talked about the baby. Or else played dominoes until the mosquitoes drove them inside.

From the larger view this also may be seen as the time of Polly's reentry into the mainstream of Peking life. By the end of 1953 the first five-year plan began. Eventually there were over a thousand projects, mostly industrial services. Steel production tripled, power and cement doubled. Propaganda began to focus on internal issues again, and there were clean, bold posters of hydroelectric dams, telephone poles against angular skylines. One of Polly's earliest pieces of this period dealt with the joys of steel production, and there were almost mystical overtones to his description of the smelting process.

Additionally this period was marked by a return to the secret life, and a theme which, in subtle variations, would dominate his efforts here until the end. In essence this theme involved what Polly would come to call the fundamental split in party thought, a split that found its earliest manifestation in the opposing attitudes of ranking party members to the Soviet presence in China. Later this same split would become manifest during the Cultural Revolution, and then again on the subject of United States rapprochement. But at this early stage the focus of attention was on Russia.

There is a letter from this period, written in response to a list of questions by Simon Crane, forwarded by Neil Dray and finally deposited behind a loose brick in a courtyard wall. The letter ran about fifteen thousand words, and had been done in a style not unlike the style of the later work. The main thrust dealt with this split as exemplified by the differences in political thinking between Lin Piao and Chou En-lai. There were also some rather uncanny predictions of the future.

Appropriately enough this letter began with Lin Piao, who was still a rather unfamiliar figure to the West. By way of background Polly cited the major events of the man's career: his record as a military leader throughout the thirties and forties, his intervening illness, his impressionable stay in Moscow, and his then current position as vice-chairman of the Standing Committee in the Central Political Bureau. As for the essential man, Polly wrote that Lin was generally regarded as a rigid force, rarely if ever wavering from the party line. He was also known to have particularly hated both the Americans and British, and firmly believed that individual liberty would only lead to domestic chaos. Among his closest allies Polly cited Han Chow of the Public Security apparatus.

Opposing Lin was the mercurial Chou En-lai who would of course become exceedingly well known in the West, but at this time was only a familiar figure to informed observers. As for Chou's background, Polly again briefly sketched the outstanding details of Chou's life, including his entrance into the revolutionary vanguard abroad and his early relationship with Mao in Hunan. There was, however, one passage of note regarding Chou's youth in which he was said to have been very fond of acting, particularly in the more emotional roles. Polly cited this fact, perhaps in an effort to help explain the man's singularly charismatic effect on those around him. At the time of Polly's writing Chou was still formally directing foreign policy with an emphasis on flexibility and rationality. Among his closest allies, Polly noted Tommy Ling.

Of particular interest were the closing paragraphs of Polly's letter:

> It is easy enough to fall into the trap of believing that because Mao has come out with some new and horrifying example of party intransigence at one moment, while Chou speaks softly and moderately on the same subject, that there must follow a division between these men. But this does not necessarily follow at all. Rather each may well be merely acting in a complementary role to the other. It is only when Lin Piao enters that the definitive split may be seen.
>
> And what about Lin? To be sure he is a hard man, certainly as hard as Han Chow. Personally I prefer to believe that Mao merely uses him as a tool, a hammer or chisel, but does not extend to him the confidence that he ultimately extends to Chou. If my supposition is correct then our position here is far from hopeless. Yes, there are contradictions but there is also, I think, a clear path to reconciliation.

In terms of that path there were several subtle programs of this period, some of which Polly was involved in, some not. All were aimed at simultaneously dividing the Asian Communist bloc, and minimizing the influence of those in Peking who were particularly vocal supporters of the Soviets. Notable among these programs was the dissemination of the Ivolov letter under Operation Rain Feast.

The Ivolov letter, which was not really a letter at all, but a Kremlin

144

directive, had supposedly been intercepted by Israeli intelligence and then traded to Langley in exchange for certain Middle Eastern secrets. In general the letter was said to have been a guideline for Soviet ministers in dealing with Peking and specifically emphasizing what the Soviets believed was a Chinese ideological naivete and recklessness. There was an additional cautionary note regarding the establishment of a Chinese nuclear arsenal, the authors of the directive believed that Peking was not politically astute enough to bear the responsibility.

Although details of how the Ivolov letter was leaked to the Chinese never surfaced, it was assumed that the route had been through Albania. As for immediate effects, the letter undoubtedly constituted a tiny crack in the relations between Moscow and Peking, a crack that was soon to grow wider.

In the months following Rain Feast there were half a dozen similar operations involving news stories planted in the European press and rumors circulated through the diplomatic channels. Polly's role in these affairs were relatively minor. He was known to have supplied the initial background material, and later played a small part in discrediting certain Soviet advisors. But in retrospect, this would always stand out as the period when the line was clearly drawn between friends and enemies.

Such was Polly's external, secret life as it stood early in 1954. He was no longer randomly responding to requests from Washington, but instead methodically working on a larger plan. In a letter dated April of that year he advised Simon Crane to begin pressing Washington to start exploring diplomatic channels to Peking and thereby validate those like Chou En-lai who were in turn pressing Mao for a position of peaceful coexistence. "Tell Washington to seek a new Asian reality," Polly wrote. And then added, "Tell them that at heart these people are just like us."

As for his personal life, he supposed that he was as content as he could have hoped to have been. He continued to study the *Tao,* mostly in the late evenings. He kept trying to understand the meaning of certain passages, passages as fragile and straight as tiny beams of light. He also continued to think of Kim, and occasionally woke in the night, forgot and reached for her. Then too there were those brief moments when he would catch her shadow on a screen, the scent of her perfume. She was also there in the evening streets, in every image of China that he loved: the outline of cypress groves in moonlight, mist on the sandbars, rain hissing in bamboo.

But if there were bad moments, there was also his daughter. Sometimes when he worked in his study she would sleep on his lap. Then on warm evenings he would sit with Maya in the garden. If she woke crying in the night he would take her to his bed, then lie down and listen to her breathe. He could hardly wait until she was old enough to tell him what she needed, because he was not always sure how fathers were supposed to love their daughters.

Chapter 6

IN HIS role as case officer Crane was expected to distort certain facts about John Polly's life in Peking in an effort to involve Cassidy totally in the subject. Small details regarding Maya Polly, for example, were exaggerated to heighten Cassidy's concern for her, and of course details of Polly's life were changed in the interests of security. But on the fourth day of conversation Crane began an aspect of this story that he truly did not understand. It was the start of Jay Sagan's middle period, a period of profound mystery.

At approximately the same time that John Polly was entering a quiet and orderly stage of his career, Jay Sagan was at last returning to the forefront of the secret China wars. He had been living a life of tedium: sour coffee, paperwork and lunches with people he did not like. Fridays he dined with his British colleagues, but he had never liked the British either, what with their obtuse innuendos and voices as logical as typewriters. Occasionally he was asked to entertain some visiting senator, and then over sandwiches, he always found himself explaining why the whole of Asia would soon be swept away by communism. Nearly every evening Hong Kong seemed to close in with mist that smelled of rotting fish. In September he was down three weeks with the flu.

Sagan supposed that the setback of his career had been the Yunnan disaster. He had never been formally admonished by his superiors, but soon after the invasion it was made clear to him that he was expected to maintain a low profile. So for months he walked the narrow line, assiduously concerning himself with only the day-to-day tedium of spying.

By this time the British had established an extensive refugee interrogation program; any refugees believed to possess information of value were taken to one of three designated centers. There they were given a bowl of rice, a tin of milk and sometimes even cigarettes. The questioning was generally pleasant, lasting no more than a couple of hours. Transcripts of these interrogations were then condensed and passed on to Sagan's office. Unfortunately most of the material was poor.

Far more valuable to the overall effort were those networks that Sagan had set up with the cooperation of Feng Chi. He requested, and was granted appropriations for, cameras fitted with long-range telephoto lenses to be used aboard the junks that worked the south China coast. Initially the captains of those junks had been reluctant to carry the equipment, fearing that the Communists would revoke their fishing permits. But in the end Feng interceded on Sagan's behalf, and the equipment was fitted to the top of the stern masts where it could be activated electronically.

Additionally there were Feng's links to Shanghai, Canton and the larger villages throughout Kwangtung Province. For the most part these links were maintained through the remnants of the Triad networks and extended family ties that even the Communists had not been able to break. Product passed out of the country in a variety of ways, most notably through the fishing fleets and selected couriers recruited from mainland trading concerns. Finally there were still the Kuomintang armies in northern Burma. Their intelligence resources were minimal, but at least they were able to watch the boarder areas, and occasionally send reconnaisance forays into Yunnan.

There were several attempts in these early years to graphically map Feng's world, with lines in blue to represent the courier routes, lines in green for the networks. Accompanying these illustrative guides were fifteen pages of explanatory notes concerning the interlocking structure of the Triad community upon which Feng's world depended. Although neither the maps nor accompanying explanations gave actual details of how the networks were run, it was nonetheless clear that by now the Bamboo Curtain was not as impervious as it seemed.

In general Sagan ran his station on a fairly casual basis. Once a month he met with Jerry Woo and presented a target list. For the most part these lists were aimed at easily penetrable areas: Red Army deployment, the northern hydroelectric projects, coastal fortifications. If ever a request could not be fulfilled, Sagan would merely shrug and thank Woo for trying. He liked to think that he was at last learning how to deal with these people.

There was only one truly unpleasant incident of this period, which occurred on a sultry night after three days of freak rain. Norman Pyle had made another rapid tour of the sector, and arrived in Hong Kong on a Friday evening. He and Sagan spoke briefly on the telephone, and later met for drinks in a bar called the Seven Dragons.

Here it was dark and there were odors of strawberry incense. Light fell from a string of blue lanterns. The walls were deep red in fake velvet. Above the fireplace hung an oil painting of a very young girl. She wore only a tattered shirt, torn to reveal her belly, shoulders, thighs and one small breast. Her hands were tied above her head to the limb of a tree. Her mouth was parted in terror and her eyes were dilated by what she saw: an enormous tiger stalking forward. The artist's name was illegible, but etched on a small strip of brass attached to the bottom of the frame was the painting's title: *The Sacrifice.*

Sagan and Pyle discussed the general direction of the Asian effort, particularly the potential of Feng Chi's mainland links. At one point Sagan felt a presence behind him, turned and saw a girl trying to sell him an orchid. For an instant in the green light she looked remarkably like the girl in the painting. Then he realized that she was not as lithe and waved her away.

Suddenly Pyle said, "There is something else I want to talk to you about."

"Oh yeah? What's that?" Sagan was watching a waitress who had bent to take an order. There seemed to be welts on the back of her thighs.

"It's about John Polly."

"Polly?" Sagan reached for his glass of scotch. "What about him?"

"His wife is dead."

"Really? That's too bad. She was a pretty girl."

"It seems that she was murdered."

"Murdered?"

"That's right."

Across the room a tall man in a dark fedora had cornered a woman against the wall. As he spoke to her he actually traced her bare shoulder with an ivory cane.

"And I'm wondering if you had anything to do with it?"

"Me?"

149

"Yes, Jay. You."

"What are you talking about?"

"Let me put it like this. Feng Chi hates Polly, and you'd do anything for Feng."

"Oh come on, sir. You know me better than that."

"Do I?"

The girl at the end of the room was smiling at the man with the cane, but clearly there was fear in her eyes.

"Why don't you tell me what kind of deals you've been making with Feng?"

"Look, sir. I really think you're way off base here."

"Maybe. Maybe. But I think you should know that Polly is not the sort of person who forgets. You understand what I'm saying? The man does not forget."

Sagan had only one more reminder of Polly that summer. On a Sunday afternoon while leafing through a stack of foreign journals he came across an article that Polly had written for a Peking magazine. The article was entitled: "The Red Sun Burns off the Marshland Fog of Ignorance." It was filled with metaphors of blind men stumbling over cracked plains and thousands of clenched fists above a winter landscape.

If there was a single turning point to Sagan's career, it would have been in the autumn, the first week of October. All during the month of September Sagan had had the feeling that his life was due for a change. Then early one evening he went to the Feng residence to collect a batch of photographs from Jerry Woo. The photographs were supposed to have been taken from the interior of a Shanghai ball bearing plant. He had requested them because Washington had always been impressed with visual proof. The day was overcast and cool. The late-blooming roses were dying.

Sagan met Woo in the library. The shelves were filled with volumes on international law and finance, probably purchased in bulk by the decorator to match the brown tones of the room. While waiting for Woo, Sagan noticed a sculpture he had never seen before: a terra-cotta dragon in combat with a tiger. The tiger, he knew, stood for temporal power. The dragon he did not understand.

Woo seemed particularly relaxed that afternoon. Instead of his usual gray flannel, he wore black slacks and a shirt in pale green silk. Instead of tea he offered chilled wine. Through the half-open door lay a view of the juniper trees and a woman in marble, kneeling at a fountain.

Woo handed Sagan the photographs. Sagan glanced through them quickly. Finally he said, "These are very good. Very good. You don't happen to know what kind of lens he used, do you?"

"I'm sorry. Photography is not an area of expertise for me."

"Well just the same, they're good. Very good."

Then Woo withdrew another stack of photographs. "Perhaps you will also be pleased with these. The quality is not as precise, but I think you will find them interesting."

There were four photographs in this second stack. Each was dark, printed on grainy paper. At first glance they seemed to show only thatched shapes, like the outline of forest pines. But looking closer Sagan saw that something was hidden in the disintegrating shadows. It looked like the blurred form of a gun barrel, but long and pointed. There were also triangular fins.

He continued to stare at them intently. Then casually said, "Jerry, where did you get these?"

"They come from the north."

"Do you realize what they are?"

"I believe they are missiles."

"That's right. They're missiles. Now where exactly in the north were these shots taken?"

"Manchuria."

"Manchuria? You never told me you had someone in Manchuria."

"He has only recently arrived."

"Who is he?"

Woo had begun to study his wineglass. It was crystal with a pattern of fish cut into the stem. "He is a young man who was once employed by Mr. Feng, and whose family continues to be employed by him."

"What's he doing in Manchuria?"

"I believe he's an engineer now stationed in that district with the military."

"You mean he's in the Red Army? He's in the army and he sent you these?"

"I imagine he is concerned about the prosperity of his family. He was told that photographs like these would help insure their prosperity."

Now Sagan was also turning his glass in the light. "I'm going to have to have these shots analyzed."

"Of course."

"And I'll need some background information."

"I'm sure this can be supplied."

"I'll need to know exactly where the shots were taken, and how many missiles he's spotted. I may even need more of the same."

"Of course, but you must understand that this is a very dangerous venture for him."

"My people will make it worth his while."

There was a final exchange in the garden, one which Sagan had expected given the value of the photographs. He and Woo were strolling between a willow pond and the junipers. On a rise stood the fountain with the characters chiseled into the stone: *Emotion is born out of habit.*

Woo said, "As far as Mr. Feng and myself can determine, this young man in Manchuria is in an excellent position to continue supplying information."

"I'll be looking forward to that," Sagan replied.

Then the last turn of the knife: "But you must understand that it is much more difficult and dangerous for us to deliver this sort of material to you than the material we normally deliver."

Sagan said nothing. The garden light was pallid, milky. There wasn't a breath of wind.

"Now, of course, Mr. Feng is not interested in material gain. He is helping you for purely ideological reasons. However, there may come a time when you might be able to repay us for this extra work we are doing for you. If you understand my meaning?"

There was the oddest vapor rising through the white trees ahead.

"Mr. Sagan?"

"Yes. I understand."

The photographs were sent by courier the following morning. The reply from Washington took seven days. The initial response was encouraging, but not overwhelmingly so. The missiles were identified as Soviet medium-range, linear descendants of the German V-2. After the usual precautionary note, Sagan was given permission to continue cultivating the source.

A full seven weeks passed before there was a second Manchurian delivery, but this time the material proved far more dramatic than the photographs of Soviet missiles. Indeed, what Sagan eventually received was nothing less than the fragments of plans for China's first isotope-producing experimental atomic reactor. The plans included a prospectus

152

for a chemical separation plant, as well as a plan for a gas diffusion plant. The construction sites were not, however, in Manchuria, but at Lanchou in the Kansu Province and at Pao-tou in the Inner Mongolian Autonomous Region.

Two more Mongolian deliveries followed. The first dealt with the discovery of uranium deposits in Kansu and Tsinghai provinces. The second described the findings of a joint Chinese-Soviet mutual assistance atomic research program. When the material was finally analyzed it was further discovered that this second delivery actually contained a direct copy of the program notes, as well as subsequent recommendations.

Having sent off these packages, Sagan now played his cards very well. He knew that it was not enough to produce brilliant material. You also had to present it brilliantly. So rather than the usual extravagant sales pitch, his reports were accompanied by only the most minimal explanations:

"Source in question is the fruit of long cultivation," he wrote. "I am not yet able to divulge the details of that cultivation, nor the details of the agents in position with the Mongolian research effort. Suffice it to say there are more than one. I can, however, predict that further reports are expected, although with no estimate of delivery."

This written, Sagan sat back and waited. The ensuing three weeks were the best weeks of his career, and he spent them leisurely, usually not arriving at the station before ten o'clock. He drank his morning coffee as he reviewed the previous night's telex cables, then spent another hour over the translations of Peking press. One Friday, while returning from lunch, he saw an exquisite ivory tiger in a shop display on the Hollywood Road. Its eyes were pearls, and clutched in the claw was a tiny gold ball. It cost more than twelve hundred dollars, but Sagan paid for it out of the operational fund, and then had it sent to Feng Chi.

Toward the end of the third week Sagan received another cable from Washington. This one requested additional information regarding the technical qualifications of the source. Sagan, however, who was now more certain than ever that he was holding all aces, simply repeated his original explanation. The implication being that this source was too hot to discuss from a distance.

A few days after this exchange, Sagan received still another Mongolian delivery from Woo, a calculation of the uranium yield in Sinkiang and detailed activities at the Soviet-built reactor in the same region. Again these deliveries were sent to Washington with only terse explanations,

153

and again Sagan dodged the ensuing questions by stressing the sensitivity of the source.

Finally, there came a cable that Sagan supposed he had always been waiting for: a formal request that he return to Washington for an extended debrief and program planning session. The night that this cable arrived he was alone in the station. After he read it he stepped out on the consulate balcony. A fine mist was descending. He was thinking about what he would wear for his return. In the street beyond a girl stood under a paper parasol. The colors of her dress were reflected in the wet pavement. For the first time in months he felt like the whole of Asia was his again.

In all Sagan spent ten days in Washington. There were four extended conferences in Langley, and many more casual talks with Norman Pyle. As a result of these talks there were two items of note: a special line for handling the Feng Chi product was established, and Jay Sagan was officially acknowledged as an indispensable force within the south China sphere. Of course there were those who would never trust Jay, not to mention Feng Chi. There was even a discussion at one point in which Simon Crane unreservedly told Norman Pyle that something was rotten in the Hong Kong station, intolerably rotten. But in response Pyle said only what he would continue to say about Jay Sagan: regardless of one's personal feelings the man definitely delivered.

In the evenings there were informal gatherings at the homes of various Asian hands, with a lot of talk about China before the war. It seemed that Sagan was always meeting women that he wanted, but under the circumstances knew he must refrain. So at the end of a night he simply had a drink in the hotel bar, and went upstairs to his room. He did not know the Washington girls, nor did he want to be seen prowling the streets.

There was only one off-color incident during his stay. It occurred on the last night. There had been an early supper at the home of another Orientalist, then cocktails for perhaps fifty guests. But at one point, feeling vaguely nauseated from the sherry, Sagan stepped out onto the balcony above a garden. It was a warm night, warm and moist. There was the sound of laughter behind him, and passing traffic beyond. Then he heard a distinct clear voice to his side.

"Hello, Jay."

154

It was Simon Crane, as gaunt and forbidding as ever.

"I heard you were in town." Crane smiled.

"Yes, sir. How are you?"

"I've been worse."

"But you look well." Actually he looked like a ghost.

"And you're looking well too, Jay. But then I suppose that's what success does for a man." Crane continued to smile.

"Oh I can't complain, sir."

"Of course you can't. In fact they tell me you've been doing splendidly. Got yourself a real gold mine."

"Just luck really."

"It's never luck, Jay. The Chinese believe in luck, not me."

The conversation could have ended here. Sagan could have said how glad he was to have seen Crane again, then shaken his hand and walked away. But it seemed that Crane wouldn't let him go.

"I'm glad I ran into you tonight," said Crane suddenly. "I've been wanting to talk to you."

"Talk to me, sir?"

"Yes. There's something I wanted to clear up."

"Well, sir, if there's anything I can help you with . . ."

"It's about John Polly."

"Oh," and again Sagan felt his stomach tighten.

"A few months ago Norman asked if you had anything to do with the murder of Polly's wife. Do you remember?"

"Uh, that would have been when?"

"Of course you remember. But what you probably don't know is that Norman asked you because I told him to."

"You, sir?"

"That's right."

"But surely you don't think that I had anything—"

"Yes, Jay. I do. Oh maybe not directly, but you knew about it. I think Feng talked to you first."

"I'm afraid I don't understand, sir."

"Of course you understand. Feng Chi murdered Polly's wife. You knew about it, perhaps even helped with certain details, and in most societies that would make you an accessory to murder."

At which point Sagan nearly smirked. "I wasn't aware that killing an enemy in time of war was murder."

155

But Crane just kept looking at him. "Stay away from John Polly. You've heard it from Pyle. Now you're hearing it from me. *Stay away from Polly.*"

Then Crane turned and padded off. He was wearing a rumpled suit that looked like one he used to wear in China.

Sagan left for Hong Kong the following morning. He arrived at three o'clock in the afternoon. The sky was gray with matted clouds, threatening rain. After trying for an hour to sleep, he rose and drove down to the Wanchai district. The only girl he could find was a sullen child, about fourteen years old. Her body was thin, and there were running sores on her shins. She was too pitiful to take to bed, so he just sat in a chair while she knelt. The entire affair lasted only a few minutes.

Now came a period of maturation. Within a month there were two more submissions from the mainland, both containing high-quality material from the scientific sector. Next there was a lengthy report on naval maneuvers in the south and northern air-strike capacity. Finally there were rapid deliveries concerning Central Committee disputes and a magnificent piece on the mechanization of the Red Army. Within Langley each of these submissions was met with greater praise, while Sagan's annual budget rose another quarter.

December and January saw the steady flowering of the operation now known as Moonset, with two submissions a month. Again the product met only the highest praise, even from traditionally difficult clients. Those close to Sagan would recall that if he had become unsufferably vain, at least his vanity retained some style. He was dressing exceptionally well.

There was, however, still one dissenting voice amidst the celebration. A memo from Simon Crane to Norman Pyle after a lengthy evaluation on the seventh week: "Admittedly the material is good. Indeed, it is very good. But given the individuals involved, I can only wonder what the ultimate cost will be."

If at the time there were those who were confused by Crane's terse pronouncement, in retrospect it can only be said that the memo must stand as one of the keenest indications of foresight. It was just into the new year, a Monday morning, and Sagan had come together with Jerry Woo once again.

As before, their conversation was held in the library of Feng's home.

156

Again there was a piece that Sagan had never seen before: a silk screen of three gibbons perched in a tree, the shadow of a man passing beneath them.

Woo himself was like a shadow today, entirely in black silk. His hair was combed back, accenting the bones in his face. Their opening moment together was stiff. Sagan inquired as to Feng Chi's health, but received no definite answer. Then tea was served, and as Sagan drank he felt Woo's eyes on him. From an adjoining room came the faint notes of an out-of-tune piano.

Then Woo said simply, "Do you recall when I told you that the day would come when Mr. Feng would ask a favor of you?" Sagan let his eyes fall away to the corner of the room. A bowl of lilacs had been laid on a black table. "Well, it would appear that day has come."

Then Sagan raised his eyes again and said, "What do you want?"

"We are having difficulty with the transportation of certain products."

"What products?"

"I think you know."

"Opium?"

"Yes."

"And you want to use my planes to bring it out of Burma?"

"Yes."

"It's out of the question."

But Woo only smiled. "We calculate that merely two or three aircraft would fulfill our needs. And of course the pilots would be generously paid."

"I'm sorry, Jerry. If it was anything else, but Washington will never stand for something like that."

"But, Mr. Sagan, this is not Washington's concern. This is a personal matter between you and Mr. Feng."

Later, by the outer gate, Woo once more became convivial, explaining that Feng would very much appreciate Sagan's presence at a dinner that had been planned for the following Saturday evening. Sagan could bring a woman if he chose.

Sagan's actual involvement with the transportation of opium began in March of 1954. Initially there were only two American pilots and three Taiwanese, and Sagan's role was minor. He merely spoke once with the pilots, negotiated their fee, then spoke with the Agency station in Bangkok. All was kept on an informal basis. There were no records of the actual transactions. Also, Sagan never actually saw the product, and so it remained simply another abstraction.

But with this initial step there began a subtle change in his relationship with Feng and Feng's associates. There were evenings with Feng, personal evenings when the two would talk in a gallery open to the garden. Along a black shelf were those ivory figurines: women astride dolphins, monkeys intertwined to form a ball, men wrestling with demons. Of Feng's early life he once described a tree with interlocking roots, where at night there were always human forms in the branches. He also once described a journey he had taken with his father, the road like a twisted sheep's gut.

On another night Feng talked about the Triads, but indirectly, with obscure references to a seventeenth-century murder. There was also something about a tiger, a headless cock and people secretly linked to one another. Power flowed vertically, then horizontally through the mainstream of the Chinese community. The dominant image was unseen power rising, and continual struggle from within.

Eventually, however, Sagan came to see that the Triads were far more pervasive than he had previously imagined. There were continual references to cities with no apparent connection to the East: Los Angeles, San Francisco, New York, Amsterdam. There was also money, large amounts with no apparent source.

"We are concerned with certain people in your employment," Feng told Sagan one evening.

"What people?"

"Certain boys you occasionally use for small services in the city."

"Chinese boys?"

"Yes. Chinese boys. We are concerned about them."

"Why? They're only stringers. They don't know anything."

"Perhaps, but they do not belong to the organization."

"I'm afraid I don't follow, sir."

"They are not one of us, and this is not acceptable."

During this period Feng formally consolidated his hold on the opium production and distribution routes. Chemists from Hong Kong were sent into Burma and Thailand to set up laboratories for converting the raw opium into morphine and then finally to heroin. Twice a year Feng met with distributors in Bangkok. Business was usually in a hotel room on the Patpong Road. Sagan, on the periphery of these networks, was again left only with vague impressions.

158

Sagan's life had once more lapsed into another orderly routine with specific days allotted to specific actions. There was golf on Thursdays with friends from the consulate. On Monday afternoons he played handball at the club. Eventually after a month of Saturday evenings in bars he met a girl who seemed to be worth more than a one-night stand.

Her name was Lucy Han. She worked as a dance hostess in a club called the Night Without End. She was twenty-two with a slender body and the classic features of the south China girls. From the first sight of her Sagan knew that she wasn't just another prostitute. She had her price, but it was not to be paid outright in cash. For several weeks all she permitted was a kiss.

Then one evening after he had taken her to dinner at an unusually expensive restaurant, she told him that she wanted to see where he lived. When they arrived at his apartment he mixed her a drink, and they stood out on the balcony in the warm night. There was the fragrance of summer trees and earth after a rain. She was wearing an organdy dress that unzipped from under the left arm. He told her that she was the first girl he had met in a long time that he could respect. Then he leaned on the iron railing and kissed her. She responded by pressing her body to his. While he felt for that hidden zipper, he looked past her hair at the distant headlights of cars moving up the mountain road.

In the darkness of his bedroom he sat on a chair as she walked slowly toward him. Half-leaning, half-sitting, she finally allowed him to inspect her. His hands and eyes lingered over her breasts, her hips, her waist. Then he looked into her eyes, but they were blank and impersonal. As he peeled off her dress it was as if her body rose up before him. Her nipples were almost transparent, but when he tried to touch the left one, she pushed his hand away. In the end every movement became mechanical, and her eyes remained empty. Except once, when he tried to touch her left breast again, then there was something alive.

He continued to see her regularly. Twice a week he took her to dinner, or else they went dancing. Afterward he brought her home and they made love. They never discussed anything of importance. Once he asked her about her background, but she changed the subject. Occasionally he bought her small gifts, but she never permitted him to touch her left breast.

*   *   *

Jack Cassidy, Billy's father, made his brief appearance in this story in 1956. He was then thirty-two years old. He had entered the secret world on a provisional basis after distinguished military service in Korea. Like others with his background he was clearly not destined for executive status, but because of certain practical skills he could have undoubtedly enjoyed a fruitful career as a mid-level intelligence officer. His posting at the Hong Kong station came after nine weeks of orientation in Langley, and his ultimate position was in essence the same position that Sagan himself had held years before in Shanghai.

Cassidy had initially struck Sagan as a personable young man. He was of medium height with light hair and even features. During their initial conversation Sagan had inquired about Cassidy's education, which apparently proved to be something of a sore spot. Cassidy had never attended college, and had always regretted it. Cassidy was married at this time with a very pretty wife and the one child, Billy.

Sagan and Jack Cassidy immediately developed an amiable working relationship. As a junior officer Cassidy was obedient, diligent and he listened well. Sagan was heard to remark that if Cassidy was not particularly clever, at least he knew it and never overstepped his bounds. In later years there would naturally be comparisons made between Jack Cassidy and Billy Cassidy, but few of these would be valid. Whether by design or experience, Billy was cut from a very different mold.

There were evenings spent together, quite early on in their relationship. Usually Sagan would invite Jack out for a beer at one of the nicer local clubs. Their discussions here were generally tame. For the most part Sagan did the talking either about his personal vision of Asia, or else some current project. In turn Cassidy would listen politely, nodding and adding the encouraging remark.

Of Sagan's specific memories of the man, there were two that initially stood above all others. The first involved Cassidy's family. Then followed the ceremony wherein Cassidy laid out photographs of his wife and the infant Billy. Next there was an afternoon at the station when Cassidy returned from a lunch with a magpie in ivory hung on a gold chain. He said that he had purchased it for his wife, and made a great deal of showing it to Sagan, who saw immediately that it was the sort of trinket that was manufactured expressly for tourists, and that the magpie was not made of ivory but fishbone.

160

As for Cassidy's duties at the station, he generally spent his days with paperwork. He seemed especially fascinated by the coding process, but unfortunately had no talent for the work. In time, however, Sagan came to see that the man was rather good on the streets, with an instinctual ability to handle himself in a crowd and a firm background in close-quarter fighting. It was not long before Sagan began to use the man as cover to follow his tracks whenever agents had to be met on their own ground. In all other areas Cassidy's behavior was seemingly marked with a certain naivete, perhaps even a certain unfounded optimism. He believed, for example, that basically there were no differences between the East and the West that could not be reconciled through discussion.

Had Jack Cassidy been sent deliberately to Hong Kong station to ferret out evidence regarding Sagan's involvement in the opium trade? Simon Crane, who supposedly knew the answer, never mentioned the subject to Billy, nor later was he willing to speak of it. Nevertheless, there were indications that Jack Cassidy's position in Hong Kong was not all that it seemed.

The story was this: a week prior to Cassidy's posting there had been a conversation between Cassidy and Norman Pyle. Without making accusations Pyle explained that he was concerned about Jay Sagan's relationship with Feng Chi and others in Feng's circle. Ostensibly Pyle was not so much interested in collecting evidence specifically against Sagan as against Feng Chi and the greater Triad organization. Consequently Cassidy was instructed not to forward his findings to Langley, but rather to the Royal Hong Kong Police.

In a variation of this story, Pyle was not even acting on his own volition, but upon pressure from the British, who at this time had grown painfully aware of the Triad influence in their colony. Others refuted this story by claiming that the British were never in a position to exert that kind of pressure, but of course this observation did not—could not—take into account the relationship of the British Secret Service to the White Mandarin.

Regardless of the actual details, not long after Cassidy's arrival at the station, there was a series of investigations made into Feng Chi, the Triads and Sagan's dealings with both. The material was routinely passed on to the Hong Kong Narcotics Bureau, material that could have only come from station records.

From these initial investigations came certain facts: by 1956 Sagan was coordinating seven weekly flights out of Burma, carrying both morphine and opium into southern Thailand. Payment for the pilots and ground crew was laundered through the operational accounts, while the flights themselves were logged as supply runs for the entrenched Kuomintang armies.

For Sagan, the first indication of Cassidy's investigation did not come until nearly sixteen weeks after Cassidy's arrival. It was a Friday evening about nine o'clock. Sagan had promised Lucy Han that he would take her dancing, but finding himself short of money, had returned to the station to draw from the petty cash. There he found Cassidy sitting at his desk behind a stack of buff-colored folders. There was an ashtray filled with cigarette butts, and the air conditioning had failed so Cassidy was perspiring badly.

When Sagan asked what Cassidy was doing, Cassidy replied only that he was trying to catch up on some work. In the morning, however, after going through the withdrawal slips, Sagan discovered that Cassidy had been studying the payment ledger, the files on Burma and Thailand and the correspondence from Rangoon. Presumably because he was unwilling to force the issue, Sagan said nothing to Cassidy, and the following Monday the two men again met for drinks at a club called the Emerald Pond.

It was three weeks later when Sagan discovered his second indication that Cassidy was looking into the darker side of the station's activities. This time the discovery was made in the afternoon, but it was not until the early evening that Sagan finally decided that he had no alternative but to confront his junior. Sagan casually invited Cassidy out for a beer at the end of the day. In the interests of security Sagan chose one of the quieter bars in the banking district.

Initially their conversation was no different in tone from others on evenings like this. Sagan spoke of a recent ideological profile of the mainland which described an internal party dispute growing from the fundamental differences between Chou En-lai and Lin Piao. This dispute was precisely the same dispute that had so concerned John Polly, but of course Sagan's understanding of the problem was by no means as complete as Polly's.

While Sagan talked Cassidy again listened, occasionally nodding, now and then commenting. In the adjoining booth sat two English clerks discussing women, while another two men sat in the shadows at the end of the bar. A waiter in a red jacket was chatting with two Eurasian girls.

An aquarium was set into the far wall. At least two of the fish were dead.

Sagan had been talking continually for about twenty minutes. Then came a probing silence and he said, "You know, Jack, I've been meaning to tell you how happy I am with your work."

Cassidy grinned. Whenever he was nervous his smile became lumpy, stupid.

"The fact that you've been staying late, that impresses me. It shows you care."

"Well, thank you, sir."

A girl in amber now stood beside the aquarium. Sagan met her glance, then looked away.

"But there is something that concerns me, Jack."

"What's that, sir?"

"Who are you working for?"

"Sir?"

"Come on, Jack, don't play games. Who told you to run down Feng Chi? Who told you to look into the Burma routes?"

"No one told me, sir."

"Oh yeah? Then what the hell have you been doing?"

Cassidy lowered his eyes to the table. He was running his finger along the rim of his glass.

"So what about it, Jack? You going to tell me what's going on?"

Then without raising his eyes: "Well, it's wrong, sir."

"What's wrong, Jack?"

"What you've been doing. You know, the opium."

"What do you know about it, Jack?"

"I know that the pilots get a percentage of the take. I know that they're using Company planes."

"So?"

"So we're supposed to report things like that. It's not right."

"And who are you going to report it to? Huh?"

Cassidy shook his head. "I don't know."

"Because the cops don't want to even know about it, Jack. That's how much they care. And Langley already knows. So who are you going to report it to?"

But Cassidy just kept staring at the table, tracing circles in a puddle of beer.

"So I want you to just forget it, Jack. You understand me?"

"Yes, sir."

"It doesn't concern you."

"Yes, sir."

"And if someone in Langley put you up to this then he's a bigger fool than you are, because this station performs, and if I have to make an occasional compromise to keep it running that's my business and no one in Langley with any real clout is going to see it otherwise. Okay?"

"Yes, sir."

"Now let me buy you another beer."

Events now began to move with such rapidity that Sagan had no chance to alter them, or at least no chance that he was willing to take. These events began, on an afternoon of thick fog when the entire city was reduced to gray. From his office window Sagan had been watching trams vanish into the mist for hours. It was a slow day. He was on the verge of leaving altogether. He had even taken his coat off the back of a chair. Then the telephone rang. It was Jerry Woo demanding that they meet in an hour.

Sagan met Woo in a park up on the Harlech Road. Below the fog had enveloped the entire harbor. When Sagan arrived at the park Woo was sitting on a bench smoking a cigarette. Here was a midsummer day set completely in winter tones.

"Thank you for coming," Woo said, but he did not turn, and his eyes were blank.

"You mentioned there was a problem?" Sagan asked.

Woo said, "Tell me about your assistant."

"Jack? What about him?"

"Why has he been supplying the authorities with information concerning Mr. Feng and Mr. Feng's associates?"

Sagan slowly raised his hand to his head, ran his fingers through his hair. In the distance a child was dragging a dog across the lawn.

"Why don't you just tell me what happened?"

"Yesterday your Mr. Cassidy met with Detective Chief Superintendent Brooks. Apparently they discussed evidence which Mr. Cassidy has found in your files. This would be evidence linking Mr. Feng and particularly associates of Mr. Feng to the transportation of opium. Naturally Mr. Feng and his associates are deeply upset about the situation. It raises many questions of loyalty."

"Jerry, you know I don't have anything to do with this."

"We are not suggesting that you did. We are merely suggesting that

164

you have a talk with your Mr. Cassidy. You might tell him that nothing occurs in this city that Mr. Feng doesn't know about. You might also tell him that his personal safety cannot be assured if he continues disseminating false rumors. Do you understand?"

Sagan nodded. There were two lovers sitting by a tree further down the grassy slope. They kissed. The boy kept trying to slide his hand underneath the girl's blouse.

Woo said, "You might also think about the possibility of sending Mr. Cassidy away for a little while."

"What's that supposed to mean?"

"Simply that there are those involved who may not be as forgiving as Mr. Feng. So perhaps Mr. Cassidy would consider leaving the city. This is what I suggest."

Sagan left Jerry Woo and returned to the consulate. There he was told that Cassidy had gone for the day, but when Sagan telephoned Cassidy's home there was no answer. It was seven o'clock in the evening and the fog had still not lifted.

Sagan arrived at Cassidy's apartment at a quarter to eight. There were no lights in the windows, but he rang the doorbell anyway. After a few minutes he walked back to his car, which was parked in the courtyard underneath the pines. He had originally thought that he would wait twenty minutes, an hour at the most. But it was nearly ten o'clock when he returned to his apartment.

There he found Lucy sleeping on the couch. He knew that if he wakened her she would sense that he was worried and start asking questions. So he let her sleep, ate a handful of cold rice, a dried fish and washed it down with scotch. A dozen more times that night he tried to call Cassidy, but the telephone just kept ringing. Then just after midnight Lucy rose, and found him sitting at the kitchen table, staring. He asked her mechanically if she had slept well. She said that she had had a bad dream. He replied, "Dreams can't hurt you." Then the telephone rang. It was a doctor from the hospital on the other side of the harbor. Apparently Cassidy was dying.

Cassidy never fully regained consciousness, so that all Sagan had in the end was one garbled story, the fragments of a medical report, and a cursory investigation by the Hong Kong police. When Sagan arrived at the hospital he found Cassidy with bandages on his head and hands. He was heavily sedated. The room was dark. The shades were drawn. Sagan sat by the bed until Cassidy began to speak, then listened as Cassidy rambled on about how three men had attacked him earlier that afternoon. He said that he kept asking them what they wanted to know, but they did not answer. Finally a doctor entered and told Sagan that the patient needed to rest.

Later in the corridor the doctor also told Sagan what had happened from a medical standpoint. He said that Cassidy had been beaten badly, and five fingers and his left ear had been severed. As the doctor explained he pointed to his own fingers and ear, saying that the appendages had been severed here and here.

In the morning, Sagan telephoned the hospital and was told that there had been no change in the patient's condition. He contemplated waiting there anyway, but instead called Jerry Woo. It was an impulsive act. His finger simply started dialing the number, while he could only passively watch.

Sagan met Woo in that same park where he had met him the day before. Earlier there had been rain. Now there were brown pools of water on the lawn, newspapers battered into the mud. There were women hanging out the wash on distant tenement balconies. Farther down the road three teenagers were vandalizing a car.

Sagan waited on the bench almost thirty minutes before Woo came. It was cold, and there were birds fighting against the wind. When Woo finally sat down, Sagan did not turn to look at him.

He only said, "Thank you for coming."

Woo replied, "I've heard what happened to your Mr. Cassidy. We are deeply sorry."

"Yeah? Well, that's not enough."

"I understand your anger."

"Good, then maybe you can tell me who did it."

"That will accomplish nothing."

"Why don't you let me be the judge of that?"

"The truth of the matter is," said Woo, "I do not know who was responsible for what occurred. There were several who would have had a reason."

"Fine. Just give me all the names."

"For what purpose? For the momentary satisfaction of shooting them? At the expense of your position here? Surely you can see that there is no logic in that?"

While Sagan thought simply: *these people are animals.* •

166

"Now of course if there is something we can do to help...some sort of compensation?"

But all Sagan said was: "I'm going to have to tell Washington something. It would help if you backed me up."

"Of course."

"So if anyone asks, Cassidy took it from the Reds."

"Ah, yes, this is what they would prefer to hear anyway, isn't it?"

"Yeah. That's what they would prefer to hear."

At the hospital Sagan was told that the patient had still not improved, but when he entered Cassidy's room, Cassidy recognized him and smiled. They even spoke for a few minutes. Then Cassidy dozed off again. Later it occurred to Sagan that Cassidy did not know the extent of his own injuries. He did not know that he no longer had his left ear or the fingers of his right hand.

Cassidy regained consciousness once more that evening. Sagan had been sitting in the corner of the room, listening to the hospital sounds from the corridor. There was someone calling out in Chinese, and another voice in English crying: "Turn off the light please. Turn off the light. It's blinding me." Then Cassidy began speaking, but Sagan could not quite understand what he was trying to say. Finally he realized that the man was calling for his wife. This continued for a minute. Then his voice trailed off. About an hour later Sagan realized that Cassidy was no longer breathing. A doctor was called in, and the man was officially pronounced dead.

Later Sagan would tell a very different story of Cassidy's death. He would say that his friend had died in a moment of absolute clarity, asking that Sagan look after his wife and child. In reality Cassidy died sometime between seven o'clock and seven-thirty on a Sunday evening while Sagan had been reading an old issue of *Life* magazine.

There was another lie connected with Cassidy's death, one which Simon Crane, among others, would question, but could never formally challenge. According to Sagan's final report Cassidy had been murdered by Communist agents while attempting to crack one of the Red networks on the Kowloon side. As Sagan related the story, Cassidy had been on the verge of success when he was captured, tortured and finally killed by a mainland effort trying to infiltrate the labor unions. Sagan wrote that despite torture Cassidy had not betrayed station secrets, including Sagan's identity and the details of the Feng Chi connection. In summation Sagan recommended a commendation. Eventually a declassified version of this report was sent to Cassidy's wife, along with an Agency commendation, which she had framed and hung in the living room, just as she was to do some fifteen years later with the commendation that they gave her son, Billy.

In the weeks following Cassidy's death, Sagan's feelings for Feng changed. He no longer felt bound to come when Feng called, no longer enjoyed those evenings with the Chinese elite. Once, not long after Cassidy's death, Sagan was invited to dinner at Feng's home and simply did not go. He did not even call to excuse himself. He just didn't show. Then one morning he found a message on his desk from Jerry Woo, and again did not respond. Instead he spent an hour tearing open useless mail, browsing through the *South China News:* all the while imagining Jerry Woo waiting by the telephone in the gloom of Feng's home.

Yet through these days Sagan still continued to collect the mainland deliveries, and in time there was actually a rather exciting piece on the internal strife within Lin Piao's military council. Now, whenever he saw Woo, Sagan found himself behaving differently, found himself waiting for Woo to ask another favor simply so that he could hear himself say no.

If events had taken another course, Sagan might very well have broken with Feng completely. Certainly there were signs that he wanted to, definite indications that at last he was prepared to draw the line on the opium question. In a September brief to Norman Pyle, Sagan outlined the essential structure of the Triads and their interlocking structure with the greater Chinese community. There were speculations regarding the extent of Triad activities in the United States, and the possibility that those activities were directed from a single source. In itself this brief was not revelatory, but it was the first material critical of Feng that Sagan had ever submitted.

But if that summer of 1956 was a time of vacillation, a time when Sagan honestly looked at his life while gathering momentum to change, then by the fall it was clear again that there really was to be no change. In October the first of several cables came in from Washington requesting information about the now widening gulf between Peking and Moscow. Next there were cables asking Sagan to verify certain rumors regarding a feud within the National Party Congress. Specific targets had always

168

been difficult for Sagan to penetrate, and so once again he found himself returning to Jerry Woo.

Woo received Sagan in the garden room. Through an open screen lay a view of the junipers and arched palms. Cut into the molding were three symbols of fortune: a lotus, two fish and the endless knot. Sagan was not kept waiting here. Woo was standing by the open screen. There was tea on a tray brought in by a young girl in a white apron. On her second finger was a ring in the shape of a crouching tiger, the natural symbol of Feng's strength.

In all Sagan spent two hours with Woo that afternoon, and each remained polite and obliging. Toward the end Woo even laid his hand on Sagan's shoulder. There was no mention of Cassidy's death. Two weeks later Woo delivered some of the best material that the mainland link had ever produced, and Sagan reciprocated with another small gift: a beggar in Burmese jade.

So at the end of this stage in Sagan's career he supposed that there were no longer any choices left. Nearly every Sunday evening there was a dinner at Feng's, while on Tuesdays he met with Woo. Later that winter Lucy Han left him for a Chinese boy who promised marriage. There was no advance warning. One day he returned home and found her gone, the closet empty, the photograph of her father taken from the mantelpiece.

Now without her Sagan again returned to Wanchai in search of women. When he found none he would simply pass the evenings in a bar. His favorite was a place on the waterfront where he could watch the ships moving in black water. There were moments when he hated this city, desperately hated the whole of Asia, but more and more he had begun to realize that he would probably never leave.

Chapter 7

IN THE fall of 1956, while Jay Sagan's mainland networks were again seeking answers to questions about Peking, John Polly now lived in the heart of the Communist Revolution. Here there was still deprivation; machines continually breaking down and no one to repair them; a sense of the future but no sense of the past; knowledge without wisdom. In the mornings after hot water and soybean curd Polly would move through streets where there was no end to the crowds. In the evenings he could not depend on the electric lights. In answer to a message from Simon Crane, Polly wrote: "I will not be content to stay here the rest of my life."

It had not been a good year. The previous May had seen the beginning of the Hundred Flowers campaign, aimed at encouraging free criticism of the cadres and bureaucracy. But like every campaign there were deeper hidden purposes. In September there had been the Soviet denunciation of Stalin, and tensions between Peking and Moscow were sharpened by obscure disagreements over ideology. In October there were shortages in the northern cities, and typhoid in the south. Then came November with an intense review of the year's progress, then December and more arrests.

But as relevant to this period as any political development there was Polly's personal life: his relationship with his daughter and his own inner thoughts. Maya turned four that summer, and in Polly's eyes she was as perfect a child as he could have ever hoped for. She honestly did look like her mother, with her mother's gestures and her mother's way of gazing off into the distance. Whenever Polly would talk about Kim, the child became very still and grave. He was not certain that she understood everything; but he knew that in time she would understand.

Not long after she had begun attending school she started coming home mouthing political slogans and quotations from Mao. Once she even returned with a slogan that Polly had written. He supposed it must have filtered down through the ranks. At first he had been concerned that the state would turn her into one of those people that were always putting the party above all else. Everywhere one heard stories of children informing on their parents, or throwing themselves under tractors to save a commune ox. But eventually he came to see that none of what she learned was really sinking in. It was all just nursery rhymes.

Sometimes in the evenings she would ask him about America, just as her mother used to do. He was always careful of what he told her because he knew that she might later repeat what he said. So mostly he just talked about the countryside around Santa Barbara, the forest animals, the cowboys he had never seen. At night he still loved to watch her sleeping. He wished that he could give her more.

Also part of this stage of his life were the first translations of poetry he made on behalf of the ministry. It had all started in the early part of the year when a national drive to encourage poetry had been launched. Regional winners were ultimately sent to Peking and their works were published by the state press. Most of what Polly saw was crude, filled with images of turbines and semiautomatic rifles. There were thousands of hymns to production quotas and functional technology. But every now and then he came across a work of real beauty, evoking his own secret conception of China at the age of twenty-seven.

By the time that Polly was twenty-eight he had achieved no small degree of notoriety among the literate circles of modern China. He was regularly invited to the state affairs, occasionally corresponding with Chou En-lai. Now and then he was stopped on the street by an admiring reader of his articles. Twice a month he lectured at the university.

With fame came special privileges, including the opportunity to travel beyond the city and the occasional use of a car. Now on Sundays he was able to take Maya into the western hills and the rock shrines. Further on lay mountains that were violet in summer evenings, blue-gray in winter. Off the road were bamboo forests entirely deserted. There was a brook between the mountains. Polly would ask the local residents, but nobody knew its name.

At twenty-nine he published his first collection of stories, written quickly in the belief that a body of fiction might help his social stature.

The work was entitled *In Praise of the Pig Breeder*. There were twelve stories in all, each with an obvious revolutionary theme. One dealt with a boy from Tibet whose tongue was cut out by a monk for reading Marxist literature to the villagers. At the end of the story the boy finds that he miraculously speaks again when he is called upon to express his thanks to Mao. Another story dealt with a girl who becomes the national woman's Ping-Pong champion after she is imbued with the spirit of Mao. On the whole these stories were extremely well received. There was even talk of adapting one for film.

Often in the evenings he would sit with Maya as she lay in bed. Life in China could be hard for children. So much was expected of them, so little tolerated. She was always asking questions that he did not know how to answer.

"Was mother a Communist when you first met her?"

"No, not really."

"And you weren't a Communist either?"

"No."

"What's it like not being a Communist?"

"I don't know. I guess you worry about money a lot."

She thought about this for a moment. Then she said, "If you and mother weren't Communists then what did you talk about?"

"Different things."

"Like what?"

Then he tried to explain how there were ultimately more important things in life than politics.

Through these years Polly's secret career had achieved a new level of stability. If the art of spying is a matter of adhering to an unvarying routine, then by 1960 Polly had begun to practice the art as adroitly as any within the secret world. Letters to Simon Crane were filed every six weeks. The drops were serviced monthly. Only a few submissions were considered truly revelatory, but all were reasonably strong. Then very suddenly that stability began to crumble.

It was in the fall that Neil Dray's tour of duty ended and he was replaced by a thin reticent man named Roger Hall. Hall was four years older than Polly. He had brown hair and gray eyes. Although he never spoke of his past, Polly was later to learn that he had previously served in North Africa, which was generally considered a murderous assignment.

Within the trade, the passing of an agent from one controller to another is often fraught with difficulties. In John Polly's case this was no exception. Polly and Roger Hall met for the first time beneath a bridge west of the the diplomatic quarter. A stretch of unattended park rose from a muddy slope. Clumps of trampled azaleas grew beside a stone pavilion. When Polly arrived he found Hall waiting in the shadow of the trestles. There was an artist's sketch pad under his arm, presumably for cover.

"I have a message from Neil," Hall began. "He wants you to know that he's sorry that he was unable to give us a formal introduction. He also wishes you the best of luck."

Polly nodded. "Yes. Well tell him thank you."

"Oh I won't be seeing him again. I merely wanted to pass along the message."

Hall withdrew a pack of cigarettes. Polly watched his hands, his eyes, his clenched jaw.

"I'd like to start by saying that the basic procedure remains unchanged. Simon still controls. I just service the drops."

"What about the meetings?"

"That remains the same too. Ring three times and hang up."

"And the cover?"

"We met at a party. I suggested that you consider writing some articles for the English press."

"Not very convincing, is it?"

"Let's just hope we don't have to use it."

It was four weeks after the entrance of Roger Hall that the events of this episode began. Polly had made another submission, this one consisting of documents he had photographed relating to the ideological differences between Peking and Moscow. The documents had come his way by accident, after circulating throughout the ministry. In all there were only four pages, but because the light had been poor Polly had been forced to use nearly an entire role of film. For the drop he bought a fish cake from a vendor by the market square, peeled away the brown greased paper, wrapped the film and dropped it down a rusting pipe that protruded from a ruined garden wall.

As always the hours after the placement were marked by a certain restless elation. Instead of returning directly home he wandered north past the central lake to the Pei Hai Park. There were passing storm clouds, intermittent thunder, but no rain. On a long gray stretch of road he heard the wind rattling through a line of carob trees. Eventually there was also the white flash of lightning.

In the morning, a particularly damp Tuesday, Polly rose early. There were sesame rolls with weak tea, then a cigarette by the window above his garden. A night of wind had left the air clear. He walked as far as the gravel crossroad with his daughter, then tramped slowly along the half-paved lane into the city.

As he walked he thought of nothing specific, only an article that badly needed attention, the coming new year, tea with Ling in the afternoon. Above the gymnasium lay a white line of stones. There were alleys littered with cabbage leaves, heaped sand and crates of hawthorn apples. Nearing the garden wall where he had dropped the film the night before he thought of Crane and remembered him as he had seen him last on that mountain above Shanghai. *Simon who spends every day of his life thinking of me.*

Then Polly stopped, and felt the blood drain from his face. A woman brushed past his shoulder as he spun closer to the wall. While in a wave of nausea lay a vision he had once seen a dream: a dozen men in uniform and a pile of bricks where his drop had been. *The film!*

He was aware only of the small details, mechanically reaching for a cigarette, reeling back to a row of leafless trees and mud. *The film.* Among the soldiers stood two men in gray. One was taking notes in a pad. The other held that length of rusting pipe. *The film.*

A crowd had gathered across the lane. There were children eating peanuts, littering the concrete with shells. Another child watched from behind an uprooted shrub. Polly turned and met their eyes, then glanced at his watch and told himself to go. *Go and don't look back.*

He walked slowly, breathing deeply, telling himself that if they knew that the film was his they would have arrested him hours ago. Which meant that it must have been a chance discovery. Some zealous citizen poking among the bricks. He saw a girl in a doorway and once, between the sound of passing trucks, he thought he heard someone call his name.

He had to rest at the ministry gates, lean against a dirty patch of stone and wipe the perspiration from his face. A typewriter clacked from an upstairs window. Two boys were unloading reams of paper from a van. There were puddles inside the corridor. Another pipe must have burst in the night.

All through that morning he did not move from his desk. He hardly raised his eyes from an article in praise of a southern commune. Accompanying the article were photographs of brown water in a dead ravine, an electrical cable strung between clay shacks. He kept reading sentences

174

that seemed to make no sense, and others filled with hidden meanings. There was also the memory of a recurring dream: inking-in commas while waiting for the People's Police.

There were three intervening hours between Polly's signal to Roger Hall and their meeting by the northern lake. Polly passed those hours wandering among the crowds of the railroad station, lingering at shop windows. Then he followed the wet paths down to the water and waited beneath the bridge.

"From what I can gather they were just children," Hall said.

"Children?" Polly was cold. He had been cold all day.

"The ones who found the film. They were just kids. Apparently they had been playing by the wall."

"So they don't really know anything, do they?"

"Not yet."

"What do you mean?"

"I mean that it's only a matter of time before they start to narrow down the possibilities. Let's face it, there aren't too many people who could have had access to that material."

Earlier there had been a woman sifting through the sand on the far banks of the lake, but now this stretch of land was empty.

Hall turned away to watch a light moving through the trees. Then he said softly, "It's a question of redirecting their attention. Now, I think I can fix it so that the Russians appear to be on the receiving end of this, but we're still going to need someone to take the fall, someone from your office, someone who also would have had an opportunity to photograph those papers."

Polly shook his head before he spoke. His arms were pressed against his ribs. "I can't let you do that, Roger."

"It's the only way."

"You're talking about murdering an innocent man."

"I'm sorry."

"No!" They were both left staring at the black vegetation, the water and a tower against the sky.

"Well, it's not your decision anyway," Hall said after a moment's silence. "I'm going to get in touch with Simon, and I'm certain he'll agree with me. The Chinese are going to be looking for an agent inside your ministry and they'll not be satisfied until they've found one."

Again Polly was vaguely aware of the silence, and the cold that seemed to rise up from the ground. "This isn't going to solve anything. Can't you see that? They'll hold an inquiry, maybe even a trial. Our only chance is to—"

"No, John. It'll all be over in a week."

"What are you talking about? How can you possibly say—"

"We're going to make it look like a suicide. It's perfectly logical. Agent knows he's about to be blown so he kills himself. I've already begun to make the arrangements."

Through the rest of that disintegrating night Polly sat by a window in his bedroom. There was a photograph of his daughter on the desk, an empty bottle of gin on the floor. Earlier he had started a letter to Crane, but broke down when he saw that the pen he was using had been a gift from friends at the ministry.

There was a note from Simon Crane to Roger Hall written three days after the body of a ministry clerk was found floating in the canal at the edge of the city. "Do not attempt to console John Polly," Crane advised. "He will come to terms with this in his own time."

It was in 1962 that the China letters began to dwell on the antecedent struggles of what would eventually become known as the Great Cultural Revolution. In the beginning Polly perceived these early signs of strife as peripheral, perhaps even disconnected from what he perceived as the essential division within the party. In time, however, he would come to amend his view so that in terms of his personal life the Cultural Revolution also became part of the whole.

Eventually there would be those who argued that Polly's perception of the Cultural Revolution had not been entirely accurate. There would be particular criticism of his theories regarding Lin Piao's duplicity and Mao's final direction. Additionally it would be said that Polly's judgment of Mao was too forgiving, possibly owing to Mao's role in the earlier release of Kim Lee. But his chronicle of letters was never intended to serve as an encompassing history of the event, merely a sporadic commentary of what he saw around him.

In the letter of November 1962 Polly first defined what would later be seen as the earliest manifestation of struggle: the growing rift between Mao and his chief of state, Liu Shao-chi.

As in other letters of this kind the opening paragraphs were given to the biographical essentials of those involved. There was a brief synopsis of Liu's life, which Polly was only vaguely familiar with. Like Mao, Liu

176

was originally from Hunan. He had worked with Mao in the underground years of the 1920's, and later became one of the foremost organizers within the urban areas. At the time of this letter, Polly noted that Liu's chief supporters were still entrenched in the cities, while Mao's orientation remained with the peasants.

Central to the differences of these two men was, as Polly put it, a fundamental conception of China's future. Liu, with his basic urban stance, was said to have believed in an institutional order with an emphasis on the practical. Mao, on the other hand, was said to have distrusted the urban elite and and their tendency toward organization and keener specialization. "It is," Polly wrote, "a question of voluntarism versus planning. Mao has always believed that correct attitude and determination take precedence over any pragmatic system of advancement."

Initially this dispute between Mao and Liu was only manifested in subtleties. There were rumors of internal debate, and cryptic editorials denouncing bureaucratic evil and political apathy. By the following summer there were veiled criticisms of Mao's rambling industrial programs, and corresponding complaints that ideology and political faith were not enough to solve complex economic equestions. Additionally there were ambiguous references to a new rationality, with a hint of material incentive. Apparently there was even talk of a coupon system wherein the highest-producing workers could purchase bicycles, wristwatches and portable radios.

Even in these early stages Polly was able to perceive that at the bottom of all criticism was nothing less than a calculated attack on Mao. Sufficiently weakened by age and illness, Polly wrote, Mao was essentially under fire from Liu and others within the party.

As for the conclusion of this first November letter Polly wrote that, although Mao's position currently seemed stable, it was still a real possibility that the chairman could be swept away. Were this to occur, Polly maintained, the subsequent China would become far more rigidly committed to the Soviet model and political isolation from the West.

With this first formal statement, Polly's next series of letters remained relatively devoid of theory and simply described what happened. By the autumn of 1963, Polly wrote that there were continued rumors of disorder throughout the party superstructure, disenchantment with the central committees, inequities between officials, and charges of internal corruption. Mao had more or less abandoned Peking and moved the center of his counterattack to Shanghai. There he began to rally not only the general administration but students as well in what would eventually be known as the Red Guard movement.

Polly wrote of sliding stability, leaving Mao without an effective party base. As a result there was talk that the chairman would take the fight to the streets. "The students," Polly wrote, "continue to adore their leader."

Another letter of the same month spoke of a gradual civic decay. There were regular power failures and occasional lapses in telephone service. There was also talk of food shortages in the south, gasoline in the north, while newspaper editorials continually contradicted one another. "Something unpleasant is happening here," Polly wrote. "But I do not know what it is."

Finally in December of 1964 there was a letter unlike any other. It was a letter that immediately met with criticism within Langley. At the heart of this letter lay Polly's primary theory of the Cultural Revolution, and for that matter, his theory on the course of modern China. It was not an unfamiliar theory. In essence it dealt with that same basic rift that Polly had noted more than three years before: the unrelenting feud between Lin Piao and Chou En-lai.

Simply put: Polly maintained that as serious as the confrontation between Mao and Liu Shao-chi was, their struggle would not represent the final determination of power. Rather it was Lin and Chou whose differences would prove most critical in the end.

In terms of a sequence Polly wrote that he believed that in the initial stages of the Cultural Revolution there would be an apparent solidarity between Mao, Chou En-lai and Lin Piao, each allied with the other against Liu Shao-chi and the formal party structure. But once Liu was eliminated from power, the Revolution would enter a second stage wherein Lin Piao and Chou En-lai would be left in opposing ideological corners with no alternative other than open confrontation.

As for Mao, Polly's viewpoint was generally defined in the closing paragraphs of his letter. He wrote that although the chairman probably still favored Chou En-lai, both politically and personally, he was not now, nor would ever be in a position to challenge Lin so long as Lin retained control of the Red Army. Consequently Mao's position was fundamentally neutral. He may have preferred the moderation of Chou, but he needed the severity of Lin, and so remained in the middle. As to whom the chairman would support once Liu Shao-chi was eliminated and the nation was polarized between Lin and Chou, Polly could only guess. He said that the chairman's position would probably depend upon outside factors such as the relative stance of the Soviet Union and the United States.

In summation Polly left his readers with perhaps his most intriguing image when he wrote:

> There are times when it seems that Lin and Chou are actually representative of two psychological traits within one man—the chairman. Given this hypothesis China is essentially schizophrenic. There is the soft and there is the hard—occasionally in harmony, but more often in opposition. As I've said before it would be nice to believe that Lin Piao is the chairman's darker side, and the chairman knows this, while Chou symbolizes his more fundamental self. But even if this analogy is incorrect, the fact remains that this nation is now, and will continue to be, divided between two opposing forces that may very well draw these people into civil war.

According to the China letters the Cultural Revolution began in late 1965. But in November 1965 Polly wrote: "It is growing increasingly chaotic. I do not know where it will end."

This same letter spoke of the still growing tension, a pervasive fear, restless crowds in the twilight. The trains, Polly noted, were no longer running on schedule. There were incidents of vandalism. A warehouse filled with newsprint had been burned, an armory burglarized, the windows of a gymnasium broken. There were also rumors of political arrests, but no one seemed to know who had been arrested and why.

Polly's next two letters mainly dwelled on what he called a political decline. From the higher rungs of the party structure came new rumors of struggle. Mao, it was said, had begun to consolidate his Shanghai base, while Liu Shao-chi was following much the same strategy in Peking. Lower ministries, particularly the propaganda sector, seemed hopelessly caught in the middle. Polly's own work of the period reflects this, with articles that had no identifiable direction, no central theme.

One conversation representative of the mood through these days occurred about three weeks into the new year. It was cold, and for days there had been shortages of coal. Polly had been at his desk for more than nine hours, rewriting an article that had filtered down from the district committee. Across the room sat Tommy Ling. There were wadded

179

pages scattered on the floor, erasure shavings and pencil stubs. It was dark, and the electric lights kept dimming out.

At one point Polly read a passage from the article he was working on aloud and then asked, "Does that make sense to you?"

Ling had not been listening, and so Polly repeated the question. "This part about Engels, Hegel and Saint Simon; does it make sense to you?"

Ling ran his fingers through his hair. He was also fairly exhausted. "Yes, I believe it makes sense."

"Then tell me what it means?"

"It means that the Engels saw Hegel and Saint-Simon as the enlightened of the eighteenth century."

"I know that, but what's it got to do with anything?"

"Hegel and Saint-Simon were the enlightened of their century. Chairman Mao is the enlightened of our century."

"Fine, but the sentence doesn't make sense."

"It makes sense in Chinese, John."

"But I'm not writing it in Chinese. I'm writing it in English."

"Some people don't admit that there are geniuses, but this is not Marxist. That is the point of the sentence."

"Great, but it still doesn't make sense."

"It will make sense to those receptive to the spirit of the Revolution."

Then Polly rose from his desk and walked over to the window. The moon was white above the outline of a steel tower. It was nearly midnight, but there were still people moving in the streets below. They carried lanterns on long poles.

"It's got to stop," Polly whispered. Then louder, "It's got to stop."

"But, John, it's only just begun."

By 1966 Polly wrote: "There seems to be an increasing emphasis on symbols. These people are becoming obsessed with them." On Thursdays he produced two thousand words on such topics as, "Why Is History a Moral Drama and Revolution a Moral Crusade?" or "What Sustenance Can Be Obtained from Rousseau?" On Wednesdays he helped edit the foreign journal where each week the ambiguity became more and more pronounced. On Fridays there were general staff meetings with arguments over the shades of meaning in a single phrase. One night someone threw an inkwell and opened up another's scalp.

In March and April there was another brief series of letters again dealing with the broader issues of the Revolution. This time the central

180

theme was revisionism, which Polly claimed was the popular term for the final loss of revolutionary spirit. Yet every week the definition became more embracing so that anything representative of an older order was revisionist. "There is," Polly wrote, "a growing sentiment that only through absolute anarchy can those revisionist elements of society be purged, and again I do not know where it will end."

In a later series Polly addressed the question of tactics, and explained that if Mao was met by overwhelming opposition within the party, he would probably work to destroy the party from without. To this end Polly outlined what he called Mao's blueprint for revolution, including a total mobilization of students and an unrestrained campaign of criticism. As for Polly's own position, he wrote that he would remain ideologically attached to Mao and Chou En-lai for as long as possible, but feared that eventually even this stance would become tenuous. "It will soon become difficult to know," he wrote, "precisely what the chairman's wishes actually are."

Two months after the delivery of these letters Mao returned to Peking and issued what would later be known as the May 16th Circular. It was addressed to all party functionaires and mass organizations. It contained a general condemnation of all those opposed to Mao, and appealed to the youth to rise up against all bourgeois existence.

Two days later Lin Piao announced the publication of the Little Red Book of *Quotations from Chairman Mao*. Initial distribution went to the army and larger universities, but there was also word of a second, third and fourth printing. Seven days following this announcement students at the Peking University attacked Peng Chen in a large hand-lettered, ink-drawn poster which was fixed to a factory wall. There was a subsequent demonstration, then an edict forbidding further character posters, but this was summarily ignored.

At the end of May the first Red Guard units were organized from the middle-level students. By the end of June there were thousands of them, by the end of July hundreds of thousands.

In July and August there were another four letters, each brief and seemingly written in haste. They dealt with the overall form of events, likening Mao's tactics to a guerrilla operation. There was, as Polly explained, a definite rhythm: attack and pause, destruction and consolidation. Polly cited Mao's initial move on the cultural and educational commissars, then his advance on the Eleventh Plenum, all while continuing to rally the youth beyond the party apparatus. By autumn Polly

181

had estimated that nearly thirteen million Red Guards had descended on Peking, with another three million still in the provinces. "There is no longer any sense of stillness in this city," Polly wrote. "Even at night— no sense of stillness."

In a second group of letters from this same period Polly attempted to define the more salient directions of the movement. The most obvious targets, he wrote, were those suggestive of the formal party structure and reigning bureaucracy. Simplified for the masses these targets became the Four Olds: old ideology, old thought, old habits, old customs. Yet even before these letters reached Langley the direction had shifted again, widening, losing even more of its definition.

Regarding an article that Polly had written for the journal, Ling commented, "I'm afraid that this is not explicit enough of the chairman's wishes."

"What are you talking about?"

Again it was late, and again the electricity kept failing. There were also odors from the ministry corridor, odors of perspiration and congealing plates of vegetables.

Ling circled a passage from Polly's article in red crayon. "Here you say that the time has come for energetic revolution. Wouldn't it be more accurate to say that energetic revolution is long overdue?"

"What difference does it make?"

"A great difference. Your sentence does not reflect the intense frustration that the chairman is supposed to have felt when he saw the corruption within the party."

"Tommy, it doesn't matter."

"But your wording is not—"

"It doesn't matter."

In the morning the streets were littered with broken glass and chips of plaster from shops that had been demolished the night before.

By October and November the letters described a still widening revolutionary front. There were references to the persecution of intellectuals, particularly those with foreign interests. There were further references to public trials, torture, the destruction of books and musical instruments. "This city," Polly wrote, "has become a shadowland with madness that surpasses all understanding."

Later he wrote that every night one heard crowds moving to and from the central square. Every morning there was new evidence of violence. There were always people lined against the walls, munching rice with

182

persistent stares. On the streets Polly kept to the alleys and factory districts to avoid the wandering gangs. He dressed in gray or drab green. He did not meet passing eyes.

In December and January there were only two letters, the first hardly more than a paragraph, the second long and disjointed. There were references to sporadic cruelty, students turning on their instructors, setting their hair on fire, breaking their fingers. Everywhere, he wrote, there were individual breakdowns. One evening in the ministry a young man simply rose from his desk and began to beat his head against the wall. Suicide was rampant, conversations seemed to have no beginning or end, there was no concept of past or future.

As if in reaction to the slow deterioration around him, Polly eventually found himself spending every spare moment with his daughter. Maya was thirteen years old in the spring of 1966. She wore her hair in braids, no longer cut straight across her forehead. In many ways she was a quiet child, and photographs of the period attest to her beauty. But there was hardly anyplace for beauty now. Like other children she always wore the same uniform, trousers unpressed and a shapeless blouse like something a prisoner might wear. The only bit of color was her red scarf that she wore on Sundays. Regardless of propaganda, regardless of what Polly himself was continually writing for the journals, this was no country for children, particularly young girls.

Of these days he would always retain an image of her trudging up the brown road on her way home from school. Once Polly had seen her like this, while standing at the window of his bedroom. She had been walking steadily for over half a mile, never taking her eyes off the ground. But just before she reached the garden gates she looked up and saw him watching. He often thought it was just he and Maya against all of China.

From late summer on the Red Guard had been urged to carry the Cultural Revolution into the provinces. By winter nearly a fifth of the nation's transport system was engaged in shuttling the youth to the countryside. There were reports of youths fighting farmers, stealing food, killing livestock, but on the whole life was supposed to have been better, and for this reason Polly allowed his daughter to travel south with a unit from her school.

She left not long after the first hard frost. The night before her departure Polly had been unable to sleep. He kept wandering to her bedroom door, then turning away again. In the morning he cooked two eggs, which were now a rare commodity. Then he packed her belongings in a canvas bag, the kind of bag that all the children were carrying these days. When he printed her name neatly on the strap, he could not believe that any of this was really happening. He simply could not believe.

Later that morning he took her to the station and the waiting trains. There were thousands milling in the yards, but Polly and his daughter had a few moments alone behind the turnstile. He kissed her and told her to write, although they both knew that the mail service had broken down weeks ago.

Now alone, Polly wrote: "I'm all right. Physically, I'm all right." But he was tired, and just when he would think that the worst was over a new crisis would arise. There were terrible stories. A girl had been mutilated with a razor. A boy had simply disappeared. At night there were gunshots and distant explosions. In the morning new posters went up on the walls. By now these posters had become horribly sinister—crude drawings of dogs, mushroom clouds and demons. The radio stations taken over by students were broadcasting repetitive slogans like garbled messages from the moon.

Finally it seemed to Polly that his life and the lives of those around him had become entirely redolent of dreams. Those were dream crowds he saw in the streets, dream stories he wrote every day. From the ministry window the city looked like a mirage. In the mornings there were compulsory readings of Mao. At night you still heard the voices: *A good government is like wind over the grass.*

It was in the spring of 1967 that Polly entered the last and most personally intense stage of this crisis. By this time the Revolution had become anarchic, with over a hundred separate Red Guard factions at the academic level, each claiming sanctity from Mao. In place of the former government there were now revolutionary committees at all levels, consisting of an alliance between the army, Red Guard and workers. In practice, however, these committees only led to a multiplication of warring factions. In Wuhan there had been heavy fighting between Red Guards and the local military authority. Street fighting had also broken out in Shanghai, with weapons stolen from the central armory. Commenting upon this internecine strife, Polly wrote: "I do not believe that the chairman is wholly responsible for what is occurring."

To some extent Polly's belief was later confirmed by Sagan and others. By late 1966 the Cultural Revolution had moved tactically beyond Mao's direction into entirely unchartered areas. Some responsibility for the violence has been leveled on Mao's wife, while others have blamed Lin Piao, who was said to have used the Red Guard factional strife to his own ends.

Central to this latter theory was an ultra-leftist group popularly called the May 16th. Like other Red Guard factions, the May 16th was primarily composed of youths, particularly the ranking party officials. They were far better financed than other factions, with electronic communications facilities, a fleet of automobiles and access to sophisticated weaponry, including hand grenades, automatic rifles and light artillery. They were said to be under the covert control of Lin Piao and there is some evidence to this effect, evidence which Polly himself would eventually present.

Polly's first exposure to the problem of the May 16th came in the spring of 1967. It was the season of dust and high winds, adding to unreality. By now Polly had come to see that politically the safest position was no position at all. His articles of the period were elaborate statements of nothing. Sentences were disjointed, paragraphs unconnected. His articles were like chips of glass. They changed depending upon the angle from which they were viewed.

In terms of Polly's own sense of a beginning he would always recall a particular conversation with Tommy Ling on Monday of the last week in March. Through this period Ling had been existing much the same as Polly: continually on the edge, clearly afraid. Since the hard fighting had begun he and Polly had met nearly every morning in the ministry courtyard, or else behind the ventilation shafts. From here there was a view of the adjacent street and a line of trees with hacked off limbs. On this particular morning the cobbles were littered with plaster and splintered wood. The telephone lines were down.

Ling said, "I received a memo from the Shanghai bureau."

"What did they want?"

"They were concerned about the phrasing in your article."

"What about it?"

"They were concerned about your description of the chairman as becoming angered by revolutionary excess."

"So? What's wrong with that?"

"Apparently they felt that it's improper to portray the chairman as becoming angered. Rather he should be portrayed as being saddened."

"They sent a memo about that?"

"Yes . . . no. Actually the memo was an excuse."

185

"What do you mean?"

"John, listen to me. They say that we are no longer safe."

"What do you mean?"

"I mean that they are planning to attack anyone associated with Chou."

"They?"

"The May 16th and other units in alliance with them."

"So? We've heard that before."

"Yes, but this time I believe it's true. I believe that the May 16th is about to move against anyone with moderate positioning."

An occasional wind brought sounds of a distant crowd. There were trails of smoke rising from the factory district.

"I think I should tell you, John, I have a certain hypothesis about this May 16th."

"Yes?"

"I believe that they are being used by Lin to eliminate his enemies. I further believe that he controls them through Han Chow."

There were footsteps on the balcony above, soft laughter, then a shutting door.

Ling added, "If I'm correct then it won't be long now."

"What won't be long?"

"Before we are sent down to one of the communes or a reeducation center."

"So what happens if you're sent down?"

"It depends. I'm told that the communes are not so bad. But the reeducation centers, these are very bad. People are dying there."

They came for him in the night, exactly how he had been told they would come: in a group of about fifteen, armed with obsolete carbines. They identified themselves as deputies of the Public Security Bureau, but from their age and their clothing it was clear that they were only students. Their leader was an intense boy with cropped hair and bad teeth. When Polly had been taken from his bedroom and brought downstairs he was read a list of formal charges. It was an awkward moment with Polly standing casually, his arms at his side, the young men all around him obviously unsure of what was expected. After the reading Polly was permitted to dress and then led to a windowless van. Almost as an afterthought one of the boys smashed a vase with his rifle butt, while another kicked the leg out from under the table.

Polly did not know where he was taken, but judging from the length of the journey he assumed that it was someplace just beyond the city limits. Here lay a converted factory yard, surrounded by high brick walls and barbed wire. There were rows of mud-brick bungalows, roofed with tar paper, the windows fixed with steel bars. There were guards milling by a truck, others squatting on planks of wood in the mud.

At some point after dawn Polly was taken to what must have been a warehouse. There he was forced to stand on a packing crate with a dozen men and women seated before him. There was only a single, naked bulb and he could not see their faces, but again he could tell that they were young, in their early twenties. After another list of charges had been read, he was told that due to severe counterrevolutionary tendencies he would be held in this reeducation center until those tendencies had been eradicated. Through it all Polly said nothing; his eyes remained blank, impassive.

When they were finished with him in the warehouse he was taken to his cell, although it was not really a cell, just an unlit mud room with an aperture cut a foot below the ceiling. A wooden shelf, barely wide enough to sit on, ran along the wall. There was an empty bucket, presumably for waste, a pallet of straw and nothing else. The first night he did not sleep.

Now began an unvarying routine that would mark the first week. At dawn Polly was taken to the warehouse along with sixty other prisoners. Here were held the compulsory readings of Mao, then sessions of self-criticism wherein prisoners were forced to stand on packing crates and enumerate their crimes against the state. Generally the prisoners were cooperative, even occasionally enthusiastic. There were, however, those who continued to resist, and for these treatment was harsh.

The prisoners worked in a factory, dyeing and cutting coarse fabric. There were also sewing rooms, but Pully never saw them. All clothing that was manufactured was purely utilitarian: winter tunics, field trousers, military uniforms. Possibly, because he was foreign, Polly was given the simpler tasks of tending the dyeing vats and trimming ragged edges. At the end of the first day his hands were stained dark brown, and no amount of rubbing could get them clean again.

In the evenings there were again political assemblies; confessions, readings from Mao. Generally these assemblies ended at midnight, but occasionally they went on until dawn. Then in half-light, the dampness and exhaustion, the voices of speakers became almost hypnotic, while the words lost every shred of meaning.

Polly came to realize that nearly all of his fellow prisoners were from among the Peking elite, particularly from the cultural bureaus. There were writers, painters, poets, musicians, an architect whom Polly had vaguely known for several years, an editor who had helped with the production of the foreign journal. There was even another American, an economist named Donnelly, who had become an expatriate in 1959. Polly, however, did not have much to say to the others. For the most part they were concerned with their salvation and the outward show of their loyalty to Mao. They were continually trying to outdo one another at the warehouse assemblies, continually trying to demonstrate their contrition and newfound zealotry.

There were moments here when it seemed to Polly that the mood of this camp was distinctly religious. Prisoners, speaking on the packing crates in the tallow light of oil lamps, were as fervent and dogmatic as any convert to one of the more fanatical religions. There was a distinctly religious overtone to the idolatry of Mao. His portrait hung at both ends of the warehouse, while another and larger one had been pasted on the inner wall. It was the concept of Mao as godhead and the revolutionary immortality of the proletariat.

What would eventually be seen as the single most important development of Polly's stay in this camp, perhaps even the most important development of this period, occurred during the second week of imprisonment with the introduction of General Ko Ming. Ko was one of the more formidable guerrilla strategists from the Japanese campaigns. He was particularly remembered for his critical role in the extraordinary Hundred Regiment campaign of August 1940, and his later efforts as an elusive night fighter. If he had not been seriously wounded in 1946 he would have eventually risen to the summit of the Chinese military authority. As it was, however, a shrapnel burst left him virtually bedridden for three years following the war, by which time advancement had passed him by.

At this point of introduction to Polly's life, the general was fifty-two years old. He was still partially crippled and occasionally suffered from severe intestinal pains. He was also afflicted with a weak heart and bad teeth. Mentally, however, he alert, and they had not succeeded in breaking his spirit. They had not even come close to it.

Polly's first meeting with the man came one Sunday evening, the one night when work and political assemblies were suspended. Polly had been working in the dyeing shed with the others. Then the curfew sounded and the prisoners were herded back into their cells. Darkness had already begun to fall so that when Polly entered his cell he saw only the shapeless form of a man sitting on a wooden ledge. He asked in Chinese who was there, but received no response. He repeated his question, but again there was no reply.

Then in English he heard, "Sit down and do not speak to me."

"But who are you?"

"I told you not to speak to me."

By this time Polly's eyes had become sufficiently accustomed to the darkness so that he was able to see the general outline of the man's face. It was a rough, deeply lined face, with prominent bones and large, hollow eyes. He was also able to determine that the man was old and very thin.

"Look, my name is John Polly. Why can't you—"

"I know who you are, Mr. Polly."

"You do?"

"Yes."

"Then how about telling me—"

"This is a joke, a very poor joke."

"What's a joke?"

"That they have put us in the same quarters."

"I don't understand."

"You are John Polly, friend and admirer of Chou En-lai? Well, I'm Ko Ming, administrative aide to Han Chow. Or should I say former administrative aide."

By now the cell was entirely dark, with only a narrow track of starlight through the ventilation slit. It was also silent, except for the occasional courtyard sounds of passing guards and the dropping tailgate of a truck.

After a long time Polly said, "If you're with Han, then what are you doing here?"

"I'm a casualty, same as you."

"What do you mean?"

"This is war, and we are the casualties. You were on one side. I was on the other. But we are now both dead, so what does it matter?"

In the days that followed other conversations were unavoidable. All were held in darkness, all fairly terse. Eventually Polly came to understand that the general had been the victim of an internal war within his own Public Security Ministry. He refused to believe, however, that the ministry director, Han Chow, had been responsible for his incarceration. Rather he laid the blame on a younger man who had been jealous of his

189

relationship with Han. When Polly intimated that perhaps the general's perception of what had happened was clouded by his loyalty to Han, the general became indignant, demanding to know exactly what Polly had been implying.

Polly answered, "It would seem that if Han wanted to he could get you out of here."

This made the general even angrier. "You don't know what you're talking about. Can Chou En-lai get you out of here? Can your comrade Ling Sheng get you out of here? Well, it's the same with Han. He is not yet in a position to oppose these children."

"Children?"

"The Red Guard. Han is not in a position to oppose them."

"And you honestly believe that, general?"

"Of course I believe. Why should I not believe?"

"No reason."

"Why should I not believe?"

"I was merely under the impression that Han Chow can do anything. And what he can't do, Lin Piao will do for him."

"That's ridiculous."

"Is it?"

"I will not talk about this anymore."

Later that night Polly was wakened by the general's labored breathing and soft moan. When Polly asked what was wrong the general told him to go away. "Go away and leave me alone, Polly. Leave me alone."

Polly came to understand that the old man's health was actually quite frail. They had him turning the dyeing vats, and although he never complained, Polly could see that the heat and effort was slowly draining his strength. More than once Polly had seen his knees buckle so that he had to brace himself against the wooden tub. The general also had difficulty walking in the morning, and because his eyes were weak, he could not avoid the standing puddles of water in the yard.

But if Polly ever expressed concern, or offered to help, the general only rebuked him, saying, "Go away. Leave me alone." And once, "Why concern yourself with me? You have just as much chance of dying here."

Again it was late, and again the cell was black, when the general cried out in pain.

"As soon as Chou En-lai is eliminated you will be killed. So will your friend Ling Sheng. They are only waiting until Chou is gone so that no questions will be asked. Now what do you think of that, Polly?"

He could hear the general breathing, hear his fingers rubbing on the wooden plank. "I think you should try and get some rest."

"Oh, there will be plenty of time to rest, Polly. Because if Chou is victorious and Lin Piao is eliminated then it will be me and Han Chow who will die. But either way one of us will die. That you can believe in."

In response to all this Polly did not have anything in particular to say. He supposed that there was a chance that the general was correct. Certainly if Chou En-lai was politically overwhelmed, Lin would probably begin eliminating those who had been known to support him, just as Chou would eliminate Lin's supporters were the circumstances reversed. There were, however, other factors to be considered, factors such as Mao's position and possible intervention. The general, however, discounted Mao's influence. He claimed that the chairman would not intercede because, in the general's eyes, Mao was like an indifferent primitive god. He had created the world and was now content to let things run their course regardless of injustice.

But on the whole there was never any sense of reality to what the general said, only a sense of detachment, as if what Polly heard was simply a story from one of the older classics wherein characters were one-dimensional, with simple motivations and predictable responses. Occasionally there were rumors of tense fighting between split factions of the Red Guard, but again there was no sense of reality, no sense of an orderly sequence through time. There was only a sense of deterioration and building madness.

Finally it seemed to Polly that even his captors had lost sight of their position in the larger conflict. There were disputes as to how prisoners were to be treated, fights between guards, unnecessary incidents of cruelty. Then there were rumors that an opposing Red Guard faction had made plans to overrun the camp and liberate the inmates. In response thirty-five prisoners were forced to lay sandbags until they collapsed from exhaustion, while riflemen watched from the rooftops.

It went from bad to worse. One night a prisoner was shot attempting to scale the outer wall. On another night a woman was beaten to death. There were shortages of food and water, and continual reverberation of mortar fire from the southeast. More than once a prisoner simply disappeared, while a line of guards were seen returning from the hills with shovels.

In July, with the descent of heat, emotions became even less predictable. The warehouse assemblies were filled with isolated fits of weeping, sporadic violence, momentary hysteria. There were three suicides in the first week, two hangings and a throat cut with a shard of glass. Every morning the inmates were tramped across the dusty yard, their eyes like plugs of glass. Every afternoon they were permitted to rest in the shade of the wall, staring at their feet.

If there was any single climax to these days it would have been in August with the consummate assault on Chou En-lai. Once more accounts vary as to precisely what occurred, with only the broader events remaining undisputed. It is known, for example, that at the peak of the crisis more than a hundred thousand demonstrators filled the Tien An Men Square, demanding Chou's resignation. It is also known that a contingent of Red Guards actually stormed Chou's office, held him captive for more than twenty-four hours, and released him only after intense debate.

There were those, Polly among them, who eventually came to see these three days in August as perhaps the most visible manifestation of Lin Piao's political strength of the time. Of course, no outward evidence has ever been produced to show that Lin was specifically manipulating the demonstrators, but sources close the the Red Guard leadership would later reveal that all through the crisis Lin had maintained links with the students both directly through his own office and indirectly through Han Chow's. Then too there would also be evidence of an attempted assassination while Chou had been en route to Shanghai.

For Polly, who at the time was largely cut off from reliable information, these three days would always number as the darkest of the Revolution. Polly's first knowledge of the crisis came from Ko Ming, who had presumably heard rumors from other inmates. Initially these rumors were vague, with only the sketchiest details. It was first said that Chou had been killed or at least badly wounded. Then in the evening the general told Polly that Chou had definitely fallen, and it was only a matter of time before all of Chou's supporters were killed. This had been on an evening of hot winds with dust spreading from the south.

There was no absolute sense of resolution to the crisis, not within Polly's mind. There simply came a point when the movement aimed at deposing Chou suddenly faltered and lost momentum. Politically Chou was said to have been substantially injured by the affair, while Lin Piao was said to have benefited, but the essential balance between the two men remained intact. Lin still held sway over the army; Chou over the moderate line.

192

For Polly the resolution was no less ambiguous. On the third evening he heard that Chou was no longer under fire, and later this statement was corroborated by the general.

He said, "It appears that you won't be executed after all."

Polly, who had already heard the news about Chou, said, "Is that so?"

"Yes. It is so. Not that anything has been settled, but at least there is a stalemate, and consequently neither of us will die."

"You don't seem particularly happy."

"I do not like unresolved conflict."

Later that night there was thunder from the mountains, but sterile thunder without rain. The wind also brought a swarm of flying ants under the door, and through the break in the wall. After several hours of stomach cramps Polly managed to fall asleep, but was wakened suddenly by the general who seemed to be whispering to himself.

In the final days of Polly's confinement, which in turn would mark the end of this chapter in his life, there was an incident that involved the general, who was by this time fairly ill again with a low but persistent fever and had difficulty breathing. Twice Polly had tried to bring the general's condition to the attention of the camp administration, but was met only with indifference. The general was neither excused from rigorous work, nor the long hours of indoctrination.

Finally one night during an unusually strenuous political assembly, the general was called upon to speak, or, as the term went, to make self-criticism. There were perhaps seventy inmates and guards present, some lining the mud walls of the warehouse, most seated on crude benches. After the general had been singled out, there was an obvious hush, because all knew him as a particularly truculent and uncompromising offender. Then slowly, deliberately, the general rose from his bench at the back of the room and began to limp forward to the packing crates.

He took a long time to climb the crates, looking inordinately frail, and gaze at the faces in front of him. His words were wholly derogatory, with classic peasant insults aimed at the administration and all those who willingly supported it. Following his brief speech, there was a moment of total silence, then the guards leapt out and dragged him down. The general offered no resistance, but just fell with the first blow and then balled himself up to protect his head and groin.

Exactly how Polly managed to appear so suddenly, no one would ever be able to explain. He seemed to have dropped from the rafters, intercepting the arm of a boy who was about to strike the general, twisting it back savagely. When another boy jumped on Polly's back, Polly threw him hard into the first row of benches, then spun and struck a third boy full in the mouth.

Finally Polly stood alone on the crates. The general lay at his feet. Around them stood several guards and inmates, poised to attack again, but something held them back. When Polly let his arms fall, the tension in his shoulders subsided, but nothing in his eyes changed, the gaze like clear water, encompassing the entire room now in total silence.

In the end Polly bent and gathered the general in his arms. As he made his way down the aisle no one tried to stop him, no one even spoke. A piece of decency had suddenly become more revolutionary than Mao.

Three days later Polly was released. He was in the dyeing shed, stacking bolts of uncut cloth when two young guards came for him and led him into the director's office. Tommy Ling was waiting. He wore a green, unpressed boiler suit. There was a vinyl briefcase under his arm. On a table were two chipped cups and a pot of tea. A steel filing cabinet had been set on cinder blocks.

"Hello, John, how are you?"

Polly nodded. He seemed neither surprised nor relieved.

"I would have come sooner, but I had some difficulty myself."

Then Polly smiled. "I understand."

It seemed there was nothing else to say. Outside in the courtyard another rain had left pools of standing water. Planks had been laid across the mud, a broken window had been filled with cardboard.

But by the compound gates Polly suddenly stopped, and looked back over his shoulder. Then he said, "There's something I want you to do for me. There's someone else I want released."

"But, John, I only have the authority to—"

"It's Ko Ming."

"The general?"

"Yes."

"But, John, he is not even—"

"I know who he is. Now can you get him out of here or not?"

There was a final conversation between Polly and the general, which occurred approximately two months following their release. It was by now the late fall, and a new sense of order had finally descended upon the

194

city. There were still reports of fighting in the outer provinces, but Peking had grown quiet again with the emergence of a new moderate line.

On the day of the conversation Polly had spent the morning in the ministry, but in the afternoon, without knowing quite why, he decided to take a walk. The light was gray, with gray crowds along the boulevards. Everywhere there was still evidence of the fighting: demolished storefronts, heaps of charred rubbish, scattered bricks. Finally, while browsing at a display of procelain animals in a dusty shop window, Polly heard a voice from over his shoulder. He looked up, and in the reflection of glass saw the general.

"Hello, Polly. Surprised to see me?"

For a moment Polly hardly even recognized the man. His eyes were no longer dark, his face no longer hollow. His teeth had been repaired.

"You think I was following you, Polly? I wasn't. I merely observed you walking and thought it would not be improper if I spoke to you. Perhaps even thanked you."

"Thank me?" The general was clearly smirking.

"For saving my life and securing my timely release."

"Oh that," as if he had actually forgotten.

"Curious thing to have done, wouldn't you say?"

Polly shrugged. Passing shoppers kept glancing at the general's coat, green wool and tailored snugly.

"Now if our positions had been reversed, I am not at all sure that I would have saved you."

"Oh yes?"

"It's foolish to save an enemy."

Then softly, almost in a whisper, "Is that what we are, general? Enemies?"

The general stepped forward and lowered his voice. "I will tell you something, Polly. I will tell you because of what you did for me, and because it probably doesn't matter anyway. Did you know that for many years Han Chow and others in the ministry have suspected that you are a spy? That is, a real spy, with external contacts? Now what do you think of that?"

"What do I think of that?" After all these years of waiting for an accusation.

"Yes. What do you think?"

"I don't know, general. What do you think? You think I'm a spy?"

"Perhaps."

195

When their eyes met, it was impossible for Polly to know whether he was serious. *Inscrutable Orient, indeed,* Polly thought.

From the start Polly tended to stress the roles of those around him, while ignoring many of the larger issues of the Cultural Revolution. He did not, for example, particularly concern himself with the early conflict between Mao and Liu Shao-chi, but rather focused upon the less visible conflict between Lin Piao and Chou En-lai. The Cultural Revolution was really little else than a skirmish in a greater war that was still several years away from culmination—this was essentially the sentiment of Polly's letter of September 1967, written at the end of his seven-week imprisonment.

> In the months that follow you may hear a lot about the fact that Lin Piao has been named as Mao's successor. Do not be deceived by this. The title of "successor" holds no weight at all, but is indicative only of certain arrangements that Mao may have been forced to have made with Lin in exchange for Lin's aid during critical points of the Cultural Revolution. As for the actual status of power, I suppose we are again entering a stage of strained stability. Mao, they say, is about to rebuild the party, while the differences between Chou and Lin remain breathing faintly in the darkness.
> In the meantime Ling *tells* me that I'm safe. Perhaps another collection of stories is in order, and Maya is due back in a month.

Maya returned from the commune in the middle of October. Polly met her at the station. It was the first cold day in a long time. There were fallen leaves on the pavings and steps, mist coiling in the skyline. Maya appeared as a slender girl, standing apart from the others. She did not embrace her father. He did not embrace her. There were too many people around them who would disapprove.

Chapter 8

"**MAYA WAS** sixteen then?" Cassidy asked.

"That's right," Crane replied. "She was sixteen."

"Is there a photograph?"

"No. I'm afraid not."

"Any idea how she spent her time at that commune?"

"Oh, I imagine she went through the usual rigmarole. Up at dawn for the daily reading. Then out to the fields until noon. Another political session over lunch. More work after that, and more politics throughout the evening."

Cassidy was silent for a moment, fingering a rock he had picked up without thinking. Then he said, "They're all fucking crazy."

It was still quite early in the morning. Again they were sitting on the point. An offshore wind was leaving whitecaps across the bay, and there were white clouds unraveling to the west. Last night, unable to sleep again, Cassidy had risen from bed, walked to the window, and the bay had been like black slate. Maya, he had thought, had probably never even seen the sea.

"Would you like some breakfast?" Crane asked suddenly.

"No thanks."

"I could have Eliot make us some eggs?"

"Look, I'm not hungry."

"I only thought you might want to eat before we get started again. We have a rather hard stretch ahead of us."

"What do you mean?"

197

"I'm afraid I'm going to have to ask you about your personal role in things."

"So it's time for that, huh?"

"Yes. It's time."

In truth, however, it was not quite yet time for Cassidy's story. There were still those intervening years between Jay Sagan's final commitment to the Chinese elite and his rise to ultimate power. For this chapter of the story Crane did not have to consult his notes.

It was Crane's opinion that the final and current phase of Jay Sagan's career actually began about 1965. Sagan was then forty-four, his hair was graying at the temples, but he had still remained fairly trim. By this year he was no longer living in the apartment on Victoria Peak, but had purchased a house farther up. It was a small house, but modern, with a magnificent view of the harbor. A terrace had been cut into the hanging gardens, and at night there was the scent of jacaranda. Whenever Sagan brought colleagues here they were always impressed with the view, but may have also wondered where he had got the money.

These were prosperous years for the station. By now there were regular yields of high-grade intelligence from all over the mainland. As attention in Washington began to focus on Vietnam, Sagan too began to turn to the southeast and soon had a string of agents from Mandalay to Bangkok and into the Mekong Delta. But as always here was a price to pay for these networks, and by 1966 the price had grown high.

One characteristic of Sagan's career was that the more he became involved in something the less visible that involvement was. Such was the case with his relationship with Feng Chi. Up until 1963 Sagan had continually pressed for Agency support of the twenty thousand Nationalist Chinese still encamped along the Thai-Burmese border. As justification for this support, Sagan cited the burgeoning Red Meo insurgents of northern Thailand, and of course the ever-present threat from the mainland. It would never be said that Jay Sagan did not know how to sell a product.

In all, Sagan made several formal proposals to Washington between 1960 and 1963. No two were exactly the same in content or approach, although the essential aims were the same. Given modern weapons, Sagan argued, the Chinese irregular armies could prove the most effective buffer against Communist insurgency in the entire Southeast Asian triangle. These soldiers had thoroughly integrated themselves into the local

198

hill tribes, their knowledge of the terrain was unmatched, and their ability to wage a protracted war was already a matter of record.

Langley, however, was unimpressed. The Yunnan failure was still fresh in many minds, and there were still those embarrassing questions of diplomacy. Then, too, there was also the question of opium.

Naturally, none of Sagan's proposals ever mentioned the opium routes. Not that there was any need to mention them, because by 1963 all those connected with the secret Asian wars knew very well that the Chinese irregulars in Burma and Thailand were heavily involved in the trade. Feng Chi was acting as broker for these Chinese. The exit points for opium or processed morphine were Bangkok and Haadyai in southern Thailand, then to the international airports of Penang and Kuala Lumpur in Malaya—all conclusively Jay Sagan's world.

It was in June 1966 when the issues raised in Sagan's petitions were finally answered directly. Norman Pyle and other executive officers from the Asian Desk had traveled to Saigon for a review of the intelligence marketplace. Then the party dispersed and returned to Washington, all except Pyle. He took a military transport to Tokyo, then a commercial flight into Hong Kong. It was a gray muggy day. There had been talk of a typhoon. Pyle had made the last flight.

Sagan would always remember Pyle's voice, and that unmistakable clarity of a local call. While in the train of false enthusiasm there was a dark pause. They agreed to meet for lunch. Sagan knew of a restaurant where only tourists ate. He also may have known or sensed the falling shadow.

It was three o'clock when Sagan and Pyle actually met. Pyle looked as neutral as ever in a pale summer suit with a stain on the lapel. His hair was by now fairly gray. He had also gained a little weight. They had drinks in a place where the doorways were tipped with chrome. The light was tinted through blue silk. For the first half hour the conversation was congenial, although Sagan kept avoiding Pyle's eyes and the stickier questions.

Finally Pyle said, "I'm going to have to ask you about those Chinese, Jay. I mean the irregulars."

"Sure." Sagan was spearing a vegetable with his chopsticks. He had never learned how to use them properly.

"Is that General Khan character still in command?"

"It's Tuan. T-u-a-n. And yes, he's still in command."

"What's he calling his people these days?"

199

"Fifth KMT."

"And there's about twenty thousand of them?"

"That's right."

"I imagine a lot of them must be second generation."

"Second generation?"

"Well, we're certainly not talking about the original team that fought in '49, are we?"

"Oh I see. Well, yes, some are in fact second generation. Others are from the local hills."

"Why do they do it? I mean the hill tribe boys. They're not Chinese, are they? So what makes them follow the leader?"

Sagan smiled. "You've got to understand that over the last twenty years there have been a lot of family ties. Nearly every boy in those villages has got an uncle who's somebody in the KMT."

"And their antipathy toward communism, that's a family affair too, is it?"

"Come on, Norm, what do you want from me?"

"The truth."

By now the restaurant had become fairly deserted. It was that uncertain hour before the evening cocktails. The waitresses were chatting by the potted palms.

Pyle said, "You know people in Washington are concerned about this sphere, Jay. They're concerned about Feng Chi. They're very concerned about the dope."

"So? What do they want from me? They want me to cancel the game? Because that's what it's going to come to. If we're not willing to play in Feng's court then there's no game."

Pyle said softly, "You know, Jay, some of Feng's stuff has been turning up in Saigon. They've been finding it on our own boys. And I'm talking about the processed stuff. The Double-Globe number four."

"Feng doesn't handle Saigon."

"I know, but it doesn't make people in Washington feel any better. I'm getting a lot of heat over this. Your friend Tuan is growing it, and your friend Feng is selling it. Okay? It looks bad. It gets people upset."

Sagan pushed his plate away. The whole mess disgusted him now. "So what do you want me to do, Norman? You want me to drop it?"

"I'm not saying that."

"Then what?"

"Talk to Feng. See if he can't do something to keep the stuff away from the boys. We're starting to get Congress on our backs. Kids are coming back strung out. Their parents are starting to write letters. It's a very uncomfortable situation."

A waitress in blue had slipped behind the palms. Another was seating a solitary woman.

"I wonder," Pyle said suddenly. "I wonder if either of us really knows what's going on anymore."

Sagan frowned. "What's that supposed to mean?"

"It's just a thought. Did you know that there are a lot of people in Washington now who are starting to feel that it might be time to talk."

"Talk?"

"To Peking."

Sagan started fingering his chopsticks. Across the room the solitary woman was toying with her pearls.

"I'm referring to influential people, Jay. People on the Hill. People with a firm connection to the White House."

While Sagan continued testing the point of his chopstick.

"They're saying that the stance we've taken is all wrong. They're saying that we're not offering solutions, only solidifying the problem."

Then Sagan glanced up. "And you, Norman? What do you say?" After twenty-five years of fighting Reds.

"I don't know. I say maybe they're right."

By nine o'clock Sagan found himself in another tropical bar, alone, fairly drunk on scotch. There were women all around, but he did not seem to have the strength.

With the expansion of fighting in Vietnam, Sagan soon found that professionally his life was more fulfilling than ever before. When Graham Cheever of the Taiwan Central passed away in 1966, Sagan became provisional head of the entire Southesst Asian sphere, a title that he was to hold through the end. Now answering only to Norman Pyle in Langley, Sagan controlled more than two hundred agents with links from Canton to Macao, across the Gulf of Tonkin and down to Singapore. Supporting these links were twenty-seven long-line junks fitted with high-frequency receivers. Once again there were those, most notably Simon Crane, who vocally protested Sagan's promotion on the grounds that a man of his moral and ethical standards could not be trusted with power. Yet as

201

Norman Pyle pointed out, the only valid measure of Sagan was his performance, and by that standard he was having an undeniably marvelous war.

But regardless of these small victories it was not Sagan's professional life that would eventually lead him into the next phase of his story. It was his personal life, and his relationship with Billy Cassidy's mother, beginning in 1961.

Since Jack Cassidy's death, Sagan had written perhaps two dozen letters to the widow. Each had a formal, slightly solicitous tone. All contained questions regarding the boy. In addition to the letters there had been two occasions when Sagan had actually seen the woman. The first had been at a dinner for husbands and wives of all the Asian Desk employees. Obviously Alice Cassidy had been invited out of respect for her husband. Then in 1960, while passing through Los Angeles, Sagan had telephoned her out of boredom. In the end he took her to dinner, the boy too, and the three of them ate cheeseburgers and talked about Jack.

But in June 1961 Sagan's relationship with the woman became, by all accounts, far more complex. The circumstances leading to this relationship are relatively unimportant. Sagan found himself in Southern California for a meeting with the Pacific Area directors. On the third day of talks, again out of boredom, he decided to telephone the woman. An hour later they met for dinner at a steak house.

She was not an unattractive woman, and that night she looked particularly striking in a black-and-white dress. Her hair was long and sandy blond. Over drinks Sagan kept stealing glances at her slender legs, while she kept fumbling with her handbag. For the most part they discussed Jack, because it could not be avoided. Sagan told her one or two anecdotes which gave the impression that he and Jack had been the closest of friends. Finally he began to talk about China, or at least about a vision of China he thought she would enjoy.

After dinner she invited him in for a nightcap. The walls of her home were done in light pastel. There was a photograph of Jack on the mantelpiece. Another on the wall showed the man in uniform against a half-veiled mountain peak. Billy in the background looked as spectral as any ghost-child.

At some point during the conversation Sagan found himself sliding closer to the woman. By now they were both slightly drunk. She kept picking at the threads on the arm of the sofa. His hand lay on her shoulder. In moments of silence there was only the dripping faucet and

202

the drone of the Frigidaire. "I've been lonely," she told him. "So lonely." Then she kicked off her patant leather heels and kissed him.

As always he had misgivings while they moved toward the bedroom. There were glowing streetlamps through the pleated curtains, shining on another photograph of Jack. Then in his arms her mouth was a separately living thing. She could not seem to get enough of her dead husband's boss. Except once, pausing for air, she told him that maybe they should slow down a little. But Sagan had already found her breasts and white thighs, which he had wondered about for years.

Afterward they both lay on their backs, not touching. She may have felt a little guilty, while he was merely trying to show that he wasn't entirely exhausted.

"So how's Billy?" he asked, because he wanted to avoid the deeper questions.

"Billy's fine," she breathed. "He thinks the world of you."

"He's a great kid. I'm only sorry I missed him."

"He talks about you all the time."

"Really?" *But what would he say if he saw us now?*

"He says that when he grows up he wants to work for you and pay the Communists back for what they did to Jack."

Sagan was not sure what was called for, whether sympathy or a patronizing smile.

He saw her only once again before he returned to the East. This second evening was easier. They both felt less haunted by her husband. She made a passable lasagna. He brought a very good Chianti. They discussed life and listened to Wagner. After several glasses of wine she told him that he had always struck her as invincible, as some kind of Asian lord in an oriental palace. In return he called her an eternal beauty, a woman of sorrows. When she took him into the bedroom he noticed that she had removed the photograph of Jack.

In the years that followed Sagan saw Alice whenever he passed through Los Angeles. Once they spent eight days together in a cabin near Lake Tahoe. When he was away from her she hardly entered his thoughts. When he was with her he told her what she needed to hear. He always looked forward to seeing her, particularly after those laconic Chinese women.

There was, however, one catch to the relationship—Billy. By the time the boy was sixteen, Sagan had discovered that he was expected to be a kind of father. Or at least an uncle. The boy was always trying to sit him down for probing conversations about the future and political stance of the secret world. One conversation that Sagan would always remember occurred on a Sunday afternoon. He and the boy had just returned from a baseball game, and had stopped in a coffee shop off the Santa Monica Freeway. A gasoline truck had run the center divider, and the traffic was backed-up for miles. Billy had ordered a milkshake. Sagan was sipping tea.

"I want to ask you something," Billy said.

"Sure." Sagan was tired, headachey. His tea tasted like nickel.

"It's about my future."

"What about it?" Bracing himself.

"Well, I've been thinking. I mean what would I have to do in order to get into your line of work? The Agency?"

"The Agency?" He should have known this was coming.

"Yes, sir. I mean, to work with you?"

For a moment Sagan went completely blank. He had no idea how people wound up in China. Then he muttered something about a college degree with a firm grounding in languages.

"And when it's time to apply, do you think maybe I could get a recommendation from you?"

"Well, that's a long way off, Billy."

"I know, but do you think I could?"

Then, because there was no other way out: "Sure. Sure I'll give you a recommendation."

Nearly every month for several years Billy continued to write. His letters were filled with questions about how things were actually done within the secret world, and some of those questions were remarkably astute. He became particularly intrigued with the political sphere of clandestine operations, the concept of covert dissemination. In time Sagan supposed that he could not help but admire the boy's persistence. Photographs of Billy at this stage in his life show a well-groomed young man with intelligent eyes. He was also known as a diligent student, who always received the highest academic honors. He had a particular flair for mathematics and held the district record for the mile.

One of the last photographs of the boy, taken before he entered college, showed him standing on the steps of his high school. He was wearing brown corduroys, a letterman's jacket and penny loafers. The milky afternoon light made his eyes look very blue and hair blond. Behind him, cut into the frieze of the school administration hall, were the words

Character and Truth. Eventually Billy's mother sent a copy of this photograph to Sagan, who laid it in a drawer along with a lot of other letters and papers he considered unimportant, but never got around to throwing out.

This, then, constitutes the background to Cassidy's story as outlined in conversation with Simon Crane. From this point forward the narrative was carried by Billy, while Crane merely listened. Whenever the boy spoke of his past his voice became soft, almost distant. By way of his own introduction he said only that his past was neither a decline nor an ascent in any moral sense. Things just happened.

Billy was twenty-two when he entered the Central Intelligence Agency. As with his father his entrance point had been the military. He was initially assigned to one of the White Star teams operating in Laos, but after an intercession from Jay Sagan he was transferred to the Taiwan-Hong Kong circle. For a while he lived in a Taipei villa. His apartment was white, white plaster walls and white curtains. In the mornings the terrace was covered with lizards.

Of these days Cassidy said that his life revolved principally around the American military and intelligence community. His contact with the Chinese was minimal. He neither liked nor disliked them. He also said that at this point in his life he believed that knowledge was derived solely from experience, but after meeting John Polly he came to see that there was another, infinitely more subtle knowledge.

Cassidy's first encounter with Feng Chi occurred after only three weeks in Taipei. Naturally it was Sagan who brought the two men together. The occasion was a cocktail party at the home of a Feng associate. It was a balmy night. What might have been the rain was only the sound of leaves in the wind. Guests were spread out in lantern light on three descending terraces.

"I was privileged to have known your father," Feng said.

"Yes, sir. Mr. Sagan told me that he worked with you."

"He was a great anti-Communist."

"Thank you, sir."

"And now you have come to avenge his death."

"Yes, sir. I suppose you could say that."

"Then this is very good, because it is only through a commitment of successive generations that we will ever achieve victory."

There were other words, but they were of no consequence and Cassidy would never remember them. What he would remember was Feng's profile against the scalloped roof, the thick fingers on the railing, the pug nose, wide lips, the entirely bald head. Below lay a patch of windblown magnolias, then sand dunes. While behind, through an open screen, lay a room so still it was as if you could hear the falling dust.

In later weeks Cassidy's initial impression of Feng was embellished with various stories he heard from Sagan and others in the station. Until finally Cassidy, too, came to associate the man with a preternatural power: the springing tiger.

It was ten weeks after Cassidy had first entered the East that he had his primary briefing with Jay Sagan. Sagan was in Taipei for talks with Chiang Kai-shek, and on a Thursday evening he took the boy to dinner at a famous garden restaurant. When Cassidy arrived he found Sagan at an iron table on the terrace. The man seemed to be watching a dark girl in a white dress. Later Cassidy said that while hesitating at the edge of the terrace he had been very conscious of a beginning, although the eventual purpose was far beyond what he had ever imagined.

Initially they discussed only trivial subjects. Sagan asked if Cassidy had settled into a comfortable routine. The boy said that he had. Drinks were served, the glasses in bamboo sheaths. Then without preamble Sagan began talking about China as it stood at the final phase of the Cultural Revolution.

"Tell me something, Billy. If you had to choose a side what would it be?"

"You mean between Lin and Chou?"

"Or Mao and Lin as the case may be."

Cassidy shook his head. "I don't know, sir. I guess I'd go with Mao. I mean he seems a bit more flexible, doesn't he?"

"Flexible, Billy?"

"Well, that's what I've been told, sir."

Suddenly Sagan said, "What if I told you that it was within our interest to support the radicals. Lin Piao and that whole group?"

"Sir?"

"Support them. Fan the fire. Keep them alive."

"How?"

"Leaflet drops for starters."

"But why?"

"Because as long as those people remain in a state of civil war they are an ineffective force in this area. For example, six weeks ago an ultra-

206

left faction derailed a train bound for North Vietnam. That train was carrying weapons and medical supplies. Apparently the Red Guards wanted the weapons for a strike against a garrison in Hunan. They didn't need the medical supplies so they burned them."

"And leaflet drops will actually have an impact?"

"I think so. The Chinese are very receptive to anything that's printed on paper."

"Who flies the planes?"

"I've got some local boys."

Four Chinese girls stepped onto the terrace. They were all tall and very thin. They wore short skirts and spiked heels. They may have been prostitutes or simply shopgirls dressed like prostitutes for the night. Sagan watched them for a moment.

Then he said, "To be quite honest, Billy, I've been looking for someone like you. Someone I can trust. Someone who can think for himself."

"To do what, sir?"

"To run the show. Frankly I'd like to see those leaflets printed and dropped within a month."

"But surely Langley has facilities—"

"I'd rather not go through Langley, not at first. That's not to say that there's anything improper about this. It's just that—well, occasionally Langley isn't as sensitive to certain opportunities as those of us within the sphere. You see what I'm getting at don't you?"

"Yes, sir. I believe I do."

But in fact Cassidy did not understand. He did not understand at all. Only seven months earlier, Sagan had proposed a similar plan, involving the drop of politically inflammatory leaflets over three Yunnan villages. The strategic aim had been to incite discord, but the plan was immediately rejected on two accounts. Langley simply did not believe that the Yunnan villagers would accept the leaflets as genuine issues from the Central Party. The second objection involved two China letters from March and April of 1967. In essence these letters described the Cultural Revolution as a bag of snakes, impossible to meddle with and not get bitten.

Billy would always remember these next fourteen weeks as votive, energetic days. There were evening meetings with the pilots, all dark wiry boys from Taiwan. Three hours before dawn Cassidy would brief them in a concrete shed at the end of the airstrip. He had a map tacked to the fiberboard, drop points circled in red crayon. The airstrip ran through a field of willows and swamp grass. There were wooded mountains to the north, supposedly inhabited by local witches, ghosts, even a phoenix. Just before sunrise the sky was usually white. Cassidy liked to stand underneath the corrugated iron until the planes were out of sight. Then he would turn and walk back slowly into the shed for coffee in a plastic cup. As a last resort he knew there were always nuclear weapons, some of them right there in Taipei.

In these days, China was a problem that supposedly could be handled with American technology and a bit of flair. Fairly early on Billy learned to think of the mainland in terms of demographics. There were close to a billion Chinese, but in modern warfare that meant next to nothing. All that mattered were the strike points, and like Sagan, Billy had them mapped out with blue drawing pins. His glimmering map was the dominant feature in his office. He loved those stray moments in his swivel chair, rocking back in front of his map. At the end of a month he knew the names of every river, every mountain range. He was particularly intrigued by Peking.

But if China as a concept was a problem solvable through an orderly process, the Chinese themselves remained the mysterious variable. Not only the Communists, but the so called Free Chinese as well. Three times Billy had accompanied Sagan to Feng Chi's home, and on each occasion he felt as if he were entering a secret netherworld. Even the approach to Feng's door was like an apparition. The white gravel path was lined with plum trees, barely kept alive in this heat and moist air. In mosaic above the gatepost were the characters for the tiger, and another tiger in marble stood near the ornamental pond. The house itself was laid out in long corridors like the ventricles of a heart.

An evening with Feng in his Taiwan home—Cassidy always had the feeling that they were staged, that every sentence had been rehearsed and the lamplight or lantern light on the terrace had been calibrated to specifically set a mood. Some of Feng's associates had faces like wax, eyes like porcelain. The Chinese would rather die than break a promise, Sagan had said. But promises were negotiable, every bit as negotiable as jade, women, opium and favors.

Then there were also secrets, perhaps the most respected commodity of them all. Once Sagan had briefly toyed with a plan to place a microphone in Feng's ancestral shrine. Presumably Feng was always telling his ancestors secrets that he would tell no one else, not even Jerry Woo. But after careful thought Sagan decided that it might not be wise to spy on allies. There were also the technical complications of getting a soundman into a windowless room that always remained locked.

Eventually Cassidy came to understand that Feng Chi's world would never be totally comprehensible, just as dreams weren't comprehensible. Merely shaking the hand of a Chinese was like touching something not quite real. Once, while strolling through the garden, Feng told Cassidy that two shrieking birds were ghosts. In fact they were two gulls drifting through the fog above the pines. Then Feng called, "Go away, ghosts!" But the gulls merely circled again and then landed on the telephone wire, nodding together. Later Feng said that there were no longer ghosts on the mainland. Chinese ghosts had all gone to Taiwan where people still believed, still put out rice, still listened to them whispering. On other occasions, however, Feng would only joke about the ghosts. "These things are of the imagination. All that is in the head."

Cassidy would say one day that Feng Chi's world was one dark shadow laid upon another. Only the symbols were obvious, particularly that pouncing tiger. Thinking of Feng was like trying to remember and not quite being able to remember. All that was clear were the peripheral images: a cluster of white flowers, lacquer, cinnabar, smiles that were not really smiles.

Finally one afternoon Cassidy could not help asking Sagan, "Sir, what are these Triads anyway?"

It was another muggy, tepid day. Gray clouds had formed a sheet across the entire sky. The Taiwan station was nearly deserted. Everyone seemed to have come down with the flu.

"Triads?" Sagan always grew sleepy in these hot afternoons.

"Yes, sir. The Triads."

"Well, they're sort of a fraternal organization, aren't they? A little like the Masons."

"There seems to be an awful lot of of them."

"Yes. There's quite a few."

"And what is it exactly that they do?"

"Oh, mutual aid. That sort of thing."

"Then why all the secrecy?"

"I don't know. I guess it's just part of the game."

"And there's nothing else to it?"

"What do you mean?"

"Well... like opium."

Sagan grew very still, and against the stillness were waterdrops thudding on a soggy towel. Finally he said, "Look, Billy. I'm not going to deny that some of that goes on, but it's—well, you know how the Chinese are."

To Cassidy, this was Sagan's excuse for everything.

In the early fall the events that marked the real beginning of Cassidy's story started to unfold. Within the larger scheme this was also about the time that John Polly's daughter returned from the commune and Lin Piao was rapidly moving to the height of his career. The Cultural Revolution had moved into a dormant stage, but more violence was expected in the spring. Among those involved in the mainland overflight programs there was a new sense of urgency. Bad weather was coming.

By now there were more than four overflights a week from Taiwan, all night flights, all in B-17's fitted with cameras. Cassidy himself was flying once a month. In September the unit had lost their first plane, hit by antiaircraft fire on the south China coast. There were no survivors, and a memorial service was held in the mountains surrounding the airstrip. From this highest peak there was a view of a plain of wild flowers, then rice paddies and finally the ocean. Cassidy did not know how the Chinese mourned their dead, so he stood a few paces behind and said nothing.

There would later be a lot of controversy over the events which led to Cassidy's capture. Why had Cassidy been aboard the flight in the first place? There had been no technical reason why he had to fly. The obvious answer was that his ability to maintain the respect of his unit demanded that he make at least a flight a month. Additionally he would have been in no position to evaluate the potential of his program unless he periodically ran the routes himself. But there was also another reason why he had made that flight, and all the flights before. By that early autumn he had come to love it. He honestly loved every minute of it.

By this time the field had been expanded. There were new sheds at the western end of the airstrip. Barbed wire had been laid along the main road. A full stand of grass had grown up through the mesh of pierced steel that served as a parking ramp. There were also three new pilots.

Whenever Cassidy did not fly he was always in the briefing shed, waiting to hear the drone of returning aircraft. With cold weather he had started wearing black gloves and a black leather jacket. A photograph of him flanked by the Chinese crew showed him in this jacket and a pair of bush green trousers. In the background lay swamp mist and the sun catching long streaks of rust on the iron roof of a supply hut.

The morning of Cassidy's last flight had a feel like the one captured in that photograph. There was mist on the swamp, thicker fog moving in the mountain hollows. Cassidy had risen early and driven out to the field in a jeep that was always having carburetor trouble. He chatted with the ground crew who were loading bales of leaflets into the bomb bays. After an hour he returned to his apartment to rest.

For a while he read a paperback novel, for a little longer he sat by the open window above the canal. Now and then young women would pass along the muddy track. In odd moments Cassidy always thought about girls. Once in Hong Kong Sagan had offered to buy him one of the expensive Wanchai whores, but Cassidy had only smiled and shook his head.

It was dark by the time he reached the airstrip. In the main shed two mechanics were chatting and drinking Pepsi-Cola. This room had remained unchanged since the early days. There were still only steel chairs, card tables and bamboo mats on the bricks. The heater was a fuel drum with a length of galvanized pipe through the roof. Taped to the plaster was a portrait of Mao that no one had bothered to deface.

After an hour the crew began to assemble. As always the briefing was short, more of a pep talk than anything else. Cassidy said that their drops had already produced long-range effects, but this was actually untrue. In the cities the leaflets were a nuisance. In the countryside they were used for toilet paper. In addition to the drop there was also to be a low-level reconnaissance scan of the southern China basin. At the end of the brief, Billy asked if there were any questions. As usual there were none.

Regarding the flight and the immediate aftermath Cassidy would retain only the most fragmented impressions. Departure had been at twenty minutes to midnight. Cassidy sat in the aft fuselage with the cameras. They encountered a brief pocket of turbulence over the South China Sea. Then it was calm and extraordinarily clear. Now and again there were white patches of light on the water like icebergs. Otherwise the sea was black. As always, the strangest sense of peace came over Cassidy once they had risen above twenty thousand feet. He had never seriously considered the possibility that a Chinese MIG could nail them to the spike.

For a while there had been idle chatter among the other members of the crew. Then it seemed that they remembered that their immediate senior was aboard and the chatter died. Cassidy fell into drowsy thought about a certian type of woman's face he had seen in Hong Kong and then again in Taipei. It was not the face of a full Chinese, but the face of a Eurasian girl with almond eyes and high cheekbones. He had only seen that face for a moment in a passing crowd, but for some reason the memory remained. Apart from these thoughts there were glimpses of the sea and finally the coastline. Descending through the night was like descending through a swamp. There was no sensation of speed, only blind drifting toward the Peking area.

During the last three or four minutes Cassidy would remember the voice of his pilot and a few Chinese words spoken so quickly that he could not make them out. He would also remember a vision of a village like a handful of gravel, and distant city lights. On the horizon was a glow like a polar sun, but it may have only been the moonlight on a plain.

It would later occur to Cassidy that the MIG had risen from beneath them, swaying in an odd angle. At first he heard nothing above the drone of the engines. Then there was a sound like pebbles drumming on metal. Next someone was screaming through the microphone. While someone else was speaking rapidly. They were rolling down and port. There were odors of burning rubber. Bits of canvas, aluminum and plexiglass seemed to be breaking away and floating off. Now the screams had turned to soft whimpering, and there was a hollow rumble like a rock dropping through a chute. Finally Cassidy was conscious of rolling, then falling.

In the end he would recall mainly the darkness, waiting, the hand of his pilot, seeping water and the outline of a jagged landscape. There would also be a few impressions of the landing, but these would not return until much later when he was told that the plane had skidded into a rice paddy, which probably kept the fuel from igniting. He had also lost his sense of time.

Over an hour passed between the moment they touched ground and the capture, but to Cassidy it had seemed like only a few minutes. When the first trucks appeared, Cassidy was kneeling with the others on a grassy mound above the paddy. Two members of the crew had been seriously hurt. One of them kept coughing up blood. Cassidy had a deep cut behind the ear, and thought that he may have broken a rib. Later, in the truck, watched by soldiers, he heard what sounded like hoofbeats, but it was only the mudguard knocking against the tire.

At first Cassidy would say that it wasn't all that bad. He and the other crew members were taken to an infirmary that may have been attached to a military base. There was a gate, a wall with barbed spikes, a steel tower against the sky. The infirmary was a long narrow room with a brown linoleum floor. The doctors did not speak, except softly to themselves.

For a while Cassidy was concerned only with immediate sensations. The scent of alcohol was reassuring as was the sound of bottles clinking together on a wooden tray. Toward dawn he was thinking about more consequential details. He supposed that after the plane was searched there could be no pretending their flight had only been a routine weather check that had inadvertently strayed over the mainland. He was also thinking about stories he had heard of how the Communists broke their prisoners. Supposedly methods of torture were used in combination with one another: pain, hunger, sleeplessness, sensory deprivation, possibly ultrasonics.

In the beginning he was moved from room to room. Most of these rooms were small concrete boxes. Some were very hot, some terribly cold. On the first day they had taken his clothing and his shoes. Now all he had was a thin cotton uniform, like pajamas. Food consisted of watery gruel that tasted faintly sour. He was fed a cup of this twice a day. Occasionally there were cockroaches at the bottom of the cup. He imagined that the insects were placed there intentionally, because he had heard that normally the Chinese were fairly clean people.

There was no day or night. A light bulb, recessed into the ceiling and protected by a wire mesh, burned continually. On what Cassidy believed was the third or fourth day the interrogation began. Cassidy was brought into an oblong room. He sat in a straight-backed, wooden chair that was set in the center of the room under a bright lamp. The lamp was arranged so that the corners of the room were lost in blackness. The interrogator was a small intense man with a scar running across his left temple. He spoke a concise, grammatically perfect English, although some of his phrasing was a little out of date.

From the start Cassidy had no intention of trying to remain completely silent during these interrogations. Silence, he knew, was impossible. There had to be dialogue, and at the end of it they had to think that he had told them all he knew. Alone in his cell, and in accordance with what he had been trained to do in Langley, he prepared his line of defense. As his main strategy he decided that he would answer certain questions truthfully in an effort to steer his interrogator away from the really vital areas. Details of the propaganda unit he believed were ac-

213

ceptable smoke, because the Communists already knew most of it anyway. He also decided that he could safely give them certain information about the reconnaissance flights, because this too was stuff they already had. As a last resort he told himself that he could talk about his early training and the personnel on the Asian Desk. He could give them Norman Pyle, because Pyle was untouchable, and if they still weren't satisfied he knew the names of a few blown agents in Taipei.

After what must have been several hours of concentrated effort, Cassidy began to think of his strategy as a series of interlocking truths and half-truths. The truth would peel off in very thin layers, and then only after days of resistance. He imagined how he might stick to one story for a week before seeming to break down in confession. Then he would start the sequence all over again with a new set of lies. With any luck he believed he could fight them for months, while always burying deeper and deeper every thought of Jay Sagan, Feng Chi and the south Asian networks.

For a while Cassidy believed that his strategy was successful. The routine was unvarying. Two guards, one with an automatic weapon, the other with a piece of rubber hose, would drag him from his cell to the oblong room. There he would face his interrogator. Usually there were others in the room, behind him in the darkness. He never saw their faces. He heard them whispering. The questioning would begin in a businesslike manner, the interrogator's voice dispassionate. Sometimes he would pace back and forth in front of Cassidy's chair. Sometimes he would lean against the wall with his arms folded across his chest. Interspersed between the direct questions was a lot of political rhetoric. He kept asking if Cassidy understood that he was only a pawn of the imperialist masters. Cassidy said he had never looked at it that way.

After several bouts of questioning Cassidy threw his interrogator the first bone. He admitted that his mission had been to drop politically hostile leaflets with the express purpose of inciting factional strife between Red Guards and workers. After this admission the questioning stopped for a moment, and the interrogator took a minute to confer with the other men in the oblong room. Cassidy heard them talking softly among themselves. Then the interrogator returned, and Cassidy was asked if he really believed that a few scraps of paper dropped from an airplane could influence the astute mind of the Chinese Communist. In reply Cassidy made a crack about the wall posters, and he was taken back to his cell. So it went hour after hour, and through it all there was a part of Cassidy's mind which kept repeating that there was no one named Sagan, no one named Feng, over and over again.

In the next stage of questioning Cassidy was asked specifically about the organizational structure of the propaganda unit. Who drafted the leaflets? What made them decide to drop a particular leaflet on a particular city? How did they presume to know about the factional strife of the Cultural Revolution? How would Cassidy like it if he were made to swallow every single leaflet that was found on his plane?

It was also during this stage that the torture began. First there were beatings, presumably as punishment for refusing to answer a question or denying what was obviously a lie. Again the sequence was unvarying. An orderly, almost sedative line of questioning would suddenly stop. The interrogator would simply walk away. Two guards would approach with rubber hoses. Then as if nothing had happened the questioning would calmly start again. Later, however, there were beatings in his cell. Here the punishment was always less severe. It was as if the guards did not really have their hearts in their work, and only when the interrogator was present did they feel compelled to make any real show of brutality.

Sometimes after a particularly savage hour with electrodes he was treated to small acts of kindness. His wound might be cleaned and dressed. His interrogator might enter his cell and, holding Cassidy's hand, would speak to him as if they were old friends. Cassidy knew that these gestures of kindness were only part of the program to break him, but knowing he was being deceived did not keep him from accepting the gestures, even praying for them.

There were periods when he wept for hours, only stopping when exhausted, then lapsing into a reverie filled with odd memories, snatches of old songs, girls he used to know. There was one recurring vision of a black train, the tracks fading into the horizon, the chugging engine, the trailing whistle.

Finally it occurred to him that the sounds of the train he thought he had heard were in fact recordings played into the room from the ceiling. There were other sounds: scraping metal, air squealing out of balloons, footsteps, teeth gnawing on bone. At times he could not be certain if what he was hearing was real or not. The problem became particularly acute when he started hearing voices: Can you tell me the time please? Can you give me a cigarette? Can you tell me what you're thinking?

One night, or at least he thought it was the night, they gave him an orange. He even devoured the peel, but then started wondering if it hadn't been spiked with something, maybe mescaline. When he shut his eyes he saw himself in the shadow of a windmill. As a child he had had a book about windmills, but had never seen one like this: the blades turning in shadow at the edge of a dark field. A few skeletal trees stood out in silhouette against rain clouds. At the center of the wheel was the face of that Eurasian girl. Her face was also reflected in a patch of stirring tulips, her voice all around. Then there was nothing to do but wait for the wind that chills the dead land.

On another night the dominant image was of himself as a mouse, cornered in a filthy room. The questions by now had grown pretty direct. The interrogator wanted to know who was at the head of the Hong Kong Station. Cassidy said that he didn't know. The electrodes went back into his mouth, ears, nose. Finally he must have screamed Jay's name, because he later found himself in his cell with a dish of mashed papaya on the floor.

As intervals between questioning grew shorter Cassidy found that he kept forgetting the subtler aspects of his strategy. Once he have them an obvious lie, and in return was given a slice of watermelon. Then without thinking he gave them Feng Chi. Later he heard more voices, two women. There was something about a girl, an island, a shark and a coconut. While Cassidy listened he developed a spasm in his throat. He could not stop salivating.

Now for hours he would lie on his cot waiting for his heart to miss a beat. Possibly the shock had damaged a valve. Possibly he was hallucinating again. Either way he told himself he couldn't go on much longer. Then the guards came and walked him back to the oblong room.

The first three questions concerned Jay's Cambodian networks, but at the mention of Cambodia all Cassidy could think of was another jungle hollow, helicopters descending on elephants, a solitary python's egg. The question was repeated, but Cassidy simply could not remember. He truly could not remember.

Then there was a moment of silence. Then the interrogator spoke quickly to the guards. Cassidy was thrown to the floor. His arms and legs were spread and pinned. The interrogator laid the toe of his boot on Cassidy's genitals, repeated the question, then gradually increased the pressure. Cassidy assumed that he had about fifteen seconds to scream.

In past moments like this there had often been some vapory image just before pain. Once he had seen a collapsing dinosaur, once a naked woman, once the skyline of a white city. But never had there been a

216

vision as real as the face now starting to form in the center of the light bulb. While other faces around him faded, the walls grew transparent. The interrogator was speaking, but Cassidy could not hear. He could only hear another voice, or the memory of a voice—his father.

Now his father's face had drawn closer, down from the light bulb, lips nearly touching Billy's ear to whisper secrets he had never told another soul. *This is what they did to me.* Even when Cassidy went blind with pain, screaming in the blackness, the image of his father remained.

The interrogator stepped back. His lips were moving, but Cassidy could only make out that phantom voice, merely a whisper, but very clear: *even rats fight back in the end.* And when Cassidy shut his eyes he saw that rat, hunched against the wall with perfect yellow teeth. You could cut the spinal cord and the jaw would still be locked.

Which is how you've got to play it, he told himself. Or heard his father whisper, because all the voices were running together, saying the same thing. *Wait. Wait until he comes closer, draw him very close, then don't stop, never stop, even when you're dead don't stop.*

He began to cry, to beg for another chance, words that he had practiced a thousand times before. And when he felt the pressure ease he started crawling forward. The game he had also practiced to perfection: beaten dog at his master's feet. Except that he did not feel like a dog, not with his jawbone narrowing into a rat's snout, teeth pulling from the gums, sliding down closer.

Past the interrogator's sleeve he could see the shadows of the guards, obviously a little sick of all this degradation. But Cassidy didn't care about the guards, with his head pressed against the interrogator's chest, sobbing, feeling a hand smooth the back of his neck. *Let him hold you. Let him pull you closer.*

And in the end he almost couldn't help smiling. So very close, while the interrogator kept explaining how nobody liked to cause pain.

But Cassidy knew he would like it. Like it enormously. *Is it time? Is it time?*

Yes, it's time.

He struck for the groin, then clawed up for the face. When he felt the fingers trying to push his head away he shook until he had them in his mouth. Then bit down to the bone. And the harder they tried to pull him off, the harder and deeper he burrowed. Until he finally understood that giving pain was just as engrossing as receiving it.

How long Cassidy remained unconscious he would never know. When he woke his entire body was in pain, but as far as he could tell there was no permanent damage. His initial thought upon waking was that he was still locked onto the interrogator, but it was only the mattress of his cot. He was alone in his cell.

For a while he lay very still. He was almost afraid to move. He knew there was something different, but he could not figure out what it was. Then he realized that the cell was dark—darkness and the scent of fresh air. He rose to one elbow and ran his fingers along the wall. Yes, this was a different cell, larger than any of the others, and there was a window above him.

He pulled himself up slowly. A wire screen was set into the stone. A pane of thick glass swung outward on a chain. Beyond lay a nightscape of low gray barracks, a water tower and barren hills. Above the hills hung a quarter-moon. Cassidy clung to that screen for a long time, wetting his lips, feeling the wind.

Through that night he heard nothing but night sounds: guards chatting softly, the throb of a generator, a bird. When he fell asleep he was conscious of the dark. When he woke he turned on his side to see the ice blue sky again. In the morning he was examined by a doctor. Apparently his ribs had been reinjured and there was some internal bruising. But when he was alone again he lay down on his bunk and wondered if the doctor who had attended him was also attending the interrogator for rupture, multiple lacerations and three severed fingers, right hand.

Throughout the next day and into the night Cassidy kept waiting for retribution. He believed that if they had any sense of sportsmanship they would honor him with a bullet behind the ear. More than likely, however, they would make it slow and painful, not that he really cared. Regardless of how terrible the future might be he was certain that he would never regret what he had done. So in a way Cassidy spent these next several hours in an odd state of contentment. He had no expectations, no concept of the future. He supposed that he was glad to be alive, but he also supposed that he was unafraid of dying, truly unafraid.

Such was Cassidy's frame of mind as he entered the mainstream of the John Polly story. Three days came and went. Other than the guards who brought his food he saw no one. His food was far better than what he had been previously fed. Now instead of gray pap there was rice, a few raw vegetables, fruit, occasionally even fish.

In the beginning of this stage he suffered from abdominal pains and there had been traces of blood in his urine. But the doctor had returned with injections, and eventually the pain stopped. Then the most pressing problem was simple boredom. When he felt well enough he began exercising mornings and evenings to keep up his strength. But apart from these exercises he had nothing to pass the time. Through entire afternoons he would just lie on his side and pick at the seam of the mattress. Once or twice he tried to invent some game, but in the end he always just fell into thought. He would think about people and places he had known, fragments of past conversations, the ghosts of tunes from the radio. Eventually the long hours of isolation led him down an unfamiliar path until he almost began wondering if there really was a world beyond this, beyond that brown landscape, the rusting metal, the rice, the tin plates of slug-riddled vegetables. And would it all be different if they had given him a woman, a radio, a few paperback books and a jigsaw puzzle. He did not think so, not anymore.

There remains a fairly lengthy letter describing the first encounter between Billy Cassidy and John Polly, but of course it was Polly who wrote this letter, and he described only his own impressions. As far as the Chinese were concerned Polly's interest in the prisoner was primarily personal. He told Tommy Ling that he wanted to speak with the boy both to satisfy his curiosity and as research for a series of articles he was planning. Undoubtedly Tommy Ling believed that Polly's motives were actually more complex and involved his feelings toward Sagan and Feng Chi. But if this is what Ling suspected, he said nothing. He was the sort of person who felt that close friends were entitled to their secrets.

In requesting permission for Polly to visit the prisoner, Ling noted that because of Polly's past association with Sagan and Feng he might be in a position to verify certain apsects of the prisoner's confession. Also because of Polly's background, Ling pointed out that the prisoner might even be more inclined to speak freely with John Polly than anyone else. In the end, of course, Cassidy would speak freely about Polly, but for very different reasons from what either Ling or anyone else could imagine.

The original concept of the meeting, however, did not begin with Polly. It began with Norman Pyle who believed that if Polly could make contact with Cassidy he might be able to determine precisely what Cassidy had told the Chinese about Jay Sagan's south Asian networks. This proposal was then passed along to Simon Crane's office and formally dubbed Operation Wounded Gull.

219

It was well known within the secret world that there was no small amount of bad blood over Wounded Gull. Jay Sagan may not have known all the details of the operation, particularly the role of John Polly, but he knew that Simon Crane was encroaching on his territory and he resented it. Crane in turn resented having to use Polly to tidy up a mess that Sagan had made, a mess that could have been avoided had Sagan only listened to Crane's recommendations in the first place.

As for Polly he neither knew nor probably would have cared about this interoffice strife. He was now in his eighteenth year in Peking. His daughter had recently come back to him, and he saw his private life as once more complete. Professionally he had published another collection of essays which were currently being praised all over China. Wherever he went they would say: there is a great man and a great Marxist.

The only remaining question regarding this first encounter was Billy Cassidy's actual status with the Chinese and why he was permitted to see Polly. The most probable explanation was the one given to Polly himself by Tommy Ling. According to Ling, Cassidy's fate had actually been uncertain. There were those within the Chinese apparatus who simply wanted to kill him, while others believed that he should be sent another interrogator and the process begun all over again. Finally there had been talk of an interrogation personally directed by Han Chow.

It was during this period of indecision that Ling's proposal to send in Polly was submitted. Perhaps if a second interrogation had been in progress, Ling's proposal would have been denied and this story would have had a very different ending. But as it happened the suggestion came at a time when most of those concerned had simply given up on Cassidy, and no one thought there was much to lose by giving John Polly a try.

The encounter took place in the late morning. Ironically the prison complex where Cassidy was being held was the same complex where Kim Lee had been briefly held twenty years earlier. Although the prison had been enlarged, the surrounding landscape had remained unchanged. There were still those empty hills, some peaked high against the sky. The light this morning was blanched. There were no glaring reflections. Through willow groves lay the dragon's teeth of white stone. When Polly reached the prison he was met by three guards and the district security officer. As always he was treated with respect.

Cassidy had wakened early, but had stayed unmoving for over an hour, listening to the hum of the generator. Finally he pulled himself up to the window and saw the false dawn receding, then darkness, then light.

He watched until each barb on the fence was distinct against the sky. There were thirteen barbs to every coil of wire. He had counted them once out of boredom. Later, just as he was preparing himself for another stretch of nothing, two guards entered the cell carrying buckets of water, soap, rags and a razor. Cassidy was washed and shaved, and then left alone again, wondering. It crossed his mind that this might be the day he would die, or else be released. He was surprised at how dispassionately he could view these possibilities.

Now for the actual metting. Polly's letter to Crane gave only a sparse, objective description of the boy. He wrote that the prisoner appeared to be in fair physical condition, although he was understandably wary and bitter. Cassidy on the other hand would later say that Polly had been nice enough, but it had been difficult to tell what he really wanted. The boy further remembered that Polly had brought him a package containing several hundred cigarettes, a copy of *Huckleberry Finn* and a tennis ball. When Cassidy asked what the tennis ball was for, Polly shrugged and said that he had thought that Cassidy might amuse himself bouncing it off the walls. Then there was an awkward silence and finally both men laughed. But this occurred much later. The initial moments were cold.

When Polly entered the cell he found Cassidy hunched on the edge of the cot shredding a bit of straw he had pulled from the mattress. His eyes were ringed with red. His lips were cracked. There were perspiration stains all over his clothing. The day before Ling had told Polly that the guards were generally terrified of the boy, and Polly had not been able to imagine how this was true, how prison guards could be afraid of a prisoner. Now, however, Polly understood. He understood the instant the boy raised his eyes and looked at him.

"Hello. My name is John Polly."

The boy did not respond. His face might have been dirty wax, eyes glass, staring up from the bottom of a pool.

"I'm wondering if you've heard of me?"

"Yeah. I've heard of you. What do you want?"

"Talk?"

"About what?"

"About what happened. About your alternatives."

The boy had ripped another straw from the mattress and started sucking on it.

"Look, there's a chance I can help you," Polly said.

"Help me do what?"

"Get out of here."

Then Cassidy smiled, but it was a horrible smile, a smile that had lost all direction. "Oh I get it. They couldn't close the deal with hard sell, so now they send you with flowers."

"I understand how you must feel, but I honestly want to help."

"Go fuck yourself."

"I suppose you realize that if you don't cooperate they'll probably execute you."

"I've been through worse."

"Yes. I suppose you have, but I wonder if you realize that your death would be entirely meaningless now."

"What are you talking about?"

"Simply that the information you're withholding is of no consequence to anyone, not even Jay Sagan."

There was a pause, the boy watching him carefully. Then, "How the hell would you know?"

And Polly smiling faintly, "I know, Billy. Believe me I know."

After this first encounter the game became far more complex. Given that the cell was undoubtedly wired for sound Polly knew there was a very thin line between what could be said and what could not be said, between encouraging the boy to speak freely, and keeping him from giving away too much. The problem was further complicated by Cassidy's own sense of caution, and the fact that the Chinese expected Polly to make progress and would terminate the discussions if he did not. In order to help Polly thread his way through the morass Simon Crane drew up a set of general guidelines regarding what information was expendable and what was sacrosanct. This memo was then coded and telexed to Roger Hall, who passed it along to Polly, who was in turn up half the night trying to memorize it.

Still another complication arose after Polly's second meeting. It seemed that Crane and others in Washington now decided that it might be possible to turn the entire affair to their advantage by using Polly and Cassidy as a route to feed selectively the Chinese false information. Of course Cassidy would remain unwitting so that it was once more Polly's sole responsibility to steer the conversation into the proper channels.

By the third meeting, and with the rules of the game fairly well established, Polly got down to business. He began by leading Cassidy into those areas which would most intrigue the Chinese who were obviously listening. This was done in accordance with Crane's theory that if you gave them candy up front they would be less inclined to inspect what came later. Next Polly tried to determine precisely what Cassidy had said under torture, and here the road became rougher. There was much that the boy truly could not recall, and much that he was ashamed to admit.

"You told them that you knew Jay Sagan," Polly asked at one point.

"So?"

"Well, I wonder if we might talk about him?"

"What's to talk about?"

"I suppose he never mentioned me?"

"Why should he?"

"Oh I don't know, except that I used to be a friend."

The boy smirked. "You?"

"That's right. He and I worked out of what was then the Shanghai station. Our senior officer was a fellow named Simon Crane, although Jay didn't have much to do with Crane. He spent most of his time with an opium trader named Feng Chi. And I understand that he still spends a lot of time with Feng."

Once again Cassidy was tearing at the mattress, shredding bits of straw.

"How about it, Billy? Does he? Does Jay sill spend a lot of time with Feng?"

The boy shrugged. "I wouldn't know."

"You sure about that, Billy?"

"Yeah. I'm sure."

"But I was under the impression that you already admitted knowing Feng."

"I didn't say I knew him. I said I met him. There's a difference."

"Yes. I suppose there is. What else did you admit?"

"I don't remember."

"Did you tell them that Feng and Jay have an arrangement?"

"I don't know what you're talking about."

"I'm talking about the south Asian networks."

Cassidy tore out another clump of straw. "Look, I don't know anything about them. Feng has some contacts, family ties. Sometimes he gets them to pass on a little stuff to Sagan."

"Are those mainland ties?"

"Maybe."

"Have you ever seen the product?"

"Of course not. It's all high security. It's routed directly to Langley."

223

"What's the route? Is it processed locally, or sent raw?"

"How should I know?"

"When did you actually meet Feng?"

"I don't know. About eight months ago."

"What did you talk about?"

"Nothing. He knew my old man."

"Your father?"

"Yeah. Feng knew my father."

"So your father is in the game."

"Used to be. He's dead."

"I'm sorry."

"Yeah. I bet you are."

"What do you mean by that, Billy?"

"I mean you killed him. You and the rest of these fucking animals. You killed him just like you're killing me."

There had been moments like this before, moments when the heat inside the cell left Polly drained, limp, staring into one drab corner.

Until he finally said softly, "Did you know that Feng killed my wife?"

"Huh?"

"I said that Feng Chi killed my wife."

A spell of silence fell over them.

At the end of this session there was another development which substantially changed Polly's operating basis. From the start of these interviews, Polly had also been meeting with the district security officer, two representatives from the General Administration of Intelligence and an auditor attached to Han Chow's Central Ministry. Polly's discussions with these people were initially brief and informal. They asked for his impressions of the prisoner and his feelings as to whether the boy was telling the truth. They particularly valued Polly's opinions because of his supposed intimate knowledge of the western spy mentality.

Yet after Polly's second session with the prisoner he began to realize that these Chinese intelligence specialists were actually depending upon him to continue the interrogation for them. He was continually given questions to put before the boy, and the answers were later evaluated against Polly's knowledge of the subject. All in all, however, there was a relaxed, convivial feel to these meetings.

By the fifth session with Cassidy, the Chinese had decided that Polly could be wholly trusted. Now when he would enter the conference room he was shown a transcript of the original interrogation and even copies of the subsequent analysis. Then followed a series of questions, which Polly answered with, "Yes, this is possibly correct," or "No, to the best of my knowledge." But through it all he was also very conscious of the fact that operationally he had succeeded beyond anyone's expectations.

There was at this juncture a second theme involving Cassidy's story, a theme which would directly lead to the conclusion of his stay in Peking. By all accounts the first mention of this theme occurred during a conversation between Polly and Roger Hall. This conversation, like others before it, was held along a thirty-mile stretch of highway between the prison complex and the outskirts of the city. Technically Hall was not permitted into these hills, but given the urgency of the situation he believed the risk was well worth taking.

It was still the early morning. There was light only along the horizon. When Polly reached the rendezvous he found Hall sitting on the hood of a black sedan. All around lay tangled forest, fog among the pointed rocks. There were birds calling from the isolated clumps of bamboo.

Hall began by saying, "Simon is extremely pleased, John. In fact they're all extremely pleased."

Polly was watching a crow move through the cypress leaves. He said, "So what happens now?"

"Telex says pull out. One more session to wrap up the loose ends, then pull out."

"And Cassidy?"

"Well, we're going to try to get him out, aren't we?"

"How?"

"I really don't know the details, but I imagine that Simon has something up his sleeve."

Polly said, "I want to get him out now."

"What do you mean?"

"I mean I want to try and get him released right away."

"But, John—"

"You people have no idea what it's like for him in there. He may not make it."

"Of course he'll make it. They're not going to shoot him now."

"I wouldn't be too sure about that. I'd like you to contact Simon. Tell him that I want the authorization to bargain with them."

"What sort of bargain, John?"

225

"I'd like to offer them a limited confession from Cassidy in return for releasing him into my custody."

"John, this is very extreme..."

"We're talking about the boy's life, Roger. You say Simon is working on a deal. I say it could take months, even years. You have any idea what it's like in there?"

Hall was very still, gazing out to the willow mounds and an isolated clump of pines. "You realize that this is going to raise all the old questions, don't you?"

"What old questions?"

"Whether or not you really are a spy. I mean let's face it, John, the Chinese have got to wonder about your motives on this one."

"Maybe, but it's a chance we've got to take."

"And there's the boy to think about."

"What do you mean?"

"Well, what happened to that chap he attacked? Is he dead?"

"He's all right."

"But he lost a hand, didn't he?"

"Just three fingers."

"And Cassidy bit them off?"

"There were mitigating circumstances. Like six weeks with the electrodes."

"But even so he attacked and mutilated one of their own, and now you think they're going to make a deal? He nearly kills a man, and now you think they're going to do him a favor? Not to mention the fact that he'll be living in your home, an extremely unstable individual. And there's Maya."

But again Polly said only, "Let me just give it a try, Roger. Let me just try."

That afternoon Polly began the long and complex process of securing Cassidy's release. Initially he discussed the question with Tommy Ling, who, like Hall, was pessimistic. Next he took the matter to the General Administration. There he was listened to, but no one would comment on his chances of success. Finally he met with officials from the district security center. This meeting was held in the prison annex less than two hundred yards from Cassidy's cell. Polly was questioned in detail, but the general tone of discussion remained cordial. There seemed to be particular interest in Polly's motives. In response Polly explained that he too had once been an American spy, dedicated to the destruction of the People's Republic. Now he had the opportunity to pass along what he had learned to another in the same position. He said that the experience would be invaluable to him both as a propagandist and a Communist. There was no clear indication at first as to how his argument was received, but later he said that Roger Hall may have been correct. There was the ghost of an old suspicion in that room, and as he spoke he kept glancing from face to face but all he saw were eyes like glass marbles.

Then toward the end of the week there were subtle signs that possibly his proposal would be accepted. First came a list of questions from the Central Security Bureau regarding particulars of Cassidy's proposed confession. Would the prisoner be willing to submit to newspaper interviews, the bureau wanted to know? Polly assured them that he would. Would the prisoner sign statements categorically condemning United States espionage practices? Polly said that this point was negotiable depending upon the wording of the statements. Finally, after several conversations with Ling, Polly succeeded in obtaining official support from his own ministry, and a letter in Ling's own hand stating that the propaganda potential of Cassidy was nothing short of extraordinary.

Concurrently Polly continued to meet with Roger Hall who was in turn exchanging cables with Crane. It seemed that Crane's primary concern was also ideological, centering on his concern that Cassidy would compromise the reputation of Langley and the stature of the Asian Desk. To assuage these fears Polly promised that he would personally review all public statements, and if necessary rewrite them to insure that the general drift of Cassidy's confession emphasized not the condemnation of the United States intelligence community, but the need for better understanding between Washington and Peking. Two days later Crane cabled back that the deal was now acceptable, which left only Cassidy.

A full week had passed since Polly had last visited with the boy, a full week and Cassidy again saw himself as living on the dark side of the moon. He suffered from intermittent cramps, vomiting and dreams in which he saw himself stabbing people with a rusty kitchen knife. He would also later admit that murder was continually on his mind: the guards, the doctor who had treated him, occasionally he had even thought about killing Polly.

At this stage of his imprisonment he was seeing no one. They had moved him to still another cell, similar to the first, but at the bottom of the steel door was a sliding panel. Now washcloths, water, plates of rice and shredded vegetables all slipped through without human contact. This cell also had no view. The window faced a sandstone wall. Light filtered in, but he could not see the sun. So once more there was a suggestion of timelessness or stuck time.

But if loneliness was complete, there were also possibilities he had never glimpsed before. On the second day he had managed to pry loose an iron slat from the cot. He expected to have a nicely ground edge in a week. But even more important was the mental edge. He loved the concept of himself slowly mutating in a nine-foot room, the aberrant specimen with no instinct for self-preservation except to prolong the killing time.

But there were other moments when he could not help thinking about a simpler freedom, say on the San Diego beachfront. Local girls would be slouched in the doorway of a penny arcade. Surfboards up against a darkening sky. He would toss a Coke bottle off the jetty, then tread back across the sand. There would be the girls watching from a distance, waiting to hear him speak. But all he would have to tell them was, "I've just been to China."

Such were Cassidy's thoughts the morning that Polly finally returned to the cell. He was again trying to shape that metal slat to a point, and when he heard the approaching footsteps he had to slide it quickly beneath the mattress. Then he was just lying there.

Polly entered without speaking, and sat on the varnished chair. His hands were folded in his lap. He may have sensed that something was wrong with this room, like an odor that he could not identify, but still said nothing. The boy watched him with heavy-lidded eyes.

Finally, "How are you, Billy?"

"Great." But Cassidy was smirking. His secrets may have been splattered all over the walls.

"They tell me that you've been very quiet."

"Yeah." Although inside his head it was always loud as hell.

"Are you still in pain?"

"No."

"Well, that's good."

Then a whole taut minute passed while Polly just kept looking at his hands, and Cassidy continued to stare.

Finally Polly said, "Listen to me, Billy. I believe I can get you out of

228

here. It's not firm yet, but I think there's a good chance that I can get you released into my custody."

"What's the catch?"

"You'll have to make a few statements. Public statements."

"Forget it."

"Look, this isn't what you think. No one is going to ask you to compromise anything. All they want is an admission of guilt, and an acknowledgment of Chinese sovereignty."

"Tell them to go suck on a doorknob."

"They'll also release your crew."

Cassidy started to speak, but then stopped. For a moment he did not even breathe. "My crew?"

"That's right. If you're willing to cooperate the Chinese have agreed to release your crew."

"Release them where?"

"Hong Kong."

"How do I know this is real?"

"I imagine they can furnish you with any reasonable proof."

"And all I've got to do is sign a statement."

"Essentially, yes."

"What do you mean essentially?"

"They may ask you to make a verbal statement for public broadcast."

"What about when I'm out? Where do I go?"

"You'll stay with me."

"With you?"

"I have a fairly large place. I think you'll be comfortable there."

"And then what? What am I supposed to do?"

"Whatever you like so long as you don't violate the terms of your custody."

Cassidy started tapping his fingers on the mattress. It went on for a long time. Finally he said, "So who else is going to be there? Your wife?"

"My wife is dead. As I told you. But I have a daughter."

"Yeah? How old is she?"

"Sixteen."

Again Cassidy began tapping his fingers on the mattress, staring at Polly's shoes. "Tell me something. Why are you doing this? I mean, what's in it for you?"

Polly did not answer.

229

Later, Cassidy would recall this conversation and comment only that he had underestimated John Polly, underestimated him pretty badly.

Cassidy was released from prison three days later on a clear morning after a night of southern winds. The evening before his release he had signed three prepared statements admitting involvement in a covert political offensive. There had also been a kind of manifesto endorsing the recognition of Peking. Throughout the signing of these documents Cassidy hardly spoke, except once when he refused to have his photograph taken. In the end, however, Polly took him aside and convinced him that the photograph was only for local distribution. This, of course was a lie, and a copy of that photograph still remains within the Langley record. It shows a lean, very pale Cassidy in a pair of baggy trousers and a white, short-sleeved shirt. In the background stand three Chinese. They might have been carved out of wood. To the left of Cassidy stands John Polly with the merest half-smile on his lips. His hair is quite long and streaked with gray. He is looking directly into the camera.

Regarding the actual release and the first few hours with Polly, Cassidy would say that his feelings had been ambivalent. He had been led to the prison gates where a driver waited with a gray sedan. The countryside was greener than he had imagined, with miles of hanging willows, bamboo in the valleys, silvery thatch where the morning light struck the peaks. Cassidy watched for a while, then lay back and shut his eyes.

When he opened his eyes again they were passing through a pine grove to the ocher brick and terra-cotta of Polly's home. There was a sense of something in this house that Cassidy could not account for. The door stood ajar. The light fell in defined shafts, except where the curtains had been drawn. Rooms were filled with underwater shades: a vase in green tones, three jade fish, another darker vase with fresh magnolias, an unframed canvas of the moon above a swamp.

They drank tea in the kitchen over strained conversation. Between their silences was the deeper silence of the house. Apparently the daughter had already left for the day. There was also a woman who cooked and cleaned, but she was not due in until later. With the rising sun the light converged on the carpet to suggest an intangible cocoon, while details of other rooms were still lost in the shadows.

After tea Cassidy was shown his room. It may have once been used for storage. There were still books stacked against the wall, wooden crates filled with paper. The bed was narrow, but soft, a European bed. Above

230

the bed hung a print, possibly torn from a magazine: green valleys descending out of Asia, powdered with reddish dust.

When Polly left for the ministry, Cassidy went into his room and lay down on his bed. An hour passed, and still he could not sleep. So he rose and started prowling through the house, picking up objects, examining them, then putting them gently back. There were two ivory nightingales on the mantel, a bronze dagger and three wooden Buddhas: one solemn, two laughing. Other rooms were fixed in bluish tones, with carpets boardered by blue lilies.

Finally there was one object which seemed to stand apart from all the others: a tiny gold dragon with extraordinary pearl eyes. For over a minute Cassidy could not seem to bring himself to touch the thing. But then he did, and felt each scale along the spine, and claws sharp enough to hurt. He might have spent all afternoon with that dragon. There was an old wing chair by the window, and he could have sat there with the dragon on the arm. But across the room on a lacquered chest stood two photographs in sandalwood frames. The first was of a woman and a child asleep, the second of a girl. After several seconds he moved closer and picked up the photograph of the girl. Then held it to the light and saw: *that face.*

Cassidy never made much of his first encounter with John Polly's daughter. He never mentioned that afternoon with her photograph, nor his subsequent thoughts. He told Simon Crane only that he had believed she was a pretty girl with a certain kind of face he had noticed on other Eurasian girls. He also mentioned that initially she had been shy, while he must have appeared indifferent. He said that they had first met over tea with her father, but this was a lie.

In fact he saw her first from the veranda. She had emerged from the shadows of the pines along the road below the gates. It was late afternoon, and the sky was changing from blue to gray. She wore a gray blouse and carried a canvas bag. Once she stopped to rest, and he liked the way she brushed her hair from her eyes. Then she stopped again to examine something in the dust. He could not see what it was, but he saw it glinting in the light.

Closer now, he heard her unlatch the garden gate, then saw another glimpse of her blouse through the foliage. When she passed behind the bamboo he could only see her trailing shadow. Then she emerged again, facing him on the path.

"Hello." Her voice was soft. She may have been slightly breathless.
"Oh hello." He also felt a little breathless.
"You are Mr. Cassidy?"
"Yeah." He couldn't stop looking at her face, into her eyes.
"I'm Mr. Polly's daughter. I'm very pleased to meet you."
"Thank you."
"My father told me that you were coming to stay with us for a while."
"Yeah. I guess I'll be here for a while."
"Is my father home?"
"Your father? No. No, he's not home."
"Well, I have to go now."
"Sure."
"It was nice meeting you."
"Yeah. It was nice meeting you too." After six fucking weeks in a concrete box.

In the days that followed Cassidy only saw the girl in passing, at meals, in the evenings when she had finished studying. Their conversations were usually uneventful. She would ask innocuous questions about America, particularly about the youth. She wanted to know what kind of clothing they wore, what kind of music they listened to. Mostly he did not know what to tell her, so he talked about the Beatles.

On other days their discussions were wholly political. She claimed that there was a certain sympathy among her schoolmates for the American students who were protesting the war in Vietnam. She wanted to know what sort of people these students were. She said that of course they were probably idealists, but did they understand the deeper ramifications of the revolutionary manifesto? Again Cassidy did not know how to answer, and so again he talked about the Beatles, the Rolling Stones and three weeks he had once spent in San Francisco.

Eventually their conversations also covered Chinese politics, not that Cassidy was interested. But he loved to hear her talk, loved the way she used her hands to emphasize certain words, the way she would wet her lips and gaze up at the ceiling. On the whole he supposed that her beliefs were largely a reflection of her father's beliefs. She was a great admirer of Mao and Chou En-lai, but thought less of Lin Piao and Han Chow.

Sometimes he heard only her voice, not her words. He would slouch in one of the rattan chairs on the veranda while she explained that unity within the ruling circle was only an illusion. But Maya means illusion,

232

he would tell her. Then she would smile and forget what she was saying. This was also the time of late summer storms, and she loved the thunder, the wet leaves in the wind. Even through her shapeless clothing he could sense that she had a fine body, and late at night he often found himself imagining her naked on the bed beside him.

Once, on a Sunday, she and Polly took him to a park. Here there were lines of willows by a lake, tall reeds at the water's edge. For a while he talked with Polly about China in transition. Then later Polly strolled off and left Cassidy alone with the girl. They were both stretched out on the reeds: she on her back to watch the light among the branches, he looking at her breasts, her eyelashes, her hair spread out around her.

All afternoon he had wanted to ask her about how young people fell in love in China. But all he said now was, "Do you know many boys your age?"

"Oh yes, there are many boys that I know."

"Anyone special?"

"Well, there's Lao Chen."

"Who's he?"

"He's one of the brightest students. He's studying electronics, but he's also a strong political leader within the university."

"And you're good friends with him?"

"Everyone likes him."

"Do you like him?"

"Naturally."

"I mean do you like him a lot?"

She smiled. "Oh I see what you are asking. No, it's not like that. Lao Chen and I are not—you know."

"But is there someone else that you're like that with?"

"No."

"No one at all?"

She turned to face him. "I think this is one of the differences between the United States and China. Here we don't have very much time for those kinds of things. Most people marry when they are much older."

"Why?"

"There are several reasons."

"Name one."

"Well, it's important to become established in a good position first."

"But what if you meet someone and you can't stand to be apart from him? What happens then?"

"This never happens."

Then he almost reached out and touched her, almost took her hand. He wanted to very badly, but instead he simply said, "I bet it happens. I bet it happens all the time."

Finally it seemed to Cassidy that China had become a dream that he did not want to end. Not that this was really China, not this house and garden all enclosed by a nine-foot wall. China was rivers of factory workers in the morning streets. China was no soap and rationed meat, all-night discussions, dissecting political theories. It was that concrete cell. But here in Polly's house, always fixed in stillness and cool light, it was enough to forget.

Cassidy was continually asking himself what could be said about Polly. The man was like someone you might meet on a train, or the only other guest in some tropical hotel. He was the kind of person you knew you would remember for a long time, but not for any reason you could name.

Often in the late evenings Cassidy and Polly would sit in the kitchen and talk, usually politics, more often the past. Of his early days in Shanghai Polly described himself as having been one more civil servant with cropped hair and a closetful of shirts in bone white Egyptian cotton. He said that he smoked Camel cigarettes and worried that his clothing might mildew in the monsoons. Regarding Jay Sagan, he said that the man had been concerned about advancement and not offending clients, particualrly Feng Chi. And as for Feng, much of what Polly said later turned up in Cassidy's own testimony to Simon Crane. It was Polly, for example, who first called Feng the last of his kind, the last of the old opium tigers.

On another night Polly discussed what he called the reality of rapprochement that was building up. He said that in all actuality it was only a matter of time before the political climate was right for an East-West reconciliation. Naturally, he said, there were elements on both sides that would oppose such a reconciliation: Lin Piao and Han Chow in the East, Jay Sagan and Feng Chi in the West. But there would come a point when even the opposition must realize that their position was untenable, or else be swept away by history.

For his own part Cassidy never had much to say in reply. Mostly he was simply content to listen. These were the final days of summer, the leaves had already begun to turn. He had been told that in the winter this city became devastated, with every street frozen in a gray chill. But he did not think he would see the winter in Peking.

234

* * *

Neither Norman Pyle nor Jay Sagan was instrumental in the maneuvering which eventually led to Cassidy's homecoming. It was not that they lacked the motivation. On the contrary, both men continually called for the boy's release. It was simply that their positioning was all wrong. They had neither the contacts nor the orientation for dialogue with the mainland, not after all these years of conflict.

The experience Crane gained while establishing an open channel to Peking would later prove invaluable in setting up those celebrated talks between Henry Kissinger and Chou En-lai. The Cassidy affair gave Crane his first real opportunity to test his intermediary sources and certain theories he had about how one should conduct oneself when dealing with the Chinese.

In all, these negotiations took about seven weeks. For Cassidy this was a period of strange ambivalence; hope mixing with hopelessness, enthusiasm and regret. One conversation of note took place. It occurred during the second week of negotiations, the morning after Polly had been given a rapid brief by Roger Hall. It was still early, but Cassidy had been up for hours, leafing through one of the history volumes by Will Durant. Also on the window box was a slim volume on the mystical process within the Oriental mind, and a Classic Club edition on the symbolism of the dragon. When Polly entered the room, Cassidy looked up from his reading. Through the window lay a view of Peking in low mist.

Polly began by saying, "Apparently this deal is going through after all."

Cassidy asked, "How soon?"

"Six weeks, maybe less."

"How is it going to work? Me for one of their people?"

"No. You for information. Probably something on the Russians. Maybe photographs of the border installations."

"Big stuff, huh?"

Polly did not smile. "You should realize that it's not going to be the same for you once you're back. It may be better or may be worse, but once you leave the mainland you're going to see that it's not the same as it was before."

Cassidy nodded. "I know."

"So what are you going to tell Jay?"

Cassidy shook his head. "I don't know."

"Maybe you should tell him that the war is over. Know what I mean?"

235

"Yeah. I know what you mean."

"Because pretty soon Jay is going to find himself in an awkward situation. Next year, maybe the year after—it won't be long now. First there will be rumors, people talking about the possibilities of dialogue with Peking. Next there will be some real feelers. Then it's going to happen. They're going to sit down and talk."

The first dawn birds were calling from the trees. Maya was running water in the upstairs basin.

Polly said softly, "Jay is never going to be able to adjust. You know that, don't you, Billy?"

"Yeah. I guess I do."

"He's too far committed. He's staked his entire life on a war against these people, and that war is over now. Does he still sleep with every woman he can find?"

Cassidy smiled. "Yeah. I guess he does."

"Too bad. I always used to think that if he could meet the right woman—then again maybe not."

In the last days Cassidy found that his life had grown very slow, very detached from things around him. Usually in the afternoons he would read for two or three hours, then sleep or else wander through the garden. These were the transitory days between late summer and early fall. All over the far end of the garden were small white flowers like premature moonlight. Cassidy's favorite place was by the rising bank on the reflection pool. He also liked to wander some distance from the house, especially in the gathering darkness. Then he would return and wait in that frayed wicker chair until John Polly's daughter returned from school.

He was thinking more and more about her now. Often he would wonder what it would be like to marry her and live here for another four or five years—reading in the afternoons, watching her grow up. Of course these thoughts had their limits. The most obvious one being the garden wall where beyond lay an entire nation of blobs. But even so he could not help wondering.

Then with the autumn winds came storms, sometimes draining the landscape of color, sometimes turning the sky deep red. Now he was always waking suddenly in the night and wondering what had happened to his former self, and why he only hated aspects of China instead of the whole fucking place.

236

Finally word came to Polly that Cassidy would definitely be leaving the mainland. Apparently certain last minute details still had to be arranged, but it was imminent now—the boy would be going. That evening when Polly returned from the ministry he asked Cassidy to step out on the veranda. When the boy was told the news he nodded and asked only: "Does Maya know?"

He waited until the afternoon of the following day to say goodbye. For hours he had been thinking about what he would say to her, what she might say to him. Her father would be at the ministry until fairly late, which would mean that they would be alone for hours. Then anything could happen, and while he waited he kept imagining how it might be: she leading him up the stairs by the hand.

As always he saw her first far in the distance, tramping along the ocher road, against a rising mist that would soon envelop the landscape. The sky was also gray, but deepening to mauve in the south. Maya was moving slowly. Once she stopped to shift her satchel of books from one shoulder to another. Then she stopped again to adjust her sandal. It seemed that she had broken a strap.

When she saw him standing on the terrace she did not wave or call out as she usually did. There was simply a hesitating moment when their eyes met. Then she continued walking. Today she was dressed in gray-green trousers, a blouse and thin cotton jacket. The top button of her blouse was undone, and Cassidy was watching her slender throat. When she reached the terrace she let her satchel slip off her shoulder and sat down in the wicker chair next to his. She must have sensed that something was wrong, and was waiting for him to speak first.

So he told her, "Maya, I'm going to have to leave soon."

She turned away. "When?" barely above a whisper.

"Tomorrow morning, early."

"Are you coming back?"

"No."

"Where are you going?"

"I don't know. Maybe Hong Kong, maybe Taiwan. Then I'll probably be sent home."

"To America?"

"Yeah."

"How come they're letting you leave?"

"Well, it's kind of complex."

"Are you glad?"

237

"Sure," but his voice was cold and dry.

"What's the first thing you're going to do when you get home?"

"I don't know. Maybe turn on the tube."

"The what?"

"The television set."

"Oh."

Then they sat for a while in silence. Her head was still turned away. She was looking out across the tops of the cypress trees. Finally he realized that nothing else would happen. This was it. After all these weeks this was what their farewell would amount to: silence in the late afternoon.

For the remainder of the evening Cassidy was quiet. During dinner he kept looking at her, but she did not return his glance. Except once in passing, but he could not sense a deeper feeling behind her eyes. After dinner Polly opened a bottle of pale yellow wine and asked Cassidy out on the terrace to drink it. They sat in the same two chairs that Cassidy and Maya had sat in earlier. At some point in the halting conversation Polly told Cassidy that Maya would probably miss him. Cassidy replied, "Yeah. I'm going to miss her too."

Then Cassidy rose from his chair and went into his room. He did not turn on the light. He just lay in the darkness thinking that Jay had been right. This country was for shit.

He supposed he slept, but badly, never really losing consciousness of the insects in the garden, the settling floorboards. When he shut his eyes he tried to envision her face, but saw nothing. Until in a dream he heard the door open slowly, saw her standing above him. Except that it wasn't a dream.

"Maya?"

She stepped closer and put a finger to her lips. "We have to be quiet."

"But, Maya—"

"I knew you wouldn't mind if I came. You don't mind, do you?"

"No, but—"

"Because I want to lie next to you, just for a little while."

Neither of them smiled nor spoke. She lifted her nightgown in a simple gesture and let it fall away. At first she seemed ashamed and lowered her eyes, her arms across her breasts. Then he told her that everything would be all right. For a while she lay very still in his arms, breathing deeply, and once with her eyes still shut she smiled, but said nothing. Her fingers curled tighter around his wrist. When he finally fell asleep he dreamed about a flawless red sun rising out of the sea. He wanted to stop it, but couldn't. When he wakened the first light was breaking. She stayed until the last possible moment, then left as silently as she had come.

In the morning there were undertones of feelings that no one wanted to discuss. So they talked about minor details, while Polly helped pack a few things into an old suitcase. When the ministry detachment arrived to take Cassidy to the airport Polly walked down as far as the gates to say goodbye.

"Well, I guess this is it," Cassidy breathed, but could not quite manage a smile.

"Yes," Polly said quietly. "This is it."

"What can I say? Thanks?"

"You don't have to say anything."

"Yeah. Well, thanks anyway."

Polly took a small object out of his jacket. It was wrapped in tissue paper. "I thought you might like to keep this," he said.

"For me?"

"Yes. I thought you might want it."

Cassidy tore away the paper. It was that tiny gold dragon. "I can't take this."

"Please. I want you to have it."

"But it's got to be worth—"

"Please."

Then Cassidy put the dragon in his pocket where the claws proceeded to rip out the worn lining of his coat.

As for his return to the West, Cassidy would only remember a stream of air-conditioned rooms, and a pervasive sense of timelessness. People were mostly conciliatory, concerned about his happiness and physical comfort. The first three days were spent in isolation, because they wanted to make certain that he wouldn't come unglued. Next came the debriefing, which was amiable enough. Sessions were regularly spaced between long walks under the palms. The food was also very good.

In the case summary of the entire affair Cassidy was commended for holding up extremely well under what they called severe interrogatory stress. He was further said to have only marginally compromised the south Asian networks, while there was no tactical compromise of the Taiwan station. Of course those who drafted these final comments knew nothing of John Polly's role in the affair and Operation Wounded Gull.

Nevertheless Cassidy still came out of it all looking very good. There was that commendation eventually hung on the living room wall of his mother's place, and a substantial cash bonus in addition to his regular accumulated salary.

Immediately after debriefing Cassidy was given an extensive battery of psychological tests with questions like: Do your muscles occasionally twitch even though you are not physically tired? And, does the world sometimes seem unreal to you, even if pleasantly so? Rather than answer these questions truthfully, Cassidy tried to answer them like a sensible young intelligence officer. In the end they were all impressed with what they termed his psychological resiliency, although they had no idea that every night he went to sleep thinking about John Polly's daughter.

Cassidy's reunion with Sagan took place about two weeks after Cassidy's passage from the mainland. He and Sagan met in a restaurant on the outskirts of Taipei where there was a view of the dark countryside on the cusp of a squall. Long gusts of wind were blowing in from the sea. Birds had taken shelter in the estuary. They had finished eating and then strolled out past an inner courtyard to a thorn-patch gate and rock. Overhead hung paper lanterns that had been shredded by the wind.

"I spoke to Norman Pyle," said Sagan. "He told me that you can return to active duty whenever you want."

"Yeah," Cassidy breathed.

"And of course I want you back. More than ever, really. There are some big changes coming down, exciting changes. I want to be able to count on you."

"Sure." But he still hadn't even looked at Sagan. He was looking at the blackening sky.

"I realize you've been through a lot, Billy. I mean if you need some time to yourself I'd understand that too."

"No. I'm ready."

"I did mention a transfer to you, didn't I?"

"Yeah. You mentioned it."

"Well, I was serious. I'd like to get you off the island. I'd like to get you working closer to me. Is that something that interests you?"

"Sure."

"You don't sound very enthusiastic."

"I guess I'm just tired."

But all evening this had been the pattern of their conversation: Sagan

240

speaking to a hopelessly listless boy. It had begun over whiskey sours, then picking at filet of sole, now facing the wind.

"Listen to me," Sagan was saying. "There really are big changes coming down. We're going to be operating with a new sense of autonomy. That was the real problem, you see. I like Norman, but you know that I can't work with someone on my back all the time. I mean who can? So it's going to change. I've got an entirely new set of rules. It's wide open. Absolutely wide open territory now."

"Is Feng Chi still going to be around?" Cassidy asked.

"Yes. Feng will be very much in the picture. Sure, I know what you're thinking, Billy. And yes, there's been some trouble with Feng, but it hasn't come from his end. It's come from Norman's end. You know that Norman has never liked Feng, never understood the man. But then how can we expect him to? I mean he's been off the front line for years. And it's not just Norman. It's the whole Desk. But as I said all that's going to change."

Now long strands of clouds were crossing the landscape, some with vaguely human shapes. While all the distant trees were bent and scraps of paper swept across a sunken lane below.

"I've been meaning to ask you," Sagan said suddenly. "What's he like now?"

"Who?"

"John Polly."

Cassidy shrugged. "I don't know. He's a Communist."

"Would you say he's content?"

"Yeah. I guess so."

"Did he talk about me?"

"A little."

"What did he say?"

"He said he used to know you."

"That's all?"

"Pretty much."

"Did he talk about Feng?"

"Yeah."

"Did he tell you that he killed Feng's brother?"

"Yeah. He told me."

"Did he tell you why?"

"He said there was a woman. The mother of his daughter."

241

"That's right. Polly shot Danny Feng because of some slut. Then he turned and nearly blew the whole Asian front right out of the water."

"That wasn't exactly the way he said it happened."

"Yeah. I bet it wasn't."

Far out at sea there may have been a foundering steamer. Cassidy kept watching the running lights vanish in the swells.

"You realize that one day Feng is going to have to deal with Polly. He's going to have to even the score."

Cassidy said nothing in reply. He was still facing the wind with his hands in the pockets of that now famous raincoat he had purchased two days before. He was thinner and paler than ever, and his hair badly needed cutting. In the not-too-distant future he would begin to carry the 9-millimeter gun and the stiletto, which someone had given him as a joke, but by early summer was no longer a joke.

Cassidy would look back at this period as one long, dark descent into a netherworld which they called the foundation of Asia. In time he began to realize that the Hong Kong station was on a very divergent path. He knew that Jay was avoiding certain issues with Langley, regularly lying, occasionally falsifying reports. He also knew that the involvement with opium had got way out of hand. There were people on the payroll, and no one knew what they did. There were more and more night flights into the Golden Triangle, unaccountable income, everyone living above their means.

As for Cassidy's own life, he did not know what to say or think. For a while it seemed that opium was the only absolute. It was that recurring dream that you had every night and could not help playing out in the day. It was the rhythm of your heartbeat, and it was the heartbeat itself. Sometimes Cassidy smoked in the early evenings when the breeze off the bay cooled the damp heat. Then there was usually the flap of pigeon's wings on the rooftops and the solitary piano from a dance studio below. He liked to sit and watch the young girls slip out into the streets. He never saw one as beautiful as Maya.

Chapter 9

WHEN CASSIDY finished speaking Simon Crane asked, "Tell me, why do you suppose she did it?"

"Did what?"

"Go to you that night?"

"What the hell is that supposed to mean?"

"Given the traditional Chinese piety and strictures on morality it's certainly not the sort of thing that would come naturally to a girl like Maya."

Cassidy had picked up a lump of driftwood. All morning he had been steadily and unconsciously grinding it to a point. "She told me that her father would understand."

"Yes. I imagine that's true, but still it couldn't have been an easy decision for her."

For a moment Cassidy did not respond. Then he said, "She told me that she had thought about it a long time."

"Yes. I imagine she did."

Then Cassidy suddenly tossed the lump of wood across the rocks. "Look, she really liked me, okay? Is that so strange?"

But Crane merely shrugged. "I suppose I'm the wrong one to ask."

Afterward Crane and Cassidy walked slowly back to the house and ate two shrunken veal scallops. The house was heavy with silence. The light was thin. For a while Cassidy sat at the window in the alternate shadow of a drawn blind. Then he fell asleep. When he awoke Crane was waiting for him on the porch. It was the lucid hour just before twilight. Shadows were falling across the open land. There was the call of unseen birds from the grass.

Once more Crane began with a brief introduction explaining that most of the events that he was about to discuss were drawn from the last nine months of entries in the main Polly case file. There were the initial Nixon overtures to Peking, the celebrated Ping-Pong response and finally the Kissinger talks with Chou En-lai. This phase was the fulfillment of Polly's career in that it was the time when he began to work most openly for rapprochement. Within Polly's mind, however, there was no sense of fulfillment, not until much later.

There was no single point, no one conversation wherein Polly was suddenly informed that at last the United States had decided to normalize relations with the People's Republic of China. Rather there was simply a gradual awareness on everyone's part that the time had come to begin thinking in terms of a major policy shift.

There was, however, one letter of note which may be seen as the beginning of this phase. At the heart of this letter was a theme which would continue to dominate Polly's life until the end, involving what Polly called the inevitable backlash to rapprochement. "There are," he wrote, "certain people who will fight tooth and nail to stop any move toward normalization." Specifically he cited Lin Piao and Han Chow, while in a more general sense he cited the old guard of the Kuomintang, Feng Chi, Chiang Kai-shek and the ones like Jay Sagan whose entire careers were based upon United States hostility toward China.

In a sense there was an irony here. All forces which Polly had been fighting for so long were now about to confront him over the one issue that was honestly close to his heart—peace. In some ways he felt ready for this confrontation. In other ways he did not. He was by now past forty. His friend Tommy Ling was close to fifty. Both had loved ones which made them extremely vulnerable, and both had achieved a certain comfort and stature which they were reluctant to throw away. Beyond all this Polly still dreamed of returning to America with his daughter and a trunkful of old notes.

What Polly would remember as the first clear indication of Washington's intentions toward Peking came on a Thursday, the beginning of October. Two months earlier Roger Hall had left Peking and was replaced by still another British link, a mild and amiable man called Michael Dart. Unlike the previous transition from Dray to Hall, Michael Dart entered Polly's life with hardly more than a whisper. Their initial meeting took place in a hawthorn grove west of the city. Then on this memorable Thursday in October they met again in the ruins of a temple known as the Hollow Bell.

Here among the willows at the mouth of a dry riverbed Polly found Dart sitting on a fallen stone. Dart was a slender man with a young face and long, slender features. He wore a new winter coat, gray with slightly darker trim along the collar. He seemed extraordinarily calm, digging into the sand with the point of a walking stick. Through the trees lay a view of clouds over shabby homes.

Dart began by explaining that the first real expression of Nixon's desire to hold talks with Mao had occurred two nights earlier. When Polly asked for the details, Dart explained that the incident took place when Nixon had met with Charles de Gaulle. Polly then asked if Dart believed that Nixon had been serious. Dart explained that he had, adding, "He also wants to relax the trade restrictions."

"When?"

"Sometime next year."

"I hope he understands that it won't be enough. It's a start, but it's not enough. He's also got to pull out of Vietnam."

"Oh I think he knows that, John."

Past a sunken gate lay the temple walls and a trapezoid palace in black moss. There was also a scorched Buddha in the grass, and Dart was tracing its lips with his stick.

"Tell me something," he said suddenly.

"What's that?"

"How long do you think it will take Mao to reciprocate?"

"What do you mean?"

"Well, Nixon has sent the invitation, hasn't he? Now how long before we know that Mao's coming to the party?"

They began to walk, following the riverbed deeper into the trees.

"It's a question of face as much of anything else," Polly said. "Mao has got to show that he's approaching the West from a position of power. If he makes a mistake Lin Piao will be on him like a pack of wolves."

"And when you say Lin, you mean the whole establishment?"

"I mean the military. And Han Chow's people."

At the edge of the ruins lay a row of dying junipers, then a waste of gray concrete leading to the city.

"Incidentally I wanted to ask you..."

"Ask me what?"

"How *you* feel about it? I mean personally."

"How do I feel?"

"Well, you've been working toward this for a long time, haven't you? So I wonder how you feel now?"

Polly shook his head. "I don't know. I guess I feel scared. You work, hope for something for this long, it's kind of a shock when it seems like it might happen."

In the weeks that followed Polly began what would be one of the more penetrating letters of his career, one which covered the full gamut of problems that had to be resolved before talks with the Chinese could actually begin. Foremost among these problems was the obstruction Polly noted in his conversation with Dart:

> How far Lin Piao will go to stop rapprochement is a question that no one can answer. My feeling, however, is that he will go a very long way. He knows that Chou En-lai is politically committed to a normalized relationship with the United States, and should Chou fail to achieve this his career might well be ruined. On the other hand Lin's career is equally at stake, and so we have a breaking point. There will be no compromise. Chou needs rapprochement, and Lin cannot afford to let him have it. As for Mao, I am certain now that he wants normalization, but for the moment he must be content to allow Chou to speak on this issue for him.

Polly further defined the differences between Chou and Lin over rapprochement by noting that central to the problem was the Russians.

> Lin argues that China needs neither the United States nor the Soviet Union. Perhaps he believes this, or perhaps he merely thinks that the argument is politically appealing and in secret still has plans to eventually rebuild a relationship with Russia. I believe the latter. But either way, the line is firmly drawn. Chou hates the Russians, and it is no longer any secret that Mao feels the same way.

Polly sketched a political division which was essentially the same as that division he had perceived three years before. On the one side there were Mao and Chou En-lai, sincerely open to a new and friendly relationship with the United States. On the other side, there were Lin Piao and Han Chow adamantly against any such proposal. Still relatively undecided were powerful elements in the Central Committee and Standing Committee as well as the Party Congress. As for Washington's stance through all this, Polly wrote, "We must show these people that we care. We must show them that we can be trusted. And please stop playing patsy with the likes of Feng Chi."

Ten days after this letter reached Crane Polly received a reply. As usual the reply was terse with no real indication of how Polly's recommendations had been received. Twenty days later, however, there was another event which was regarded as a clear sign of American intentions: the quiet withdrawal of the Seventh fleet from the Taiwan Strait. Then, in December, subsidiaries of American business concerns were given permission to begin trading with the mainland, and finally there was talk of a cultural exchange. In celebration Polly opened a bottle of rice wine that was on the verge of turning to vinegar, drank a few sips, then walked back into his study and wrote a rather insipid essay on the role of a dialectic materialist in the postindustrial age.

The end actually began in the early winter of 1970. John Polly was at the very height of his career, although with power there was also vulnerability. A month before he had consented to meet with western journalists, and there was eventually a string of articles in the European press regarding his past, his political beliefs and his outlook on life after twenty years in Peking. Perhaps the most perceptive of these articles was written by the French journalist Julian Jeannel. There was an accompnaying photograph of Polly standing beside Jean-Paul Sartre. In the background was a windblown cypress and a leaning pagoda.

It was in December that Polly first began to take an active part in the primary campaign to sell rapprochement to the political establishment. In a letter describing his involvement he wrote:

> Once again we are probably seeing still another internal struggle. I assume that because Chou En-lai is presently in a weakened position he feels that he can launch only an indirect campaign. There is, however, no doubt that Chou's ultimate aim is to weaken Lin Piao and Han Chow, while at the same time building up himself and Mao. To this end my services have been enlisted. I begin publishing the first of a series next week.

Once again there was a closing reference to the Nationalist power base in Taiwan and Hong Kong, Polly noting: "Washington's position in Taipei is politically indefensible. And Feng Chi represents everything these people hate."

Polly's initial article was actually written in conjunction with Tommy Ling. It was elliptically constructed with ideas dovetailing into one another so that the whole was slightly ambiguous. Specific names were not mentioned, and concepts were also fairly vague. In general, however, the article attacked the extremist behavior of the May 16th and other radical organizations ostensibly allied with Lin Piao. Additionally there was a call for unity and support for the chairman.

Polly's second article was closer to the bone. There were unmistakable references to Lin Piao's allies in the Central Committee, and an obvious reference to Peng Chen of the Standing Committee. Once more, however, the overall thrust was elliptical. Every major theme had at least two meanings, while specifics were interwoven with vaguer concepts.

Finally there was a fairly well remembered article entitled "China and the Turning World." As with the others of this first series the essential message was somewhat veiled, but in the final paragraph there was a definite allusion to the United States and the possibility of rapprochement. "All things change," Polly wrote. "He who was first may find himself last, while he who was last may soon be first. Nothing is static. Nothing is impossible."

Following publication there was what Polly called a strange stillness in the city, not a total stillness, but rather a sense of slow movement. Wherever Polly went it seemed as if people were avoiding his glance. A letter to Simon Crane on the last day of January noted: "It appears that this entire campaign is like a military operation wherein three sections of an army attack in combination to achieve their objective."

This letter was among the most optimistic of Polly's career, ending with: "When this is all over I think you should tell N.[ixon] to pack his bags. Or maybe K.[issinger]. In the meantime I'll be packing mine."

If there had been any doubt regarding Polly's interpretation of the November and December events those doubts were dispelled by the February announcement that Peking would be willing to meet the Americans in Warsaw. In celebration Polly again spent another quiet night alone.

In the beginning of March Polly began his second series of articles, and although Lin Piao's name was still not mentioned there were obvious references to his career and political stance. Unlike the previous series these articles were published erratically over several months. There were two in March, one in April, and another five in June, July, August and September. Perhaps the most notable feature of this series was the use of allegorical conceits to denote the more sensitive issues at hand. There were images of swans fighting with recalcitrant dogs, tigers limping across deserts in search of truth, pandas, the symbol of peace, weeping in the forests. Of these articles Polly wrote to Crane: "I like to think they're pretty good. Are they?"

In the fall these articles were collected and reprinted in booklet form. On the cover was a white mouse against a blue field. The edition was dedicated to Chou En-lai, lest anyone miss the point. Also, the reviews were very favorable, and in time there were evening readings of the work on radio. Apparently the stories had become popular with the children, who may not have understood the politics, but were enchanted by the animals.

Also of consequence through that summer, fall and winter were the more obvious events, such as the lifting of restrictions prohibiting tankers of American oil companies from refueling in China. Next were the celebrated House Foreign Affairs Committee hearings on China, and finally there was President Nixon's off-the-cuff comment to Yahya Khan of Pakistan regarding his desire for high-level talks with Mao. After each of these incidents Polly sent brief letters of encouragement to Simon Crane, and rumor has it that a copy of the most effusive note was actually shown to Henry Kissinger, although he was not permitted to keep it.

The months between the winter of 1970 and the spring of 1971 constitute a period in which the historical perspective of events was profoundly altered by the release of the China letters. Previously this era was generally regarded as a time when the United States had been gently wooing an unresponsive Peking. Today, however, it is felt that Peking was not unresponsive, merely more subtle and indirect.

For example, eleven weeks after the United States authorized the selective licensing of goods for Chinese export, Peking reciprocated by a caustic denunciation of the Soviet Union's policy in Rumania. The implication was that a Chinese blow against the Soviets was in reality an amiable gesture toward the United States. To many in Langley the full significance of this kind of gesture was lost until many years later when a Polly letter was released containing this sentiment: "It would do well

249

to remember that these people (the Chinese) have always believed that an enemy of their enemy is as good as a friend."

In the same context Mao's November criticism of Lin Piao was another sign of encouragement to the United States, as was China's extraordinarily mild condemnation of the American invasion of Cambodia or the *People's Daily* eulogy to the four Kent State University students shot during a protest of that same invasion. "Remember," Polly wrote in late October, "there is a purpose to everything that Mao does, only sometimes that purpose is beyond the end you imagine."

This was essentially the same viewpoint that Polly presented to Langley at the start of what would later be termed "The Era of Ping-Pong Diplomacy."

It was early April when Crane cabled Polly regarding Ping-Pong. Initially the concept was something of a joke. There had been rumors that Mao was considering inviting the United States Ping-Pong team to China, but nothing had been confirmed. Crane's cable referred sarcastically to bouncing politics and a pervasive Agency fear that the American team would be beaten rather soundly. Polly's letter in reply said that a defeat at the table might be wiser than victory. The point, however, was really academic, because the Chinese always won at Ping-Pong.

Next there were expressed concerns that an American Ping-Pong team might not have the political savvy to successfully play their way across China without incident. Wouldn't the Chinese rather see the Ice Capades? Norman Pyle was said to have asked. Or how about John Denver? To which Polly replied: "Just be glad that they haven't asked to see The Grateful Dead."

On two occasions Polly met with Michael Dart and was questioned about the propriety of traveling athletic teams in China. Questions included: What exactly will be expected of these young people? Will they actually meet Mao? And if so how are they to behave?

In response Polly wrote one of the drollest letters of his career, a three-page tract on Ping-Pong as an intellectual but symbolic exercise in China's *Realpolitik*. "Here is a game premised on adversity. The bat is small, hardly larger than a muscular hand. The ball too is small. Strike too casually and the ball hangs, falls short of its intended destination. Strike too vigorously and it shoots beyond the suburban confinement of the board."

Next there was a passage on Ping-Pong as a lesson in guerrilla warfare wherein human resourcefulness was the essential theme. "When the

250

player has achieved the precise position," Polly wrote, "the blow itself is incidental." In the same spirit Crane wrote back asking for clarification. "Please explain the long strategic odds and the short tactical odds. Also, do the Chinese really play for keeps?"

On April 6, when the invitation actually became a reality, there was another exchange, this in a more serious vein. Polly was asked if there were any liabilities in requesting permission to send accompanying journalists to cover the festivities. Polly replied that the request was unnecessary because plans to invite newsmen were already in the works. Further, Polly was asked to comment on the political effect of the invitation within the Peking elite. Polly wrote: "Obviously the American tour is not something that Lin Piao, Han Chow and others of their camp particularly favor. They are not, however, in any position to protest."

Polly was not invited to attend the exhibition games nor the April 14 party during which the American team was presented to Chou En-lai. By way of explanation Polly wrote that his invitation had probably been withheld out of respect for the Americans, because after all he was still technically a traitor and fugitive from justice.

So once again Polly celebrated alone with a glass of wine by the window above his garden. The night air was mild, the first mild night in weeks. Later he received a telephone call from Tommy Ling, and they chatted about a future that looked very bright.

The end of the White Mandarin began in the last days of May. If there had been a definite pattern to the months before, that pattern was outlined in a metaphor which Polly used to describe his life at this time. He wrote that he was like some secret valve linking two enormous machines—the United States and China. If the workload was often exhausting, he was also deeply satisfied. Never before had he enjoyed the kind of support he was getting now. Never before had there been such a concentrated effort to achieve a single purpose. About this time Polly began to realize that there really would come a point when his services were no longer needed in Peking. He wrote: "Since Nixon and Mao both want the same thing, wouldn't it be simpler if they just eliminated the middleman (me) and hashed it out between themselves?"

And the response from Simon Crane: "It won't be long now, John."

Such was the optimism immediately prior to the final confrontation. By now Polly was working on his third series of articles, honing the issues to an even sharper point. There had been bad storms throughout the

251

spring, but the days were mostly clear now. Sometimes after working late Polly would walk down the Avenue of Protracted Peace, then wander into the outlying sections where the streetlamps were dimmer, and the buildings uniform and unbroken.

It was such an evening like this that marked the beginning of the end. For hours Polly had been penciling notations in the margin of a paper entitled, "Mobilize the Whole Nation and Go in for Agriculture in a Big Way." At four o'clock he decided that he was too tired to concentrate, and thinking he could work later that evening he put on his coat and left the ministry through the rear entrance.

There were rain clouds above the city and low fog in the streets. He was walking slowly, thinking that perhaps he would take a longer route home, until, without realizing it, he found himself in a neighborhood he rarely visited. Here lay a warren of narrow cobbled lanes, crumbling sandstone and brick. There seemed to be no life at all behind the courtyard walls, no lights, no voices, only rising smoke from the factory district.

He had been walking only about twenty minutes when he sensed the figure behind him. He was not certain what first made him aware of this presence, whether it was a faintly heard footstep or the glimpse of a tall, crooked shadow. He knew only that it was a man, and the man was definitely following him.

For another quarter of a mile Polly walked, altering his pace, turning suddenly, waiting, then turning again. Twice through the fog he again saw the shadow and heard the clap of footsteps on the cobblestones. Then, still walking, thinking that given these twisted streets and this fog he could easily hide, he heard a voice call out, "Wait!"

Polly stood motionless while the figure approached stiffly through the fog. At the end of the lane there were a few skeletal trees dying of factory smoke, and water tanks against the skyline. Even when he could see the face he wasn't certain. There was only the half-memory of a face in a cramped mud cell and the reflection of the same face in a storefront window.

Then he heard, "Hello, Polly."

"General? Ko Ming?"

"The same."

"What are you doing here?"

"What do you think? I was following you."

Closer now Polly could see that the general looked about the same as he had looked the last time they had met. He wore a long green coat and

252

heavy boots. He stood very straight, shoulders back, arms at his side.

"I want to talk to you, Polly."

"What about?"

"The future of this People's Republic."

"Are you sure you wouldn't like to go someplace more comfortable?"

"I think it would be better if we spoke here."

"Here?" There was only a windblown courtyard under fog, a ditch of black water and a rubble heap.

"I know you think this is strange. We have not seen each other for almost three years and suddenly I come to you like this. Well, you won't think it strange when you've heard what I have to say."

They began to walk past earthworks overgrown with withered vines, a juniper left white with ash, a deserted foundry.

"Tell me, Polly, do you ever reflect back on the time we spent together in that detention center?"

"Not really."

"Well, I do. As a matter of fact I have given a great deal of thought to it in the last few days."

"Is that so?"

"Yes. In particular I have been thinking about certain political discussions we had together. Also I have thought about the fact that you saved my life. It proves that whatever else, you are basically an honorable person. Which is why I've come to you now."

Ahead lay another open stretch of mud and willow mounds. There were tumbled blocks of stone, and the charred remains of a doorway on the hill.

"I have been reading your articles," the general said. "I find them most interesting."

"And that's what you wanted to talk about?"

"In part. You see there was one particular article that intrigued me very much."

"Which one?"

"It was the one in which you intimated that there were certain people in the party who were working to undermine the chairman's policies. Do you recall that one? I believe it was called 'The Crane.'"

"'The Tiger and the Crane.' It was called 'Tiger and the Crane.'"

"Yes. That's the one. You also wrote that these enemies of the chairman would go to almost any length to stop the development of friendly relations with the United States. Do you remember that part?"

"Vaguely."

"Well, now I would like to ask you just how far you really believe they would go. I mean these people in the party opposed to Mao—how far do you think they would go?"

Polly shook his head. "I don't know, general. How far?"

"I will tell you. They will go so far as to kill the chairman and seize total power."

Polly stopped walking. His hands were in his pockets. "What are you talking about?"

"An organization. Very secret, but very widespread. They call themselves the Five Hundred and Seventy-one Group."

"How do you know about it?"

"I know because I was asked to join them."

"Asked by whom?"

"Someone in the ministry."

"What's his name?"

"It doesn't matter. He's only a small fish. It's the big fish that we must worry about."

"And who are the big fish?"

"Who do you think?"

At the bottom of the gully lay a sheet of canvas beaten into the mud. For an Instant Polly thought it was the body of a child.

"I don't see why you're surprised, Polly. You yourself wrote that these people were capable of such a thing. And why not? They're convinced that the chairman has betrayed the Revolution. First it was the Red Guard, then it was Vietnam, now he's playing Ping-Pong with the Americans. Surely you can't be surprised."

"How many are involved?"

"I don't know. Perhaps fifty, but of course many of these men are commanders in control of hundreds, even thousands of trained soldiers."

"How far do you think it's gone?"

"I don't know that either."

Birds or mice had begun stirring in the surrounding vegetation. There was also a stiff wind spreading the fog.

"You think I'm lying, don't you?" the general said suddenly.

"No."

"I'm not lying. This organization does exist. Of course it's structured so that one knows only the names of those immediately above and below him, but I'm quite sure that it extends to the very top of the military and police."

254

"You mean Lin and Han?"

"Their names have not been specifically mentioned, but I believe their involvement was implied."

"When did you find out about this?"

"A few days ago."

"And why did you come to me?"

"Why not? You seem to have the necessary connections to deal with this sort of problem."

"How do you know you can trust me?"

"Because only a fool saves a man's life and then betrays him."

The wind had shifted, moving across the willows bringing odors of stagnant water and chemical waste. The general was watching the headlights of a truck on the rim of the gully.

Finally he said, "Despite what you may think of me, I am fundamentally a patriot. I would not like to see the chairman murdered."

"So what do you want me to do?"

"Talk to your friend Ling Sheng. Tell him what I've said here today. Although I'd prefer if you did not mention my name."

"What if he doesn't believe me?"

"Then tell him to look to Lin Piao's son. There's a lot to be learned from the movements of Lin's son."

They had come to a particularly wasted stretch of the city down along the canals. Here stood a mile of swamp and a steel bridge above oily water. When they had reached the banks of the canal Polly said, "You told me that they asked you to join them, is that right?"

"Does it surprise you?"

"No. I was just wondering what you told them."

"What do you think I told them? I told them I would be delighted."

"What if you had refused?"

"I'm not sure. Perhaps I would be dead by now."

"But there must have been others who have refused."

"No, Polly, you don't understand. It is not an invitation to a dinner party. It is an invitation to a military takeover of the government."

At first there was no real sense of alarm. Polly wrote only that after his talk with the general he went home and spent a quiet evening with his daughter. Apparently they played dominoes.

Early the following morning Polly telephoned Tommy Ling, and eventually met him about half a mile south of the ministry. Here Polly simply recounted what the general had told him, neither adding nor subtracting anything. By the time he had finished they had come to the end of an unpaved road and a patch of winter grass that nobody had bothered to cut and burn.

After a moment of silence Ling said, "This source of yours, do you believe he's reliable, John?"

"I don't know. I think so."

"But you have reservations."

"It's possible that he's overreacting."

"But if he's not it could be very serious, no?"

"Yes. It could be very serious."

"So what do you think we should do?"

Polly shrugged. "How about taking it to Chou?"

"Do you know how many rumors of this sort are brought in to Chou's office every month?"

"It may not be a rumor, Tommy."

"Still, I think it would be better if we first tried to verify if what he said is true. For example, this business about Lin's son, this is intriguing to me."

"How so?"

"Lin's son is in the air force. Now, certainly if one were to instigate the sort of action that these people are supposedly contemplating one would need the air force. Also there is the matter of the organization's name. Do you know what those numbers stand for, John?"

"I don't know. I guess they could stand for anything."

"No, not anything. These numbers have a specific meaning. It's phonetic. Say it in Chinese. Five hundred and seventy-one. It sounds exactly like armed revolt."

Later, as the two men were again moving back along a cobbled lane, Ling said suddenly, "Tell me, John. This source of yours, is he really so secret?"

"Yes. He's pretty secret."

"Do I know him?"

"Yes."

"If you were to tell me his name would I think more or less of his story?"

"I don't know, probably less."

"Why do you think he asked you not to tell me his name?"

"Because regardless of our opinion, he's scared. He's very scared."

The first reaction in Langley to this information was also relatively

256

casual. Apparently there was a cautionary memo sent to the White House, but no definite alert. Simon Crane made no effort to pursue the matter through any of the outlying stations, nor was there any internal research.

But then very suddenly the mood began to change. "We have underestimated the severity of this situation," Polly wrote. "We have underestimated it very badly," and in this same letter Polly went on to describe his second conversation with Tommy Ling which occurred three nights later.

It was a Monday night and Ling had come to Polly's home unexpectedly. When Ling arrived he found Polly sitting at the kitchen table with his daughter. There were three cabbage heads on the windowsill, a paperback edition of *Alice in Wonderland*. On a plastic dish were the remains of two radishes. When Polly answered the door he saw immediately from the expression on Ling's face that they would have to speak alone.

He told his daughter, "I'm going to step outside for a moment."

She looked frightened, first into her father's eyes then into Ling's.

Outside in the garden Ling said, "She has a lot of Kim in her, doesn't she?"

Polly's synopsis of the conversation that followed comprised thirteen pages. It dealt with the results of Ling's primary investigation, and the conclusions drawn from that investigation. According to Polly's letter, Ling's first area of investigation had concerned the physical movements of Lin Piao's son, Lin Li-kuo. Supposedly Ling had been able to trace the boy's movements through talks with air force officials and secondary records. All inquiries were made under the auspices of research for a series for *Peking Review;* this had been the real brilliance of Tommy Ling—to work within the system, entirely undetected.

By way of background Polly wrote that Lin Li-kuo was still fairly young—middle twenties or early thirties—but he had already achieved no small degree of stature within the People's Air Force. He was also said to have been a fairly handsome man, and rather popular with his fellow officers.

Polly then went on to write:

> Apparently Lin has made no less than four trips to Shanghai
> and Nanking in the last two months. Ostensibly these trips were
> to help his father establish political activist cadres within the air
> force units, but Tommy claims that this is suspect because not

257

once did the boy meet with the political directors. Instead he spent his time renewing old friendships among the air force command, particularly among those with direct access to fighter aircraft.

With the military as his focal point and specifically the air force, Polly went on to describe Ling's second area of investigation—a series of thefts from rural police armories. According to Polly, Ling had apparently stumbled on the subject of these thefts quite accidentally, and further inquiry revealed only the most minimal details. Nevertheless it was clear that between the months of April and June there had been at least four burglaries of automatic weapons and hand grenades.

Finally there were the more nebulous, but no less disturbing consequences of Ling's investigation into the travel schedules of Lin Piao, Han Chow and six other leading military figures. By comparing departure dates, Ling was able to establish that on three occasions these men traveled simultaneously to an air force training base just west of the Kansu Mountains. There were further indications of two unauthorized flights into the Inner Mongolian Autonomous Region, and what Ling called a peculiar three-day period in which Lin Piao, Han Chow and others seemed to vanish entirely.

In the conclusion of his letter, Polly recorded this last exchange almost verbatim, noting that it had taken place as the two friends were returning to the house.

"I think this is bad, John. I think it's very bad."

"I know."

"When are you going to see your friend again?"

"Soon."

"You must ask him for more information. He's got to give us more information."

"I'll tell him that."

"And, John?"

"Yes?"

"I think you should send Maya away for a while."

Now came eight days of intensity unlike any that Polly had experienced before. "We are hunting on the run," he wrote to Crane, and went on to describe his second meeting with General Ko Ming.

The meeting took place at seven o'clock in the evening on that dev-

258

astated stretch of the city by the inner canal. Polly arrived first and waited beneath the concrete pillars of an iron bridge. There was nothing between the muddy banks and the dirty water. There were no lights, no roads, only a cart path along the rim of the embankment. From where Polly stood he had an open view across an oily swamp and heaped dirt.

Polly first saw the general from a distance, silhouetted against the night sky. The man was moving stiffly; shoulders and back straight, eyes forward, the cadence of his steps unvarying. At thirty yards Polly stepped out from between the pillars and raised his arm. The general nodded slightly in reply.

Then he said, "I take it you spoke with your friend Ling."

"Yes."

"What did he say?"

"He's frightened."

"So he should be."

From these opening words, Polly then described how the general immediately launched into a terse and rapid explanation of the organizational structure of the conspiracy and its tactics.

"Apparently," Polly wrote, "what is being contemplated is nothing less than a classic military overthrow of this government. The coup will begin with the pretense of a foreign air attack. This will provide an excuse to mobilize Lin Li-kuo's first-strike teams as well as the imposition of martial law. The civilian population will then be herded into the shelters, and in the ensuing confusion the formal government control will change hands."

Polly further noted that according to the general there were elaborate plans to take over the radio stations, and specially trained cadres for this purpose. "Units of the local military command are to be issued with light, fully automatic weapons, while larger pieces will remain in reserve."

As for the essential motivations, the general reiterated what he had said earlier: members of the 571 conspiracy were convinced that the party's direction as dictated by Mao and Chou En-lai was hopelessly aberrant. Rapprochement with the United States, the gradual trend toward a capitalist system, the increasing tolerance of political dissidents— all these were clear signs that the basic tenets of the Revolution had been violated.

As a final comment, Polly explained that it was the general's opinion that the chairman would at best be a historical figure within this new regime. When Polly asked what the general meant by that, the general

259

replied that the chairman would probably be killed, but the details of his death would be fabricated so that he would achieve the status of martyrdom.

Now came a rapid, breathless exchange from Polly to Crane and Crane back to Polly. At the heart of all communication lay three evening meetings with Ko Ming and two days of silent probing. Polly wrote urgently: "Desire any and all information regarding possible Yellow Sea maneuvers believed to have occurred during the months of April and May."

In reply, Crane cabled the reports of the South Korean coastal watch. Next Polly requested a photographic analysis of two Manchurian military installations and a breakdown of high-frequency radio traffic from the Mongolian border. Again the response from Langley was immediate, clearly attesting to the fact that by this time, the third week of investigation, all concerned were fully aware of what was at stake.

These were to be remembered as dark days, literally dark with low storm clouds and occasional rain. Afternoons were hot, nights warm. With his daughter, Polly remained distracted. Alone, he remained frightened, turning at the sound of the wind under the door, or the backfire of a passing automobile, or less defined sounds half-heard in the stillness. "I see patterns of deceit everywhere," he wrote, "but I do not think I fully understand them yet."

Then came the climactic meeting with General Ko Ming. It took place in the evening, at an unusually violet hour. There was a watery blindness to the fogbanks, and a warm foul wind.

"You might be interested to know that the Soviets are involved in this too," the general said.

"In what sense?"

"I cannot be certain, but it would seem that they may offer material and financial support. There is also some evidence of Nationalist involvement."

"What do you mean?"

"I don't find it so surprising. Surely one can see that Taiwan has as much to lose by this rapprochement business as anyone."

"But what sort of involvement?"

"I don't know, but it's possible that it will be aircraft from Taiwan that will supply the spark to start the fire."

Accompanying this report were a few brief comments from Polly. At the center of his message lay his repeated understanding that a military coup in China could be launched most effectively under the auspices of a defensive thrust against a foreign air strike. Given this, it was Polly's opinion that based upon the sophistication of mainland radar facilities, an enemy air offensive could not be faked without the actual deployment of foreign aircraft. Chinese fighters pretending to be foreign would not suffice. Thus Polly proposed that if the conspirators genuinely wanted to convince mainland defense systems that they were under attack, some sort of cooperative arrangement had to be made with a foreign power.

To this end, Polly postulated the following scenario. He suggested that a representative of the conspiracy met with a representative of the Nationalist government on at least two occasions. As a result of these meetings an agreement was made to the effect that Taiwan fighters would be flown into Chinese airspace and so trigger the mainland defense system. This would in turn serve as the plausible excuse for pilots of the 571 to launch their first offensive strike, possibly on Mao's residence in Shanghai. The strike could be later blamed on Nationalist squadrons acting without their government's sanction. There would then be talk of reprisal against Taiwan, but after much apparent debate the talk would come to nothing.

What exactly happened to this portion of Polly's letter is still something of a mystery. One story has it that Simon Crane showed it to Norman Pyle, who was entirely baffled and unwilling to distribute the piece any further. In another story it was Crane who was nonplussed by the theory, and withheld the letter in the interest of Polly's reputation. The fact remains, however, that later, after Polly's daughter had been abducted, this letter was unearthed in support of Crane's theory that Feng Chi and Jay Sagan were involved.

Immediately following Polly's second meeting with Ko Ming there was another conversation with Tommy Ling. This one took place on a Sunday behind a deserted market square. Here lay more brick-and-timber slums in a maze of unpaved streets. The two men walked briefly until they came to the gateway of an empty compound. There were odors of the communal latrines.

When Polly finished recounting what the general had told him, Ling said that he believed it was time that they approached Chou En-lai.

Polly said, "What are you going to tell him?"

Ling shook his head. "I suppose I should tell him everything."

"What if he wants to know who my source is?"

"Then I will explain the situation to him."

"But what if he pressures you? What if he wants to talk to me directly?"

"Please, John. The premier is a reasonable man."

What exactly Tommy Ling told Chou En-lai has never been divulged, not by Ling, not by Polly, not by anyone in Peking. All that is known is that Ling and the premier met privately for about two hours on a Monday evening. In response to Ling's story the premier was said to have expressed no small amount of concern, and apparently a debate later arose as to what could be done.

There were those, mainly some of the younger adjuncts, who believed that the entire 571 organization could be stopped by simply publicizing what was known and thus enlisting what had always been Mao's most powerful weapon, popular sentiment. On the other hand Chou, Ling and later Mao himself argued that the conspiracy had gone too far by this point, and public accusations could very well lead to civil war.

A letter, written by Polly shortly after the premier was taken into confidence, amply illustrates the concern:

> The problem, as it stands now, revolves around the fact that Lin Piao still commands considerable loyalty among the army. This is not to say that the common soldier does not love Mao, but merely that the soldier is bound to follow his immediate superior. Thus even a direct imposition on the part of the chairman may not prove sufficient to stop an assault once it has started.

Given these circumstances, Polly went on to describe a proposed strategy revolving around the classic guerrilla premise that nothing is so precious as the element of surprise.

> So long as the conspirators remain unaware that their plans are no longer a secret, it is felt that the advantage can still be Mao's. In accordance with this thinking, it has been suggested that the conspirators be allowed to make their first move, and only at the moment of their overt commitment will Mao's elite guard counter. To this end I am being pressed to learn the exact date of the proposed attack and the details of how and from where that attack will be made. At the moment Ko Ming does not seem to be in a position to help, but I remain hopeful.

On a less optimistic note this letter closed with a reference to a contingency escape route through North Korea, and the whispered fear that the strain of these days would prove too great for the chairman's failing health.

With the involvement of Chou En-lai and less visibly Mao, Polly's role in this struggle became almost passive; the essential background of the conspiracy had been uncovered and most of the activity within the Maoist camp now centered on building a reliable defense. There was, however, still much that was expected of Polly, and much more that he would eventually contribute.

But strictly in terms of this period before the final confrontation, there were only two last incidents of note. They were the actual abduction of Maya Polly, and Polly's earlier meeting with Mao. A letter written at the end of August discussed that impending meeting as well as Polly's own feelings of foreboding. "I wonder," he wrote, "if I'm too old for what I'm about to face. Certainly I'm tired."

Simon Crane cabled back: "It won't be long now, John."

Polly's conversation with Mao supposedly occurred in the late afternoon at a military compound located a few miles northeast of the city. In Polly's letter describing this meeting there is a brief sketch of the compound and the adjacent grounds. Apparently it lay along a wooded stretch of highway, fairly well hidden from the road by tall pines. There were two main structures. Both were low, gray concrete buildings ringed with barbed wire and sentry towers. Beyond lay open grassland and a row of white barracks. Polly also noted that an artificial lake had been dug in sight of the chairman's quarters with junipers and weeping willows along the shore.

The chairman by this time was well past his prime. Photographs of this period, and there were to be many during the Nixon visit, do not necessarily reflect his true age. "He seemed tired," Polly wrote. "He asked if I wanted tea, then smiled and said, 'Or would you prefer beer.' But as for himself he drank only bottled water, which he claimed was particularly beneficial for digestion."

Polly went on to describe how the chairman was dressed simply in a pair of light cotton trousers and a white short-sleeved shirt. When Polly entered the room the chairman did not rise from his chair, but merely extended his hand. In the background was the faint hum of generators, but otherwise it was very quiet.

263

"A long time has passed since we've seen each other, John."

Polly replied that it had been a long time, and he hoped that in the years to come they would be able to see each other more often. The chairman smiled at this, and then joked about his own mortality.

"They tell me you have done a great deal to help this office," the chairman continued. "I wish to express my gratitude."

"Thank you, sir, but I only hope that I can continue to serve."

"I'm sure you will. Although I wonder if perhaps when problems are resolved here you would not want to go home?"

"Home, sir? This is my home."

"Of course, but I was referring to your birthplace, which is also your home. The United States."

"Oh."

"Wouldn't you like to return one day?"

And then because it hardly mattered, "Yes, sir. I suppose I would like to go home."

The only other exchange of consequence described in Polly's letter came toward the end of their meeting. For a long time the chairman had been still, gazing through the drawn curtains to the distant mountains. On the far wall hung two sparsely delineated landscapes and a study of a dragonfly in green. The chairman's wrist hung over the arm of his chair, and his silence remained unbroken for nearly a minute.

Then he asked suddenly, "Tell me, John. How is your daughter?"

"She's fine, sir. Thank you."

"How old is she now?"

"Nineteen."

"Ah, nineteen. And they say she is very pretty."

"Thank you."

Then again the chairman glanced at the open window to the mountains in the fading light and the embankment of the lake in shuttered branches. "Have you thought of sending her away for the summer, John?"

"Yes, sir. I have."

"The coast is very beautiful this time of year. Perhaps she would enjoy a brief stay in Po Hai."

"I'm sure she would, sir."

"Then let me suggest you send her there, just until problems are resolved here. Do you understand what I'm saying?"

"Yes, sir. I think I do."

264

As for their final moments together, Polly wrote simply that there were undercurrents of despondency that even later he could not define. The chairman made a passing reference to the fact that a thousand years ago a bird would have been dissected in the palace yard so that the entrails could be examined for maggots. Then once more there was a word about Polly's daughter and the chairman expressed his concern.

Polly did not tell his daughter that she would be leaving until the last night, a night of high winds that brought no relief from the heat. He did not know how to say goodbye. He did not know even what to tell her now that she was almost a woman. One day, he thought, he would probably have to explain, and had always imagined leading her out into some garden to say: *Two years before you were born....*

Then at other times he thought he might never tell her, thought that he might die here and the task would fall to Simon, who would simply say: *I believe it's time we had a talk about your father.* But then what? *Your father was a spy?* or *He loved your mother very deeply?* Or perhaps even: *He tended to see his life in terms of symbols and in the end it killed him.*

As it happened, however, Polly's farewell to his daughter was nothing more than a brief goodbye on a patch of windy ground near the train station. Earlier he had told her that the city was no longer safe, and he supposed she understood. He also told her that he would join her soon, and not to worry if a month or two went by. Then he held her in his arms for a long time, which was something he rarely did since she had come to look so much like Kim.

There are only a few pertinent facts regarding the abduction. The girl was taken nine days after her arrival in Po Hai, while those disturbing photographs which showed her nude and transgressed did not reach Polly until the end of the second week. Immediately upon hearing the news Simon Crane began to draft a letter of condolence which he planned to have cabled in the morning. This letter, however, was never completed because in the face of such horror Crane did not know what to say.

Yet there were those memos from Crane to Norman Pyle, and one important memo beginning with a reiteration of Crane's basic theory that the abduction of Maya Polly was not a political act, but an emotional one on the part of Feng Chi. Then followed a brief description of three

265

methods in which Feng could have arranged for the abduction. Next there were two formal references to that mysterious British sighting of the border crossing, and finally this celebrated postscript:

> I now believe that we are no longer in a position to dismiss the theory that between the Hong Kong station and certain individuals within the mainland intelligence community there exists an interplay. Precisely what the planned end of this interplay is I do not know. It is likely, however, that both parties have agreed to some mutually beneficial arrangement involving nothing less than the death of Mao, the overthrow of the Peking government and the termination of rapprochement.

There was also a conversation between Pyle and Crane pertinent to this memo. Like others of its kind during this period it was not held in Norman Pyle's office, but outside, on the edge of the Langley forest. Here lay an acre of lawn stretching to the pines, then deer paths farther into the wood. Pyle and Crane had walked in silence to the first trees. Crane kept picking off leaves and tearing them to bits.

Finally Pyle said, "I haven't shown your memo to the others. I didn't think it would accomplish anything."

Crane was intensely shredding still another leaf. "It wasn't meant for anyone else. It was meant for you."

"And I've given it a good deal of thought."

"Fine, but it's not thought that we need. It's action."

They had reached a darker hollow. In the clearing stood two oaks that had been charred perhaps by lightning.

"All right, Simon. What do you want me to do? You want me to pull in Sagan? Because I will. I can pull him in and have him sweated within twenty-four hours."

"It's too late for that. An overt move now will only cut the child's odds that much more, not to mention any chance we might have of finding out what the hell is really going on out there."

All around them lay the stumps and withered limbs of other trees. But Crane was watching a circling hawk. "Tell me something, Norman. How many agents does Sagan budget for?"

"Two or three hundred."

"Any idea where they're placed?"

"He says the mainland, but that could be a lie."

"So then it's possible that he has a man right under our nose."

266

"What do you mean?"

"I mean that Sagan may have carved a route right through the Desk, built his own organization and gone into business for himself."

"With Feng Chi as silent partner?"

"Yes."

"I think that's a bit much, Simon."

"You want to take the chance that I'm wrong?"

They had wandered into the charred circle of oaks now. Pyle was picking at a blackened trunk. "If you're right," he said, "and I'm not saying that you are, but if you are, what will it take to clean this up?"

"A man, one man—on the inside."

"And I suppose you have someone in mind."

"Yes, as a matter of fact I have."

"May I ask who it is?"

"Billy Cassidy."

"Oh Jesus, Simon, no."

It was, however, only three days after this conversation that the first lines were cast as an overture to Cassidy's entrance. At the end of a week the Asian Desk was like some enormous microscope, with Cassidy the virulent strain under observation. From secondary sources, stringers on the fringe of the Asian circle, there were dozens of stories about that dangerous young man who was supposed to have once loved John Polly's daughter.

Chapter 10

"SO POLLY still doesn't know?" Cassidy asked. "I mean about the chance that Feng might have Maya—he still doesn't know, does he?"

"We saw no point in telling him," Crane replied. "There's nothing he can do."

"But the possibility must have occurred to him?"

"Yes, it occurred to him."

"So what do you tell him?"

"We lie."

It was now sometime after nightfall. Behind them lay the captain's house with only one light burning in an upstairs window. Earlier Cassidy had climbed down among the rocks and torn a starfish off the barnacles. But he didn't kill it. He merely examined it, while thinking about John Polly.

And now that Polly's story was complete he did not know what to say or think. The night before a wind had left the trees along the palisade even more tattered than usual. Once more this place was like the end of the world.

Finally both men rose and started tramping back across the grass. The southern sky was nearly the color of fire. The wind was beginning to sound through the reeds. Crane was limping from having sat too long, while Cassidy let his raincoat drag behind.

They moved in silence for about fifty yards, then Crane said, "You understand that this is the last night. Tomorrow you go."

"Yeah," Cassidy sighed. "I figured this would be the last night."

"So I wonder if you have any questions?"

268

"No."

"The important thing to remember is not to play your hand too quickly. Just take it one step at a time."

"Right."

"And, Billy?"

"What?"

"We'd like to avoid bloodshed. Do you understand?"

"Sure." But it was clear that the boy was thinking about something else.

There was a more formal briefing held that night in the library. There Crane talked about cover and the importance of never volunteering information. People do not expect it. In the event that Cassidy was asked about his stay in Langley, over an hour was spent memorizing the details about the two-year testing program, instructors, the layout of the rooms. There were even sample questions from the primary examination. Finally Crane talked about priorities with an emphasis on the filing systems of foreign stations. Look for the small things, he told Cassidy. And look for what is not there.

In the morning Cassidy climbed out of bed and got himself a beer. He drank it on the veranda while three white ships crossed the horizon. The bay was glazed with an offshore wind. From the crash of waves on the rocks he knew that the tide was in. When he returned to his room he saw that his knife, the Browning and two magazines of ammunition were lying on the dresser. They had even cleaned the blade.

So Billy returned to the obscure life he had left six days before. He returned and found that nothing had really changed. Three hours after landing at Kai Tak he was sitting at a bar with Jay Sagan. A sultry woman, naked to the waist, danced in a gold fiberglass cage. Sagan drank gin, Cassidy whiskey and coke. The Rolling Stones were playing on the jukebox: *By the time you're thirty you're going to look sixty-five. You won't look pretty and your friends are going to kiss you goodbye.*

"So how was Langley?" Sagan asked.

"Fine."

"You passed your exams?"

"I don't know. They send you the scores."

"I'm sure you did fine, Billy. I'm sure you did just fine."

"Sure."

Which was the entire extent of their conversation regarding those six lost days.

Thereafter Sagan talked about some woman he had met, or bought. He said her name was Honey Pie. Apparently she was one of the Feng Chi girls, and moderately strung out on smack. Around midnight, after Sagan had gone through several gins, Cassidy casually asked about the station, what was new, who was doing what. Sagan said things were great, big things were happening and they were great. Then in his wasted room above the pharmacy Cassidy cooked an egg and ate it from the pan. He couldn't stop thinking about Maya.

Station records were housed at the rear of the central annex. Here past wastes of linoleum, green plaster and rosewood laminate, lay the vault. There were chairs in buff Naugahyde and fluorescent lighting. Doors were electronically sealed, the offices partitioned with fiberboard. Adjacent to record shelves were reading cages and a video retrieval system. The entire area fell under the jurisdiction of a girl named Ruth, a washed-out blond whom Cassidy had never liked.

It was nine o'clock in the morning, and only the junior staff had arrived. Ruth was leafing through a magazine, sipping coffee from a cup with her name on it. When Cassidy entered she grinned. "Oh you're back. How did it go?"

"Great." But he wasn't smiling.

"So you passed?"

"Of course not." And he laughed.

They talked about the weather while he filled in seven yellow requisition slips. *If you need three, then take seven,* Crane had said. *Four for smoke.* Among the steel shelves he was conscious of some foul odor from the air conditioner, and the clack of a woman's heels on the floor. There were trolleys for files, but he just tucked them under his arm. Then he moved back to the reading cage, sweating badly.

The first file was an index of payment vouchers extending through mid-December. Then there was a breakdown of the telex traffic, also extending back through December. Finally there were the synopsized lists of program summaries cross-indexed with the operational groups. After twenty minutes his shirt was wet and his mouth was dry. Crane had said, *Look for the small things.*

The last fifteen minutes he spent drafting a proposal for what he called the perforated line—also Crane's idea, because you had to have a reason

270

for spending so much time down here. So on six pages of yellow foolscap he sketched his vision of a disinformation line through the radio links. *Let them think you're working on the complex route—and look for what isn't there.*

What was left of the day he wasted on paperwork and chatting with the duty clerks, smoking and drinking rank coffee. At six o'clock he met Johnny Ray at a club called the Spike, where everyone went for the atmosphere. Ray had turned twenty-eight the day before and someone had given him a crass gold chain. He was also wearing a new leather coat with a shark embroidered on the left lapel. From across the bar, hunched on a stool in bad light, he might have been just one more Hong Kong dealer. His black hair was swept up and back. There were dark circles under his eyes.

"How's it going, Johnny?"

Ray spun around and grinned. "I heard you were back. How did it go?"

"Fantastic. I flunked."

As Cassidy slid onto the stool he saw that Ray's face had been scratched. Three parallel scars ran down from the eye.

"What happened? Some girl?"

Ray smirked. "The bitch fucking loves me."

"Why don't you get yourself a nice one, Johnny?"

"Hey, this one is nice."

A lank prostitute entered the bar from the rear. Ray was watching her reflection as she passed between the potted ferns.

"So what's going on, Johnny? You miss me?"

"Sure. Place fell apart when you were gone."

"What did you do for your birthday?"

"Got drunk, got sick and got this." He pointed to the cuts along his chin.

"Sounds fun."

"Oh yeah. Best birthday yet. Which reminds me—what did you bring me?"

Cassidy smiled. "As a matter of fact I had a real nice present for you, Johnny. But when the guy at customs opened the box it started bleeding and so he wouldn't let me bring it in."

Now in the smoked mirror there was the reflection of a girl with coral lips and a bone white face. She was poised among the ferns, twisting a leaf around her finger.

271

Suddenly Cassidy said, "You know, Johnny, I've been on something you might be interested in."

"Forget it, lover. I'm busy. In fact right now I'm engaged in service for the old man."

"You and Sagan, huh?"

"That's right. Priority service."

"Yeah? What kind of service?"

"Secret."

"Real secret, or bullshit secret?"

"Real secret. Mainland stuff. We got ourselves a big score."

"Is that right?"

"That's right."

"And what are you doing? Driving the master's car?"

"Go fuck yourself. I am *the* security coordinator."

"Yeah? For what?"

"Secret."

"Come on, Johnny."

"No, man, I'm serious. This is the real thing."

"Is Feng in on it?"

"Hey, Billy, if you want a piece of the action why don't you talk to Sagan?"

"Maybe I'll just do that."

When Ray tossed back his head to swallow the last of his beer, Cassidy couldn't help but notice just how exposed the throat became.

He returned to the records in the morning. Through the sorting shelves he saw Ruth stacking papers; he nodded because they didn't expect him to be too friendly.

The path was less obscure today, every indication more distinct. *Look for what's not there.* In the first twenty minutes he scanned the previous year's expenditures for June, then July, then August. Next there were the product graphs, and yes, July and August had been unexplainably low. Southeast takes had dropped markedly, while the inflow from the mainland had been next to nothing. But the money, he noted, the money had still been pouring in and out.

Another hour passed, and Cassidy had hardly moved his hand, except to turn a page. He had finished with expenditures, and had now begun to scan the balance sheets. Again there was something not quite right, too much money on certain months, not enough on others. On the first of August seven thousand dollars left the station, but there was no indication as to what the money bought. Then two weeks later Jay and Johnny were in Taipei. They dined at Budding Grove where Jay always went to see the women. Then there were drinks at a place called the Dreaming Oyster where the women wore transparent veils and hookers waited in the courtyard. *Does Jay still sleep with every woman he can find?* Finally there was a two-hundred-dollar night on Friday, while on Monday Sagan had his teeth cleaned and two decaying molars filled.

By the end of the second hour Cassidy was done with details. Details were meaningless without the larger view. But what was the larger view? December? Yes, December. He had been living in a fog, smoking, drinking, listening to the Rolling Stones on a crapped-out portable machine. Johnny Ray had started into the big time, dealing half an ounce of the uncut stuff a week. Jay was meeting every night with Jerry Woo, and at the end of the month the whole direction of the station had changed. Everyone knew it, but no one actually talked about it. At the end of three months the first tentative steps into unauthorized territory had been taken. Expenditures were always over-budget, but there was still lots of money; if nothing else there was lots of money, because the funds were internally generated. Crane had said, *We're not interested in the opium routes. We're interested in what Sagan is doing with the profit.*

Later that day Cassidy actually saw Sagan passing through the courtyard in the rain, stepping wide to avoid a puddle, shouting something over his shoulder. While high above the second floor, Cassidy watched from the window grille. The white exhaust from a waiting car was rising above the trees.

Then at five o'clock there was Jay again, chatting with a junior clerk by the water cooler. When Cassidy approached Sagan broke off his conversation to smile. "How's it going, Billy-boy?"

"Just fine, sir."

As always Jay was dressed immaculately. Today his suit was pale green, the shirt and tie just half a shade darker.

"I understand you've been keeping pretty busy?"

Cassidy felt his stomach knot. "Yes, sir. I've been working on a few things."

"And what might they be, Billy?"

"Ah...well...it's just this idea I've had. It's got to do with setting up a perforated line."

"Get them chasing their own tails, is that it?"

"Yes, sir."

From a doorway down the corridor someone called out Sagan's name and he shouted back, "Just a moment." Then to Cassidy, "Look, Billy, I'm just a bit tied up right now. Why don't you go ahead and draft the proposal and we'll sit down and really hash it out."

"When?"

"Hell, I don't know. Next week?"

"A week, sir?"

"Yeah. My schedule should be a little more flexible in a week."

As if Jay's schedule wasn't flexible enough already. Records were clear on this point. Since April Jay had hardly spent a full day in the station. There were thirteen trips to Taiwan, three to Macao, and a two-week tour through Bangkok, Phnom Penh and the Malay Peninsula. Ostensibly this travel had been to reinforce the courier routes which fed Saigon Command, but over the months the station reserves showed a million-dollar benefit.

But if the larger figures gave a sense of the stations' scope, it was a fairly paltry sum of money which finally proved to be most critical within the larger scope of the story.

It was a Tuesday evening, the third day after his return, and again Cassidy sat down with the records. All through the previous afternoon he had been waiting for this moment, as if something were waiting for him. At six o'clock he left for an early dinner, but could not eat, not tonight. So he killed two hours in the botanical gardens. There were four pink flamingos in a green pond filled with lily pads, and at dusk he saw a girl who from a distance looked like Maya. She was moving between the lines of bamboo. He watched until she fell into the arms of a man beneath a streetlamp.

When he arrived to the station the night staff was just arriving. He showed his pass at the door, then walked down the corridor. It was quiet now, with only the distant sound of a typewriter, a shredder, someone asking for coffee and a reply that there was only enough cream for one cup.

There were notations for coffee in the records, also tea, soft drinks, chocolate bars and a subscription to a boating magazine. Another list covered maintenance costs: light bulbs, oil for the motor pool, even cat food.

274

Another hour and he had moved beyond the establishment costs into operations. Here the record was less defined, notations more ambiguous. Ammunition costs ran seventy-two dollars a month, not that Cassidy could figure where it went, not seventy-two dollars worth of 9-millimeter rounds. Next there was equipment: three subminiature cameras in the last six months, one Nikon with a telephoto lens, two Panasonic tape recorders, one voice-activated recorder and a high-speed impulse transmitter. *Jay had always believed in a well-stocked shop.*

At ten o'clock the night staff broke for fifteen minutes. There was a trolley of sandwiches and pastry in cellophane. Someone asked if Cassidy wanted a bear-claw, but he didn't answer, not now, not when something was there just beyond his reach among the expenditures for June, July and August.

June—a particularly desolate month. There had been a water shortage, all the taps running thin. Johnny had scored another kilo, and was trying to move it through a hospital on Guam. Cassidy remembered the conversation from a one-room Kowloon slum. The stuff was on the kitchen table, and it was pure, very pure.

Next came July and August, and everywhere that Cassidy went he kept hearing those breathless chuckles. "Dope is a political statement," Ray had said, which was as good a justification as any. While another kilo came on a rainy Thursday, with three more buyers waiting in a Los Angeles Holiday Inn. Then on the more legitimate line, Jay kept talking about arming the hill tribes for a sweep into Cambodia to cut the Ho Chi Minh Trail.

But there, right there during the last nine days of July, something else was happening, something vital. He read: *Four-bedroom dwelling with medical team for clandestine occupancy of ten days.* A house and a doctor for thirty-five hundred dollars. In the remote stillness of a Chinese landscape Jay had rented a house and brought himself a doctor who could keep his mouth shut.

Cassidy slowly closed the file. His hands lay on the desk. A house, when this city was filled with perfectly adequate houses where agents could live, rest, be debriefed. And a doctor, when there were already two station doctors to handle problems in the field. From down the corridor came laughter, a cough, someone asking for a date. And yes the dates matched perfectly, absolutely perfectly. Then came another voice asking for the time. Twenty-one minutes to midnight, and past the walled

275

hamlets, between Yuen Long and the wilderness, there had been a house that no one was supposed to have known about.

It took only another fifteen minutes to find Johnny's signature in the duty roster. He had logged the extra hours as hazardous work in the field. Then replacing the files Cassidy couldn't keep his hands from shaking, and he was thirsty. But the water cooler stood beside the shredder and there would be at least two girls feeding-in the evening waste. Of course there were always soft drinks, but again there would be people in the lounge. And he did not want to see them. He did not want to draw them into conversation. *Come on, what were you really doing down there?*

Past the cipher rooms he saw a boy named Wimberly who worked in codes and was supposed to be a genius. He was slumped in the doorway, faintly ridiculous in checked slacks, penny loafers and a Dacron shirt. On the wall behind was a photograph of Albert Einstein, the face forming out of a mushroom cloud.

"Hey, Billy, long time no see."

"How are you, Wimberly?"

"Not bad, not bad. How about you?"

"I'm fine." But he knew that he must have looked terrible: pale, arcs of sweat around the armpits.

"I understand you people really have something big in the works."

Cassidy shrugged. "Maybe."

"Oh yeah. I heard it was something really tremendous."

Then came an awful moment when Cassidy had nothing to say, but Wimberly continued to stare.

Until finally Cassidy managed to say, "Hey, Wimberly, you haven't seen Johnny, have you?"

"Who?"

"Ray."

"Johnny Ray?"

"Yeah."

Then Wimberly grinned. "Now what would I be doing hanging around scum like that?"

It was warm in the streets with a heavy wind off the harbor. Cassidy walked slowly, but his instinct was to run, or else slip into the alley and listen for the sound of footsteps stopping. On the Garden Road two limousines waited underneath the trees. Farther down were the street magicians and prostitutes waiting under the neon. Twice he retraced his path, but saw no one.

He waited twenty minutes before entering his apartment, watching from the dark arcade at the end of the block. Once he saw a passing van with blacked-out windows, then two lovers pausing to kiss by a clump of suffocated foliage. When he finally reached his room he drew the curtains and gently laid a chair in the doorway. Then he sat on his bed with another whiskey and Coke, the ashtray filled with cigarette butts, the far wall washed in red from a blinking Pepsi-Cola sign on the neighboring roof.

Another five minutes passed, and he supposed that he should have contacted Crane. Agent achieves primary target, case officer must be informed. But he also knew what Crane would say in that reasonable voice: *Go easy, Billy. Go slowly. Wait until tomorrow.* When it was now that he felt her very near, saw her eyes in every shadow, the memory of her hair.

He rose from that filthy mattress and walked twelve paces, counting from the corner. Then he used a bread knife to pry away the wooden floorboards. The Browning, the extra magazine of ammunition and the switchblade were wrapped in plastic sandwich bags. There was also an escape passport and eleven thousand dollars in cash. It was all the money he had in the world, and when he looked at it he thought he had better spend it wisely, because when this was all over he might not get another job for a long time.

Once more he kept seeing shadows in the streets that he couldn't quite identify. There were also lovers who may not have been lovers, and cars that seemed too slow when they passed. Three blocks from his apartment he found a cab, which was supposed to have been a dangerous way to go. But this driver looked fairly safe: a Chinese boy with a speech impediment. Then at some point along the causeway, Cassidy shut his eyes and saw one distinct image of himself wondering under fluorescent lights. *They were all part of it. Ray, Wimberly, Ruth, those girls at the shredder—all part of it.*

Johnny Ray's apartment stood on a bluff at the end of a narrow road. Cassidy told the driver of the cab to stop at the bottom of the hill. Then he paid the boy and began to walk. Through breaks in the trees he saw the harbor lights, and the lights of the lower villas. Once he paused when he thought he heard a movement in the vines. Then he paused again to cock the Browning.

There were no lights in the windows, but music drifted from an upstairs room. There were firecracker casings on the garden path, beer cans stuck in the trellis. *He's had a party,* Cassidy thought. There were cigarette butts in the fountain. Then on the doorstep he waited, breathing deeply, listening for voices. Then there was nothing to keep him from knocking; softly first, then louder.

Ray opened the door without turning on the light. He was wearing a purple velour bathrobe over black silk pajamas. There was a glass of wine in his hand. His lips looked swollen.

"Billy?"

"Hey, man, you weren't sleeping, were you? I mean I heard music."

"No. I wasn't sleeping."

"Is someone in there?"

"No."

"Can I come in?"

Now Cassidy stood by the plate glass. Across the terrace lay shadows of surrounding palms. There was another bottle of wine on a varnished chest, a lacquered fish on the wall. Ray had moved from the bar to the sofa. There was only the light from the kitchen, and the city lights through the window, reflected off a bank of clouds.

"So what's happening, Billy?"

"Just passing by."

"At two in the morning?"

"Well, you know how it is. I couldn't sleep."

There was still that faint, dreamy voice from the radio upstairs. On the mantel was a photograph of a naked girl. Cassidy stepped closer to examine her face, and saw that a cat was tattooed on her breast.

"Who is this?" Running a finger along the silver frame.

"Just some girl."

"Not bad."

"She's all right."

"What's her name?"

"Number four."

"Is she the one who scratched your face?"

"No."

"Then who was it?"

"Number six."

278

There were sounds of distant traffic, and a helicopter circling above. Cassidy put down the photograph and turned back to Ray.

"You know I've been thinking about what happened to your face, Johnny."

"Yeah?"

"I was thinking that it healed pretty fast. I mean, this girl cuts you only a few days ago, and it's already healed."

"So what?"

"Well, looking at those scratches now, it occurs to me that they must have been pretty bad. I mean what they really look like is deep cuts that have been healing for about two weeks. Know what I mean?"

"No, man, I don't know what you mean."

"Let me put it like this, Johnny. Are you sure you didn't get those scars about two weeks ago? Thursday night? August the fourth?"

Ray slowly moved his eyes from the window, past a shaft of moonlight on the carpet and finally into Cassidy's eyes. His fingers were tight around the stem of his glass. His head was cocked to the side. And in that motionless second, Cassidy withdrew the Browning, smiled and flipped the safety off.

"It's like this, Johnny. You either tell me what I want to know, or I swear to God I'm going to blow your kneecap off."

Ray just kept staring while the glass slipped out of his hand, bounced on the carpet but didn't break.

"You want to tell me what this is all about, Billy?"

"Sure I'll tell you. Two weeks ago you picked up a girl at the border. Nineteen, pretty, half-Chinese. Now I want to know where she is."

"Hey, Billy, I haven't the slightest idea what you're talking about."

"Yes you do. You picked her up about midnight. You took her to a house six miles this side of the border. There was a doctor there, and he probably gave her something to knock her out. Later maybe Feng came by, or was it Jerry Woo?"

Again Ray's eyes fell away to the harbor and the clouds have the bay. "Mind if I ask a question?"

"What?"

"Are you playing alone, or is this a group effort?"

"What do you think?"

"I honestly don't know."

"It's a group effort, Johnny. In fact it's the whole fucking Desk. Pyle, Crane, all of them."

Then Ray breathed deeply and began to nod. "Okay. Okay, Billy. What do you want?"

"Where is she?"

"At Feng's."

"What are they doing with her?"

"I'm not sure."

"Can you get her out of there?"

"No."

"Can Sagan?"

"Maybe."

"Is she all right?"

"More or less."

"What's that supposed to mean?"

"Well, it's like this, Billy. I think Feng is keeping her pretty loaded on smack. I think he plans to string her out and then turn her over to one of his houses."

There was something terrible about the way that Cassidy's mouth twisted up, and the veins stood out along his neck. But all he said was, "Get dressed, Johnny. You're going to take me for a ride in your Corvette."

It was nearly dawn when Cassidy and Ray reached the house on the point. Because Cassidy had telephoned earlier, Eliot was waiting on the veranda. When the Corvette came to a stop, he walked around to the driver's side, pulled Ray out by the arm, and led him inside. Then Cassidy was alone.

For a while he sat on the wooden steps and listened to Ray's voice drifting through the kitchen window. There were also softer tones from Simon Crane. Then without really thinking he wandered out to the point. The tide was in. He was not cold.

Crane emerged from the house just after first light. He wore a ratty cardigan and a baseball cap. The rising sun was in his eyes, the sea turning to a deeper blue. As Cassidy watched the old man approach slowly through the grass, he he had the oddest thought that time was slipping through his fingers.

Then Crane sat down and said, "You did well, Billy. You did very well."

"What's going to happen to Ray?"

"He's going back to Langley this afternoon."

"And then what?"

"I don't know."

"Will they put him in the cooler?"

"Please, Billy. I don't know."

Along the horizon were the fishing boats in black shadow. Cassidy had turned his face to the wind. He heard Crane say, "The fact that she's at Feng's residence makes it all a bit more complex. We have no legal base to send a team there, nor do the British."

"So?"

"Well, it means that you'll have to go in alone, and with no support at all. As a matter of fact I'm not even officially going to know about it. If you get my point?"

"Yeah, sure."

"You should also understand that if anything goes wrong you're on your own."

"What about Jay? Is he on his own too?"

"What do you mean?"

"I'm going to have to bring him in with me, aren't I?"

"Oh I see."

"So where does it stand?"

Crane lowered his eyes. He was looking at Cassidy's hands. "I can only tell you that I have no special instructions one way or another. Do you understand?"

"Yeah. I understand."

By the time they began treading back through the grass, the gulls had descended along the cliffs, the sun was well above the sea. They had moved in silence past the withered trees.

Then Crane said suddenly, "I suppose you understand the irony."

"Huh?" There was a cigarette between Cassidy's lips, but he did not have a match.

"Regarding what Feng is doing."

"What are you talking about?"

"Maya's mother had been in a brothel."

"So?"

"I imagine that Feng loves the irony of placing Maya in one too. Not to mention the effect something like that would have on Polly. I mean a death is one thing, but years of not knowing, or knowing and being unable to do anything about it."

Cassidy spit his cigarette out. "Look, I just want you to know what's happening here, Billy."

"I know what's happening."

"Fine. Then bear in mind that Maya has been through a lot."

"What do you mean?"

"Well she may not—I'm not sure how to put this—she may not be the same girl that you remember."

"So?"

"I just don't want you to be disappointed, that's all."

"I've got no expectations, Crane. Okay?"

When they parted Crane did not return to the house, but watched from the veranda as Cassidy stalked out through the grass, lit another cigarette, and finally slid into the black Corvette. Later Crane would be asked if he had suspected that the boy had been close to an emotional breakdown, and recalling this moment he would say no. Even at the end every movement had been controlled.

Cassidy returned to his room. He was tired and hungry, and at seven o'clock in the morning he did not know where else to go. For a while he lay down on the dirty mattress and shut his eyes. A wind had risen, whistling through the telephone lines, knocking at the double windows. Now he was too hot, now too cold. Once he dozed, only to be wakened violently by a barking dog. When he finally rose again he saw that a fog had moved in, and the ends of the city were lost.

A long time ago, at least six or seven days, he had wondered what it would be like just before his final move on Jay, his ex-patron. He had imagined all the minor preparations: sitting on his mattress and dismantling the Browning, cleaning it, reassembling it, then feeding in the magazine. He had imagined sighting into the electric light bulb, dry firing once, then lying down to rest.

By eleven the fog had drifted even farther up from the docks. Now through the streaked window he saw shadowless streets diminishing into gray. Something is different, he told himself. Something is different but nothing has changed. Then he moved slowly through the shambles of his room and turned the shower on. While he waited for the water to heat up he picked up a few bits of clothing from the floorboards: shorts, socks, a shirt that was passably clean. Then above the water basin he was once more drawn into the lure of the mirror.

It was a low fog, and on the street Cassidy could not see more than a block. Light barely touched the moving figures, gave them no shadow, no relief. At the end of an alley off Pedder Road he saw a swinging lantern in a window, and beggars in a circle tossing bones. There was a toy shop farther on that he always passed on his way to the station. He had never seen the door unlocked, only the toys rusting on the shelves.

The station seemed more subdued than usual. Typists were chatting quietly in the lounge. Down a corridor there were muffled voices. Someone was talking about the weekend and a Chinese girl at the dog races. The other doors were shut, and there were no other sounds, except the occasional telephone and the squeal of a trolley file.

Cassidy wasted the first hour scanning through consulate circulars. Employees were advised about a softball game on Saturday, and a rise in local rape and beatings. Women who lived alone were particularly vulnerable.

At noon he wandered out to the streets and a bar for a sandwich that tasted like cardboard. Newsmen ate here, sometimes the junior clerks from trading houses. But nobody knew Cassidy. Nobody spoke to him, nobody even looked at him. He ate staring at a page from the local *Times.* There had been another skirmish along the Mekong Delta, and there was black smoke rising from the jungle. It was said that the war had killed emotion, but this was untrue. Merely, one did not take sides with what was happening in Vietnam, not when the opium routes were making more than a million dollars a month.

The afternoon was even slower. Cassidy killed two hours glancing through the transcripts of a refugee report. There was also a low-grade brief from Macao. Apparently terrorists had killed a Japanese businessman. At four Cassidy noticed a thin, dreary boy named Lumwell who worked for the transport pool. He was dressed in black gabardine, bent over a trolley sorting through the mail pack. Cassidy came up from behind him and said, "Hey, Lumwell, seen the man?"

The boy did not look up from the stack of envelopes and Cassidy was left staring at the back of his neck. There seemed to be some kind of rash at the hairline.

"Mr. Sagan will be in later today," he replied.

"Are you going to see him?"

"Possibly."

"Will you give him a message for me?"

"Put it in writing."

"Come on, Lumwell, just tell him that I want to talk to him, okay?"

"Maybe."

At five o'clock there was a commotion in the lounge. Somebody said something about a bomb, but it was only a traffic accident. A child had been struck by a car. His body had been thrown across the pavement onto the steps of the consulate. Cassidy watched with the other station employees from the third-floor window. Finally one of the older clerks told everyone to return to work. "Go back to your desks, people. There's nothing more to see." But nobody moved. The women in particular could not stop looking.

Cassidy spent the last torpid hour of the day leafing through memos from Singapore, Rangoon and Manila. These memos were supposed to have been kept in the vault, but somehow they always wound up in general circulation. As usual there was nothing notable, except a few words regarding the suicide of a trade commissioner in Kuala Lumpur. According to the Singapore station the man's death was still a mystery. The commissioner had not been homosexual. He had not been in debt. There was simply no reason why he would have wanted to kill himself. In the end they chalked it up to psychological, which meant that it was nobody's fault.

At ten minutes to six Cassidy laid aside the last memo and went into the lounge to get a drink of water. From the window he saw that the fog had turned slightly yellow. There were headlights strung out for miles along the point, and a faint odor of burnt ash. For more than fifteen minutes he stayed fixed at that window.

Until he heard Jay Sagan's voice softly from behind. "What are you doing, Billy?"

Sagan was leaning in the doorway, one arm draped across the water cooler.

"Hello, sir."

Sagan's blue blazer was slung over his shoulder. His pale red tie was unknotted at the collar.

"I understand you've been looking for me."

"Yes, sir. I have."

"What for?"

"As a matter of fact I was wondering if we could possibly get together later. Maybe have a drink or something."

Sagan frowned. "Well, Billy, you know I'm a little busy these days."

"Yes, sir. But if I could just talk to you for an hour. That is, it's sort of important."

Sagan thought for a moment, then looked at his watch. "Okay. I've got to meet someone off the Hennessy at nine. Why don't you drop by that little place near the Ice House at ten. We can have a drink there."

"That would be fine, sir. Thank you."

"Oh, Billy?"

"Sir?"

"You haven't seen Johnny, have you?"

"Johnny?" With the taste of adrenaline in his mouth.

"That's right. Have you seen him?"

"Uh, yeah. I saw him last night."

"Can you tell me where he is now?"

"Well, not exactly, sir, but I think he's taking a long weekend. That is, I know he met some girl and well..."

Then an image that Cassidy had seen a thousand times before: Jay chewing his lip in disgust.

"Christ, I wish he would tell me before running off like that."

"Yes, sir."

When Sagan had gone Cassidy turned back to the window. The yellow fog was sliding faster now along the street below. Two boys in black pajamas were dropping something down an open drain. Cassidy remained poised at the glass for a long time.

Cassidy returned to his room at seven o'clock. He knew that waiting here in this shabby stillness would be hard, but once again he had no place else to go. He was a stranger in the local bars and restaurants, and he did not have any friends. For a while he tried to read an old issue of *National Geographic*. It had been lying on the bathroom floor for almost a year. The pages were stuck together. There was an article on the monkey cult of Katmandu, and a photograph of a woman suckling an ape.

After another half hour he thought that there was a chance he would be able to eat. He wasn't certain, but there was a chance. He boiled two eggs and heated a bowl of rice. He sprinkled the rice with curry powder and laid the eggs in a dish. In the end, however, he could only manage a few bites of rice. The eggs were disgusting.

After he finished eating he returned to the mattress and sat down slowly with his back against the grimy plaster. After another half hour he sank down even lower. At some point before he fell asleep he thought of Polly's daughter again. For quite a while now he had almost been afraid to think of her too often because he had forgotten what she looked like. So he kept her memory for special moments. Then, as if running his

285

eyes across a faint horizon, he could usually recall something she had said or done, some way she had looked at him.

There came a point when he was ready, but it was still too early to leave. He stood by the door and switched off the light. Then there was only the reflection of that neon sign on the far wall, and a few city lights through the curtain. He was conscious of the weight of the Browning on his shoulder, the knife strapped to his calf. One half-formed memory passed of a room in black walnut, a bottle of vermouth on the table, an elephant's tusk on the mantel. And there was Jay pointing to a map of Asia, saying: *That's the playground.* Then very quietly Cassidy stepped out into the foul hallway.

The bar was dark, lit only by a string of green bulbs and candles in wine bottles. All around were slender Chinese girls. Tacked to the walls were fishnets, life preservers and lacquered starfish. Crab shells served as ashtrays. Every waitress wore a sailor's cap, silk jersey and black stockings. There was a garish portrait of a naked girl among mauve orchids. Her legs were entangled in jungle vines.

Cassidy took a table at the rear and ordered a beer. A dry voice sang to a steel guitar: *One of these days I'm going to see you again. One of these days for sure.* In the booth next to Cassidy were two drunk American soldiers. One of them kept whispering, "You got to put a little fear into his life. He needs a little fear." Another soldier was chatting with a girl in the doorway. He ran his fingers down her shoulder to lower the strap of her dress.

To avoid trouble Cassidy did not look into anyone's eyes. He looked only at the pattern on the surface of the table and the reflection of light in a mirror. So when Sagan finally arrived it was as if he had materialized out of the smoke and gloom. Cassidy glanced up to the entrance and there was Sagan, hands on his hips, back arched slightly.

"Sorry I'm late," Sagan said as he sat down. "Some asshole thinks I've got nothing better to do than listen to his bull."

"It's okay," Cassidy said softly. "I only just got here myself."

A girl on a stool in the corner was examining a run in her stocking. There was also a dark bruise on her thigh. Sagan called for a waitress. When she came he ordered scotch. As she moved away he made a joke about her breasts.

"So how are you, Billy?"

286

"I'm okay, sir."

"I know I haven't been around too much, but this has been a very rough period, very rough."

"Yes, sir. I understand."

"Not that it won't pay off. I can promise you that it's going to pay. And I'm talking the big table. But it takes a lot of time."

Another willowy girl appeared beneath the fishnets, smoothing her dress, wetting her lips. Sagan glanced at her briefly, shook his head.

"You haven't had too much action lately, have you, Billy?"

"Sir?"

"With the women."

"Oh. No, I guess not."

"You know I'm not running a monastery. There's no reason why you shouldn't go out and have some fun."

"Yes, sir."

"In fact I think it might do you some good. Now I admit that some of these girls here aren't what you'd want to take home to mother, but they're fine for a night. Some of them are just fine."

But closer now Cassidy could see that the girl that Sagan had been watching was probably a junkie. Or at least she had a junkie's walk, and slow eyes that kept restlessly scanning the faces at the bar.

"Maybe you'd like me to set someting up for you, Billy. I know some nice girls, extremely nice girls. How about it?"

"Well, I guess that would be okay."

"I could even get something going for you tonight."

"Tonight, sir?"

"Sure. Why not?"

"Well, I'm a little tired tonight."

The laughter was fading. The women disappearing.

"But there was something else, wasn't there, Billy? Something you wanted to talk to me about?"

Cassidy smiled. "Yeah, but I guess it doesn't seem that important now. I guess I just needed somebody to talk to."

"Was it about that mainland line of yours?"

"Yeah, but it can wait, sir. Really."

"But I want you to know it's a sound idea, Billy."

"Thank you, sir."

"And I haven't forgotten."

"No, sir."

"So as soon as I'm out from all this pressure we're going to take a look at it again. You can count on that."

"Yes, sir. Thank you."

The night air smelled of the sea. There was the blur of neon from other clubs along the waterfront, the wind stirring in the palms. The two men walked slowly over pavement that was slick from the mist. The riff of a clarinet was trailing from an open door.

"I'd like to thank you for meeting me here tonight," Cassidy said.

"My pleasure, Billy."

"Yeah, but I really appreciate it."

"Anytime."

"And I wonder if I could ask you for one more favor."

"Name it."

Then the line he had been waiting all night to deliver. "I don't have a car, and I was wondering if you could give me a lift home."

In the final minutes Cassidy was very conscious of every small detail: the nightscape, a schooner in the bay, a clanging jetty bell. Jay's Cadillac was silver gray with tan upholstery. There was a tiny mirror on the end of his key chain, a stain on the sleeve of his blazer. He drove with the window down, resting one elbow on the door. Beside him Cassidy had one knee wedged against the dashboard. They were moving through a neighborhood that was supposed to have been overrun with cats.

"Heard from your mom lately?" Sagan asked.

"Yes. She's doing fine." Except that he hadn't thought of her in months.

"That's good. She's a great lady."

"Thank you."

Past the neon strip lay the factory yards. The street was littered with shredded newspaper, tin cans, crushed packing crates. The mist was still rising from the sea.

"Next time you talk to your mom, tell her hello for me."

"Sure."

"Because I never find time to write. You know how it is."

And then in a voice entirely hollow and flat, "Yeah. I know how it is," as he slipped the Browning from his jacket and cocked it.

"What are you doing, Billy?" Staring at the gun on the boy's knee.

288

"Just pull over."

"Come on, Billy. What's going on?"

"Just stop the fucking car."

There was a brick wall near a loading ramp, and past the wall were the dock lights and black water. A wind through the alley brought odors of decaying fish.

"What's this all about, Billy?" His voice was still very calm.

"I want you to drive to Feng's house. I want you to drive real slow. If you hit the gas I'm going to shoot for the left foot."

Sagan smiled. "Why don't you tell me what this is all about?"

"Just drive."

"Come on, Billy. Is it the girl? Is that it?"

"Drive."

"Jesus, Billy. You have no idea what the hell you're doing. You just don't have a clue."

Then Cassidy raised the gun. "Don't make me kill you, okay?"

The road was empty and unlit. Past the deeper bay lay flooded paddies and distant village lights.

"Tell me one thing, Billy. How long have you been working for them?"

"Don't talk."

"A month? A year? How long, Billy?"

There was a stretch of swamp, then a row of banana trees. A fire was burning in the northern hills.

"Or maybe you just started? Is that it, Billy? They picked you up when you flew back to Langley? What did they tell you? What?"

There were pine trees against the far sky. The air was colder.

"Come on, Billy. What did they tell you?"

And then because it didn't matter: "I saw the photographs of Maya."

At the start of the long curve before Feng's villa, Cassidy told Sagan to cut the ignition and coast to a stop. There were lights in the upstairs window and the sound of insects washing down from the reeds.

Cassidy said, "Tell me who's up there."

"Look, Billy, why don't you just tell me what you want out of this?"

"Who's up there?"

Sagan began to grind his teeth. "A couple of Feng's people."

"What about Feng?"

"No."

"And Jerry Woo?"

"They're both on the island."

Then slowly, still not lowering the gun, Cassidy slid out of his jacket and draped it over his arm. "We're going up there. When we get to the top you sound the horn until one of them comes out. Then you tell him to bring out the girl."

"Christ, Billy, if you want the girl—"

"Fuck it up and I'll kill you."

The road to the villa rose up from the highway through the trees. There were lights beyond the mulberry vines, then white brick and green shutters. When the headlights swept through the iron gate a figure emerged from the portico, a thin, wiry boy. He was dressed like all of Feng's boys in a short leather coat, blue jeans and sneakers.

As the boy approached the car, Sagan called out, "Hello, Larry. How's it going?"

"Mr. Sagan?"

"That's right. How are you?"

"Mr. Sagan, everything okay?"

"Sure. Everything okay."

A second figure was watching from the window, half hidden by the fringe of leaves.

"Listen, Larry, I want you to go in there and bring the girl out here."

"Girl?"

"You know what I'm talking about. Now you go in there and bring her out."

The boy glanced over his shoulder, then ran his hand across his mouth. "I don't know, Mr. Sagan. I don't think I'm supposed to do this. I don't think Mr. Feng—"

"I'll take the responsibility, Larry. Now you just go in there and bring out that girl."

"Okay, Mr. Sagan."

"And hurry."

"You did good," Cassidy told him. "Keep it up."

Now more leaves were tumbling over the gravel, rising up in the headlights. There was also a sound like an incoming train.

"Billy. Billy, listen to me."

"Shut up. They're coming."

Cassidy did not turn his head, only shifted his eyes. Two figures stood

290

in the porchlight—Maya and the Chinese boy. The boy was holding her by the arm. He seemed to be whispering in her ear. Then he pulled her roughly down the steps and out across the gravel.

Days ago Cassidy had envisioned this moment, imagined the approaching footsteps while he told himself: *Be still, watch for the small movements, the hand slipping down inside a coat, glancing eyes, a nod.* But he could not help himself from looking at her now: hair blowing across her face, the thin dress, the bare feet. Once she stumbled, but the boy caught her and they kept on coming.

"Talk to him," Cassidy whispered. "Be friendly."

Now the boy was pulling her around to Sagan's open window. Her eyes were blank. Her lips were slightly parted. Even when the boy released her arm she did not move.

"Now I want you to put her in the car, Larry." But Sagan's voice was taut. He might have been in pain.

"In the car, Mr. Sagan?"

"That's right, Larry. Just put her in the car."

But again the boy looked over his shoulder, then down to Cassidy's jacket. "Everything okay, Mr. Sagan?"

"Yes, Larry. Everything is fine." But his voice was still too cold, hands rigid on the steering wheel.

And the boy leaned farther into the open window. "You sure, Mr. Sagan? Mr. Sagan?"

Into the dead silence. Where for one fragile instant no one moved, no one spoke. Only their eyes met, and glanced away. Then slowly the boy began to raise his arm, to slip his fingers inside his coat. While Sagan started screaming, *no,* Cassidy pulled the trigger.

The boy's head jerked back. His eyes widened. He may not have even understood what had happened. Then the shock passed, and he actually seemed to recover. He straightened himself as if trying to regain his composure in an embarrassing situation. Until he realized that blood was pouring from his throat.

Cassidy couldn't help watching as the boy slumped over the fender, fingers reaching for something, leaving tracks of blood. Even as Sagan lunged forward, throwing his shoulder, trying to wrench away the gun, Cassidy couldn't keep himself from the lure of that boy's eyes.

Sagan held Cassidy's wrist with one hand. His other hand was locked around the barrel of the gun. He twisted it up, trying to bring the muzzle into Cassidy's chest. Once their eyes met, and Cassidy said, *wait*, but Sagan kept twisting until the gun slipped free, clattering past the dashboard, the steering column, the brake pedal.

And again Cassidy said, *wait-a-minute-please*, but Sagan did not understand, probably wouldn't have waited if he had. Because after all he was still the King of Asia, while Billy Cassidy was just a Third World man. So in the end Sagan reached down, picked up the gun and swung back around to fire. But turning, he saw the glint of metal, then Cassidy's knife and the searing pain.

Cassidy felt the blood on his hand, felt Sagan's breath, and felt his weight working against the blade. And as the eyes started clouding over, that questioning look: *What did you do that for, Billy?* Until Jay's body slipped away, and Cassidy called out Maya's name.

She did not respond, only stared back like all the others had stared. So in the end he had to drag her, to push her down on the back seat. As he drove off he saw the outline of another boy in the porchlight, lifting a rifle to fire. But there was no shot, probably because that boy also wasn't certain what had happened.

Cassidy drove for about five miles, watching the highway passing under the tires. Finally he glanced down, saw that Jay was still breathing, and pulled off into the trees and a bamboo grove. When he cut the engine there was only the sound of crickets and breath escaping from Sagan's wound. When he pulled Sagan from the car and laid him on the cool ground, the girl sat up in the back seat and began to cry.

The ground was soft, the leaves damp. Cassidy knelt beside Sagan, and the moisture soaked into his jeans. When he pressed his hand to Sagan's chest he knew that the man was going to die. He had also left the headlights on so that the mangoes seemed ghostly, spread out for a hundred yards.

After a long time of labored breathing Sagan managed to whisper, "I think I need a doctor, Billy."

A wind had brought the scent of violets, and odors you smelled in every Asian forest. There was also the rattle of dry bamboo. Sagan asked, "Is that really John Polly's daughter?" Cassidy nodded.

"Yeah," Cassidy nodded. "That's his daughter."

Sagan smiled, "Pretty girl," and died.

There was an old government-issue blanket in the trunk of the car. Cassidy spread it over Sagan's body, then opened the rear door, and softly

292

asked Maya to step out. She looked at him briefly but there did not seem to be any recognition. She was still in shock, or else heavily drugged. While he lifted the body into the back seat, she stood gazing into the opaque light and stirring leaves.

They drove in silence. He did not look at her, although he wanted to. She sat very still with her hands braced against the dashboard. The rice fields gave a depth to the landscape that Cassidy had never noticed before. There were villages behind the paddy dikes he could not recall ever having seen before. Twice he tried to speak, but could not think of anything meaningful to say. Then out along the marsh he finally asked if she was all right. She did not answer, but when he turned to look at her he saw that her face was tracked with tears.

Suddenly she whispered his name, "Billy?" In his dream she had put her head on his shoulder and encircled her arms around his waist. As it happened, however, they both just sat, staring at the road passing under the wheels. *Billy?*

When they reached the house on the point she was taken from him almost immediately. Apparently Crane had brought in a doctor from Langley, a woman who supposedly specialized in these kinds of cases. There had also been a room prepared, one of the nicer rooms with a view of the bay. As they led her away Cassidy watched from the doorway.

Then for a while Cassidy sat in the kitchen with Eliot and a bottle of inexpensive brandy. Earlier Eliot had tried to strike up a conversation, but Cassidy told him to shut up. In an adjoining room Crane was speaking on the telephone. Cassidy could not hear all that was said, but he heard enough to know that there was still some question as to what was to be done with Jay Sagan's body.

Finally there were also a few brief words between Cassidy and Crane, spoken once again out along the palisade. It was another gray dawn. A cold wind had driven the gulls inland.

"Do you want to tell me what happened?" Crane said.

Cassidy shrugged. "I had to kill him, that's all. There was also a boy, one of Feng's boys. I guess I had to kill him too."

"Did anyone see you?"

"No."

Crane turned back to the sea. Even with the sun above the horizon the water remained the color of lead. After a moment of silence he said, "I can't promise you that everything will be all right."

293

"I know."

"Naturally I'll speak in your behalf, but I can't promise."

Cassidy shrugged. "It doesn't matter," and started to turn away. But stopped. "Hey, Simon. Maya is going to be okay, isn't she?"

"Yes. She's going to be fine."

"Because I thought maybe they really hurt her."

"They did, but she'll be fine."

"That's good. And Simon?"

"Yes?"

"She didn't—that is, she didn't say anything about me, did she?"

"No. I'm afraid she didn't."

"Oh. Well, I guess that doesn't matter either," and walked off through the grass.

But later that afternoon as he was once more sitting on the rocks, Crane came up from behind and said that she wanted to see him. For a moment Cassidy did not respond. He did not even turn his head. Then he stood up quickly, and lobbed a beer can over the cliff.

The door to her bedroom was shut, and he hesitated before knocking, then lightly tapped three times. And again.

"Billy?"

He entered slowly. She was lying on the bed. The light was faintly blue through blue curtains. There was a vase of rosebuds on the nightstand, a sea urchin on the windowsill, a mirror set in a ship's wheel.

At first neither seemed to know quite what to say. He had taken a few steps into the room, and then stopped. She had propped herself up on the pillows, and he saw that she wore a red flannel nightgown. His hands were jammed in his pockets. She was winding the frayed end of the quilt around her finger.

Finally he managed to say, "How are you?"

She answered, but did not look up. "I'm better, thank you."

"I guess they told you that your father will be coming here pretty soon."

"Yes. They told me."

He glanced down at his canvas shoes. The bloodstains had turned brown. "Look, I'm sorry about what happened back there."

She shook her head. "Don't be sorry. I'm glad you did it," but she might have been talking in her sleep. Her voice was toneless. She was still knotting that stray thread around her finger.

While he thought: *This is bad. This is really bad.*

294

"Are you going to be here much longer?" she asked.

He shrugged. "I don't think so."

"Why not?"

"Well, it's kind of hard to explain...."

"Is it because of what happened? What you did to those men?"

"Yeah. That's part of it."

"Where are you going to go?"

"I'm not sure."

"To America?"

"Maybe."

The conversation did not end, it evaporated. Suddenly Cassidy felt very awkward facing this remarkably beautiful girl with bloodstains on his shoes. On the wall to his left was a watercolor of the Chinese coast, and another of a schooner in high wind. He had never much liked ships, and the nothingness of the sea.

"Look, Maya. I think I'd better get going now."

She did not reply, still unraveling thread from the quilt.

"Maybe I'll stop in before I leave, okay?"

Again she said nothing, until he was actually turning the doorknob. Then she called, "Billy, wait." And when he turned around to face her: "I love you."

Which only proved what he had always believed—sometimes even losers get lucky.

In the late afternoon Crane drafted a cable to Michael Dart regarding the rescue of John Polly's daughter. Early the next morning Dart left the coded transcript behind a loose brick in a wall that ringed a grove of chestnut trees, and there it lay for five critical days.

Had Polly read that cable the day on which it was delivered, the ending of his story might have been very different. But probably not... all that really might have changed would have been his perception of events and the tone of his closing letters.

Polly to Crane: "We are all living erratically now, with a sense of forces closing in. They tell me that three days ago someone tampered with the premier's limousine. There have also been problems with the telephone service. For myself I am not frightened, but for Tommy and the others. ..."

Additionally he wrote of stagnation and lingering suspicion. Chou En-lai, he noted, was said to have spent much of his time in relative solitude,

295

seeing only a handful of advisors late in the evenings. There were also power blackouts and radio broadcasts frequently broken by static. Every evening at nine o'clock the crowds began to thin so that by ten the streets were virtually empty, except for the urban militia and passing government troops. Finally Polly wrote that the children had vanished, or at least he rarely saw them playing anymore.

Attached to this letter were two pages summarizing the tactical status of Chou En-lai's main defense line against the 571. As outlined in an earlier letter, Polly described that defense as largely dependent upon the element of surprise. There were twelve loyal units from the urban militia in Peking and another eight in Shanghai and Nanking. "The numbers will suffice," Polly wrote, "if the timing is correct."

In the postscript to this letter there was another reference to those fairly secret plans for an executive evacuation, and a tacked-on sentence regarding Polly's daughter. Of the evacuation Polly wrote only that no one was certain where Mao and Chou En-lai could possibly go, perhaps into the Tibetan hills or farther into the eastern wastes. As for his daughter, his brief note of sorrow seemed particularly pitiful, in that it was actually written the morning after her rescue.

This was the setting for what the Chinese would always recall as Polly's greatest single contribution. Every morning of every day was underscored with fear. Ling had developed a wasting cough and complained of sores in his mouth. Later Polly would admit that twice he had passed that wall by the chestnut grove, but did not stop to look behind the loose brick because he did not believe that there could have been anything of consequence from beyond the mainland, least of all concerning his daughter.

Those in Peking's inner circle were certain never to forget John Polly's final conversation with General Ko Ming. It was Saturday, very late. Polly had been lying on his bed unable to sleep for several hours. Earlier he had opened the shutters, but there was no breeze. The sheets were damp with perspiration. Then from what seemed like a long way off, he heard the telephone ring. He sat up quickly and drew apart the mosquito netting, but the ringing had stopped. By now his heart was beating very rapidly, waiting for another three rings. When he heard them, he lit a cigarette and dressed.

There was no moon and the canal was very dark. Polly walked quickly until he came to the steel bridge where the asphalt fell away to the gravel.

Then he descended the banks, scanning the mud flats for moving shadows.

It was sometime after midnight when the general finally arrived. As always he came from the west, over the marsh, and from the way that he walked Polly could not tell if what he would say would be good or bad. But when they came together at last underneath the bridge, the first words that the general said were, "I believe that I have discovered what you wanted to know."

Later Polly would be asked how he felt listening to the general speak, and in reply he would say that he had felt relieved, even happy. In fact this was a lie, because even during moments of intensity there was still his missing daughter.

But regardless of Polly's personal feelings, his fatigue and distraction, his eventual account of this conversation was remarkably detailed. He noted that he and the general had sat on a rusted girder. They had lit cigarettes to kill the odor of the foul water. Now and then there had been the faint sound of rising bubbles from fish or vegetation. Otherwise there was only silence.

In all, this conversation lasted only thirty minutes, but within that time the general was able to tell Polly nearly everything that is known about the 571. Much of this information was further contained in the 571 manifesto, which was later leaked to selected journalists.

Of particular note was the general's opening statement: Lin Piao had finally emerged openly as the conspiracy leader. Next there was a lengthy description of the basic strategy, involving the seizure of key installations in Peking and other cities by Lin's crack guards. Finally there were specific details regarding the proposed assassination of Mao, which was supposedly to occur while the chairman was en route to Peking.

At this point Polly asked the general when the coup was to take place, and in response the general looked at him in surprise. Obviously annoyed, he said, "I thought I told you. It's the eleventh."

"This month?"

"Of course this month."

"Oh, I see. Thank you," which, Polly would later write, had concluded the conversation.

There was a stunned, frenetic quality to what remained of the night, and each man who played a part in the events would only remember small

297

portions of what happened. Immediately upon returning home Polly telephoned Tommy Ling, and within the hour Ling had met with Chou En-lai. While this meeting took place Polly remained in Ling's apartment, mostly sitting by the window, gazing out to a block of oblong dormitories and patches of racked dirt and concrete. When Ling finally returned home he told Polly that the premier was extremely grateful for all that he had done, and that once this conspiracy had been dismantled, the full resources of the People's Republic would be mobilized to search for Maya. In reply Polly expressed his gratitude, but later, alone in his house, he once more broke down and wept.

Now the letter in which Polly would record the final confrontation. From a careful reading of this letter it is clear that it was actually written in two separate sittings, with a space of about five hours in between.

The first portion of the letter is a fairly disjointed account of Polly's experiences on the night of September 11, while the second portion is a much more objective view of the broader scheme.

According to the letter, Polly was nowhere near the center of the struggle. In fact, he spent the night in a pale green room, drinking tea with Tommy Ling, the radio playing selections from the repertoire of the Shanghai Municipal Orchestra.

Here first reports of the fighting were vague. Polly wrote that all he had initially heard were that the advance strikes had been carried out exactly as was expected with an early morning warning of Nationalist fighters off the coast. In response twenty-two MIG-14's were launched, and the Nationalist aricraft were routed without fire. Then all but two of the MIG's returned to their base, and those two proceeded to Shanghai where they were believed to have strafed the chairman's residence. The chairman, who was nowhere near Shanghai, was of course unharmed.

An hour after this report there was allegedly a second attempt on the chairman's life, this just north of Nanking where the chairman was said to have been on his way to Peking by train. Once again, however, the chairman was nowhere near the area, and so this attempt too was a failure. There was, however, a later discrepancy regarding the details of this attempt. There were those who claimed that the commando team assigned to kill the chairman had been forcibly restrained, while others claimed that the entire plot aborted when the commando leader suffered an eleventh hour fit of guilt.

Later through that night there were sporadic reports of street fighting, with heavy casualties in a village near Hsin-hua. There was also appar-

298

ently mortar fire along the far canals and several deaths at an electrical plant. Polly further noted that at one point there had been rumors that the radio facilities had fallen, thus accounting for an interruption of the music.

Shortly before dawn, after many hours of silence, Polly was taken to an adjoining room, also pale green and windowless. Here there was a narrow bed, a toilet and a photograph of the chairman on the wall. The door was left ajar, and as he lay in the darkness he heard voices from the corridor. Two young men were speaking, and there was something about a maze of clay walls, burning oil on water and a severed artery tied with a shoelace. When Polly awoke again the garrison was silent and the lights extinguished.

The second portion of Polly's letter begins sequentially with his own experiences at about ten o'clock in the morning. He wrote that after lying in the stillness for about an hour, Tommy Ling entered his room with a thermos of lukewarm tea. As they drank Ling explained that from what he had heard, only the advance rebel units had actually engaged in combat, while the reserve units surrendered or fled without a fight. Two military caravans had been intercepted on the road from Nanking. Another three were routed outside Shanghai.

"In most cases," Polly wrote, "it seems that the individual soldier had not even known what it was that he was fighting for. When it became clear to him that the issue was internal and political, the rebellion lost momentum. Now there is some relief, but with six hundred deaths no one is cheering."

As for Lin Piao and the eight others of his immediate circle, even today the mystery remains. According to Polly, Lin had spent the night of the attack at his country residence in Peitaiho. When it became clear to him that the coup had failed, he was supposed to have telephoned four comrades, possibly Han Chow among them. Within minutes an escape route was activated, and there were several reports from witnesses who claimed to have seen a convoy of limousines speeding to an airfield outside of Peking. It was also rumored that the body of a limousine driver had been found in a field not far from Lin's residence. The driver had been shot through the neck and pushed from a moving vehicle.

Once the convoy reached the airport there were again discrepancies as to exactly what occurred. One report said that there had been more shooting, while others denied this. It was, however, generally agreed that

299

at some point before midnight Lin and eight others boarded a British-made Trident and took off in a northeasterly direction toward the Soviet border.

The next developments were even more ambiguous. Polly maintained that the first clear indication of what happened came when the Ulan Bator regime requested information from Peking regarding the crash of a Chinese aircraft of British make deep in Mongolia. There were references to half-burnt corpses, documents and weapons. Next there was a Soviet query also regarding the crash of a British-made Trident with Chinese markings, and again references to documents and weapons. In response to all this Peking remained silent.

In conclusion Polly wrote, "It seemes clear only that Lin Piao is finally dead, and what he stood for has died with him." As for himself, Polly added that he felt as he was now living life from a great distance. He had eaten very little. He had smoked too many cigarettes. There was no direct mention of his daughter, but his feelings were implicit in these closing lines: "I cannot say now what the future will be, nor even if I can face it."

Which later may have struck him as a little too maudlin, because it was only an hour later when, while placing this letter for Dart to retrieve, he found that cable from Simon Crane: *Your daughter is well and safe.*

At some point during the twenty-four hours immediately following the events of September 11, John Polly actually spoke with Simon Crane by telephone. When Polly had learned that his daughter was safe, he went to Michael Dart in a fit of excitement, and against all laws of the trade demanded that he speak with her directly. Dart protested, but eventually a call was placed from the British consulate on a scrambled line. For roughly seven minutes Polly spoke with his daughter, then with Crane for another three minutes. As for what passed between the two men, Michael Dart later claimed that Polly said simply, "Hello, Simon. How are you?" while Crane kept asking, "Do you know what happened to Lin Piao?"

Two days later Polly responded formally to this question, but found that really he had little else to add. In the end there were several theories, none confirmed, but all plausible. An article of interest from the period, which appeared in *La Nouvelle Chine,* referred to the fact that the Soviet Union had nothing to gain from an immediate announcement that they had discovered Lin's body, but everything to gain from secrecy. Consequently, there would always be some mystery. As for the crash, some

300

said it was caused by a poorly drawn flight plan and questionable weather, while others maintained that the plane had been shot down. Then there was a third theory, and some evidence to support it, that the passengers had quarreled and a bullet through the fuselage had depressurized the cabin.

"I suppose," Polly wrote, "that we will never know for certain exactly what occurred. So be content to tell Kissinger that Lin Piao is dead and the time has come for Nixon to pack his bags."

In response Crane cabled, "Soon, John, very soon."

On the morning of the fourteenth, Polly met Ling in a cake shop not far from one of the battle sites. There was a view of a pockmarked wall, a few blown windows and a burnt tree. Later Polly spoke briefly with the proprietor's son, who claimed that on the night of the fighting he had seen three men die along a sandstone wall. As the boy spoke he pointed to traces of blood and a row of trampled sunflowers.

Then there was an incident which Polly supposed was as proper an ending as could be expected. It occurred in the early morning after a night of rain. He was sitting at the kitchen table, leafing through a week-old copy of the *New York Times,* when suddenly he heard a knock on the door. He rose and found Tommy Ling on the porch with wet shoes and his cap in his hand. He looked very tired. Polly offered tea, but Ling declined, explaining that there wasn't time. A limousine and driver were waiting by the garden wall.

"Are you going to tell me where we're going?" Polly asked.

"I have just been informed that Han Chow was not aboard that Trident," Ling said. "In fact, he has been captured and is now being held at the central garrison."

"So?"

"So he wishes to see you, John."

"Me? He wants to see me?"

"Yes."

"What for?"

"I wasn't told."

"Well, what the hell gives him the right to—"

"John, the man has been condemned to death. Don't you think he deserves this last request?"

The cell was much like other cells that Polly had seen before. The walls were unpainted concrete. There were no windows. There was a cot and a bucket for a toilet, another bucket for washing. The dominant odor was unscented disinfectant. There was a stool bolted to the floor.

When Polly entered he found Han lying on the cot, dressed in blue denim, socks but no shoes. He looked very pale and thin, but his face was unmarked, which probably meant that he had either confessed or else the torture had been electrical. Even after Polly had sat down on the stool, Han remained prone, watching. Then he raised himself on his elbows and said, "Thank you for coming."

There was a magazine on the floor by the cot. Beside the magazine lay a copy of Polly's own *Stories for Children.* When Han noticed that Polly was looking at the book he said, "I asked them for something to read and that is what they gave me."

"Did you enjoy them?"

"Not particularly, but then I suppose they were not intended for someone like myself."

"No," Polly said, "they weren't."

Then there was nothing else to look at in this room, except each other's eyes.

"You're probably wondering why I asked you here," Han said, "particularly since we were never friends."

"No, we were never friends."

"And yet of all the people you were the one I requested to see. Doesn't that surprise you?"

Polly shrugged. What surprised him was why he had come in the first place.

"Do you know," Han continued, "that for years you have been on my mind?"

"Me?" while his hands were folded in his lap.

"Yes. You have been on my mind quite a lot. I suppose the obsession was due to the fact that I could never quite confirm my suspicion. With the others I was always able to gather evidence and clear away the doubt, but not with you. No, you always eluded me, John Polly. This is why I've asked you here now. Because I have to know. For my own peace of mind."

And into the tightening silence. "Know what?"

"Whether or not you have always been a spy?"

Polly's chin was resting on his palm. "What makes you think that even now I'd tell you the truth?"

Which made even Han smile. "Yes, that's a very good point."

302

There was a parting word as Polly stood at the cell door. Han had slumped back down to the cot. His head was resting on his arm. Polly had risen and said simply, "Goodbye," then banged on the panel for the guard to let him out.

But as he stood waiting at the door, Han called out, "Mr. Polly?" Polly could feel Han's eyes on the back of his neck.

"As one great deceiver to another I have decided to reveal my last secret to you."

Then still waiting, staring at the blank steel door.

"Be careful of Feng Chi, Mr. Polly. He is not satisfied. He's never forgotten."

On September 16 President Nixon, in an unscheduled news conference, declared that the United States would support Peking's admission to the United Nations Security Council as a reflection of an Asian reality. Two days later Henry Kissinger announced that the president would visit China within six months.

Then Polly to Crane: *Is it time now?*

And Crane in reply: *Yes, John. It's time.*

So he left on the following Tuesday, much as he had always expected to leave, more or less just slipping away with two trunks of old books, papers and a few objects that he wanted to keep. There was supposed to have been a final message from Mao, but all Polly ever saw was a scrap of stationery with one word scrawled across the top: *Goodluck.*

Then there was a final evening spent alone in his now extraordinary garden. Winter was coming and soon the first frost, but that night the foliage seemed as uncontrollable as ever, with the leaves radiating outward and finally spilling over the walls. "I planted all this without thinking about it," he once wrote. "Now it has got completely out of hand."

Then in the morning as he was leaving he could not help but feel as if both house and garden were simply dissolving behind him. He did not look back, but he felt as if it was all just dissolving.

And as for his farewell to Tommy Ling: This took place on a patch of empty ground by the airstrip, a poor piece of land that even the Chinese had not found a use for. So there it lay, an ugly mass of scrub. Polly was wearing an old sports coat and flannel trousers, a white cotton shirt and no tie. Ling wore a green jacket with a tiny panda pinned to the lapel, the symbol of peace.

At first Polly simply shook Ling's hand, but this did not seem enough,

303

so they embraced. There were no words that mattered, no questions, nothing. Except later, as Polly was tramping out to the waiting plane he heard Ling call out his name. *John.* Then across thirty feet of dead grass they looked at one another for a little while longer.

Unfortunately there were no existing letters describing Polly's feelings on his final passage from Peking to Hong Kong. Instead we have only Simon Crane's impressions, and these are terse. Apparently Polly landed in the early evening after a delay in Shangai. He stepped off the plane in Canton carrying only a paperback volume of poems from the Tang and a tuna fish sandwich that he had not felt like eating earlier. The majority of Crane's other notes concerned the details regarding security and clearance through Hong Kong customs, after Polly reached there by train. There was no word regarding Polly's physical appearance, his first conversation or his reunion with Crane. There was, however, a brief catalogue of Polly's personal effects including: two statues of the Lord Buddha, one in jade the other in ivory, the enameled claw of a dragon encircling a pearl, an autographed volume of *Mao's Thoughts,* three porcelain vases, a tortoise shell, a lock of a woman's hair and that battered copy of the *Book of Changes* with a bundle of yarrow sticks taped to the spine.

Later in the evening Crane climbed the staircase to his makeshift study in the western wing of the house on the point. From where he sat at the rolltop he had only to lean a little and there, through the window, stood Polly and his daughter on the rocks. Below, in the kitchen, Eliot was preparing what would undoubtedly be the last dinner. Somewhere else, probably prowling among the tide pools, spearing sea anemones with a stick, there was still Billy Cassidy.

For a long time Simon just sat, toying with a brass clock, leafing through the case files and Polly's more recent letters. Since late the night before he had been searching for some appropriate note upon which to end this story, whether political or emotional, or else an all-encompassing image—the sort of thing that Polly had always been very good at. (If nothing else, after all these years, Polly had certainly perfected the form of a letter.) But from any angle that Simon chose to view this ending he could not help but think that something was still not right, as if running his fingers over one of John's vases and always stopping at a tiny crack— something was still not right.

After a while he lay down on the bed and listened to the ticking clock,

304

and the fainter surf through the open window. He had tried to bear in mind the broader sequence beginning with Shanghai and ending in this room, but all that came back were odd phrases he had no reason to remember, images that did not fit the pattern. In a shaft of sunlight there was Polly on the banks of the Whangpoo, then Jay Sagan in a darkened bar. He recalled Kim Lee with a blue scarf to hide the bruises, Norman Pyle on the edge of the Langley forest. On the eve of Henry Kissinger's departure for Peking, Crane had met with him briefly in the Oval Office. They had discussed Mao, particularly the chairman's personal habits and a politically suitable gift. Next there was Billy as Crane had first seen him, slumped in a prison chair, obviously contemplating someone's murder. Tommy Ling, whom Polly had called the hope of China, was known only to Crane through a photograph and the letters, while Han Chow, Lin Piao and Chou En-lai were fairly well covered in the Langley record. And finally there was the city itself, although Polly's descriptions of Peking were unlike any other. Lying between the distant past and a horrifying future, he wrote: "I do not expect this place will ever draw a substantial number of tourists."

Then after a dinner of broiled chicken in soy sauce Crane walked out along the exposed shore. He found a battered oar, a broken lobster pot, but still no satisfactory ending to this story. When he returned he passed Cassidy and Eliot playing cards in the kitchen. Polly and his daughter were talking softly in a bedroom. There was a message from Pyle finalizing arrangements for departure, and a query from Taiwan Central regarding the disbursement of travel expenditures. There was also the shell of a horseshoe crab on the mantelpiece, perhaps something that Maya had found.

By nine o'clock he was back in his room, scanning notes he had made earlier, half-consciously clinging to one image of Polly loitering in a Shanghai back street. There was a sound like the kicking of an empty pail, although it was probably only one of the jetty bells. "Dragons are real," Polly had once written, and for some reason this too had found its way into Crane's final notes. There was also a note regarding Cassidy and a related note on Polly's daughter. As Crane reread their names he suddenly thought: *I should never have let them all stay in this house together.*

By midnight, half dozing in the wing chair, he kept telling himself that there had to have been another pattern, something he had missed. Again there was the jetty bell, then a shutting door and a footfall on the

305

staircase. When he shut his eyes he saw John's face, and also the face of another he could not quite identify. "What you are looking for," John had written years ago, "is only the shell, the husk of a deeper motive. Politics do not matter—passion matters."

And then Crane understood. It wasn't *something* that he had missed. It was *someone*. And out of an internal darkness came Feng Chi, the springing tiger.

It is clear today that Polly's own conception of an ending had been no less exact than Crane's. There remains a letter to Polly's daughter, left with Cassidy, and then Cassidy's own testimony of his final conversation with Polly. According to the boy, Polly had entered his room just a few minutes before midnight. When Cassidy was asked if he had been surprised to see Polly, he said no. He had not been surprised...

"Billy?"

"I'm here."

"Don't turn on the light."

They sat in the darkness, sharing a cigarette that Cassidy had found in the pocket of his bathrobe. There was a reflection of the moon on the bay. For a while they did not speak, listening for sounds of others moving through the house. They heard nothing.

Finally Polly said, "I need to borrow the gun."

At first Cassidy said nothing. His eyes were fixed on a light low on the water. Then he sighed, "So Maya told you what Feng did to her, huh?"

Polly nodded, and the answer was also in his eyes, in the slope of his shoulders and the way his hands pressed against the windowsill.

"You know where to find him?" Cassidy asked.

"Yes."

"You want me to go with you?"

"No."

"Are you sure? It might make a difference."

"No. I want you to stay with her. Do you understand? Stay with her?"

"Sure."

There may have been another storm at sea, a late summer squall.

Cassidy said, "Do you have any idea how you're going to do it? I mean, it could get kind of tricky trying to get at him from the inside."

"I'll find a way."

Then Cassidy started to speak again, but stopped. The Browning was

306

in the top drawer of a heavy oak chest. As Cassidy handed it to Polly he said, "You know you don't have to do this."

But Polly said nothing. He felt the weight of the gun, drew back the bolt, dry-fired once and then inserted the magazine. It was only as he was leaving that he remembered the letter.

"For Maya," he said, "just in case."

Cassidy took the envelope, turned it over in his hands, and then put it in the pocket of his bathrobe. "The keys to Eliot's car are on the mantel."

"I know." Polly smiled.

Polly drove slowly. It had been a long time since he had driven a car as large as this one, and he was not used to the power steering and the brakes. For several miles his landmarks were the blackened hills. Then the highway fell to the salt marsh and the willow fields. There had been country like this in Shanghai, he told himself, with hamlets that no one dared visit, roads to the swamp, village fires at the foot of mountains. *But then I had a Buick and a Colt revolver, not this Chevrolet and Browning.*

For the final mile he drove even slower to read the numbers on the gateposts. When he saw Feng Chi's home, he continued for another fifty yards, then pulled into the trees at the edge of the road. From here he could see the garden walls, the red tiles and a ring of chairs on the lawn. While on the cornerstone, in marble, was that tiger he had always known would be waiting for him.

But if Feng was the tiger, then tonight he was definitely the dragon, with a dragon's sense of sight and smell. A dragon, they said, could hear passing clouds and the smell of a man's breath miles away. Although now Polly only heard blown leaves on the pavement and smelled only rotting plums.

He thought of Kim, and supposed that if she had ever haunted him, she would haunt him now with eyes in the rearview mirror to say, *Go home, John. You can't ring the bell backward.*

Then he thought of Maya who would have also tried to stop him now, but when she had described what Feng had done, her voice had been cold and toneless, and afterward she had cried; she, like her mother, who hardly ever cried.

He lit a cigarette, thinking: twenty-two years later and once more flicking ashes out of the window. There was lamplight through the trellis and drawn curtains, three plaster ducks on the moss. I could enter through the rear, he thought. Or through the front. They'd never expect me to just walk in the front door.

But as he climbed out of the car, still watching the roof that rose through the trees, he saw a light fall from a door. Then he heard footsteps on the path, and when he reached the iron gate, he saw what he supposed had been inevitable from the start—Feng Chi walking slowly, leading a small dog on a leash. There was a thin cigar between his fingers. He paused to touch an orchid, then glanced at the sky.

Closer now Polly could see that the dog was some sort of white terrier, old with stiff haunches. Feng let the animal pause to urinate, then moved across the lawn. Polly waited, then unlatched the gate and cocked the Browning. Only after he had raised the gun to the level of Feng's chest did he call out the name. *Feng.*

And the response that he had always dreamed of... "Is that Mr. Polly?"

Polly stepped out to face him.

"Ah. I should have guessed. Only a moment ago I had the oddest thought about you, and here you are—to kill me."

Polly stood very straight. One arm was at his side, the other outstretched with the gun.

"Not that I can blame you, Mr. Polly. I would have done the same. In fact I tried on several occasions, but it seems that it was not meant to be."

Now the dog had begun sniffing at Feng's feet, then squatted to lick a canker on its paw. The eyes were glazed with cataracts.

"They tell me I should put him to sleep," Feng said, looking at the animal. "But I've grown so attached to him. I'm sure you can sympathize, Mr. Polly."

But Polly had still not moved, and he could not sympathize.

Feng breathed deeply and raised his head. "Well I'm ready now. You may shoot me." But it sounded pretty arrogant.

And Polly just kept looking at him.

"I said you may shoot me now, Mr. Polly. What are you waiting for?"

He wasn't certain. Perhaps some sort of revelation.

Or perhaps only an answer to a question he never understood: what was it all for, those twenty-two years?

"Shoot me, Mr. Polly. Go ahead. Shoot."

But looking past Feng's eyes, first into the dog's blind eyes, then into Kim's eternal eyes, he finally understood. And said, "I already shot you," then turned and walked away.

Epilog

JOHN POLLY returned home in the fall of 1971. He came by way of Hawaii on a military transport and reached the California coast on a warm velvet evening. He was then forty-eight years old. A photograph, taken on that day, shows him as still a tall, thin man, vaguely smiling, on the steps of a penny arcade. He is wearing a white tropical suit, a maroon tie and there is a newspaper tucked under his arm. In the background are a motorcycle and a hot dog stand. If one didn't know the story behind this photograph, how it had been taken by his daughter, one might well assume that he was just another pale stranger from abroad.

There is of course a continuation to this story, including Richard Nixon's February visit to Peking, a broadening economic exchange and the eventual diplomatic normalization. But within the scope of the secret wars there is little else to tell.

Feng Chi died in the winter of the following year. He was shot seven times in front of a restaurant called the Dream of Heaven. Later the same week the body of Jerry Woo was found in an alley near the Macao ferry wharf. He too had been shot repeatedly. These murders were said to have been the result of an internal war within the Triad community, precipitated in part by the withdrawal of the United States military presence in Asia. When the fighting was over the fundamental structure of the opium routes had changed. The situation Was not necessarily better or worse. It was just different.

That same winter Simon Crane returned to the East for what would be the last posting of his career. He spent nine weeks reorganizing the shattered Hong Kong station and the skeleton of Jay Sagan's Asian net-

310

works. Then quite suddenly he took ill, and within a month he had withdrawn from the service entirely. Now and then he still occasionally lectures at Langley, although his talks are not particularly popular. They are said to be rather dry, classic discussions of how one runs an intelligence service in a land where the art of spying is more than a thousand years old.

There remains the story of Tommy Ling. Following the final events of 1971, Ling left the Ministry of Propaganda and moved into the higher strata of the Peking elite. Until the death of Mao he served first in the National People's Congress, and then within the State Council. His career was not without adversity, but overall it was always said that he led a charmed existence. While upon a more revealing note there is this: one line from a small volume of poetry published under Ling's own name in the latter part of 1972: "Every time I pass the famous garden I still expect to see my friend."

There are also the concluding notes regarding Billy Cassidy. For many weeks following the end of this affair Cassidy remained in a no-man's-land between prosecution and amnesty. There were those who believed that regardless of the circumstances Cassidy's conduct could not be dismissed with impunity. The death of Jay Sagan demanded retribution, if not within the legal channels, then at least within the secret world. In opposition to this view there was Simon Crane and to some extent even Norman Pyle, who argued that any formal proceedings would only raise questions that were better left unanswered. To prove the point Crane submitted a partial retrospective of Sagan's involvement with the opium trade. The paper saw only an afternoon of distribution before it was withdrawn and the discussion regarding Cassidy's fate terminated.

During those indecisive weeks Cassidy found himself in a holding station, an enclosed compound deep within the Langley forest. Here were the brick and timber cabins occasionally used for interrogation. The days were fairly unvarying. In the mornings he jogged around the perimeter of tall trees. In the afternoons he played Ping-Pong with the guards. At night there were sometimes films. He also drank a lot.

There has never been a satisfactory explanation as to exactly how Billy's story ended. Presumably there simply came a day when Simon Crane drove out to that compound and explained to the boy that he would now be leaving. Where he went, whether to Europe or South America, no one knows, except perhaps John Polly's daughter.

As for Polly and his daughter, all that really need be said is that

311

eventually they found a home in Santa Barbara, where she attended the university and he began work on still another series of translations. The first, published that winter, was simply entitled *Poetry from the Tang.* Then the following spring came the far more personal *Excursion to the Dragon's Pool,* which critics pronounced intriguing, but somehow lacking an authentic feel of China.